DELORES FOSSEN's

family tree includes Texas cowboys, Choctaw and Cherokee Indians, a Louisiana pirate and a Scottish rebel who battled side by side with William Wallace. With ancestors like that, it's easy to understand why this Texas author and former air force captain feels as if she were genetically predisposed to writing romances. Along the way to fulfilling her DNA destiny, Delores married an air force top gun who just happens to be of Viking descent. With all those romantic bases covered, she doesn't have to look too far for inspiration.

Ever since she was a little girl making her own books out of construction paper, **ANN VOSS PETERSON** wanted to write. So when it came time to choose a major at the University of Wisconsin, creative writing was her only choice. Of course, writing wasn't a *practical* choice—one needs to earn a living. So Ann found jobs, including proofreading legal transcripts, working with quarter horses and washing windows. But no matter how she earned her paycheck, she continued to write the type of stories that captured her heart and imagination—romantic suspense. Ann lives near Madison, Wisconsin, with her husband, her two young sons, her border collie and her quarter horse mare. Ann loves to hear from readers. Email her at ann@annvosspeterson.com or visit her website at www.annvosspeterson.com.

DELORES FOSSEN

Unexpected Father

ANN VOSS PETERSON

Legally Binding

™ **Harlequin**®

TORONTO NEW YORK LONDON
AMSTERDAM PARIS SYDNEY HAMBURG
STOCKHOLM ATHENS TOKYO MILAN MADRID
PRAGUE WARSAW BUDAPEST AUCKLAND

Recycling programs
for this product may
not exist in your area.

ISBN-13: 978-0-373-68833-3

UNEXPECTED FATHER & LEGALLY BINDING

Copyright © 2011 by Harlequin Books S.A.

The publisher acknowledges the copyright holders
of the individual works as follows:

UNEXPECTED FATHER
Copyright © 2006 by Delores Fossen

LEGALLY BINDING
Copyright © 2004 by Harlequin Books S.A.
Ann Voss Peterson is acknowledged as the author of this work.

CONTENTS

UNEXPECTED FATHER

Delores Fossen

CHAPTER ONE

St. Joseph's Convalescent Hospital
San Antonio, Texas

"LILLY CAME OUT of the coma." Dr. Staten's voice was clinical. Void of emotion or any speculation as to the impact of the bombshell that he'd just delivered.

Detective Jason Lawrence's reaction, however, wasn't quite so serene or detached.

There was emotion. Plenty of it. And speculation? That, too. A really bad kind of speculation that knotted his stomach and tightened every muscle in his body.

Oh, man.

It felt as if someone had sucker punched him.

"Lilly's awake?" Jason managed to ask even though he already knew the answer. Still, he wanted a confirmation, and while he waited for it, he prayed.

Except he didn't know what the hell to pray for.

Dr. Staten nodded. "She woke up about two hours ago. That's why I called and asked you to come."

And at no time during the call had the doctor indicated that Lilly was no longer comatose. Of course, Dr. Staten probably thought it was news best delivered in person. Jason was debating that. Though there was nothing that could have helped pave the way for this, he would have liked a few minutes in private to prepare himself.

"How did this happen?" Because he didn't want to risk something as dignity-reducing as losing his balance, Jason dropped down into the burgundy leather chair across from Dr. Staten's desk.

"She simply woke up." The doctor lifted a shoulder and flexed his dark, gray-threaded eyebrows. "We don't know why. It's not a common occurrence, but it does happen—even after nineteen months."

Yes. These things probably did happen. But nineteen months had been more than enough time for Jason to believe it wouldn't happen.

Ever.

And he'd built his entire life around that *ever*.

Dr. Staten sat, as well, easing down into his chair, and from over the thin silver rims of his glasses, he examined Jason with sympathetic brown eyes. "I know this has to come as a surprise…"

Jason almost laughed. Not from humor. Definitely not from that. But from the irony. Lilly was awake—after nineteen months, three days and a couple of hours. After everyone, including the medical community, and he had given up hope. She was awake.

It was nothing short of a miracle.

And the beginning of what would no doubt be his own personal nightmare.

Jason pulled in his breath, released it slowly. "Has Lilly said anything?"

"A little. She's still somewhat disorientated and doesn't remember much about the car accident. That's to be expected. It'll take a while for her body to start functioning normally, but now that she's awake, I believe she'll make a full recovery."

Jason silently cursed his reaction. Cursed himself. And then cursed fate for dealing him a hand that he didn't want to play. He was happy for Lilly. Truly happy. No one deserved to be in a vegetative state, and now she would get a second chance at life. But Jason couldn't help it: her second chance changed everything.

"Have you told her?" Jason asked.

Dr. Staten paused a moment. There was no need for Jason to clarify his question; the doctor certainly knew what was foremost on his mind. "No. I figured it'd sound better coming from you."

Jason seriously doubted that. It wouldn't sound *better* coming from anyone. But it was true—he needed to be the one to tell Lilly.

So he could soften the blow.

So he could prepare her for the shock of her life.

And then what?

Would he ultimately lose everything that he'd come to love in the past year? Jason suddenly felt as if he were perched on top of a house of cards with an F-5 tornado bearing right down on him.

The doctor picked up a pen, groaned softly and tossed it onto his desk. The cool facade was broken, and for the first time since Jason had walked into his office, he saw the frayed nerves.

Not exactly a comforting reaction.

"Lilly's expecting you," the doctor instructed. His suddenly strained voice said it all. "I let her know that you were coming."

And that was Jason's cue to get to his feet. He

mustered what courage he could and tried to push aside his fears. No easy feat. His fears were mammoth, and the next few minutes would change his life forever.

"If you need more time, I can postpone the visit," Dr. Staten offered.

Man, was that tempting. But it wouldn't solve anything. This conversation with Lilly had to happen. Plus, delaying the inevitable would only prolong his agony.

Jason followed the doctor out of the office and toward the patient ward of the convalescent facility. With each step, his heart pounded and his breath thinned. Sheez. Such a wuss reaction. But he couldn't help it. Because he was a cop, his life had been on the line a couple of times, but he'd never before had this much at stake.

When they reached the room, the doctor stepped aside to allow Jason to enter ahead of him. Jason took a deep breath and pushed open the door to Lilly's room. A room he'd seen at least a dozen times. From the vantage point of the doorway anyway. He'd kept his distance, literally and figuratively. But this was different. She wasn't just lying there, eyes closed and attached to machines to monitor her vitals. One machine was still in place, as was an IV, but she was sitting up with the help of pillows stuffed behind her back.

Her gaze slid in his direction and she spotted him. Instant recognition. Jason knew that from the brief widening of her blue-green eyes followed by the not-so-brief tightening of her mouth.

"Jason," she said.

Not a friendly greeting. It dripped with questions. *Why are you here? Of all the people in the world, why would you be my first real visitor?*

Unfortunately, she would soon find out.

Because he suddenly felt awkward and fidgety, Jason stuffed his hands into the pockets of his khakis and ambled closer. "Welcome back, Lilly."

The right corner of her mouth lifted. "You actually seem sincere." Since her first attempt sounded as if she were speaking through gravel, she cleared her throat and repeated it.

"I am sincere."

And Jason was *almost* certain he believed that.

Lilly was pale, a skim milk kind of pale, but other than that and the two-and-a-half-inch whitish scar angled on the left side of her forehead, she didn't look as if she'd been through a horrifying ordeal.

However, she did look different.

Her normally short auburn hair now lay on the tops of her shoulders. Loose. Not confined in one of the not-a-strand-out-of-place styles that she usually preferred. No makeup, either.

She had freckles and chapped lips.

Definitely not the pristine, polished corporate image that Jason had come to associate with that face. Too bad. Because that executive veneer had always been a reminder that she wasn't his type. That she was hands-off.

For reasons he didn't want to explore, she didn't seem so hands-off right now. Lilly seemed very small and vulnerable, despite her defensive expression and her smart-ass reply to his greeting.

"How are you?" he asked, mainly because he couldn't think of what else to say.

She hesitated as if considering what ulterior motive

he might have for his question, and she moistened her lips. "Coming back from the dead isn't easy."

Jason nodded. "I imagine not."

Lilly made a you-don't-know-the-half-of-it sound. "My whole body's stiff, and it doesn't respond the way it should. I'll spare you most of the specifics, but I've got a wicked headache. Cotton mouth. And I understand it'll be days…or even longer before I can walk. I'm a little scared about that."

Lilly stopped, wrinkled up her forehead. And closed down. She was no doubt embarrassed that she'd revealed her fear of not being able to walk. It was a totally human, normal response, but Jason figured she would view it as a weakness.

"Of course, there's a bright side to this," she continued. It was her CEO presentation voice. Light, confident, airy. "I figure I've lost a lot of weight. I doubt I've been this thin since high school." Lilly fanned her trembling fingers through the air to indicate an imaginary marquee. "Coma—the ultimate diet."

"You'll be back to normal in no time," Jason promised her. Though he didn't know why. That certainly wasn't a promise he could deliver.

She stared at him a moment. "Oh, I get it now." Lilly's mouth relaxed and she made a clumsy swipe to push her rumpled hair off her forehead. "This is an official visit from *Detective* Jason Lawrence, San Antonio PD. You want to question me about the car accident that put me here in this hospital bed."

He wished that was the reason he'd come.

"I work Special Investigations now," Jason informed

her. "Your accident doesn't come under the jurisdiction of my department."

Something, some raw emotion, riffled through her eyes. "So, you're here to talk about Greg." Lilly huffed and coupled it with a disapproving groan. "I figured you'd give me at least a day or two to catch up on current events, physical therapy, visits from friends, trips to Krispy Kreme, et cetera, before you started badgering me again about the night Greg died."

Greg. His brother. His *dead* brother. And the subject of the majority of Lilly's and his last conversations, and bitter arguments.

Always arguments.

It didn't matter that she was trying to defuse this tension with her Krispy Kreme style of humor. The emotion and the pain were still there, crouching just below the surface of her words.

Jason moved closer and stopped a few inches from the foot of her bed. "I'm not here about Greg, either." Besides, no amount of questioning and arguments would bring his brother back. He knew that. *Now.* But Lilly was right—nineteen months ago, it'd been a topic he'd broached often with her.

And yes, there had been plenty of badgering involved.

"All right, then." She took a sip of water from a plastic cup clutched in her right hand. "You've piqued my interest. If you're not here to talk about Greg or my car accident, then this'll be a very short visit. Because I think we both know there's nothing else for us to discuss."

Jason couldn't fault her defensive attitude. He

deserved it. After all, this was the woman he'd accused of contributing to the death of his brother. Despite the fact he'd known Lilly for more than six years before his brother's death, it was hard to stay friendly after an accusation like that. However, she was wrong about them having nothing else to discuss.

There was plenty.

"I'll give you two some privacy," Dr. Staten announced, and he stepped out of the room, shutting the door behind him.

Jason glanced over his shoulder to confirm the man's timely exit. Staten was definitely gone. The room suddenly seemed too small, and it was getting smaller by the second with Lilly's stare drilling into him. Where had the air gone?

"Do you remember anything that happened while you were in a coma?" Jason asked.

Lilly blinked, as if surprised by the question. "No." She paused. "In fact, not only is the coma a blank, so are the last few hours before I got into the car." She stopped, angled her head, studied him. "Is there something about the accident that the police are investigating?"

Jason chose his words very carefully.

"The case is still active. I'm sure the lead detective will want to question you when you're feeling up to it."

And he left it at that.

She made a soft *hmm* of agreement. And concern. "Then something must really be wrong for you to be here."

It was, and since there was no good introduction for

what he had to tell her, Jason just started with the basics. "The night Greg was killed, you had sex with him."

Not a blink of surprise this time. More like a flash of anger over his bluntness. "I don't want to discuss this—"

"I know it happened because he called and told me. In fact, he told me just minutes before he died."

Since this was only a recap and since he hadn't wanted to start an argument with her, Jason left out one important detail: Greg had thought the sexual encounter might lead to a permanent relationship with Lilly rather than her shutting him out of her life.

But she had shut him out.

And because of that, Greg was dead.

There it was. The flood of old memories. The still-fresh pain. Always the pain. Jason knew for a fact he wouldn't forget that grief anytime soon. Nor would he forget, or forgive, what Lilly had done.

"Is this actually leading somewhere?" Lilly prompted in that crisp voice that he'd learned to hate. "Because I'm not in the mood for a trip down memory lane, especially when you're the one doing the navigating."

"It's leading somewhere." Since he needed it, Jason took another deep breath. "You got pregnant that night. With Greg's baby."

That got her attention. Man, did it ever. She did a double take and her breathing stilled. "Excuse me?"

"You got pregnant," Jason repeated. Because Lilly looked as if she badly needed it, and because he needed it, as well, he waited a couple of moments to give her some time to try to absorb that.

The plastic water cup started to collapse under the pressure of her grip. "I didn't know."

Jason had been afraid of that. So that meant Lilly was in for a double shock.

He'd have to save the third part of these revelations for another day since that news would probably stall her recovery and send her into a panic.

A hoarse sob clawed its way past her throat. "Oh, God. Oh. God. Pregnant. I got pregnant." Her gaze slashed to his, and she groaned. "The accident caused me to miscarry, didn't it?"

Her reaction surprised him, and that was putting it mildly. Jason had been expecting her to be upset at the news of an unplanned pregnancy.

Or maybe that's how he'd hoped she would react. *Upset.*

But this was a couple of steps past that particular emotion. He'd never thought of the workaholic, success-driven Lilly as overly eager to start a family, but she looked genuinely distressed over not just the pregnancy but the possibility of losing a child.

"No." Jason let her know. Not easily. But he finally got out the denial. "You didn't miscarry."

With her eyes suddenly dark and wide with concern, Lilly opened her mouth. Closed it. Frantically shook her head. "What do you mean *no?*" The question was all breath. Not a hint of sound. Yet Jason heard it clearly.

"Your injuries were mainly caused by a piece of metal railing that came through the windshield," Jason explained. "It hit you on the head, caused some major trauma. The airbag stopped any impact damage in your midsection and probably prevented you from miscarrying."

She didn't have much color in her face, but what was there, drained completely. Her bottom lip began to tremble. "I don't understand."

Jason waited a moment, until he stood a chance of his voice being steady. It wasn't a hundred percent, but under the circumstances, it was the best he could do. "You carried the baby full term, and then the doctors delivered it via C-section."

"Are you saying…" But she didn't finish. Mumbling something indistinguishable, she dropped back onto the pillows and her eyelids fluttered down.

Since Jason needed to end this conversation right here, right now, he just tossed it out there. Quickly. Before he could change his mind, turn and leave. "You had a baby, Lilly. Nearly a year ago."

She lay there. Not moving. Except for her lips. She continued to mumble something. A prayer, maybe. Then she opened her eyes. Slowly. As if she dreaded what she might see on his face.

"Had?" she repeated, obviously latching on to his use of the past tense. A tear streaked down her cheek.

A real honest-to-goodness tear.

In the six years he'd known her, he'd never seen Lilly cry. Oh, man. This was ripping them both to pieces—but for different reasons, of course.

Jason couldn't stand that look of undiluted pain on her face, so he put an end to it. "Not *had,* Lilly," he corrected. "You *have* a baby. A daughter."

CHAPTER TWO

IF IT'D BEEN any person other than Jason Lawrence telling her this, Lilly might have thought it was a joke. But this no-shades-of-gray cop wasn't the joking type. Heck, she wasn't even sure he was the smiling type. Still—

A baby.

How could that be?

If this was the truth, then she would have been… what? She quickly did the math. She would have been two months pregnant when she was involved in the car accident. Two months, as in sixty days.

Yet she hadn't known.

How could she have not known?

Her life had always been so organized. She'd known every appointment, every deadline. So, how could a missed period or two have escaped her notice?

Almost hysterically, Lilly slapped the plastic cup onto the table beside her bed so she could pinch herself. Hard. She felt it all right, the sting of the pressure on her skin. But that wasn't definitive. Maybe she was still in a coma. Maybe she was dreaming about a pinch and a pregnancy.

Yes.

That was it. This had to be some weird dream, even though she couldn't recall a single instance of a dream the entire time she'd been in a coma.

"It's for real," Jason volunteered as if he could hear the argument going on in her head.

He walked toward her, slowly, and held out his arm. Probably so she could touch him. Because she didn't know what else to do, Lilly took him up on that offer. She reached out. Dreading, hoping and praying all at the same time. Her fingertips brushed against the smooth fabric of his bronze-colored jacket, which was nearly the same color as his short, efficient hair.

The jacket felt like…well, a jacket.

But Lilly went one step further. She slid her fingers over the back of his hand. Warm, human skin. Comforting in a primal sort of way.

And maybe in other ways, too.

She suddenly wanted to latch on to his hand, and it wasn't totally related to her need to make sure she was truly conscious. Simply put, she needed a hug. Mercy, did she ever. Even though she was twenty-seven—no, make that twenty-nine—she suddenly felt as fragile as a newborn baby.

Ironic.

Since a baby was the exact topic of conversation that'd sent her heart and thoughts into a tailspin.

Lilly met Jason's gaze again, to see how he was re-acting to all of this touching stuff, but whatever he was feeling, he kept it carefully hidden in the depths of those smoke-gray eyes. No surprise there. She'd always believed Jason was born to be a cop.

Or a professional poker player.

Because that rugged stoic face gave away noth-ing. The only time she'd ever seen an overt display of emotion from him was the night his brother, Greg, had died. Understandable. She'd had an overt display of her own.

Well, afterward, anyway.

When Jason had gone and she had been alone.

"Are you okay?" Jason asked.

Lilly didn't even consider a polite lie. "No. I'm not. It's hard to be okay when nothing makes sense."

She moved on to part three of the reality check. Not knowing what to hope she might see, Lilly clutched the hem of her roomy green hospital gown and jerked it up. Thank goodness she was wearing panties or Jason would have gotten a real eyeful. But even if she hadn't had on underwear, she would have looked anyway. She needed proof.

And she got it.

She slid her fingertips over the thin, pinkish-colored scar. Right on her lower abdomen. Not some ragged wound caused by an injury, but clearly the result of surgery.

A C-section.

Jason leaned in closer. So close. *Too* close. He caught her gown and eased it back into place so that the soft cotton whispered over her thighs. Probably because her near nudity bothered him.

No, wait.

He didn't think of her that way. He'd covered her probably because further examination wasn't necessary. She had all the proof she needed.

Reality check was over. Now it was time to deal with the aftermath. And she dealt, all right. The breath swooshed out of her and because she didn't want any tears to escape, Lilly squeezed her eyes shut.

"A daughter?" she said.

"Yes." Jason's voice was tight. Edgy. Exactly the way she felt.

He didn't add anything else, and it didn't take long for the smothering silence to settle uncomfortably between them. Lilly used that quiet time to try to put a stranglehold on her composure, to try to grasp what was happening.

But both were impossible tasks.

Only two hours earlier she'd awakened to learn that she'd lost nineteen months of life because of a car accident that she couldn't even remember. Nineteen months. Heaven knew what toll the coma had taken on her body. And there was the inevitable toll that her absence had no doubt taken on her business. Sweet heaven, she'd lost so much. Now, Jason had informed her that she'd been pregnant and delivered a baby.

A baby who was almost a year old.

"Her name is Megan," she heard Jason say.

At the sound of some movement, Lilly opened her eyes to find him searching through his wallet. He extracted something. A photograph that was a bit crumpled around the edges. He held it up so she could see it.

Her mouth went dry.

She took the picture, hesitantly, and pulled it closer to her so she could study it. The little girl had auburn hair. Not quite a genetic copy of Lilly's own, but close. Darn close. It wasn't straight but instead haloed her face in soft, loose curls. Just as Lilly's own hair had done when she was that age.

Lilly caught her bottom lip between her teeth to cut

off any unwanted sound she might make. At this point, any sound would be unwanted. And too revealing.

In the photograph, Megan was smiling. Not a tentative one, either. It went all the way to her eyes.

"Oh, mercy," she whispered. Lilly pressed the picture to her chest.

This precious child was hers.

The connection she felt for Megan was instant. Not a gentle tug of her heart, either, but a feeling so intense, so right, that the tears she'd fought came anyway. Lilly didn't even care that she was losing control. Seeing that tiny face was worth all the tears. It was worth humiliating herself in front of Jason. Worth the coma.

Worth everything.

Her baby.

Her own flesh and blood.

"I've missed so much," she mumbled, knowing it was a total understatement. She'd missed carrying her child. Giving birth. And most importantly, she had missed nearly the entire first year of her daughter's life.

"Yes," Jason whispered.

Since there was a lot of emotion in his one-word comment, Lilly looked at him again. He still had on his cop's face, but those eyes said it all. Or at least they said *something*. Exactly what that *something* was, she didn't know.

Unless…

"She's Greg's baby," Lilly clarified. Why, she didn't know. She didn't need to explain her sex life to Jason.

He nodded. "The doctors did a DNA test on Megan after she was born."

What a waste of time. If Lilly had been awake during

Megan's birth, she could have told them there was no reason for such a test. Before that night with Greg, it'd been nearly a year since she'd had sex. And that one time with Greg hadn't been unprotected, either, which meant something had gone wrong with the condom.

And then it hit her.

Her heart practically leaped to her throat. "Who has her? Both Greg's and my parents are dead—"

"I have her," Jason interrupted.

Lilly was surprised that her heart didn't jump right out of her chest. It was already pounding, and his statement made it pound even harder. "You?"

That improved his posture. Not that he needed it. He was already soldier-stiff, which was his usual demeanor, but Jason seemed to take her simple question as a challenge.

"Me," he enunciated through semiclenched teeth.

Oh.

Even with his adamant confirmation, it just didn't register in her brain and was in total conflict with the image she had of Jason Lawrence.

He shoved his hands into his pockets; it seemed as if he changed his mind a dozen times as to what he was about to say. "You were in a coma so long that the doctors didn't think you would recover. *I* didn't think you'd recover. I was Megan's next of kin."

There was something in the way he said that. Especially the tone he used when he tossed out the last part. Next of kin. Something...territorial? Something that launched a flurry of mental speculation.

And it also launched an equal flurry of concern.

A moment later Lilly realized that her concern was warranted.

"I have custody of her," Jason finished. He paused a moment. "Legally, Megan is my daughter."

CHAPTER THREE

JASON BRACED himself for Lilly's reaction. Or rather, he tried to. It was hard to brace himself for something he wasn't sure he could handle.

"Oh, God," Lilly mumbled. Not exactly the hostile accusation that he thought she might fire in his direction. After all, he'd just confessed to claiming her child. "You took Megan in. You've been raising her."

It was a lot more than that. Yes, he'd taken the child in. Yes, he was raising her. But he also loved her. More than life. More than anything.

And he couldn't lose her.

"I'll bet taking care of a baby required some serious lifestyle changes for you," Lilly commented. Not chit-chat, though. Her eyes were too strained for that, and there was a slight tremble in her voice—which probably meant she was as thunderstruck as he was.

She'd just learned that she had a daughter.

And Jason had just learned that he might lose one.

"I made a few lifestyle changes," he admitted. He tried to rein in his feelings. Failed. "It was worth it. Megan's a sweet kid."

Now there was a reaction from Lilly. Something small and subtle. But he could almost see the realization come to her. She'd had a child, but for all practical purposes, she wasn't in the picture.

Jason didn't think it was much of a stretch that Lilly would soon want to change that.

"Well…" Lilly started. But she didn't finish whatever thought she'd intended to voice. Instead she looked down at the picture. She held it as if it were delicate crystal that might shatter in her hands. "She has my hair. Greg's eyes, though." She lifted a shoulder. An attempt at a nonchalant shrug. But there was nothing nonchalant about any of this. "Your eyes, too."

Yes. The infamous Lawrence gray eyes that seemed to be the equivalent of a mood ring. Silvery pearl, sometimes, and on those not-so-good *sometimes*—gunmetal and steel. Megan had them in spades, along with the olive-tinged complexion that was the genetic contribution from Greg's and his Hispanic grandmother. Megan was a Lawrence through and through.

But Jason could see Lilly in the child's face, too. The way Megan sometimes defiantly lifted her chin. The sly, clever smile that could melt away botched cases, heavy workloads, long hours at work and other unsavory things. At first, it'd been difficult for him to see the smile, Lilly's smile, on the mouth of the child he loved.

DNA sure had a bent sense of humor.

"I want to see her, of course," Lilly said.

It wasn't exactly a request, either. She certainly hadn't framed it with a please and hadn't left room for argument.

Though Jason wanted to argue.

Worse, he wanted to take Megan and run. To hide her so that he wouldn't lose her. But not only was that a stupid reaction, it would be wrong. He'd been the one to raise Megan—so far—but now that Lilly was awake and on the road to recovery, he no longer had sole claim to her.

Maybe he wouldn't have any claim at all.

And that sent a stab of pain straight through his heart.

"I'll make arrangements for you to see her," Jason offered, once he could speak. "When you're feeling up to it."

There was a flash of that sly smile, and it was tinged with sarcasm. "I think it's safe to say that I'll feel up to seeing her anytime, anyplace. After all, she is my daughter."

Jason had somehow known, and feared, that she would say that. "I just wasn't sure you'd want her to visit you here in the hospital."

It wasn't a lie. Exactly. That had crossed his mind. It'd also crossed his mind that he wanted to delay the visit so he could prepare Megan. How, he didn't know. It wasn't always easy to reason with a baby. But perhaps he could show Megan pictures of Lilly so she wouldn't be frightened of meeting a stranger who just happened to be her mother.

Picture recognition might help Megan. But it wouldn't do much to soothe his fears. Nothing could do that.

"Besides, it's late," Jason added. "Nearly six."

And he was babbling. Hell. He wasn't a babbler. Worse, he seemed to be grasping at straws, at anything, to postpone what he knew he couldn't postpone.

"All right," Lilly said. She kept her attention staked to him. "This definitely qualifies as an awkward moment. We're a lot closer to being enemies than we are friends, and yet you did this incredible, wonderful thing by taking in my—"

"Don't," Jason interrupted. He took a moment to gain control of his voice, and his temper, before he continued. "I don't want your thanks." He could handle her hostility, even her sarcasm, even that damn sly smile, before he could handle her gratitude. "I said I'd arrange for you to see Megan, and I will."

Lilly nodded. "I might not be reading you right, but I get the feeling there's something else. Something you're not telling me."

Well, the coma hadn't dulled her instincts. That was both good and bad news. He wanted Lilly to be healthy and on the road to recovery. He *truly* did. But Jason had been counting on having a few days or even weeks before having to tell her everything. Not just about Megan and his custody. Other things, like the events surrounding the night she'd nearly died.

Panic began to race through her eyes. "Is Megan okay? There's nothing wrong with—"

"Megan's perfectly healthy," he told her. "She's had normal childhood illnesses, of course. An ear infection. A cold or two. Nothing major."

The pulse on her neck was pounding so hard that Jason could actually see it. "However?" she questioned.

Yes, there was a *however.*

Jason considered the several ways he could go with this, including just ending the conversation and heading out. If he followed department regulations to a tee, he should just turn this over to the lead detective. But he couldn't do that to Lilly. Despite their past and the inevitable obstacles they would no doubt face in the future, there was some information she needed to know.

The operative word was *some*.

Jason groaned and scrubbed his hand over his face. "The police will want to question you about the car accident."

Her brief silence probably meant she was processing that. Not just his comment but his groan, as well. She leaned closer. So close that he could see all those swirls of blue and green in her eyes. "Are you saying they weren't able to figure out what happened?"

It was touchy territory and, as Jason had done several times during their conversation, he considered his answer carefully. "They'll want an eyewitness statement to the incident, and you're the ultimate eyewitness. It's standard procedure." He hesitated, gathered his breath. "They also want to talk to you about the information you found when you were going through your father's old business records."

"You mean, the computer files that implicated some people in my father's dirty dealings?" Lilly didn't wait for him to confirm that. "I remember copying those files to a CD."

"Yes. You'd called a friend in the S.A.P.D. and told him about them."

"Sergeant Garrett O'Malley." Lilly touched her fingers to her left temple and massaged it gently. At first. Then, as the frustration began to show on her face, her massage got a little harder until her fingers pressed into her skin. "After I copied the files, things get a little fuzzy."

Jason latched right on to that because even though

her memory might not be totally intact, she still might be able to provide them with some critical details. "Just how fuzzy is fuzzy?"

"A big, giant blur." The temple massage obviously wasn't working so she stopped and huffed. "Did I give the CD to Sgt. O'Malley?"

He shook his head. "But you'd planned to do that the next morning."

She bobbed her head in an almost frantic nod. "Now I remember. I took the CD from my computer at the office and got into my car in the parking lot." Lilly froze. Her gaze froze, too, for several long moments before slowly coming back to his. "The CD wasn't with me when I had the accident?"

"No." This conversation was quickly taking them into uncomfortable territory. Because of their history together and because it didn't fall under his department, the best thing he could do was to back away. He definitely shouldn't be the one to interrogate her. "Look, you have enough to deal with right now—"

"And stalling won't help me deal with it any faster, okay? Tell me what's wrong, Jason."

He couldn't. The timing sucked, and whether Lilly believed it or not, she wasn't strong enough, mentally or physically, to hear the truth.

"You're still stalling," Lilly pointed out.

Yes, he was.

And he would continue to do so until he'd taken care of a few things. Such as security, for instance. At a minimum, he wanted a guard posted outside her room. Just as a precaution, especially since no one other than the medical staff and he knew that she was out of the coma.

Then he needed to get the doctor's approval to allow the lead detective to tell Lilly what would essentially be yet another bombshell. One even bigger than the one he'd already delivered.

Because nineteen months ago, Lilly's car accident hadn't really been an accident.

In fact, Jason was about a hundred percent certain that someone had tried to murder her.

THE ROOM was too quiet.

No voices. No doctors. And definitely no Jason. He'd left hours ago with a promise to return. Lilly repeated his words now, using the Terminator's thickly accented voice, and she added a hollow laugh.

God, how Jason must hate her.

First, there was her part in Greg's death. Or from Jason's perspective, not her part. She was *entirely* responsible. She accepted that. She *was* responsible. And no amount of penance, wishing or grieving would bring Greg back.

Nothing would.

Of course, Jason now had a new reason to despise her: Megan. He no doubt saw her as a threat to his custody. That was true, as well, a realization that didn't make Lilly feel like issuing even a hollow laugh. This would almost certainly turn into a long battle where there would be no winners, least of all her daughter.

Lilly tried to force her eyes to stay open. Hard to do, though. If the clock was accurate on her bed stand, it was already past midnight, the end of what had been one of the most exhausting days of her life.

She could blame the fatigue in part on the physical

therapy that she'd demanded. A two-hour session. Grueling. Painful. Essentially she'd discovered during the session that her muscles felt like pudding and were just about as useful. It would take "lots of time and hard work," the physical therapist had said, for her to regain complete use of her limbs.

Lilly didn't mind the hard work, but she wouldn't settle for the *lots of time*.

She planned to be walking by the end of the week.

It wasn't exactly an option, either. She needed to be mobile so she could see her daughter. She wanted to start building a life with the child she hadn't even known existed until six hours ago.

A child she already desperately loved.

She hugged the picture to her chest and tried to stave off the tears. She failed. They came anyway. Tears of joy and sadness. The joy was there because she had a precious little daughter. The sadness, because she'd already missed so much of her baby's life.

She wouldn't miss anything else.

Thanks to Jason, her baby had apparently been well cared for—by the last man on earth whom she thought would do her any favors. Of course, Megan was his flesh and blood, as well. Greg's daughter. Jason's niece. That was probably the real reason he'd stepped up to the fatherly plate. He'd loved his brother. Therefore, he'd love his brother's child.

In spite of the fact that Megan was her child, too.

There was true irony in that. Her sworn enemy had her daughter. Not just *had* her, either. Jason was her legal custodian. A father by law. And he was the only parent Megan had ever known. It wouldn't be easy for her to try to find her place in her baby's life.

But she did have a place.

And no matter how hard it was, she would find it.

Her eyelids drifted down again, but she fought it. It was irrational, but the thought of sleep actually terrified her. Because she might not wake up. Because she might lapse into another coma and stay there. In a permanent vegetative state. Alive in name only.

"That won't happen," Dr. Staten had promised her when he'd checked on her after the physical therapy session.

However, Lilly hated to take the chance. Still, she couldn't stop her eyes from shutting. She couldn't stop the fatigue from taking over. And the quietness of the room and the night closed in around her.

Clutching her daughter's picture, she drifted off to the one place she didn't want to go: sleep.

She dreamed of walking, her hand gently holding her daughter's. Of hope. Of a future Lilly hadn't even known she'd wanted until she'd seen the photo of Megan. Her baby's smile. Her eyes.

Then the dream changed.

It became dark and Lilly felt pressure on her face and chest. Painful, punishing pressure that made her feel as if her ribs were ready to implode.

She fought the dream, shaking her head from side to side. When that didn't work, she shoved at the pressure with her hands and forced herself to wake up.

Her eyes flew open.

The darkness stayed.

So did the god-awful pressure.

It was unbearable. She couldn't breath. Couldn't speak. Couldn't move.

It took a moment to understand why. The darkness and the pressure weren't remnants of the dream. They were real. Very real. Because someone was shoving a pillow against her face. Suffocating her.

Someone wanted her dead.

CHAPTER FOUR

THE PANIC AND the adrenaline knifed through Lilly, hot and raw. It was instant. Like a fierce jolt that consumed her. Fight or flight.

Do whatever it takes to survive.

Lilly managed to make a muffled, guttural sound. It wasn't quite a scream, but she prayed it was loud enough to alert someone. Anyone. And she began to flail her arms at her attacker. She fought. Mercy, did she ever fight. She wouldn't just let this SOB kill her. But her pudding-like muscles landed as helpless thuds on the much stronger hands that were smothering her.

Who was trying to kill her?

Better yet, how could she stop it from happening?

Even over the pounding of her heartbeat and the rough sounds of the struggle, she heard the footsteps. Frantic. Fast. Someone was coming.

Just like that, the pressure stopped. Lilly didn't waste any time. She immediately shoved the pillow aside and, starved for air, gulped in several hard breaths so she wouldn't lose consciousness.

She quickly looked around to make sure her attacker wasn't still here. The room was pitch-black. Well, maybe. She couldn't tell if the darkness was real or some left-over effect from nearly suffocating.

"I need help," she called out.

The footsteps merged and blended with others, until Lilly was no longer able to distinguish which were coming and which were going.

"Hell," someone said.

Jason.

He ran to her bed and looked down at her. He made a split-second check, probably to make sure she was still alive and well. The *alive* part was true, but it might be eternity before she could achieve the *well* part. She was shaking from head to toe and was on the verge of losing it.

Jason already had his standard-issue police Glock drawn, and he whipped his aim around the room. Ready to fire at the intruder.

But no one was there.

On the far end of the room, the window was open and the gauzy white curtains fluttered in the night breeze. It would have been a tranquil scene if a would-be killer hadn't just used it as an escape route.

Jason raced to the window, and while still maintaining his vigilant cop's stance, he checked outside. Cursed again. He used his cell phone to request assistance. His hard voice echoed through the room and her head.

"Are you okay?" he asked, hurrying back to her.

Lilly tried to take a quick inventory of her body. "I think so." But she had no idea if that was true.

"We can't stay here," Jason informed her.

He reached down and scooped her into his arms. Not a loving act. Far from it. Clutching her against his chest, he rushed her out of the room. Probably in case her attacker returned.

A truly horrifying thought.

She didn't want the person to get away, but Lilly wasn't ready for round two, either. She was, however, ready for an explanation, and she was fairly sure that Jason was the person to give it to her.

"Earlier you were stalling about telling me something," Lilly said. Her teeth began to chatter and she suspected she might be going into shock. Great. As if she didn't have enough to deal with. Well, the shock would have to wait. She needed answers. "And I think that 'something' is important, that it has to do with what just happened."

"Yeah." Jason took her up the hall and to the deserted nurses' station.

"Yeah?" she repeated, amazed and frustrated that he'd dodged her question once again. "The time for stalling is over, don't you think?"

Jason deposited her onto a burgundy leather sofa in the small lounge just behind the nurses' station. The cool, slick leather didn't help with the chills that had already started.

With his own breath coming out in rough, frantic gusts, he glanced down at her. Just a glance. Before he turned his attention back to the doorway. Standing guard. Protecting her. Or rather, trying to.

"W-well?" Lilly prompted, curling up into as much of a fetal position as her stiff muscles would allow. "Don't you have something to tell me? Wait—let me rephrase that. You *have* something to tell me, so do it."

He nodded, eventually. "Your car accident probably wasn't an accident."

She watched the words form on his lips. Tried to absorb them. Couldn't. It was next to impossible to absorb that someone wanted her dead, especially since she couldn't recall anything about what had happened to her nineteen months ago.

"And what about tonight?" Lilly asked, afraid to hear the answer. "What happened?"

"This obviously wasn't an accident, either." Jason's jaw muscles stirred as if they'd declared war on each other. "Whoever tried to kill you nineteen months ago—I think he's back."

WHEN HE SAW the lanky, blond-haired detective making his way up the hall toward him, Jason ended the call with his lieutenant and stepped out of the doorway to Lilly's new room. He wanted to give his fellow S.A.P.D. peace officer his undivided attention. Unfortunately, it would be next to impossible to do that because of what the lieutenant had just requested.

Or rather, what the lieutenant had *ordered* him to do.

Talk about the ultimate distraction. That order kept repeating itself through Jason's head, and he doubted it'd go away anytime soon. Especially since he had no clue as to how he could carry it out.

"Please tell me you have answers," he said to Detective Mack O'Reilly. Jason kept his voice low so he wouldn't wake Lilly. To get her to fall asleep, it'd taken nearly a half hour of questions and assurances from him that she was safe. Jason didn't want to go through that again until he could make good on those assurances.

If that were even possible.

O'Reilly shrugged. "I have answers, but I don't think you'll like them. There's only one surveillance camera in or around this entire place. It's in the parking lot and static, fixed in only one direction."

Jason tried not to curse. "Let me guess—the wrong direction?"

"You got it. It was aimed at the center of the parking lot. Someone came up from the side and, while staying out of the line of sight, smashed the lens with a rock. All we got for a visual was a shadow. The crime-scene guys are dusting both the camera and the rock for prints, but it looks clean. Whoever it was probably had on gloves."

Definitely not good. Jason had hoped for a sloppy crime scene, even though deep down he'd known it wouldn't be. Whoever was behind this was brazen. Yes. Determined—that, too. Maybe even downright desperate.

But not sloppy.

Jason had personally gone over every inch of Lilly's room and hadn't found even trace evidence.

"How about the rookie guarding Ms. Nelson's room?" Jason asked. "Did you find him?"

O'Reilly nodded. "He was in the utility closet at the end of the hall. Duct tape on his mouth, hands and feet. He has a goose-egg-size lump on his head, and someone had used a stun gun on him, but he can't remember being knocked out."

Probably because the guard had fallen asleep.

This time, Jason didn't even try to contain his profanity, but it was aimed just as much at himself as it was at the guard. When Jason had checked on him about a half hour prior to Lilly's attack, the guy had looked a little drowsy. Jason had asked if he'd wanted to be relieved, but he'd said no, that the double espresso he was sipping would keep him awake all night.

Yeah, right.

Jason wanted to kick himself. Hard. How could he have let this happen?

He'd been positive that nineteen months ago someone had tried to kill Lilly. That's why he'd had a guard assigned to the convalescent hospital in the first place. What he should have anticipated, however, was that one guard wouldn't be enough. After all, the person responsible for this latest attempt on Lilly's life had no doubt been the one who'd forced her off the road and left her for dead.

Getting past one guard in the middle of the night obviously hadn't been much of a challenge. Murdering Lilly wouldn't have been a challenge, either, if Jason hadn't returned to the hospital to talk to Lilly's doctor about additional security measures for the facility.

Ironic.

While he'd been discussing the need for extra security, someone had been breaching it. And Lilly had nearly paid for that breach with her life.

"So far, no witnesses," O'Reilly continued. "But we're canvassing the neighborhood. Something might turn up."

Not likely. It was late. Midweek. The small downtown hospital was surrounded by specialty shops that mainly did business from ten to six o'clock. That meant there probably weren't a lot of potential witnesses milling around to see someone escaping through a window.

"I gave one of the detectives the names of two suspects, Wayne Sandling and Raymond Klein," Jason explained. "Both are former attorneys. About two years ago, Lilly uncovered some information that caused them to be disbarred."

What she'd uncovered, though, wasn't an offense that would have earned them jail time. While Sandling and Klein had been working as advisors to the city council, the two had somehow managed to get a construction company a lucrative contract to renovate historic city-owned buildings. The problem? The owners of the construction company were Sandling and Klein's friends. A definite conflict of interest. That suspicious contract wasn't enough for an arrest and, coupled with other similar unethical activity, it was barely enough to get them disbarred and fired as city council advisors.

But Jason knew there was more.

His brother, Greg, had even suspected it. After dealing with Sandling and Klein on a city contract deal, Greg, too, had noticed inconsistencies with bid dates and altered estimates that had ultimately cost him a contract to do auditing work for the city. Greg had been more than ready to request an investigation into the two attorneys' dealings. It hadn't happened, of course.

Because Greg had died in the car accident.

"Sandling and Klein have already been contacted," O'Reilly assured him. "Neither seemed pleased about that."

"I'll bet not. I want them questioned—hard."

"Absolutely."

Not that it would do much good. Questioning them hadn't been effective nineteen months ago. Jason had no doubts about Sandling's and Klein's guilt as far as unscrupulous business practices, but what was missing was solid proof that their unscrupulousness had gone much deeper than what the police had already found. There was no remaining evidence since the files that Lilly had copied from her computer had disappeared the night she'd been run off the road.

Jason knew that wasn't a coincidence.

Detective O'Reilly craned his neck to peer over Jason's shoulder. "By the way, how's Ms. Nelson?"

"Other than a few bruises, she wasn't hurt physically."

He couldn't say the same for her mental health, though. Here she was, only hours out of a coma. Hours where she'd learned she had a daughter that she hadn't even known she'd conceived. That in itself was enough trauma to face, but Lilly now had to deal with the aftermath of an attempted murder and a full-scale police investigation.

Jason looked back at Lilly, as well, and saw that she was in the exact place he'd left her. Well, sort of. She was still in the hospital bed. Still asleep. But it wasn't a peaceful sleep by any means. Her arm muscles jerked and trembled as if she were still in a fight for her life.

Which wasn't too far from the truth.

Someone wanted her dead, and wanted it badly enough to have tried not once but twice. Jason had been a cop for nearly eleven years and had learned a lot about criminal behavior.

This guy wasn't going to give up.

But then, neither was Jason.

It'd been a mistake not to beef up security, a bigger mistake to let down his guard, and he wouldn't do that again.

"Who knew Ms. Nelson was out of the coma?" O'Reilly asked.

It was a question Jason had already asked the hospital staff, and he'd gotten answers that hadn't pleased him. "Too many people. One of the nurses called a few friends to tell them the news. Another nurse called Lilly's former secretary—again, to share the good news. The doctors spoke to colleagues. Even Lilly's insurance company was contacted."

Jason couldn't consider himself blameless, either. He'd told Megan's nanny, Erica, though he didn't think Erica would pass on the information to anyone. And of course, there'd been paperwork processed at headquarters to assign the cop to security detail outside Lilly's room. In others words, at least several dozen people had learned that Lilly was no longer in a coma, and obviously one of those *several dozen* was someone who wanted her dead.

Lilly stirred again, and this time her eyes opened. In the same motion, she sat up, spearing him with her gaze. Her eyes were wild. Her breath, racing. She scrambled back toward the wall, banging into it with a loud thud.

O'Reilly immediately stepped away. "I'll let you know what the crime-scene guys say about the security camera." With that, the detective made a hasty exit, leaving Jason to deal with Lilly.

There was just one problem. Jason didn't know how to deal with her.

Seemingly disgusted with herself, she shook her head. "I keep dreaming."

Nightmares, no doubt. Jason wanted to tell her that they would go away, but he'd fed her enough lies tonight.

Reassurances that she was safe didn't contain even a shred of truth.

Not yet, anyway.

Jason eased the door shut and walked to her. He had a ten-second debate with himself before he moved even closer and sat beside her on the bed. Yes, there was plenty of bad blood between them, but he would have had to be a coldhearted jackass not to try to offer some comfort.

"You have more bad news?" she asked, her voice cracking on the last word.

She was trembling all over, and he reached out. He pushed aside any doubts he had about what he was doing and pulled her into his arms. Lilly stiffened at first. Not a little stiffening, either, but a posture change that affected practically every muscle in her body. Probably because she was shocked by his gesture. Or maybe even appalled. But by degrees, she soon settled against him, as if she belonged there.

Jason quickly dismissed that last thought. Lilly didn't belong in his arms. She didn't belong this close to him. This was an anomaly. An emotional blip created by the dangerous situation that had forced this temporary camaraderie between them.

Then he felt her warm breath brush against his neck. He took in her scent. The logic of emotional blips and anomalies flew right out the window.

Hell.

What was going on here?

The confusing yet tender episode lasted only a few seconds—thank God—because Lilly pulled back slightly and looked up at him. She squinted her eyes and appeared to be as thunderstruck as he felt.

Jason totally understood her dumbfounded state. Twenty-four hours earlier if someone had told him he'd be holding Lilly, and reacting to it in the most basic way a man could, he would have never believed it.

She swallowed hard and inched back even farther. The confusion in her eyes faded, and in its place came the uncomfortable realization of what had just happened.

Oh, yeah. They were on the same page.

Lilly cleared her throat, reached for the blanket and gave it an adjustment that it in no way needed. "You never did say—why were you here at the hospital tonight?"

Blind luck. But Jason kept that to himself. "I couldn't sleep, so I decided to drop by to check on the guard," he said, thankful for the conversation. It would hopefully take his mind off that *basic male* reaction he was still having. "When I saw Dr. Staten was still here, I went into his office to talk to him."

She paused. "Well…thank you."

Her thanks was genuine. Jason didn't doubt that. But he also didn't doubt that it hadn't been an easy thing for her to say to him. Civility of any kind was tricky between two battle-scarred enemies.

"I'm sorry," Lilly whispered, pulling away completely from him.

Jason immediately felt the loss of her body heat. A sensation that surprised and sickened him. Sheez. What the heck was wrong with him, anyway?

"What are you sorry for?" he managed to ask just to keep the discussion going.

"For borrowing your shoulder to cry on." She dusted her fingers across his jacket as if to remove any evidence of herself.

"After the scare you had, you deserve a shoulder, and the crying."

She stared at him. Paused. Stared at him some more. "You're being nice to me."

True, and he wasn't exactly pleased that she'd pointed it out. "Blame it on the adrenaline and fatigue." He groaned softly. "Don't worry… I'll be back to normal in no time."

"Good," she concluded. "Because it's easier that way."

Jason nodded, understanding. They had enough to deal with without bringing Greg's death and all those unresolved issues to the table. Unfortunately, one of those issues now seemed to be this bizarre attraction, or whatever the heck it was, that he felt for her.

Lilly leaned back, rested her head against the stack of pillows. "I wish I'd at least gotten a glimpse of the person who tried to smother me. Maybe I would have recognized him so you could arrest him."

Jason almost blew out a breath of relief at the change of subject. The *right* change. Too bad he hadn't thought of it sooner. Which only showed how dangerous distractions could be. Instead of pondering the effect of his hormones, he should be questioning her and digging for any clues to help them find the perp.

"A visual isn't the only way to recognize someone," he reminded her. "Was there anything familiar about his scent or his clothes?"

She immediately shook her head. "No."

Jason continued to press. "How about his voice? Did he say anything?"

"No to all of those. No scent. I wasn't able to touch his clothes. And if he said anything, I didn't hear it." Lilly paused a moment. "I can't even be sure it was a man. All I know is the person was a lot stronger than I am." She flexed her eyebrows. "But then, I'm not exactly a menacing threat with my superheroine strength, am I now? It didn't take much to subdue me."

So they weren't necessarily looking for a male, strong or otherwise. Just someone who had a reason to kill her. And Jason knew for a fact there were people who fit right into that category. "This has to be connected to your father. To his dirty business dealings."

"I agree. He was involved in so much. Falsifying paperwork and bids so he'd get contracts for services that he then only partially provided…if at all. He scammed a lot of people with bogus agreements to do everything from audits to major construction." Lilly grabbed a handful of the blanket and fisted it until her knuckles whitened. "He's been dead for two and a half years. You'd think the fallout would be finished by now."

It wouldn't be finished until this SOB was caught. "We still have the same suspects. Names we've gone over hundreds of times."

"And it could also be any one of the dozens of former business associates that my father scammed or involved in his illegal schemes. Once I'm back on my feet, I want to go through my office and my house—" Her eyes widened. "I still have an office and house, don't I?"

He nodded. "Your attorney's been taking care of that with money from your personal and business accounts.

But it probably won't do any good to visit your house and office. The police went through them and didn't find anything."

"Maybe they missed something." She froze, and her gaze whipped back to his. "Oh, my God. Megan. What if this person tries to go—"

"There's a cop at my house." One he could trust not to fall asleep. He wasn't about to risk Megan's life.

Lilly's breath was racing now and she placed her hand on her chest. "Thank you, again."

Jason decided it was a good time to get to his feet and put some distance between them. Unlike Lilly's other thanks, this one didn't feel so warm and fuzzy. Nothing he did for Megan required gratitude. What he did for her was totally out of love, and it riled him that Lilly even felt that she had a right to thank him.

Yes, it was stupid. Petty, even. But every paternal instinct in his body screamed for him to latch on to Megan and not let Lilly anywhere near her. He would have to override his instincts, though.

His lieutenant hadn't given him much of a choice about that.

"I'm making arrangements for you to be transferred to another hospital," Jason advised her. "Logistically, this one just isn't that easy to secure."

"And then what?" she asked, her voice thin. "I'd planned to be discharged in a day or two."

He'd already considered that, along with the lieutenant's order. "Once the doctors release you, you'll be placed in protective custody. *My* protective custody."

"Oh." Something flickered in her eyes and she stayed

quiet a moment. "Let me guess—that wasn't your idea?"

"My lieutenant's," he admitted.

Another *Oh*. "How in the world did he convince you to agree to that?"

"Quite easily. He reminded me that Megan might need protection, as well, and that I'd no doubt want to be the one to provide it."

She examined him with her firm gaze. "This way, you kill two birds with one stone."

The word "kill" turned his stomach. "I don't like that analogy." But to protect both Lilly and Megan and to minimize the disruptions to Megan's life, the thing to do was for Lilly to move in with him.

It was logical.

Mercy, he hated that frickin' word.

The move was *logical,* but nothing else about this was. This was the next step in the nightmare he'd dreaded since the moment he'd heard that Lilly had come out of the coma.

He would literally put Lilly under the same roof with the daughter he loved more than life itself.

The daughter she'd no doubt try to take from him.

Lilly shook her head. "You know this protective custody won't work, right?"

Jason shrugged. "We don't have a choice."

"Maybe we do. I could always use a private bodyguard."

Jason was about to give her an opinion on that, and it wasn't a good opinion, but something—or rather someone—stopped him.

"I will see her now!" someone yelled from the hall.

It was a man's voice. One that Jason didn't immediately recognize. That angry shout had him moving and reaching for his weapon.

"Take another step," he heard Detective O'Reilly warn, "and I promise you'll regret it."

With his gun ready and aimed, Jason hurried to the door and looked out. Hell. While he hadn't recognized the voice, he certainly recognized the man.

Wayne Sandling.

The former prominent attorney who'd done business with Lilly's father. Lots of business. And it hadn't all been aboveboard, either. Sandling was the last person on earth Jason wanted near Lilly.

"He barged his way in through the front desk," O'Reilly told Jason.

That didn't please Jason, but he would deal with the lax security once he'd finished with Sandling. "What are you doing here?" Jason demanded.

Sandling obviously recognized him, as well, because the man's mouth practically curled into a snarl. "Detective Lawrence. Long time, no see."

It wasn't nearly long enough.

Though the former attorney had no doubt climbed out of bed to make this visit, he somehow managed to look as if he were ready for the courtroom. He wore a navy suit, complete with a tie. A tie! At this hour of the morning. His ink-black, conservative-cut hair had been combed to perfection. Not even a hint of sleep was in his eyes. For someone that meticulous, it made Jason wonder how he'd managed to get caught doing anything illegal in the first place.

"You didn't answer my question, Sandling," Jason pointed out. "Why are you here?"

"Isn't it obvious?"

"Not really." Jason used his best badass-cop voice and added a glare. "Clarify it for me."

If Sandling had an unsavory response to Jason's tone and glare, he didn't show it. "One of your fellow officers called me tonight. About an attack on Lilly Nelson. He wanted to know if I had an alibi."

"Do you?"

"That's not the point. The point is I was awakened and questioned." His cosmetically perfect teeth came together for a moment. "I don't like that."

"Well, I don't like someone trying to kill Ms. Nelson." Jason stepped closer, making sure he violated Sandling's personal space. "So, where were you tonight?"

"Home, in bed, asleep. Alone," he added. Sandling came closer, too, violating Jason's personal space. "And I won't be questioned about my every move, either."

"You don't have a choice about that. You have motive and that gives me the right to question you about your *every move*."

"Is that Wayne Sandling?" Lilly called.

"Don't you dare try to get out of bed," Jason warned her without taking his eyes off the man. He didn't want Lilly to have to confront Sandling. That didn't mean she'd agree with him, and she would probably go so far as to try to get up and make her way into the hall.

That wasn't going to happen.

Jason decided it was time to put an end to this spur-of-the-moment conversation. "Detective O'Reilly, escort

Mr. Sandling out of the building. If he puts up a fight, arrest him."

"I won't let the cops and Lilly Nelson try to pin trumped-up charges on me again," Sandling insisted. "Find another scapegoat, Detective Lawrence, and leave me the hell alone."

And with that, Sandling turned and walked away. His hand shot up, to give O'Reilly a back-off warning when the detective tried to take hold of his arm. O'Reilly's escort duty wasn't necessary; Sandling left on his own, practically gliding down the hall. Jason kept his gaze fastened on him until the man was out of sight.

"Make sure he doesn't come back," Jason instructed O'Reilly. He turned to Lilly, who was indeed trying to get out of bed. "Stay put. He's gone."

Huffing, Lilly sank her head back onto the pillow. "Well, that was a special ending to a special night."

It was indeed. "I'll beef up security at the nurses' station and the front door." Just having to say that riled him, because until Sandling's impromptu visit, Jason thought he'd already done that. Which only proved just how dangerous this situation was. It was next to impossible to secure the place. He needed to have her transferred to the other hospital immediately.

"Sandling wouldn't dare try to come back tonight," Lilly said under her breath.

It seemed as if she was trying to convince herself.

"Are you still having doubts as to whether you need protective custody?" Jason didn't wait for her answer. "Then think again. Because I'm going to protect you whether you want it or not."

It was an order. Solid. Forceful. Certain. But Jason

had his own doubts about the certainty. With everything that'd happened, he had to wonder. Could he do his job and keep Lilly alive?

CHAPTER FIVE

LILLY'S NERVES WERE too frayed, and there were too many butterflies in her stomach for her to object to what Jason was doing. And what he was doing was lifting her from her wheelchair into the seat of the waiting SUV he'd rented. The rental was a necessity, he'd insisted, because his own vehicle would be too easily recognized.

By Wayne Sandling, perhaps.

Or by someone else who wanted to silence her permanently.

Carrying her was a necessary act, as well, Lilly reminded herself, because despite the past two days of intensive physical therapy, she still wasn't able to walk unassisted. That meant she didn't have a choice about his *hands-on* care. Still, there was something unnerving about having to rely on anyone—especially Jason—to make sure she got from point A to point B.

On the plus side, she was leaving point A: the hospital.

Point B: Jason's house.

Where she would see her daughter for the first time.

Lilly glanced down at the photo she had cradled in her hand. That instantly soothed the unpleasantness from having to rely on Jason to carry her. It also lessened the fatigue and the stress from the spent adrenaline and the sleepless nights. She could face almost anything now that she knew she'd soon meet Megan.

The April air was already muggy and much too warm, and the morning breeze whipped at them, bringing with it the fruity grape smell of some nearby mountain laurels. It blended with the scent of Jason's aftershave. No fruity fragrance for him. It was manly, and it reminded her of warm leather and the woods.

Jason nestled her in his arms, on the side away from his shoulder holster and weapon. Her aqua-colored silk top and pants whispered against his T-shirt and jeans. What a contrast. Her, wearing silk, mainly because that was the primary fabric in her wardrobe. Jason, wearing jeans, snakeskin boots and a plain black T-shirt. She was betting he had a lot of those items in his closet. But that wasn't a criticism. He looked darn good. In fact, his firm, nicely shaped butt was meant for jeans, and she wasn't exactly pleased that she'd noticed that about him.

"Sorry," Jason mumbled when his arm swiped across her breast. He eased her onto the front passenger seat.

After all the inappropriate thoughts she'd had about his butt, Lilly pretended not to notice the intimate contact, even though she did suck in her breath. Thankfully, Jason pretended not to notice that.

She sighed.

This protective custody wasn't off to a good start. Lilly wasn't counting on it to get much better, either. All she could hope for was that the person who'd tried to kill her would be caught quickly so that neither Megan nor she would be in danger. As long as this person was out there, the sleeplessness would continue. So would the sickening, ominous feeling that the next breath she took could be her last. Hardly the beginning of a new life that she'd wanted when she'd first awakened from the coma.

Jason got in the SUV, started the engine and drove away from the hospital. Lilly spared the place a glance in the side mirror. She wouldn't miss it. She was anxious to get on with her life, and that getting on with it started now. Of course, she would have to return every other day for physical therapy, but that wouldn't take too much time from her plans to bond with Megan. She'd missed so much already, and she didn't intend to waste even a minute more.

"What kind of security measures have you taken to make sure all of us are safe?" she asked Jason. And by "all of us," she definitely meant Megan.

"I'm taking lots of precautions." He hitched his thumb in the direction behind them. "That's an unmarked car with two officers inside."

She took another glance in the mirror and saw both the vehicle and the plainclothes cops.

"They'll make sure no one's following us and that we get to my place in one piece," Jason explained. "I also created a little diversion by telling the hospital staff and your secretary, Corinne, that you'd be going to *your* house for a few days. There's a decoy car headed there now. It'll pull into your garage, and the officers will exit through the back. So if anyone's looking for you, they won't know if you're there or not."

All in all, it was a good plan. Or rather, it was a start to a good plan. "That's one base covered. How about your house? Is it safe?"

"As safe as I can possibly make it. It's in a gated community, and I had a new security system installed. A patrol car will make spot checks at least every hour. Of course, I'll be there, too."

Of course.

Lilly forced herself to relax and to focus on the positive. "Hey, maybe with all this protection and safeguards, the guy who tried to kill me will decide it's too big of a risk to come after me again. Maybe he'll just disappear."

"Maybe," Jason mumbled.

She noted his tight jaw and the tenseness around his eyes. "You don't believe that, do you?"

"No," he readily admitted.

Neither did she.

That's why Lilly welcomed those security measures. And she even welcomed Jason. Because as difficult as this arrangement would be, it would be unbearable if her daughter was in any more danger than she perhaps already was. With all of Jason's faults, it seemed as if he genuinely loved Megan. Which meant he'd protect her with his life.

Lilly was counting heavily on that.

"So, it'll be Megan, you, the nanny and me staying at the house?" Lilly paused. "Or is the nanny there only during the day?"

"The nanny's name is Erica," Jason explained. "She's a live-in."

There was something in the way he offered that information that had Lilly picking through it to see if there was any hidden meaning. Her brain was obviously a little overactive because she immediately came up with a possible scenario.

"Erica's been with you since Megan was born?" she asked.

"Yes."

Okay. That didn't confirm her scenario that Erica might be more than a nanny, but again, Lilly was sure there was something left unsaid.

"Is—"

"Erica can be…a little possessive sometimes," Jason volunteered, interrupting her, which was a good thing since Lilly didn't know how she would finish that question anyway. *Are you sleeping with the nanny?* hardly seemed appropriate.

"She's possessive about Megan?"

That earned her a semiglare. "Yeah. Who else?"

"You, perhaps?"

Jason reacted as if he'd tasted something disgusting. "Not a chance."

All right. So, she wasn't stepping into a love-nest/wannabe-family situation, and that made her feel far better than it should have. However, the "possessive" description bothered her. After all, Jason seemed possessive. Lilly felt that way herself.

One house.

Three possessive people.

This was going to be one heck of a long stay in protective custody.

"I'm making arrangements for a nurse to come to the house," Jason continued a moment later. "But it'll take a couple of days to do a thorough security check. In the meantime, if you need help, just let me know."

There it was again. That niggling feeling that he'd left something out of his comment. "Help?" she repeated.

"Help," he verified, though he did pause after his quick response. "You know, what with the wheelchair. You, uh, might need assistance…getting around or dressing. If you do, just let me know."

She'd rather set her hair on fire.

This situation would be tense enough without him helping her in that kind of personal way.

Jason shook his head. "I don't know why I said that."

Lilly knew why. It was the same reason she'd had images of his butt and Jason and Erica in a lovers' romp. "I think it's about what happened two nights ago at St. Joseph's. That hug," she clarified when he aimed a questioning glance in her direction.

"What about it?" Judging from his stiff tone, he didn't want to discuss it any more than she did, but Lilly couldn't let this linger between them. If they were to share a house, it might be best to start with a little air-clearing.

"I don't think it was a valid attraction or anything," she concluded.

Valid? Valid! Sheez. It was a word she'd use in a corporate briefing, not in a personal discussion about inappropriate hospital embraces.

He sat there. Waiting, or something. He obviously had no plans to cooperate with the air-clearing or to question her bizarre word usage.

Lilly gave it one more try. "I think the hug and our reaction to it was some kind of, uh, knight-in-shining-armor response. You know, because you'd saved my life."

Jason shifted in his seat. "It was a hug. That's all. It can't undo what's between us."

"True." Lilly added a silent *whew* to that. She couldn't cope with hugs and possible attractions that didn't make sense.

And nothing about being attracted to Jason made sense.

She needed to concentrate on her daughter. On how she was going to deal with this first visit. On how she was going to make a place for herself in Megan's life.

And that's exactly what she did.

Lilly glanced down at the photo again. The butterflies returned with a vengeance. And the doubts. So many doubts. Including the tsunami of all doubts: whether or not she'd be a good mother.

Before the accident and the coma, she'd spent months trying to clean up the investment business that she had inherited from her father, and she'd put the notion of children and marriage on the back burner. Of course, her experience with Greg had contributed to that back-burner decision. Talk about taking an emotional toll. Yet, if she hadn't had that brief tumultuous relationship with Greg, there would have been no Megan.

Strange that the night she'd regretted most had produced a child that she could never regret.

With that, the memories came. Good mixed with the bad. It was always that way with Greg. The night that she'd had sex with him, he'd just had a huge business setback that would almost certainly lead to bankruptcy. After drinking, he'd shown up at her house. She'd tried to console him and they'd landed in bed. Lilly had immediately realized it as a mistake since she hadn't loved him and because he'd wanted more than friendship from her.

A lot more.

Greg wanted a wedding ring and the white-picket-fence fairy tale. Unfortunately she'd told him that she wasn't ready for those things. And might never be. Angry with her rejection, he'd stormed out and minutes later was involved in a fatal car accident.

It had only been the beginning of the nightmare.

Jason had blamed her for his brother's death, and there was indeed blame to place in her lap. She'd gotten so caught up in her argument with Greg that she hadn't noticed that he was too drunk to drive.

A fatal mistake.

One she'd have to live with.

Megan didn't soften that mistake. Far from it. Because even though at the time Lilly hadn't known that they'd created a child, she'd essentially let her baby's father walk out the door and die.

"Nervous?" she heard Jason ask.

That one word pulled her out of that mixed bag of memories, and she glanced around to see what had prompted his question. With one hand, she had a death grip on Megan's picture, and with her other hand, she was choking the strap of her seat belt.

She slipped Megan's picture into her pocket. "The truth? I'm terrified."

That terror went up a notch when he took the turn into the Redland Oaks neighborhood. She'd learned from one of the cops who'd guarded her for the past two days that

Jason had bought a house in the northeast area shortly after Megan was born.

"Don't expect too much for your first visit," Jason warned. He stopped at the security gate, entered his code, and the long metal arm lifted so he could drive inside. He waved at the officers in the car behind them, and the driver circled around to leave. "Megan's going through this stage where she's a little wary of people that she doesn't know. I've told her about you, but she's too young to understand."

Well, she certainly qualified as people her daughter didn't know. Lilly prayed there wouldn't be tears—from either Megan or her.

To calm her quickly unraveling nerves, Lilly forced herself to concentrate on gathering information. After all, she hadn't had much of a chance to talk with Jason about Megan. For the past two days, he'd been tied up with the investigation and security arrangements. They'd only spoken briefly on the phone, and that was only so that Jason could tell her when he'd be arriving to pick her up from the hospital. The call had lasted less than a minute.

"Can Megan walk yet?" she asked.

"More or less. She still takes a few spills, but she gets better at it every day."

Lilly had no idea if that was in the normal range of development, and she made a mental note to read some parenting books. "How about talking? Does she say anything?"

Dead silence.

Not good, considering it was a relatively easy question.

"She babbles a lot and says bye-bye and…da-da," Jason finally answered. He gave her a hard glance. "Let's just get down to the bottom line here. I love Megan. She loves me. And she calls me da-da because I'm the only father she's ever known."

Lilly couldn't dispute that, but she could take issue with what he *wasn't* saying. Suddenly this was no longer a conversation about child development. It was a conversation about all that air they hadn't managed to clear yet. "I'm her mother."

"That doesn't void the last eleven and a half months." He cursed under his breath. "Look, what happened to you wasn't your fault. I know that. But I also know I'm not just going to give Megan up now that you're out of the coma."

There it was. The real bottom line. The one they'd been tiptoeing around since the moment he'd walked into her hospital room and told her about her daughter.

Lilly shook her head. "I'm not going to give her up, either, Jason."

That hard look he was giving her got a lot harder. "Then I guess we're at a stalemate."

Not really. Yes, Jason had legal custody, but he'd gotten that custody only because she hadn't been able to care for her daughter.

Now, that had all changed.

Well, sort of.

Lilly gave herself an internal hard look similar to one she'd gotten from Jason, and she realized that their stalemate would soon turn into a huge problem. First of all, she wasn't even sure she could totally revoke Jason's custodial rights. Not without a long legal battle, anyway.

During that time, her daughter would be pulled between the two of them.

But what was the alternative?

Shared custody?

Lilly could barely contain a laugh. The idea of Jason and her amicably sharing a child for, well, the rest of their lives seemed impossible. Heck, despite the danger and that now-infamous hug, they couldn't stop snipping at each other for a fifteen-minute ride.

Yes, indeed. A huge problem.

Jason pulled into the driveway of a single-story, redbrick house with smoke-gray shutters. Modest, but pristine. Very much a family house in a family neighborhood. Unlike his former place in a singles-only apartment complex. He hadn't lived there because he was a player, either. She remembered Greg explaining that with Jason's shift work and late-night undercover duties, he preferred not to live next to families with children.

Times had certainly changed.

Lilly did a quick check in the vanity mirror on the visor to see if she looked as windblown as she felt. She did. Of course, it was hard to tell with her choppy hair gathered up into a ponytail. She wasn't a vain person, but once things settled down, she'd be making an appointment with her hairdresser.

Jason got out, retrieved her wheelchair. She considered trying to walk on her own. *Briefly* considered it. But then decided that falling flat on her butt wouldn't make a good impression on Megan or the nanny. So Lilly didn't make even a grumble of a protest when Jason scooped her up into his arms and deposited her in the wheelchair.

"You're angry," she said, noting his expression.

"You're right."

Well, that anger would likely increase a hundredfold once she informed him about the discussion she'd had that morning with her attorney. Lilly was dreading what Jason and she would say to each other once he knew. And unfortunately, she would have to tell him soon— after she met her daughter.

She placed her hands on the wheels, but Jason took over that task, as well. Again, no protest from her. During the past two days she'd discovered she was lousy at steering the chair, too. Besides, he could get her there faster, and speed suddenly seemed to be a critical issue. She didn't want to wait even a second longer to see Megan.

He pushed her up the flagstone walkway lined with Mexican heather. Actual flowers. Yep. She really was going to have to adjust the old mental image she had of Jason. She'd only known him as the brooding loner, rebel-with a-cause for justice, who was married to the badge. This wasn't the residence of a married-to-the-badge workaholic.

This was a home.

A home that Jason had created because of Megan.

That put a rather large knot in the pit of her stomach. This wasn't a competition between Jason and her, but it sure felt like one.

And he clearly had the advantage.

All the vanilla-white plantation blinds in the front window were closed. Probably a security precaution. Lilly half expected the richly stained wooden front door to open to reveal Erica and Megan standing there, ready to greet her. That didn't happen. Not only didn't the door open, it was double locked. Jason used his key so they could go inside.

The security system immediately kicked in with a buzzing sound, and he entered the code on the keypad near the door to stop the alarm from engaging. With each of these mundane, necessary actions, her heart beat even faster.

He pushed her wheelchair into the foyer. "Erica?" he called.

Nothing. No response whatsoever. And for one brief, terrifying moment, Lilly considered that the *possessive* nanny had nabbed Megan and gone on the run rather than risk losing the child. But then she heard the sound. Or rather, she heard the three sounds that happened simultaneously. Jason's cell phone rang, and there was a little high-pitched squeak, followed by a shuffle of movement.

Footsteps.

And there she was. The little girl responsible for the millions of butterflies in Lilly's stomach.

Megan Maria Lawrence.

Her daughter came barreling out of the room to the right of the foyer. Not a steady barreling, either. Every step seemed awkward and off balance, but somehow, amazingly, she stayed on her feet and didn't come to a stop until her gaze landed on Lilly.

Apparently sizing her up, Megan stood there dressed in pink overalls and a white cotton shirt with soft eyelet lace on the collar. Her auburn curls danced around her face.

Lilly's heart went into overdrive. One look, and the

love for her daughter was instant. All-consuming. And in that moment, she knew she would do whatever it took to protect, to love, to keep her.

Behind her, Lilly could hear Jason talking on the phone, but the conversation didn't register. Nothing registered except Megan. Well, nothing until a woman peered out from the room Megan had just exited.

Erica, no doubt.

No all-consuming love here. No sizing up, either. The tall, leggy brunette in the breezy khaki capris and waist-length coral T-shirt had obviously already done her sizing up. With one indifferent glance from her crystal-blue eyes, she made Lilly feel like an intruder.

"Ms. Nelson," she greeted.

Lilly settled for a polite nod and returned her attention to her daughter. Megan, however, seemed far more interested in the wheelchair than the woman sitting it in. It was no doubt Megan's curiosity that had her toddling toward Lilly and the chair.

Megan aimed her index finger at one of the wheels and babbled something incoherent. But her curiosity only lasted a few seconds before she looked at Jason.

The little girl smiled.

And the smile made it all the way to those sparkling pearl-gray eyes.

The wheelchair no longer held Megan's attention, so Lilly latched on to the chair arms and forced herself to stand. That still didn't garner Megan's attention.

With that same awkward gait, Megan made her way past Lilly and to Jason. Only then did Lilly realize that he'd finished his call and was putting his phone back in his pocket. He leaned down and scooped Megan up in his arms.

"Da-da," she said.

And there was nothing incoherent about it. The little girl gave an awkward, backhanded wave and placed a kiss on Jason's cheek.

The moment was pure magic.

Lilly could almost feel her heart breaking. Sweet heaven. Before she'd seen Megan, before she'd seen this, she'd been so certain about barging her way into Megan's life, but that kiss and smile put a huge dent in her resolve. Jason was Megan's father in every way that mattered.

Jason's gaze met Lilly's, and she braced herself for the I-told-you-so smugness that she thought she might see there. But there was no smugness. No triumphant look of any kind.

But there was concern.

"Take Megan and go to the playroom," he told Erica. "We'll be there in a few minutes."

Oh, no. This couldn't be good. Maybe now she'd get that victory speech or else a lecture on the house rules, which she'd probably already violated. Lilly eased back down into her chair and waited.

"There's something important I need to tell you," Erica said to Jason. And then she fired a narrow-eyed glare at Lilly.

A double *Oh, no.* Erica was probably ready to voice her objection to the protective-custody arrangement.

"It'll have to wait," Jason told Erica, his insistence sounding very much like an order. He looked at Lilly. Specifically, at the chair. Then he glanced at the room at the end of the hall. "That wheelchair will never fit through the door. You'd be stuck in the hall. Out in the open. That's too big of a risk."

"A risk for what?" Lilly asked, already knowing she wouldn't like the answer.

But Jason didn't confirm that answer, and he seemed to have a quick debate with himself before turning back to Erica. "Go ahead and take Megan to the playroom. And don't go near the windows. In fact, take her into the storage closet."

Now, that *was* an order. Just like that, Lilly's heart raced even harder and the blood rushed to her head. Whatever had caused that urgency in his voice, it wasn't a lecture about house rules.

Something was terribly wrong.

Erica must have decided the same thing. She took Megan, though the little girl protested a bit with more of those babbled syllables. Again, it was nothing coherent, but she voiced her displeasure with her adamant tone and by grabbing for Jason. However, Megan ended up grasping at the air because Erica complied with Jason's request and hurried the child out of the room.

"What happened?" Lilly asked.

Jason drew his gun from the shoulder holster. In the same motion, he grabbed her wheelchair and moved her out of the foyer. Away from the front door. He directed her into the adjacent living room, then hurried to the window. He lifted the blinds just a fraction and peeked out.

"That call was the security company that monitors the control panel at the gate," Jason offered. "They've already phoned for police backup because someone's trying to override the system."

It was difficult to hear him with her heartbeat crashing in her ears. "What does that mean?" Lilly waited, holding her breath. Praying.

"It means whoever tried to kill you is probably on the way here."

CHAPTER SIX

JASON HADN'T THOUGHT this day could possibly get any harder.

But he was obviously wrong.

He glanced at Lilly. She'd gone pale and had flattened her hand over her chest as if to try to steady her heart. Her lips were so tightly pinched together, they were practically white.

"Can you get out of the wheelchair and onto the floor?" he asked.

She gave a choppy nod and, hoping she could do it on her own, he immediately turned his attention back to the window. Or rather, back to the street that fronted the house. There wasn't a moving car in sight, but he couldn't count on it staying that way. If this was the latest attempt by the would-be killer and he or she could somehow bypass the security code, then they were all in danger.

Behind him, he heard Lilly maneuver herself out of the chair. He wished like the devil that he'd had time to carry her to the storage closet—aka the panic room— that he'd modified in case of a situation just like this one. But he couldn't take the risk of leaving the front of the house unguarded. That kind of move could put Megan in too much danger. And he was certain Lilly would agree with his decision. Megan had to come first.

"Will Megan be okay?" Lilly asked.

"Of course." Jason prayed that was true. He'd considered that the perp would figure out where they were, but he'd honestly believed that the guy wouldn't make an attempt in broad daylight to come after Lilly. He had also believed his security measures would be enough.

They *had* to be enough.

Because the alternative was unthinkable.

"What about surveillance cameras?" Lilly asked. Her voice was shaking. "Is there one at the gate?"

"Yes." But the security company had already told him that the vehicle had heavily tinted windows and that the driver's face was obscured. In other words, they would send the video to the crime lab for analysis, but they couldn't rely on the images to make an ID.

Hell.

Without an ID or without a face-to-face confrontation, they might not figure out who was behind this. Of course, Jason wanted to know that so he could arrest the guy. But he didn't want that info at the expense of further risking the lives of the people inside his house.

Staying by the edge of the window, he fastened his attention to the street. Still no cars. No one, in fact. That was a plus on their side. Maybe this way, no innocent bystanders would be involved.

The spring breeze wasn't cooperating. It kept stirring the thick shrubs and massive oak trees that dotted the neighborhood. Each flicker of movement, each sway of the branches, every harmless sound spiked his adrenaline and sent his gaze whipping around the visible area. Thankfully, it was only the visible area he had to be concerned with because there was no street to the back of the house. And if the person gave up trying to disarm the gate and simply climbed over it, the security company would alert him.

That thought must have tempted fate.

His phone rang, the sound slicing through the room.

Jason didn't take his eyes off the street; nor did he lower his gun. Holding his breath, he pulled out his cell phone and took the call.

"It's over," he heard the now-familiar voice of the security company employee say. "The person gave up and drove away."

Jason released his breath. "Are officers in pursuit?"

"Negative. They haven't arrived yet."

That was *not* what he wanted to hear. "Call them now. Give them a description of the vehicle." Maybe it wouldn't be too late for them to apprehend and make an arrest.

"He's gone?" Lilly asked.

"It appears that way."

Jason pushed the end button on his phone and looked back at her. She was climbing into her wheelchair. Not easily, either. It was obvious the muscles in her legs weren't anywhere close to being a hundred percent. He considered helping her, but his instincts yelled for him to continue to keep watch.

So that's what he did.

"The cops aren't going to catch him, are they?" Lilly whispered.

"They will." Though he didn't know how he would make good on that promise. He just knew they couldn't continue to go through this.

"Is everything okay?" Erica's voice poured through the house's intercom system. Only then did Jason realize she'd probably been listening since he'd installed an intercom unit in the panic room.

"It's okay," he assured her. "But just in case, don't take Megan near the windows."

Thankfully, Erica didn't ask for a just-in-case clarification. He heard the slight click to indicate she'd turned off the intercom.

Lilly wheeled her chair closer to him. She was breathing heavily, probably from the exertion and the fear. "As long as I was in a coma, Megan was safe."

It was true, yes. But Lilly hadn't been responsible for her father's business practices or her coma.

Or her recovery.

Jason was about to remind her of that when he caught the movement in the foyer. Erica. With Megan straddled on her hip, she came to the entryway of the living room. Staying away from the windows, she snagged Jason's gaze.

"Ms. Nelson's right," Erica concluded. "Megan is in danger as long as she's here."

He considered reminding Erica that it was his job to protect *both* Lilly and Megan. But it was more than that. Now that Lilly was out of the coma, Megan wasn't safe. Period. Because anyone who would attempt to murder a woman in a hospital bed probably wouldn't hesitate to use a child if it meant that child could lead him or her to Lilly.

"I have my orders," Jason explained to her, trying to keep the emotion out of his voice. It was for Megan's sake. Even though she was a baby, she could no doubt sense the tension. He hated seeing that puzzled look on her face. "And those orders are for me to protect Lilly and Megan. That's what I'll do."

Erica didn't do an eye roll, but it was close. "There's something I have to tell you," she insisted.

"Unless it's an emergency, it'll have to wait." Jason motioned toward the playroom. "I want Megan and you in the panic room awhile longer. Until we're sure this guy isn't going to try to make a return visit."

A god-awful thought.

"It's not an emergency," Erica continued. "But it's important. I don't think it should wait. Once you've heard what I have to say, you might change your mind about guarding Ms. Nelson."

He was both intrigued and baffled by that, but Jason didn't miss the catty tone in Erica's voice. He wasn't stupid or blind. He knew that Erica had feelings for him. Despite his earlier denial to Lilly that Erica's possessiveness was limited to Megan, he knew otherwise. Oh, yes. He'd seen that *look* in Erica's eyes, and he suspected that she would like to marry him so the three of them could be a family.

That wasn't going to happen.

He has no plan for marriage. Not to Erica. Not to anyone. He needed to concentrate on two things: raising Megan and doing his job. He didn't have the time or energy for anything else. And in this case, doing his job meant dealing with Lilly and all the danger that came with her.

Lilly got her wheelchair moving in the direction of the playroom. "I'd be interested in hearing what you have to tell Jason," she said to Erica.

"You already know," Erica snapped.

She brought the wheelchair to a dead stop. Right in front of Megan and Erica. Lilly stared up at the other woman and shook her head. But then, the head shaking came to an abrupt stop, as well.

Lilly whirled the chair around so that she was facing him, but she didn't get a chance to say anything.

Erica beat her to it.

"There was a call earlier, just before you arrived," Erica said. "It was from Michael."

Michael. Erica's brother. And Jason's friend and attorney, as well. In fact, it was Michael who'd asked Jason to hire Erica to be Megan's nanny. "What did he want?" Jason asked.

"I knew something was wrong when he called," Erica explained. She was nervous now. "I pressed him to tell me. And he did because he didn't want to be blindsided by this."

"Blindsided?" Jason repeated. "By what?"

"Michael got a call from Ms. Nelson's attorney."

"Oh, my God," Lilly mumbled.

Judging from Lilly's reaction, this would be yet more bad news. Jason wasn't sure he was ready for that, but it didn't stop Erica from continuing.

"Michael said Ms. Nelson started the paperwork to revoke your custody of Megan."

OH, THIS WAS GOING to get messy.

Lilly had known this moment would come, of course, but what she hadn't counted on was having to deal with it only minutes after the scare with the possible breach of security. Judging from the fierce look that Jason was giving her, dealing with the killer or security issues might be easier than the conversation they were about to have.

"I'm sorry," Lilly said. She was. Genuinely sorry. "I intended to tell you."

His left eyebrow shot up and he indicated an unspoken *When?* However, Jason didn't voice that question. "I want the three of you to go to the back of the house. If I need you to move into the panic room, I'll let you know through the intercom." He turned his gaze on the nanny. "Erica, Lilly will probably need help getting out of that wheelchair and into the room."

Okay. So, he didn't intend to let her explain. Not that she needed to shed much light on her decision, anyway. Since there was nothing Lilly could say to him to make this better, she decided to comply. Besides, Jason was right: it'd be safer for them to be out of the front room. Because if the would-be killer returned...

But she stopped.

Best not to go there.

Keeping a firm grip on Megan, Erica turned and headed down the hall. Lilly did the same. Not easily. The carpeted floor wasn't exactly a good surface for the wheelchair to maneuver on. Still, Lilly had no intention of asking for help.

Erica disappeared into a room at the end of the hall. Lilly tried to follow her, but it only took one hard bop of her wheels on the door frame before she realized that Jason was right—she wouldn't be able to squeeze through.

So Lilly sat there.

Like the rest of the house, the playroom reflected

the same homey environment that Jason had created for Megan. Cheery pastel-yellow walls. Overstuffed floral chairs. And toys. Lots and lots of toys. Not gender-specific, either. Megan had a pinto rocking horse, dozens of colorful plastic building blocks and stuffed animals. Some of them were huge, including the fuzzy orange elephant perched in the corner near the doorway to what was probably the panic room.

"Do you need help?" Erica asked.

Yes. But Lilly wasn't going to ask for it. "I'll be fine right here."

She hoped.

The front door was only about thirty feet away. Too close if someone came barging through it. Of course, Jason wouldn't let that happen. Which only contributed to the massive amount of guilt that Lilly was suddenly feeling. She hadn't done anything wrong by trying to get custody of her daughter, but then she hadn't done it the right way, either. Despite the investigation and security arrangements, she should have found the time to tell Jason.

Megan began to squirm to get down, and Erica eased her into a standing position on the floor. Lilly almost reached out her arms—an automatic gesture to welcome Megan to come closer—but she held back, hoping the child would come to her.

She did.

Megan toddled her way and gave the wheels a cursory inspection before turning her attention to Lilly. She cocked her head to the side, a gesture that so reminded Lilly of Jason. That was his expression. Along with his eyes, Megan looked very much like his biological daughter.

"Da-da?" Megan babbled, and she yawned, rubbed her eyes and pointed to the door.

"Da-da's busy right now," Erica responded, her voice strained yet somehow soothing. "He'll be here soon." Erica sank down into a rocking chair and tipped her eyes to the ceiling before her gaze came back to Lilly. "Jason had to know about that call from your lawyer."

"Yes." It was too bad, though, that the news hadn't come from her.

But Lilly immediately rethought that. That wasn't the sort of news that could be softened, so it probably didn't matter who the messenger was. Besides, she had to give Erica the benefit of the doubt here. The woman obviously loved Megan. If Jason lost custody, that would mean Erica would lose Megan, too. She wouldn't have any rights to see the child, either. Lilly understood that concern.

That fear.

Because even though she'd only known Megan for a few precious minutes, she couldn't imagine losing her.

Megan rubbed her eyes again, and while keeping a precarious balance, she stooped to retrieve a well-worn, blue polka-dotted blanket from the floor. She shoved it against her right cheek.

"It's her nap time," Erica explained. "She still takes two a day. One short one in the morning and another longer one in the afternoon."

Lilly felt a pang of jealousy in her heart. Such basic information. But it was info she didn't know. Here was her own daughter, her own flesh and blood, and she knew so little about her.

That would change.

Erica stood and gathered Megan into her arms. Lilly started to back out of the doorway so they could get through, but Erica waved her off. "She can take her nap in here. I'm sure that's what Jason would want."

Lilly watched as the nanny pulled open one of the chairs, converting it into a small but plushy bed. Erica got on it with Megan and cuddled with her. Another pang. A huge one. Erica was doing all the things that Lilly knew she should be doing.

"The guest room's right across the hall," Erica told her. "That's where you'll be staying."

A guest. Not that Erica had needed to emphasize that. Lilly knew her place. For the moment, anyway. But she wouldn't remain a guest in her daughter's life for long.

"The door's already open," Erica added. "But if you need help getting in, just let me know." The offer had a get-lost tinge to it.

Since Megan seemed to settle right into the nap and since Lilly felt like an intruder, she turned her wheelchair around to face yet another door she couldn't enter.

"Enough of this," Lilly mumbled. She put on the brake, shoved the metal footrests to the side, grabbed on to the chair arms, stood up and took a step.

Her muscles responded. Flexed. Moved. The way they should respond. *Almost.* For several moments, she concentrated just on that. It didn't exactly feel right, but it was better than being in that chair.

She took it one small step at a time and not without support, either. Using the wall and furniture, Lilly began to make her way around the room. She was doing okay until she banged her knee into the protruding Shaker-style dresser. But she didn't let a little pain deter her. She kept moving. An inch at a time toward her goal.

And her goal was the bed.

Where she was likely to drop like a landed trout once she reached it.

The physical exertion sent beads of sweat popping out on her forehead, and she felt dizzy. She ignored both the sweat and the light-headedness and continued. If she had any hopes of taking care of her daughter, it started with her regaining her independence.

"What the heck do you think you're doing?" she heard Jason ask.

And he asked it just as she made a final, haphazard grab for the bedpost. Her reach landed short, and she off-balanced herself. Lilly tried to grab something, anything, but it was too late. Her shoulder smacked against the bedpost, which felt as if it were made of granite.

Jason hurried across the room and got to her just in time to loop his arm around her waist. But it didn't stop her forward momentum. In fact, it threw him off balance, as well, and they both fell hard onto the bed.

Just like that, she was in Jason's arms. Touching him all over. That touching part was even more noticeable because her top shifted in the fall and her now-bare stomach slipped against his midsection.

Body met body.

Breath met breath.

So did their gazes. They met. Held. And kept holding

until there was a lot of unwanted energy simmering between them.

The entire encounter was powerful because it seemed to drain her brain and her common sense. For one moment she forgot all about the bitterness, she forgot all about Greg. Heck, she forgot how to breathe. And all she could remember was that being held had never felt this right.

Which meant it was wrong.

Totally wrong.

Lilly cleared her throat, hoping it would clear her head. It didn't. Worse, Jason seemed to be having the same problems with his thought process. She pulled away from him before she said something stupid like, *kiss me*. And for some reason, she did want him to kiss her. She wanted to know how that strong, sensual mouth would taste. She wanted to know how his lips would feel against hers.

She was obviously going crazy.

"We'll blame this on adrenaline again, okay?" he said.

It wasn't a suggestion.

Lilly nodded and adjusted her top so that her stomach was covered. She also quickly changed subjects. "I guess you must be sure the bad guy isn't close or you wouldn't be here?"

"The police arrived and are patrolling the neighborhood. If he's in the area, they'll find him. If he's long gone, then they'll beef up security at the gate. Double access codes. Extra security cameras."

All of those things were good ideas, but they wouldn't find him. Lilly was certain that the guy was long gone, which left them to deal with the aftermath. Unfortunately, part of that aftermath meant she owed Jason an apology.

"I'm sorry that I didn't tell you about calling the lawyer."

Jason spared her a narrow-eyed glance. "You should be sorry."

"Well, I am."

Another glance. Followed by an angry groan. Then he stared at her. Nope. Make that a glare. "I'm really pissed off at you right now, you know that?"

"Yes." She softly explained, "But put yourself in my place and ask yourself if you wouldn't have done the same thing."

His glare didn't soften one bit. "I'm not in the mood for reasoning here, Lilly. This isn't about logic or validity. It's about the love I have for that little girl across the hall."

"It's also about the hatred you feel for me," she pointed out.

"I don't hate you."

He said it too quickly for her to believe that he'd given it any real thought. "Liar."

"I don't hate you," he insisted.

"Maybe not. But every time you look at me, you remember Greg and how I could have saved him if I'd been thinking about him instead of me."

He shrugged and propped his hands on his hips. "If you're waiting for me to deny that, I can't."

"I know you can't." Lilly considered ending this air-clearing with that acknowledgment, but they were at an impasse here, and for Megan's sake, they needed to get past it. "Because every time I look at you, I remember the accusations and the hell you put me through that night and all the weeks after it."

That was only partly true. Which made it a lie. For reasons she didn't want to explore, she no longer saw the pain of Greg's death when she looked at Jason. Instead, she saw Jason, the man. The hot cop. The person responsible for confusing her more than she could have ever imagined.

"We need to put an end to this protective custody," Lilly informed him. "We need to figure out who tried to kill me so we can all get on with our lives."

No more glaring, but there was skepticism written all over his face. "I'll listen to any ideas you have as to how we can catch this guy."

"*Any* ideas?" she questioned.

He frowned. "Within reason."

Well, that probably ruled out what she was about to say, but Lilly went with it anyway. "I'd like to go to my office and have a look around."

He was already shaking his head before she finished. "Too risky."

"Breathing is too risky," she reminded him.

Jason leaned in, violating her personal space. "But some breaths are riskier than others."

She didn't think it was intentional, but she knew from the look on his face that he was probably thinking about that near kiss.

Yes, that was indeed one risky breath.

He was so close that she could see the swirls of gray in his eyes. Too close. Yet she did nothing to move away. It was a cheap thrill, except she knew this cheap thrill would have an enormous price tag with the potential for her heart to be broken.

"Besides," he continued, leaning back out of her personal space, "anything you need from your office, I can bring it here."

"You can't bring a conditioned response to me. In other words, something there might trigger those gaps in my memory so we'll know who's trying to kill me. And if we know that, we can catch him."

He stayed quiet a moment and then shook his head again.

"It makes sense," Lilly continued so she could cut off any objection he might try to voice. "We could go to my office after hours, with a police escort and without letting anyone outside S.A.P.D. know. You could have the building and parking lot checked to make sure it's secure."

"But that still wouldn't make it safe."

"A half hour. That's all I'd need. Just enough time to try to relive what happened that night before someone tried to kill me."

Lilly geared herself up to add more to the argument, but the sound of Megan's fussing had both Jason and her turning in the direction of the empty doorway. It didn't stay empty for long. With Erica in hot pursuit, Megan came racing into the room, and the second she spotted Jason, she made a beeline for the bed.

"I'm sorry," Erica said, coming after the child. "She doesn't seem interested in taking a nap today."

Jason lifted the child onto the bed with them. "It's okay. She can stay in here for a while."

That must have met with Megan's seal of approval

because she gave Jason a kiss on the tip of his nose. The little girl climbed out of Jason's lap and worked her tiny body in between Lilly and him. Erica quietly left the room.

Lilly leaned in closer, savoring the feel of Megan's soft skin. Taking in her scent. She ran her fingers through those curls. Like air and silk. It was one of those unforgettable moments in her life. A real turning point. Her first step at getting to know her daughter.

Jason touched Megan's hair, as well, and let his fingertips trail over her cheek. It was like a sedative for Megan because her eyelids immediately drifted down. It seemed as if she was interested in taking a nap, after all.

"If I forgive you," Jason whispered to Lilly, "if I forgive myself for what happened to Greg, it'll be like letting go of him."

There it was. The catch-22 that she'd been trying to come to terms with since that night. "I understand."

"Do you?" he challenged, but he immediately waved it off. "When Greg died, I thought there was nothing more painful than losing a brother. But now I know I was wrong." He looked down at Megan and brushed a kiss on her forehead. "There are greater heartbreaks in the world."

Yes. And losing Megan was at the top of the list.

Lilly stared at her daughter, who was nestled in the crook of Jason's arm. Megan's da-da. A connection she knew she couldn't—and wouldn't—break.

So, the question was, what kind of compromise was she willing to make to be part of Megan's life? What was she willing to do so this would work? There was only one answer; she was willing to do anything.

Anything.

And that included forging a truce, a compromise and perhaps even a relationship with her enemy. With Jason. Strange. It didn't seem as distasteful as it should.

While Lilly was mulling over that contradiction, the phone next to the bed rang.

Jason gave a weary sigh, leaned over and snatched it up. "Hello?"

Lilly couldn't hear what the caller said, but whatever it was, it didn't please Jason. He jabbed the button to turn on the speakerphone function.

"What makes you think Lilly Nelson is here?" Jason asked the caller. He looked at her and mouthed two words.

Raymond Klein.

Oh, mercy. She'd had enough of an ordeal without adding this. Yet, it was an important call because, after all, Raymond Klein was on their list of suspects. Had he called to issue some warning that he was after her? Lilly wished. Because that meant they'd know he was the one behind these attempts and the cops could haul his butt in.

"Where else would she be?" was Klein's chilly response to Jason's question.

"What do you want?" Lilly demanded. That demand earned her another glare from Jason. She was getting used to those.

"The cops keep calling me and dropping by to ask questions," Klein explained, sounding as if he were glaring, too. "You've already ruined my life—"

"FYI, *you* ruined your own life by getting involved with my father. If you hadn't done that, you wouldn't have been disbarred."

"I didn't do anything wrong. Someone set me up."

It was an old song and dance. One that she didn't want to hear again.

"I won't be drawn back into this, understand?" Klein continued. "My advice? Back off because I'm a desperate man, and desperate men don't play by the rules."

His words sent a chill through her. "That sounds a little like a threat, Mr. Klein."

"Maybe because it is."

CHAPTER SEVEN

IF JASON WERE to make a list of Dumb-Things-To-Do, this would be at the top.

With that reminder, he didn't curse. He'd already cursed himself enough. Nor did he try to talk Lilly out of leaving the downtown office building and immediately returning to his house. He knew now that he'd be wasting his breath.

Why?

Because after two days of arguing with her about this, Lilly had delivered the ultimate ultimatum—she was going to her office with or without him.

Right.

As if *without him* was an option.

Rule number one of protective custody was to protect. Plain and simple. And he couldn't protect her if she was halfway across the city in the absolute last place she should be. He couldn't stop her from leaving, either.

It'd done no good to remind her of the incident at the hospital. Or the incident with the security gate. Or Raymond Klein's threatening call. She was here, and it was up to him to make sure she stayed safe.

The elevator came to a stop, the metal doors swishing open, and Lilly and he came face-to-face with a massive hallway lined with office doors. Even though he was a cop who was trained and armed, it was unnerving to face all that space. All those doors. Where anyone, especially a killer, could be lurking.

However, Jason knew the place was probably safe. *Probably.* Two officers who were now patrolling the parking lot had gone through every office, every hall, every nook and every cranny. There was no one else in the building except for Lilly and him, and Jason intended to keep it that way. He also intended to make this a very short visit.

In addition to the thorough building check, Jason had taken every other security precaution that he could possibly take. He'd driven a circuitous route, backtracking and watching to make sure they hadn't been followed. He had also left a police guard with Megan and Erica in case the perp decided to go in that direction instead. Now, he had to hope that all those security measures were enough to counteract the uneasy feeling in the pit of his stomach.

Jason stepped out of the elevator onto the third floor, and he reached out his arm to assist her. Lilly either didn't see his gesture, or else she blew him off. Instead, she used her cane to walk.

"Walk" being a relative term.

She was still wobbly, and he figured she'd have bruises on her palm from putting so much pressure on the cane. He'd offered to help. Lots of times. But he had finally given up trying to convince her to take the slow and easy approach to her recovery. It was like talking to a brick wall.

Or to himself.

That thought caused him to smile. God knows why. He certainly didn't have anything to smile about. He could blame that on the below-the-waist, brainless part of his anatomy. It was a myth that men were ruled by their heads and not their hearts.

Heads and hearts indeed. Those parts were definitely involved in the process, but he knew for a fact that at this stage, lust was the number one factor.

Once this was over, he really needed to make the time to be with a woman.

Of course, his body immediately reminded him that Lilly was a woman, but he told his body what it could do with that reminder.

"Don't say it," she mumbled.

Since he was still embroiled in his own borderline lecherous mental discussion, it took Jason a moment to figure out what she'd said. Good grief, had she figured out what he was thinking?

"Don't say what?" he asked cautiously.

"About this not being a good idea."

Oh, that. "It never crossed my mind."

She laughed. One short burst of sound and air to form a *Ha!* "Sarcasm. A lost art form. I'm beginning to like you, Jason, and I don't think that's a good thing."

He didn't even have to think about that one. "It isn't. And you don't like me. Not really."

Lilly made a throaty sound of disagreement. "We're back to the you-saved-my-life stuff and that's the only reason I could possibly like you?"

They could go there. Easily. But Jason was tired of the BS. Maybe if they just dealt with it, like adults, it wouldn't be an issue.

Okay, that didn't make sense.

But avoiding it wasn't working, either.

Nothing was working.

And he'd never been more frustrated and confused in his entire life.

So, he came to a stop. Lilly stopped, too. But in the wrong place. Right in front of an open office door that had a huge window. The overhead lights created a golden spotlight above her. In fact, the light was the same color as the sleeveless top and slim short skirt she was wearing. Both silk.

How did he know that?

He'd brushed against both the fabric and her at least a dozen times. Accidentally, of course. But those inadvertent caresses still had an effect on him. A woman wearing silk. Maybe that was any man's fantasy. Judging from his reaction, it was apparently his.

Jason caught her arm and moved her to the side, away from the direct line of sight of the window, but the light still shone on her face.

Man, she was beautiful.

Not beautiful in that beauty queen, polished sort of way. But in a natural way that stirred parts of him best left alone.

She hadn't pulled her hair into a ponytail tonight, and it instead lay against the tops of her shoulders. Those dark auburn locks were a stark contrast against the much lighter fabric of her clothes. Earrings, thin threads of gold, dangled from her ears. Jason noticed it all. Even the delicate heart necklace that lay between her breasts.

Yep, he noticed her breasts, too.

And every inch of him started to ache.

"I can't believe this is happening," he mumbled to

himself. Regrettably, he didn't mumble it softly enough because Lilly's gaze whipped to his.

She stared at him, and stared. Her expression went from concern, to alarm, to disgust. Jason was sure his expression went through a similar transformation and settled heavily on the disgust part. Not disgust for her, but for himself.

"Sheez Louise. What's wrong with us?" Lilly whispered. She groaned softly. He found that erotic, too. Heck, at this point, her breathing seemed like an aphrodisiac. "And don't you dare blame it on adrenaline."

Nope, it wasn't adrenaline.

It was stupidity.

Stupidity generated by the brainless part of him that kept making really bad suggestions as to what he should do about this unexplainable attraction he had for Lilly. An attraction for his brother's lover.

Ah, there it was.

The metaphorical chastity belt. Lilly was hands-off because she was Greg's. It didn't matter that Greg was no longer alive. Just the fact that she'd slept with him—and no doubt even loved him—meant there could never be anything more than lust between them. And he had no intentions of doing anything about it.

Unfortunately, good intentions didn't always win.

"I'm attracted to you," he admitted. He heard his words and practically winced. Never, never, never did he think he'd say that to Lilly Nelson. But then, never did he think he'd want a woman this much.

She raked her finger over her jaw and shifted her posture slightly. "I'm attracted to you, too."

This time, he did wince. "You weren't supposed to say that. You were supposed to slap me or something."

Lilly lifted an eyebrow. Paused. Stared. "Trust me, Jason, over the past few days there are a lot of things I've thought about doing to you…" Her voice changed. The air changed. He changed. Everything changed. "But slapping you isn't one of them."

Oh. Hell.

"That was the wrong thing to say." Jason was surprised he could manage something as complex as human speech. His body and energy were suddenly pinpointed on only one thing.

Kissing Lilly.

"Anything I could say, or didn't say, would have been wrong." Lilly shrugged. "Or right. Depending on your perspective."

His perspective apparently wasn't that good right now. Neither was hers. He was sure of it.

"I blame it in part on your jeans," she informed him.

Even with their no-holds-barred conversation, he hadn't expected her to say that. "Excuse me?"

"Your jeans," Lilly said as if that clarified everything. She waited a moment. "You look really good in them. You look really good, period. And maybe because it's been so long since I've had sex. Or maybe it's you. Or me. Or the moonlight. Or your aftershave. Or maybe it's because I'm just going crazy."

Well, they were definitely on the same wavelength, and it wasn't a good place to be. "My aftershave, huh?" Jason questioned.

She nodded. "It reminds me of leather and sex."

He frowned. "And that's a good thing?"

"Apparently so." She touched his arm, rubbed softly. Stopped. Then started again. Her fingers moved to the front of his white cotton shirt. To his chest. And she began to play with the fabric. "When I was in the laundry room this morning, I sniffed your T-shirt." She huffed. "See what you've reduced me to? Clothes sniffing. Thanks to you, I'm now a bona fide pervert."

Lilly had no doubt meant that to make him laugh. Or at least she'd meant it to break the almost unbearable tension. It didn't work. No amount of humor or sarcasm was going to defuse this.

He didn't move.

Neither did Lilly.

But he did move closer. Yep. He went in the wrong direction. His gaze traveled over her moonlit face and searched her eyes. He saw a lot of concern there. Maybe even fear. And unfortunately there was something much, much worse. He saw mirrored in her what stirred his own body.

Desire.

Minutes earlier Jason had been certain that he'd filled his quota of doing stupid things. But he was apparently wrong. He saw a flash of the future and realized he was about to make the stupidest mistake of his life.

That didn't stop him.

Nothing would stop him. He knew that now. So he quit fighting.

He reached out, slid his hand around the back of Lilly's neck and hauled her to him. She made a soft gasp when she landed against his chest. Not a gasp of shock or discomfort. It was breathy. A quivery, feminine sound.

"We're practically at war with each other," she reminded him.

It was a good reminder.

And a useless one.

"That whole war thing between us…" he lowered his mouth to hers "…is cooling down a bit." He brushed his lips over hers and elicited another of those gasps from her. "Wouldn't you say?"

"It's a little cool. But still there. And that means we shouldn't kiss," she said, her breath clipped. She shook her head and the movement stirred her hair around her face, the wisps landing on her cheek.

"Well, we have to start somewhere. It would hardly seem appropriate if we had sex without kissing first."

Now, she laughed. It was low, rich and filled with nerves. Jason knew how she felt. Every nerve in his body was on edge.

Her scent curled around him, blending with those of the cool, damp air-conditioning and the spring night. There were undertones of her arousal. Subtle. Yet not subtle to his own body. He wanted his scent on her skin. Her scent, on his. Hell, he just wanted her.

He skimmed his thumb over her bottom lip.

"Jason—"

He didn't let her finish. Fitting his mouth to hers, he kissed her. It was quick and light. No urgency. No demands. Almost immediately he lifted his head to gauge her reaction. Her eyes were wide, her mouth pursed in what appeared to be surprise. Or maybe outrage. It wasn't quite the reaction he'd hoped for. He'd hoped to see a punch of lust in those ocean-colored eyes.

So, he kissed her again.

This time her breath quickened. Her clenched hand trapped between them relaxed, for just a moment, before she gripped the front of his shirt and pulled him closer.

It was the only invitation he needed.

Running his hand into her loose hair, he recaptured the back of her neck and gently angled it so he could deepen the kiss. She made a little sound, just enough to part her lips. Enough for him to slip past the sweet barrier of her lips and discover plenty about Lilly Nelson.

LILLY HAD BEEN so sure that Jason would taste like a combination of mint and ice. But there was nothing cool and minty about him. He was all fiery hot, as was the possessive grip he had around the back of her neck.

She didn't fight the kiss, the grip, him or anything else. The only fight she had was to get closer to him. Jason did the same. Fighting and grappling, they came together, and she felt the solid muscles of his chest. Felt the sinewy strength of his arms. And with all that feeling, the kiss continued.

Jason escalated things. If he hadn't, she would have. The kiss was already French and immensely pleasurable, but he used that clever mouth to make her want more.

He was aroused. Lilly felt his erection brush against her stomach. She wanted to feel even more of it, but she braced her hand on his chest to stop herself from doing that. It would be wrong to touch him, to move against him.

But it would feel darn good. She was sure of it.

His kiss had created a fire inside her. An ache. And that ache was already demanding relief.

Her hand on his chest must have caused him to stop, because Jason tore his mouth from hers and looked down at her. Judging from the just-kill-me-now expression, he'd come to his senses and wasn't pleased about this momentary surrender to passion. She hadn't come to her senses yet, but Lilly knew she'd have to, soon. Having sex against the wall probably wasn't a good idea.

Probably.

Even if it suddenly seemed like the best idea in the world.

"You're a good kisser," she confessed. His breath gusted against her face. "I'd hoped you wouldn't be."

His breath continued to gust, and he sounded as if he'd just run a marathon. "Then we're even. I'd hoped you wouldn't be, either. It would have put an end to this in a hurry."

"All right. The kiss doesn't have to mean anything. In fact, I insist that it not mean anything."

He nodded. "So do I."

"Good. We're in agreement. Maybe a first for us."

But agreeing didn't make it so. Lilly knew that kiss meant *something*. She could already feel the difference between them, and it wasn't just about heavy breathing, racing pulses and the most primitive of urges. There were now huge dents in those barriers between them. But maybe, just maybe, they wouldn't be adding any more dents in the near future.

"We have a lot of things to work out," Lilly reminded him. And while she was at it, she reminded herself.

He considered that a moment. Nodded again. But what was missing was the part about him truly believing that the kiss didn't matter, that it meant nothing. She could see his skepticism written all over his face.

"We won't even discuss it again," she continued, hating that she'd become a motormouth, hating even more that Jason wasn't offering a thing to explain all of this away. Heck, she shouldn't be the only one tripping over her tongue. "We'll concentrate on the case, on getting the lilos and getting out of here."

There. Finally, she saw it. The slow, necessary transformation from hot kisser to hot cop. Correction: hot, dedicated cop. Which was exactly the persona she needed with her tonight. The reminder had worked. Jason no doubt remembered the danger, the person who wanted her dead and the seriousness of their situation.

Good.

At least one of them now had the right mind-set.

Before she could do anything else stupid, Lilly moved away from him, something she should have done before they'd started their little verbal foreplay that'd led to that kiss. And she moved quickly. Well, as quickly as her impaired legs would allow. She went down the hall to her office.

Jason stepped in front of her and did his cop thing by surveying the place. He then stepped to the side. What he didn't do was say a word. Or look at her. He kept his attention on the room itself.

Oh, yeah. They'd really ruined things with that kiss.

"Your attorney had planned to move all your things out in five months," Jason explained, his gaze still surveilling. "Everything would have been placed in storage until Megan became an adult."

Five months. That would have been the two-year point of her coma. Lilly was a little surprised that her attorney had waited so long to do that. But maybe there'd been legal issues involved. Maybe even issues that involved declaring her dead. A thought that sent goose bumps over her skin.

She switched on one of the overhead lights and forced herself to concentrate on something other than the coma and Jason. She started with the basics and checked to see what was familiar and what wasn't. Her functional, no-fuss desk was there, as was a computer that was no doubt hopelessly out of date. Across from the desk was a trio of saddle-brown leather chairs and a small table—bare. No plants, but then they'd probably died and been removed. Other than that, everything was the same.

Well, almost.

Lilly certainly didn't feel the same. She felt like a visitor to a place where she'd once spent seventy-five percent of her time. The work had seemed so important then. Vital, even. It didn't seem that way now.

"Well?" Jason prompted, his voice tight and impatient. Probably because he was anxious to leave. "Does being here trigger any memories?"

"Only that I'd become a workaholic those weeks before the coma." Pressing her cane against the floor, she took a step inside and pulled in a deep breath. The place smelled like dust and lemon air freshener.

Probably a sicko metaphor for her life.

She went to her desk and opened the bottom file drawer. The folders were still there. Right where she'd left them. She pulled out the one that was marked Urgent and sat so she could study it. Or rather, study what was left in it. The file had once been huge, at least two inches thick, and now it contained less than a dozen pages. Someone had obviously removed the majority of the documents; after thumbing through the file, she decided the missing pages pertained to the investigation into her father's activities.

Jason turned on the computer, pulled up one of the leather chairs and got to work, as well. "Should I remind you that the police have already been through all of this?" he quipped.

"Should I remind you that people, even cops, miss really obvious things when they look for evidence?" Lilly countered.

He gave her a flat look. "There's a fine line between the lost art of sarcasm and being a smart-ass." But the corner of his mouth lifted into a semismile when he said it. A smile that warmed her in places it shouldn't have. Especially her heart.

Oh, sheez.

The man had dimples. What kind of defense could a woman have against those? Her twenty-nine-year-old brain had obviously regressed to that of a hormonally pumped teenager.

It was obviously time for a change of subject. And a change of attitude. Lilly knew just what it would take to do that. "By the way, I want to thank you for helping Megan adjust to being around me."

Just like that, Jason's semismile faded, and she watched by degrees as he closed down. Now he wasn't just a cop, but the hard-nosed officer she'd come to know. Kissing and becoming aroused were okay. Ditto for light flirting. But talking about Megan was still touchy territory. Lilly wanted it to stay that way for a while. Until she got over her lust-fest for Jason. She needed that to make sure she kept her hands, and the rest of herself, off him.

"I think Megan's getting used to me," Lilly added.

"Yes." Just a yes. It was practically a roadblock.

"Not Erica, though." Lilly tested the waters. In fact, this was the first time she'd been able to discuss Erica with Jason, since the woman always seemed to be around. "She doesn't like me."

He shook his head. "It's not that—"

"She's possessive, I know," Lilly interrupted.

"And she's jealous."

Okay, so Jason hadn't closed down as much as she thought. Nor was he oblivious or blind to Erica's feelings for him. "Just how much influence does Erica have over you?"

"What's that supposed to mean?" he snapped.

The water testing was over and she'd apparently jumped in headfirst. "Nothing sexual." Lilly knew that now that she had seen the two of them together. That didn't mean Erica was powerless in this weird quadrangle of a relationship. "It's just when the time comes to work out Megan's custody, I don't want Erica to interfere."

"She won't," he said gruffly. He didn't add more. In fact, he didn't even maintain eye contact. Instead he checked his watch. "I told the officers in the parking lot that we'd only be here an hour at the most."

In others words, cut the custody chat, the flirting

and any residual lusting and get down to the business at hand. She did. Lilly skimmed over a copy of the initial report that she'd sent to the police. The report that detailed some of her father's shady dealings. There was nothing surprising about it. She remembered writing it, remembered the effect it had. In short, it had led to an investigation that had in turn led to Wayne Sandling's and Raymond Klein's disbarments. She'd crossed all the t's. Dotted all the i's.

So what if anything was missing?

"Have I overlooked something so obvious that it's staring me right in the face?" she mumbled. "What if this isn't connected to my father's business?" The question was meant more for herself than Jason.

"You have another theory?" He moved closer. Probably to see what she was reading that had prompted her comment. But he also must have remembered what'd happened the last time they'd gotten close.

Jason moved back.

Lilly sighed.

"Road rage, perhaps?" she suggested. "Maybe I was in some kind of driver-to-driver altercation that night, and it turned bad."

He made a sound of disagreement. "And this person is carrying a grudge after nineteen months?"

She turned toward him and lifted her eyebrow, a reminder of the grudge he'd carried all this time.

"Sarcasm," he complained. "I've heard it's a lost art form."

Except she was no longer sure he was holding a grudge. Lilly rethought that. Or maybe that kiss was nothing more than just that—a kiss. A basic physical reaction and nothing more.

Hey, it was possible.

And what with his fatherly duties and high-pressure job, it'd probably been a while since Jason had kissed or been kissed.

He leaned closer and whispered, "Best not to think about it."

She knew what he meant. He wasn't talking about her road rage/grudge-holding theory. He was referring to *them*. And Jason was right.

"Think about Wayne Sandling and Raymond Klein," he continued.

Oh, she was thinking about them. Even the kiss couldn't diminish that. "Means, motive and opportunity. They both have that in spades. And while I know they're guilty of illegal business practices, is either of them actually guilty of wanting me dead?"

"Time will tell." He paused. "Any other names that jump out at you?"

She shook her head. "Not really. But that's what scares me. It could be some person that we don't even know about. Someone who was smart enough to keep his name from drawing attention. My father wasn't exactly discriminate about his business associates."

Jason's cell phone rang and Lilly was in such deep thought that it took her a moment to realize what it was. He snatched his phone from his pocket and answered it. And Lilly immediately became alarmed, because he'd told the two officers in the parking lot to alert him if anything went wrong.

So, had something gone wrong?

She closed the file folder and reached for her cane in case they had to dive for cover. With all the danger of the past four days, she would have thought her body had grown accustomed to the fear.

It hadn't.

Lilly reacted as if this were the first time. The racing heart. The thin breath. The sickening feeling of dread that came from having little or no control over a potentially deadly situation.

Because there was nothing else she could do, she waited, watching for any cues on Jason's face. There were emotions there, all right. Confusion. Questions. Concern. It was the concern that created all sorts of wild scenarios in her head.

"Is Megan okay?" Lilly asked the moment he took the phone away from his ear.

"This isn't about Megan. Your former secretary, Corinne, is downstairs, and she wants to see you."

Well, it wasn't the threat she'd tried to prepare herself for. "Corinne's here?" Lilly checked the time at the bottom of the computer screen. It was already past 11:00 p.m. Hardly the hour for an office visit.

"She says she was just driving by and saw the lights." Jason paused. "You want to see her?"

She almost said no, because she wanted to continue to go through the files, but there was something about Corinne's visit and her saw-the-lights explanation that piqued Lilly's curiosity.

"Sure."

Jason relayed that to the cop and ended the call. "You think Corinne knows something?" he asked.

"Probably not. If she did, she would have already

given the information to the police." Still, that didn't rule out Jason's theory about Corinne having some information. Like the cops and everyone else who'd been through the files, Corinne might have missed something.

Because time was preciously short, Lilly reopened the file folder and continued to go through it while they waited for Corinne's arrival. Jason did more than wait. He put the computer on a screensaver and withdrew his weapon.

That got her attention. "You think Corinne's an assassin coming in here to finish me off?" Lilly asked, conveying her skepticism.

"I'm not taking any more chances."

Lilly was about to point out that Corinne was almost fifty. A grandmother at that. On a profiling scale, she wouldn't be in the top one hundred suspects. Still, she didn't object to Jason's diligence. It was that diligence that'd kept her alive so far. More so, she trusted him, and she swore to herself that her change of heart had nothing to do with this odd intimacy that was now between them.

She heard the elevator door open and then the footsteps. Two sets. Probably Corinne's and the police escort's. Several moments later, both appeared in the doorway.

Like her office, the changes in Corinne were minimal. A few more gray hairs threaded through the rich chestnut strands. Maybe she'd put on a pound or two. But that was it. No sinister vibes that she was a killer. Then, Lilly hadn't expected to get such vibes, anyway.

"It's so good to see you." Corinne went to her, reached out and hugged her. "How have you been?"

"Better. I think." Lilly returned the hug while staying seated. "It's good to be among the living."

Corinne pulled back and the sadness crept into her blue eyes. "What happened to you was horrible. I still can't believe it."

Corinne glanced at Jason's unholstered gun, the file folder and finally at the computer screen that, thanks to Jason, was now spewing stars and other celestial objects. Corinne's bottom lip quivered. Not an unusual gesture. Lilly had experienced lots of Corinne's lip-quivering when they'd been embroiled in the police investigation. The woman wasn't very good at hiding her nerves.

Corinne clamped her teeth over her bottom lip to stop it from quivering and waited a moment until she'd gotten control of herself. "You think you'll be reopening the office anytime soon?"

"I'm not sure," Lilly answered.

In fact, she hadn't given it much thought. What with getting acquainted with Megan and the near-smothering, Lilly was still trying to find equilibrium. According to her financials, she had more than enough money to keep the business closed for another year or two. It might take that long to resolve the custody issues and find the person who wanted to kill her. Getting back to work definitely wasn't high on her list of priorities.

"What about you?" Lilly asked. "What have you been doing for the past nineteen months?"

"Well, after I tied up some loose ends around here and after the police were finished with their search, I went to work for an investment firm over on St. Mary's. Still, I like to drop by here every now and then to check on the place."

"And you decided to check on it tonight?" Jason couldn't keep the cop out of his voice.

"Because I saw the lights on. Usually I just stop by during regular business hours because I no longer have a key to get into the building." She blew out a nervy breath and turned her attention back to Lilly. "What about you? Where are you staying now that you're out of the hospital?"

"A police safe house," Jason volunteered before Lilly could answer for herself. It wasn't exactly a lie, but it was obvious Jason didn't want Corinne to know where she was. "It has lots of security," he added. "Someone tried to hurt Lilly while she was in the hospital, and we don't want anyone coming after her again."

"I see." Corinne's breath quickened, and she made a vague motion toward the door. "Well, it's obvious you two are working, and I need to get home. So, I'll just be going."

They exchanged goodbyes. Hasty, polite ones. And Corinne headed for the door with the police guard following right along behind her.

"Do you trust her?" Jason asked.

Lilly opened her mouth to say yes, but the one-word response stuck in her throat. Yes, Corinne had been a great secretary. Loyal. Efficient. Not from Lilly's father's regime, either. Once Lilly had discovered the discrepancies and the illegal activity, she'd wiped the slate clean. All employees had been let go, and she'd started fresh with Corinne. A woman who had no ties to her father.

But that didn't mean Corinne couldn't be bought.

There were a lot of riled people who'd been burned by her father's business practices, and maybe one of those riled people now had Corinne on their payroll.

"I really don't know if I can trust her," Lilly admitted.

"Then we're not staying any longer. Let's get out of here."

Lilly didn't argue. Corinne's visit might have been legit, but it had rattled her. She grabbed the file she'd been reading and tucked it and several others beneath her arm. Jason took the remaining folders from the drawer and took her arm to get her moving.

Despite her limp and the cane, they made it out of the building in record time. Corinne was nowhere in sight, but Lilly immediately spotted the two officers in the dimly lit parking lot. One was near their vehicle, which was as close to the building as possible without parking on the sidewalk. The other cop was at the far end at the entrance. The two were definitely guarding the place as much as they could, considering the office building was sandwiched between other buildings.

And that wasn't the only security concern.

At the front of the parking lot there was a semi-deserted street. At the back stood a row of eight-foot-high blooming mountain laurels. Fragrant and beautiful. But they'd also make a great hiding place. She hoped the officers had thoroughly searched that area because Jason and she still had to make their way down a long stretch of the sidewalk.

"Keep walking," Jason insisted.

She heard the concern in his voice and realized something wasn't right.

Lilly could feel it, and it was bone deep. A warning that speared through her until her breath was racing right along with her too-vivid imagination.

She continued walking, faster though, her cane and her flat sandals thudding like heartbeats on the pebbled concrete. She glanced over her shoulder. No one was following them. No one was lurking in those mountain laurels or in the shadows of the buildings.

So maybe she'd been wrong about things not being right.

It was, after all, coming up on midnight, the proverbial witching hour. Someone obviously wanted to kill her. That was a solid enough reason to get a case of the willies. That was probably all there was to it. A good old-fashioned case of frayed nerves and willies.

Lilly had convinced herself that all was well.

Until she heard the sound. A sort of click.

The *all's well* rationalization that she'd fought so hard to find evaporated at the exact moment that she heard another sound.

No click this time.

It was a deafening blast.

And a bullet slammed past her.

CHAPTER EIGHT

JASON DIDN'T NEED anyone to tell him what that god-awful sound was. He knew. And he cursed. Because he was well aware that someone was shooting at them.

Hell.

They were still a good five or six yards from his SUV. Too far to make it in a single dive. Especially for Lilly. As a temporary measure, Jason hooked his arm around Lilly's waist and pulled her off the sidewalk and into a cluster of shrubs. She was already headed in that direction anyway so thankfully she didn't take too hard of a fall.

Another shot tore through the night and slammed into the ground. Mere inches from Lilly's head.

So much for his temporary safety measure of being in the shrubs. To keep her alive, they'd have to move.

"Let's go," Jason ordered.

With his arm still around her, he drew his Glock and dragged Lilly out of the shrubbery and to the side of the SUV. It was safer than using the plants as a shield, but it didn't neutralize the danger, because judging from the angle of the two shots, the gunman was somewhere on a rooftop. That meant he or she was in a perfect position to adjust, re-aim and fire again.

And that's exactly what happened.

The shot skipped off the roof of his SUV, metal tearing through metal.

"Who's doing this?" Lilly mumbled. Not a question exactly. More like a furious, frustrated plea.

Jason heard the other officers scrambling for cover and position. Either or both would be able to return fire, but that didn't mean they could take out the shooter before he or she took out one of them. He moved his body over Lilly's, sheltering her as best he could, and he scanned the rooftops to see if he could catch a glimpse of the sniper.

Nothing.

For a few seconds.

The gunfire returned. Not a single shot, either. A barrage of deadly bullets that pelted the ground and the SUV. Jason felt totally helpless. All he could do was stay put and pray the shots would stop so he'd get his own opportunity to put an end to this. Unfortunately he couldn't just start firing random shots. They were literally in downtown San Antonio, and he didn't want to shoot anyone by mistake.

Beneath him, Jason could feel Lilly trembling, and he hated that once again she'd been placed in a situation where her life was at serious risk. Her question had been dead-on—*Who's doing this?* Because until he knew that, stopping it would be hit or miss.

Jason was damn tired of missing.

The shots continued for what seemed an eternity, and just like that, in the blink of an eye, they stopped.

He waited. Listened. For any sound to indicate the gunman was reloading. Or escaping. When he heard nothing other than the normal noises of the city, he turned and pinpointed the roof of the adjacent building. The spot where he believed the shots had been fired.

"Do you see him?" Lilly asked.

Because she lifted her head, Jason used his forearm to keep her down and hopefully out of harm's way. This lull could be a ploy by the gunman to get them to leave cover. He wasn't about to allow Lilly to take that risk.

"Anything?" Jason shouted to his fellow officers.

"Negative," they answered within seconds of each other.

And the silence continued. No shots. No out-of-place sounds.

Nothing.

"I've called for backup," one of the officers advised.

Good. It shouldn't take long for them to arrive, either, since they were only about three miles from headquarters. It was too bad, though, that the shooter could be long gone by then, as well.

"Keep a visual on the perimeter of that other building," Jason ordered the officers.

Because what went up had to come down, eventually. That wouldn't necessarily happen, though, at the front of the building. A more likely escape route would be the back. He considered going there, but he immediately ruled it out. The gunman was after Lilly. That didn't mean he or she wouldn't kill others to get to her, but if Jason left, Lilly would be unprotected. He could be playing right into the gunman's hands. Still, he had to do something to try to nail this guy.

While keeping a vigilant watch, Jason used his cell

phone to contact one of the officers. This definitely wasn't something he wanted to shout out for the shooter to hear. "Take your partner and proceed to the back of that building where the shots originated. Try to cut off any potential escape route."

"Will do," the officer said, hanging up.

It was a huge undertaking. And probably a futile one. The building spread across nearly a third of the city block, and it would take a dozen or more cops to secure it properly. Still, it was better than nothing, and with backup on the way, they might get lucky.

Might.

"If this is about revenge," Lilly whispered, "then we're back to Wayne Sandling and Raymond Klein."

He heard a "but" at the end of Lilly's comment, and he understood it. Maybe it wasn't about revenge at all but something that Lilly knew. Or something she could learn. Possibly from those files. Or possibly something that'd been on that disk she'd planned to give to the police.

Of course, that left Jason with a huge question. If the person responsible for these latest attempts on Lilly's life had also been the one to run her off the road and steal the disk, then wasn't it finished?

Why had the attempts to kill her continued?

Either the perpetrator believed there was other incriminating information than just the one disk—info that was trapped inside Lilly's head—or, as Lilly said, it could be for revenge.

Or...

Jason almost hated to finish that thought, but he did. This could be related to none of that. But if so, then who would stand to gain something, anything, if Lilly were out of the way?

He didn't like the first thought that came to mind, but it came anyway.

Erica, maybe?

He was about to go through all the reasons why it wasn't possible for his nanny to be guilty when his phone rang.

"Detective Lawrence," Jason answered.

"We made it to the back of the building." It was one of the officers. "But it's not good news. We saw someone speed away in a dark-colored car. The license plate was covered with mud or something."

Jason cursed. "How about a description? Were you able to get that?"

"Negative."

Not that it helped, but he cursed some more. "Find Wayne Sandling and Raymond Klein and bring them in to headquarters. *Now*. I've got questions to ask, and by God, they'd better have the answers."

LILLY COULDN'T STOP shaking.

It was as if her body had decided it'd had all it could take and it was going to punish her for the trauma. So she trembled from head to toe while she stood there, behind the interrogation mirror where the detectives had left Wayne Sandling.

Sandling certainly wasn't trembling. With his hands tucked behind his head and his legs stretched out in front of him, he practically lounged at the austere metal table, waiting for the detectives to return so they could continue the questioning. Not that the questioning was actually leading anywhere: Sandling had denied any involvement in the shooting.

Despite being called out in the middle of the night to be interrogated by police for an attempted homicide, Sandling appeared well-rested and was dressed to perfection in a flawlessly tailored business suit. He was calm and collected.

Unlike her.

"I feel like a genuine wuss," Lilly muttered.

Jason glanced at her and frowned. "Why?"

She held up her hand to show him that she was shaking.

"That makes you feel like a wuss?" he challenged. "It's a normal human response to having your life threatened."

"You're not shaking," she pointed out.

"I'm a cop. I've been trained not to shake. But if it helps, I'm shaking inside."

She didn't believe him for a minute, but yes, it did help to think that he wasn't impervious to all of this. How could murder and mayhem ever become routine for anyone, even for a cop? Lilly knew it would be a long time, if ever, before she could forget the sound of those shots. They'd gotten lucky. Any one of those bullets could have killed them.

"The incident reports are done," Jason told her. "And it doesn't appear Sandling is on the verge of a confession, so I'll make arrangements for an officer to take you back to the house, okay?"

It wasn't the first time Jason had suggested that. It was the third time in the four-plus hours they'd been at police headquarters. She wasn't any more amenable to the offer now than the first time he'd made it.

"I want to be here when Raymond Klein is questioned," Lilly reminded him.

"It might be hours before they even find him."

"Then, I'll be here for hours."

Obviously not pleased about that, Jason huffed. But the sound had barely faded when he slipped his arm around her waist. "I don't suppose you'll let me get you a chair, either?" he asked.

Ah. So the arm thing wasn't a lovey kind of gesture. It was because she probably didn't look too steady on her feet. "It's strange, but all the fear and adrenaline have made my leg muscles feel stronger. Don't worry, though. I won't be suggesting gunfire and near death as a form of treatment for rehabbing coma patients."

"More sarcasm." The corner of his mouth lifted a fraction. "You're really good under pressure, you know that?"

"Right." Just in case he'd forgotten, she gave him a repeat demo of her trembling hand.

"Proves nothing. We've already established that. And you *are* great under pressure." He stopped, mumbled something incoherent. "But then, several of my perceptions about you have changed over the past few days."

Lilly considered that. Nodded. "I could say the same for you." She considered that some more. Shook her head in disgust. "But those perceptions have changed mainly because we have the hots for each other."

Judging from the look in his eyes, he wanted to deny that. Lilly knew he couldn't. "I shouldn't have kissed you," he concluded.

Yes, that particular intimate act was the proverbial point of no return, but she wouldn't let him shoulder the entire blame for this. "I kissed you back."

"It shouldn't have happened. I feel guilty as hell. Like I've betrayed my brother—"

"I know. I feel guilty, too." Not that it helped.

She'd known all along that Jason would see any attraction for her as the ultimate disloyalty to Greg. And there was a reason for that. Greg was…well, unrealistic when it came to her and the future he'd wanted them to have together. He certainly wouldn't have given Jason and her his blessing to jump headfirst into a relationship.

"I'll tell you what," she suggested, because they both needed an out. "Let's not kiss again, and that way we avoid this whole big guilt-fest. Agreed?"

Jason stared at her. "You think agreeing will make it happen?"

No way. But she kept that to herself. "I think we have to accept that abstinence is the way to go because we don't have time for the alternative." She tipped her head to Sandling. "We only have time for that. And by *that,* I mean I don't want us to die. I want Megan to be safe. The only way all of that can happen is for us to prove Sandling's responsible or else find the real culprit and put him or her behind bars."

It was a good speech. And it was even true. Well, for the most part. Lilly did want to keep Megan and Jason safe. She wanted the would-be killer stopped. But she didn't think all the distractions in the world would stop her from wanting the man beside her.

She'd relived that kiss a half dozen times. The taste of him. The way she'd felt when he'd held her in his arms.

Everything about it was wrong, especially the timing. And yet, everything about it felt right. As long as it continued to feel right, she didn't think she had a snowball's chance in Hades of stopping what had already started.

But what exactly had started?

"Only a pathological liar could be that calm during an interrogation," she heard Jason say.

She followed his gaze, and it was fixed on Sandling and the detective who'd just reentered the room. "He probably knows we're watching him, and he wants to rile us with this iceman routine."

"Well, it's working," Jason snarled.

Yep, it was. She glared at Sandling as he gave a flippant chuckle when the detective reminded him that he had a motive for the shooting. A motive for the attempted smothering. And a motive for trying to get through the security gate in Jason's neighborhood.

That motive was *her*.

"So do a lot of other people," Sandling calmly concluded while he examined his nails. "Including, but not limited to, my former law partner, Raymond Klein. I trust you'll ask him these same boring questions?"

The detective didn't respond, and instead paraphrased a previous question about Sandling's whereabouts during the shooting. As he'd done before, Sandling denied everything. What Lilly couldn't decide—was he telling the truth? Sandling seemed a little too meticulous for what was essentially a string of incredibly non-meticulous crimes.

That didn't make him innocent.

The inconsistencies between his somewhat prissy demeanor and the crime scenes could have been intentional. A way to throw them off his trail. The tactic could stall them for weeks.

Or forever.

That created a sinking feeling in the pit of her stomach, and she groaned softly. "What are we going to do about Megan? How can we keep her safe?"

"We'll have another guard at the house starting today." Judging from his quick response, Jason had given this lots of thought. "A sort of cop-nanny. I might go ahead and try to set up a safe house. I'm not sure if it'd be any safer than a gated community, but I'm still considering it."

Lilly sorted through all that info and immediately discovered what he *hadn't* said. "What about Erica?"

"I think it might be a good idea if she isn't staying there with us any longer." He slid his arm from her waist and checked his watch. "I'll see if they've managed to locate Raymond Klein. I also need to call the crime lab to find out if they got anything from the video surveillance camera they took from the security gate."

She caught his arm to stop him from leaving. "Wait a minute. You didn't think I'd just let that part about Erica pass, did you? Why are you giving her the boot? Is it because she doesn't like me?"

"No." He hesitated and then repeated it. "No. It's because I'm not sure I can trust her."

It was like being hit by a big sack of rocks. Trust was the issue here? Lilly hadn't seen that one coming. Jealousy, yes. Possessiveness, definitely. Too many cooks in the kitchen scenario—that, too.

But not lack of trust.

Lilly would certainly have grilled Jason until he told

all about this distrust issue. She would have if there hadn't been a knock at the door. Just one sharp rap, and it opened. It was Detective O'Reilly, the officer who'd been assisting Jason on the case.

"We found Raymond Klein," O'Reilly told them. "He's being taken into interrogation now."

That got Jason moving. He stepped around O'Reilly and into the hall. Lilly followed him. Or rather, she tried to. Jason turned and tried to stop her. But that didn't work, either. Because instead of deterring her from seeing her possible attacker, Klein came straight to them.

Lilly had no trouble recognizing the man. After all, they'd run into each other plenty of times during the investigation that'd led to his disbarment.

Klein hadn't changed at all in the past nineteen months. The same slightly shabby salt-and-pepper hair. The overly round face that was cragged with too many wrinkles considering he was only in his late thirties. All those wrinkles and his heavy brow gave him a permanent sourpuss expression.

"I thought we'd settled this," Klein greeted. He looked right past Jason and O'Reilly and aimed his greeting at her.

Jason stepped protectively in front of her. Lilly huffed and tried to reestablish her ground, but Jason would have no part in that. The best she could manage was to move to Jason's side so she could face Klein head-on.

"I want him tested for GSR," Jason relayed to O'Reilly.

"Gunshot residue?" Klein supplied. "You'll need a warrant for that."

"We already have it," Jason confirmed.

Klein's chin came up. "You're wasting your time, Detective."

That was probably true. Klein's hair was still damp, indicating a recent shampoo. If he was the shooter, he'd no doubt have worn gloves, showered and changed his clothes. He wasn't the sort of man to get caught with the obvious. It'd taken her twice as long to connect Klein to her father as it had for her to do the same for Sandling. In the end, the authorities had gotten him for a suspicious report he'd made to the city engineers. A report that had ultimately allowed her father to receive a contract where he'd taken a ton of money and provided minimal services in exchange. Klein's part in that deal had been barely enough to get him disbarred.

And he wasn't about to let her forget that.

Raymond Klein hated her. Lilly had no doubts about that. But the question was, had he done something about that hatred, or was this anger simply because he felt he'd been railroaded again?

Though it seemed a senseless exercise, Lilly tried to remember what'd happened that night of her accident. Had she seen her attacker's face? Was it Klein's face? And was that the reason he now wanted her dead— because she would be able to identify him if and when her memory returned? Unfortunately she could insert Sandling's name into that particular scenario and it would ring just as true.

Klein took one step toward her, halving the already meager distance between them. "I guess I wasn't clear enough when I phoned you. I told you I wouldn't be pulled back into this, and I meant it."

Jason put his hand on the butt on his Glock. "Since we're clearing things up, you won't be calling Lilly again. And you won't be getting in her face to issue any other threats."

No more steps toward her, but that didn't stop Klein's expression from tightening. "She and her father ruined my life."

"And you had no part in that?" Lilly asked.

"None," Klein quickly answered.

Jason obviously didn't buy a word of it. Glaring, he motioned toward the room behind them. "Escort him into interrogation," Jason told O'Reilly. He waited until O'Reilly had done that before he continued. "I need to be here during the questioning, but I'll get someone to give you a ride back to the house."

Yet another head-against-a-brick-wall moment. "And if I don't want to go?" she asked.

"Tough. You're going." He leaned in closer, until his mouth was practically right against her ear. "You've had a long day, an even longer night, and you need some rest. Please, just go. You don't have to worry about being there alone with Erica. I'll make sure an officer stays there with you until I get back."

She was about to argue, but O'Reilly came out of the interrogation room where he'd deposited Klein.

"Before you listen to Klein being grilled, you might want to hear what the crime lab had to say about that surveillance video taken from the security camera at the gate of your neighborhood." O'Reilly closed the door to the interrogation room. "They were able to partially enhance the image," he explained.

Lilly couldn't help it. Her hopes soared. This could be the break they'd been praying for.

"And were they able to determine who was behind the wheel of that car?" Jason asked.

"No."

She'd had mere seconds of that soaring hope, but that dashed them.

"But they were able to get a better look at the license plate," O'Reilly continued. "They only got a partial, but it was enough to run it through DMV and come up with a name."

All right. That was a reason to hope again. "Which is it—Wayne Sandling or Raymond Klein?" Lilly asked.

O'Reilly shook his head. "Neither. The car is registered to your former secretary, Corinne Davies."

CHAPTER NINE

JASON UNLOCKED THE front door to his house, stepped inside and listened for any sound that shouldn't have been there. He could hear the hum of the air-conditioner. The rhythmic swish of the brass pendulum in the grandfather clock in the foyer. The TV was on low volume in the living room.

All seemed well, but he wasn't about to take that at face value.

Yes, he was paranoid.

That could happen when only ten hours earlier someone had come close to killing Lilly and him.

There was a plainclothes cop watching TV from the sofa in the living room. Jason nodded and tried to convey his appreciation that the man was guarding the place in his absence. Unfortunately, the guards were a necessary precaution that might have to continue for a while.

Jason didn't even want to think about how long a *while* might be.

He continued down the hall. Listening. Staying vigilant. Erica was in the playroom, and even though she was holding a magazine, Jason didn't think she was reading it. She tossed it aside and practically leaped to her feet when she saw him. But Jason motioned for her to sit back down.

"Where's Megan and Lilly?" he whispered.

There was little change in Erica's expression, just a soft intake of breath that had a hint of frustration to it, and she aimed her index finger in the direction of Lilly's room. "Lilly insisted on having Megan with her," she said.

Uh-oh.

That had probably caused an argument or two. Not from Megan. But from Erica. Things had probably not gone smoothly while he'd been at headquarters. Still, it couldn't be helped. He'd had to do reports and he'd wanted to help with the investigation and interrogation of the suspects. Plus, Lilly had needed some rest. And it was a necessity to get her out of headquarters, away from Wayne Sandling and Raymond Klein. For that to happen, he'd had no choice but to send her with the police escort back to the house. Unfortunately, that meant Lilly had had to deal with Erica on her own. He was sorry he hadn't been here to run interference.

Jason turned toward Lilly's room, and because the door was open, he spotted her immediately. She was napping not on her bed but on a brightly colored patchwork quilt stretched out on the carpeted floor.

She had a sleeping Megan cradled in her arms.

He smiled, leaned his shoulder against the door frame and watched them. This was one of his favorite moments—watching Megan sleep. When she was awake, she was always on the move, and it was impossible to concentrate on the sheer joy she'd brought to his life. But now, with her resting peacefully, Jason could study her tiny face and relive all the wonderful things that he loved about her. If he accomplished every career goal he would ever have, it wouldn't come close to the fulfillment he'd gotten just by being Megan's dad.

And that brought him back to Lilly.

She could take fatherhood from him, but he no longer thought that she would. He mentally shrugged. Maybe that was what he wanted to believe, anyway.

The files that Lilly had brought from her office were scattered on the desk tucked in the corner. She'd no doubt been reading through them while watching Megan. Double duty. He'd done a lot of that himself over the past eleven and a half months.

"Lilly's rushing things," Erica whispered, walking up behind him. She folded her arms over her chest and didn't take her gaze from Lilly. "It'll confuse Megan."

Jason made a sound to indicate he didn't agree. "Megan doesn't look confused or rushed." She looked as if she belonged right there in Lilly's arms.

Erica stayed quiet a few moments, and Jason braced himself for the fallout. It came. "I don't know how you can welcome her into your home. Not after what she did to Greg."

Fallout, indeed. Any other time, he might have agreed. But this wasn't any other time. It was *now,* and whether he wanted it or not, things were changing between Lilly and him. They had to change, for Megan's sake.

"Oh, I get it," Erica concluded on a rise of breath. "You're being nice to Lilly because you're worried she'll take Megan. That's it, isn't it?"

He wished that was it. Jason wished the attraction he felt for Lilly was all part of the custody issue and the love both of them felt for Megan.

But it wasn't.

He wanted to kiss Lilly. He wanted her in his bed. Hell, he just plain wanted her. That didn't have a thing to do with Megan.

"Please don't tell me you're willing to have a relationship with Lilly for Megan's sake?" Erica went on.

Jason didn't know the answer, and he didn't want to explore it now. Especially not with Erica.

Because this wasn't going to be pleasant, he gently took Erica by the arm and led her down the hall so they wouldn't wake Megan and Lilly. He only hoped there wouldn't be shouting, but it was a distinct possibility.

He considered several ways to go about this, but decided to use the direct approach. "Erica, I think it's time for you to leave."

She went board-stiff. Stared at him. And then jerked away from him as if he'd slapped her. "What do you mean?"

He continued with the direct approach. "I mean that Lilly and I have enough to deal with right now, and your being here isn't making things easier."

"I see." Keeping her gaze pinned to him, she stepped back. She swallowed hard. "Did Lilly talk you into doing this?"

"You know I can't be talked into anything that I don't feel is right. This was my idea. Lilly needs time to be with Megan, and Megan needs time to be with her. That won't happen with you around. Megan will keep turning to you, and that'll only cause friction between Lilly and you."

Erica pulled in a breath and gave a shaky nod. "You're certain about this?"

"Positive. I'll give you a month's severance pay and

a reference, but I want you to consider this your two weeks' notice—"

"Two weeks' notice isn't necessary. I'll leave today— for Megan's sake. And yours." Erica looked down at the floor. "I'll pack a few things and arrange for someone to pick up the rest. I won't be long."

"There's no need for you to rush."

"Yes. There is." When she lifted her head again, Jason had no trouble seeing the tears in her eyes.

Great. He felt like a jerk. But he would have felt like a bigger jerk if Lilly had had to battle Erica just so she could spend time with her daughter. This was definitely a case of one too many moms.

Swiftly wiping away her tears, Erica headed in the direction of her room, but then stopped and turned back around to face him. "I'm sorry things didn't work out so I could stay. And just for the record, no hard feelings." With that, she walked away.

Jason was a little surprised with her reaction. It was amicable and the decent thing to say. The *right* thing. If Erica was sincere, that is. But he wondered if she truly was.

"Anything wrong?" He looked back to see Lilly standing in the doorway of her room.

Man, she was a welcome sight, and there was no amount of denial that would make him feel otherwise. There went another slam of guilt. First, over Erica. Now, over this giddy feeling he got whenever he saw Lilly. It'd been that way since he'd kissed her the night before at her office.

Since giddy and guilt just didn't go together with a police investigation, Jason renewed his vow to start rebuilding some barriers between Lilly and him. Not anger barriers. Not hate. Just a few mental fences to remind him that this was a woman his brother had loved. Even if he wanted her—and, yep, he did—having her would make them both miserable.

He needed to remember that.

She'd changed since he'd last seen her at headquarters and now wore a sleeveless silk dress that was the color of ripe peaches. One of the articles of clothing she'd no doubt had the cops pick up for her from her house. The dress suited her, skimming along her body and stopping several inches above her knees so that it exposed a great deal of her legs.

She was barefoot, and he could see that she'd painted her toenails pearl white. For some reason, even with the guilt-producing discussion he'd just had with Erica and the guilt/giddy pep talk he'd given himself, those bare feet captured his attention.

"What happened?" She followed his gaze to her feet and flexed her eyebrows. "Am I about to get a lecture on the dangers of going barefoot?"

"Not from me." He forced a smile because he thought they could both use it.

"So, what's wrong?"

"Erica's leaving." He kept his voice low so he wouldn't wake Megan. Erica would want to say goodbye to her, of course, but he hoped she would save that goodbye for another day. "She's packing her things now. Once she's done, I'll have the officer drive her where she wants to go."

Lilly's eyes widened, and she walked closer, until

they were only a few inches apart. She touched his arm and it soothed him far more than it should have.

"I'm sorry," she whispered.

"Don't be. It's for the best." He hoped. Jason also hoped that Erica's cool farewell wasn't a smoke screen for some sinister plan.

Yep.

That paranoia was still hanging around and was snowballing out of control. It was mixing with Lilly's scent and creating a fog in his brain. She smelled like cinnamon applesauce. Not exactly a scent that would normally turn him on, but it seemed to be doing the trick today.

"How's Megan?" he asked. Best to keep the conversation on a safe topic.

She gave him a suspicious look, as if she'd expected him to say something else. But what he had on his mind, he had no intentions of saying.

"Megan's napping." Lilly checked her watch. "She fell asleep about fifteen minutes ago."

So, it'd be at least an hour, probably twice that long, before she woke up. That would give Erica plenty of time to pack and it'd give him plenty of time to fill Lilly in on what had happened.

"Did you find out anything about Corinne's car?" Lilly worked her fingers through the crown of her hair to scoop it away from her face.

"Yes." And Jason hadn't cared for the news any more than Lilly probably would. "Corinne reported it stolen, but she didn't do that until several hours after the incident at the security gate."

Lilly bunched up her forehead. "Why'd she take so long to report it?"

He'd asked himself the same thing. "Corinne said she didn't notice that her vehicle was missing until she left work that evening. It wasn't in the parking lot so she claims she has no idea who took it or when."

"Do you believe her?"

Jason shrugged. "I don't know what to believe. And it gets even better—guess who works in the same building as Corinne? Raymond Klein and Wayne Sandling. They're partners in the consulting business these days, and they work just three offices away from her."

"Sandling and Klein," Lilly repeated. She pulled in a hard breath. "Their names keep coming up."

Yeah, and not in a good way, either. Either of them was brassy enough to have taken Corinne's car and driven it to the security gate.

"So, we're not taking Corinne off our list of suspects?" Lilly asked.

"No one's coming off that list just yet," he mumbled, rubbing his hand over his face. "Worse, I might have to add a name to it."

Lilly didn't have to think about that for very long. "Erica?"

Jason didn't know why it surprised him that Lilly had come up with the correct answer so quickly. After all, they'd had that whole trust discussion at headquarters. Plus, Lilly had spent the better part of a week under the same roof with Megan's soon-to-be-former nanny. Lilly probably hadn't missed the jealousy in Erica's eyes. He certainly hadn't. Just as he hadn't missed Erica's cool pseudo-goodbye that he feared would come back to haunt them.

Was Erica bitter enough to do something to get rid of Lilly?

Maybe even bitter enough to want to kill her?

"The day that Corinne's car was at the security gate, Erica was here inside with us and couldn't have done it," Lilly pointed out.

Jason had already considered and dismissed that. "It doesn't mean she's innocent, though. She could have hired someone to do the job."

"You mean a hit man?" Lilly shook her head. "No way. She wouldn't have risked that, not with Megan in the house. I might not be on her list of favorite people, but she loves Megan, and she wouldn't have put her in harm's way."

He couldn't dispute that. But there was another angle to this. "Maybe the person in that car was never meant to come inside and hurt you. Maybe it was simply a scare tactic to send you running so that Erica could have Megan all to herself."

"I'm sorry you believe that," he heard Erica say.

Oh, sheez. Open mouth, insert size-twelve boots. And here he hadn't thought this could get any harder.

Erica was at the end of the hall, her suitcase in her hand, and she had a fierce grip on the handle. She didn't come any closer, but her eyes darkened when she looked at Lilly. "You might have won this round, but this isn't over."

"This *round?*" Lilly repeated. "This isn't a competition, Erica."

"Isn't it? You think because you share DNA with Megan that it'll make you her mother? It won't."

"DNA is just for starters," Jason countered. He maneuvered himself in front of Lilly in case Erica decided to go berserk. "The rest will come with time. Lilly has a right to be with her daughter."

He hadn't choked on the words, either. And he wasn't especially shocked that he'd meant every word.

Erica stared at him. "Does she?"

Well, it wasn't the pseudo-cool goodbye that she'd issued just minutes earlier. "I'm ready to go now," Erica said to the officer in the living room. She didn't wait for him. She practically stormed toward the front door.

The detective followed Erica, and from over his shoulder, he issued Jason a nod. Probably of sympathy. Man, he'd really gone about this the wrong way. Of course, maybe there was no correct way to dissolve a relationship like the one that Erica had with Megan.

Erica didn't look back at him when she left, and Jason stood there and watched as the officer shut the door behind them.

"I'm sorry," Lilly repeated.

"So am I, but this had to be done. It's bad enough having suspects out there in the city. I couldn't have one under the same roof."

"Still, that didn't make it easier."

No. It didn't. But he thought his decision might allow him to sleep a little easier tonight.

"There's another problem with Erica being a suspect," Lilly continued. She went to the door, locked it and reactivated the security system. "Wasn't she here at the house with Megan the night someone tried to smother me?"

Since he'd already mentally gone over this info, he knew the answer to that one. "Erica had the night off, and my neighbor was here to watch Megan."

"Oh." She leaned her back against the door. "Okay, so that really could mean that Erica's a suspect."

It did. And it completely changed the motive for what was happening. Of course, that didn't mean Erica was the sole culprit. Jason simply couldn't picture Erica perched on a rooftop shooting at them with a high-powered rifle. So, did that mean there was more than one person after Lilly? Was this some conspiracy, or was it simply two people with two totally different sinister agendas?

"You look exhausted," Lilly observed.

Maybe because he was. Past exhaustion, really. He kept that to himself and switched to a more comfortable topic. "What did Megan and you do all morning?"

Her mouth curved slightly. A brief, amused smile. And she took a step toward him. Slowly. Not some calculated saunter, either. The limp threw off any chance of a seductive stance, and yet that limp, that slight imperfection, made her look all the more human.

As if he needed anything to do that.

"Hmm. Is that question a ploy to distract me from telling you that you look exhausted, or do you really want to know?" Lilly asked.

Well, it was clear that Lilly wasn't going to allow this to be a safe conversation. "Both."

No amused smile that time. Instead, Lilly cleared her throat. "When did we start being so…honest with each other?"

Jason went to her. So they could keep their conversation soft and not wake Megan. Or at least, that's the reason he gave himself for closing the already narrow distance between them. However, to stop himself from doing anything too stupid, he crammed his hands into his jeans' pockets and promised himself that that's where he'd keep them.

"You think we're being honest?" he asked.

Caution flickered in her eyes. They were more blue today than green, and shimmered. "Probably not. It's hard to have a momentous air-clearing that could lead to total honesty meltdown while people keep trying to kill us." She paused. Frowned. "And there is an *us* in danger now. Thanks to me. Just call me Typhoid Lilly."

"So you're blaming yourself for some homicidal maniac shooting at us?" Jason asked.

"The gunman was aiming for me, and that's what put you in danger." Groaning and burying her face in her hands, she slid down and sat on the floor with her back against the front door. "I keep going over what happened. I keep kicking myself. Conditioned response—indeed. Go to my office to try to trigger some memories. And what happens? I nearly get you killed in the process."

Jason waited a moment. "Are you finished beating yourself up?" He went closer, eased his hands from his pockets and stooped down so they were at eye level.

Lilly met him at that eye level when she lowered her hands from her face. And she ignored his question. "It wasn't enough for me to be negligent in Greg's death, but last night, I almost did the same to you."

Jason didn't like the sound of that. He waited another moment. "*Now* are you finished?"

"No. I'm just getting started."

That pained look on her face intensified. It made him want to comfort her. But pulling her into his arms would mean touching her. And he knew for a fact that just wasn't a good idea. Not with the fatigue and this dangerous energy between them.

Still, he couldn't make himself turn away.

He couldn't stop himself from listening.

And he couldn't stop the ache he had for her.

Because this was forbidden. Taboo. And for some reason that only made him want her more.

"I replay the moments leading up to the shooting," Lilly continued, obviously not willing to drop the subject. "I replay the moments before Greg walked out of my house. I keep thinking if I could just go back and change things—"

"You can't."

Lilly blinked and seemingly listened for answers he couldn't give her. "But then how do I get past it, huh? How do you ever get to the point where you can forgive me? Where I can forgive myself?"

It was a question he'd asked himself at least a thousand times. "I don't know," he said honestly. "But I know blaming yourself won't do any good."

"Maybe not any good, but I don't see how we can avoid it." She raked her finger over her eyebrow. "And how do we get past this…stuff we're feeling for each other?"

"That's a fantastic question," he mumbled.

"Do you have a fantastic answer?"

He shook his head and met her gaze. Not good. It only made him want to move closer to her, and he was already too close as it was. "Lilly, I don't even have a bad answer. Truth is…I don't have any kind of answer at all."

"But you agree that feeling this way is wrong, that it'll only make things more complicated?"

"I agree. Massive complications. And there's that part about it causing us to lose focus while there's all this danger around us."

"Good point," she conceded. She didn't exactly sound thankful for his reminding her of that, either. Which was a good thing. Because Jason hoped the reminder would make her move away.

It sure as heck wasn't working for him.

But she didn't move. Lilly sat there, her attention fastened to him. She gave him no sultry come-on looks. No whispered invitations. No anything. Still, it happened. The air stirred between them. Everything stirred.

Especially his body.

Jason might have talked himself out of what he was thinking about doing. *Might.* But he didn't even try. Somewhere along the way, he'd lost the battle with reason and was functioning on some primitive level where desire replaced common sense.

Cursing himself, cursing her, cursing this unquenchable need he had for her, Jason leaned forward, slid his hand around the back of her head and tugged her closer to him.

The fire was instant. No more smoldering flames. This was white-hot, and it burned through him. Consuming him. He couldn't think. Couldn't talk. But he could feel. And right now, that was the only thing he wanted to do.

He wanted to feel Lilly in his arms.

Feel his mouth on her.

He wanted to feel everything.

Jason took her as if he owned her. Her lips, pressing against his. Her body, moving against his. Soon, it wasn't enough. Not nearly enough. He tested the taste of her, touching his tongue to hers, and he quickly realized that her taste only made him want her more.

The battle started. The frenzied need for them to touch each other. They fought, grappling for position until Lilly maneuvered her way into his lap.

The kiss continued.

They took and ravished. And took some more. Both starving for what the other was so willing to give.

Jason finally broke the intimate contact when he remembered that he needed air to live. Lilly gulped in some much-needed breaths, as well, while she clung to him.

"What about Megan?" she asked, her voice broken by her breathing.

He'd already thought of that. "We'll hear her if she wakes up," Jason promised.

Lilly nodded, obviously not ready to question that, and she latched on to him and went back for more.

The second battle was just as intense. No longer content with just her mouth, Jason took his kisses to her neck. Lilly made a sound. A low, sensual moan. Definitely not a request for him to stop.

So, Jason didn't stop.

CHAPTER TEN

SOMEWHERE IN THE back of her mind, Lilly realized this was a massive mistake.

She knew all the arguments and knew them well. Jason was Greg's brother. The man who could challenge her for custody. The man who had in the past and could continue to make her life a living Hades.

But she no longer cared about arguments and such.

She took things from Jason that she hadn't even known she wanted. The strength from his embrace. The mind-blowing thrill of his kisses. And, mercy, he was a good kisser. The gentleness of his touch. The need. Most of all, the need. She could feel it all through him, and it only fed her own desire for him.

Lilly decided to take everything he was giving her since there was no chance she'd talk her body, or his, into slowing down. There was a frantic urgency in their kisses. It was a race, but against what she didn't know. All that mattered was that they had to have each other now.

He took her neck. She took his. And she touched. Really touched. Letting her palm slide down all those toned, firm pecs. And his rock-hard abs. She was guessing that he had a six-pack, and she shoved up his shirt to confirm that.

Yes, the man was built.

Jason touched, too. And he was decidedly better at it than she was. While he cupped her neck with one hand and kissed her blind, he let that other clever hand wander in the direction of her right breast. Somehow, even through the fabric of her silk dress and her bra, he managed to locate her nipple, and he pinched it lightly. Just enough pressure to make her want him to do it again and again and again.

"Yes." She let him know in case he'd missed the needy sounds she was making.

"Yes?" Jason questioned, meeting her gaze. But he obviously already knew the answer because he gave her another of those little pinches.

"Yes," she assured him.

Maybe because they now had eye contact, it occurred to her that she should suggest that they stop. But her body promptly disagreed with that. She was hot and aching for him to do more than merely pinch. Mercy, she wanted him.

He pulled her back to him and buried his face in her hair. His breath hit against her neck. It was warm. Quick. His pulse and heartbeat must have been pounding because she could feel it wherever they touched. And they seemed to be touching everywhere.

Except in the very place she wanted him to touch most.

Jason obviously guessed what she wanted because he looped his arm around her waist and pulled her against him. Lilly made adjustments. No easy feat with her legs still not functioning a hundred percent, but she somehow managed to put her knees on each side of his hips.

She moved forward. Saw stars. Really big stars. Then

the vee of her panties struck right against the front of his jeans. Lilly could feel him. Every inch of him. That hard ridge straining against the denim.

His mouth was on her neck. Pressing. He slid his hand up her thigh to the front of her panties. Since she'd already moved past into the shameless zone, because every part of her was on fire, Lilly moved against his fingers. Intimately. But not gently. She didn't want gentle. She wanted to feel alive. She wanted to feel needed. She wanted to—

He hooked his fingers onto the elastic of her panties.

And he slipped his hand inside.

Every coherent or semicoherent thought she had flew right out of her head.

"Touch me," she heard herself whisper.

Jason cooperated. He touched her, and he didn't have any trouble finding the right place. Nor was he especially gentle. He made rough, almost frantic slippery strokes. While his mouth feasted on her cheek and neck. While his erection pressed against her thigh. Until she couldn't think. Until she couldn't breathe. Until she didn't care if she ever did either of those things again.

But even without the ability to think or breathe, Lilly knew it was time to take this to the next level. She reached for his zipper. Jason took it up a notch, as well. He shoved her dress up to her waist.

Then he stopped.

And stared at her.

Lilly blinked, trying to focus. Trying to figure out what had happened to bring everything to an abrupt halt.

"I don't have a condom."

Oh, great. Somehow, even through her passion-hazed brain, she understood that. She also understood she didn't have an immediate solution. "Neither do I."

He cursed. It was a four-letter word for what they would be doing if they'd had a condom.

"I don't guess there's one in the house somewhere?" she asked. And she was hoping the answer was yes.

Jason shook his head. "I haven't had a woman here."

Because of Megan. Lilly understood that. Her body didn't like it, but she understood it.

Logic and normalcy slowly began to return, little by little, and with each passing second, she began to feel more and more self-conscious. The passion began to fade. So did the immediate, pressing need to have wild sex on the floor with Jason.

All right, she couldn't lie to herself. She still had that particular need for wild sex, but it was stupid to have pushed things this far without at least making a few rudimentary plans—like buying a condom.

Frustrated, she eased out of his lap and pulled her dress back into place so that she was covered. She hadn't minded her seminudity during the crazy foreplay, but it seemed awkward now.

"Please don't say you're sorry that happened," he whispered.

She dodged his gaze. "Sorry isn't the correct word. Embarrassed."

"Why? Because we acted on what we've been feeling for days?"

Lilly debated several answers but went with the truth.

"This whole lack-of-condom thing reminds me a little of teenagers with their hormones out of control. Plus, I'm not sure sex would have been a smart idea."

"It wouldn't have been smart," Jason readily concurred. He paused, smiled. Dimples flashed. "But it would have been damn good."

She couldn't help it. She laughed. Lilly savored the light moment, but at the same time she knew it did nothing to cut the tension that was so thick she could taste it.

"Once we find out who's trying to kill us," he said, sounding as disappointed and as unfulfilled as Lilly felt, "we can concentrate on what's happening, or not happening, between us."

Yes, that was logical.

Maybe a little too logical, considering that he was still aroused. And that got Lilly thinking.

What *had* just happened?

She thought about keeping the question to herself. Maybe mulling it over for a while. But Jason was here, right in front of her, and before the kissing and touching, they'd had this whole honesty discussion going on between them.

"I have to know. All this kissing and touching—does it have anything to do with Megan?" Lilly asked.

That seemed to freeze him for several seconds. "Excuse me?"

After seeing his reaction, she instantly regretted her question. But there was no turning back now. Even if it hurt like the devil, she had to know the truth. "Is this your way of working out a custody arrangement?"

No freezing that time. Her question earned her a

scalpel-sharp glare, and he had to unclench his teeth before he could speak. "I'm going to pretend I didn't hear that."

She caught his arm to stop him when he started to get up. "No, you're not. You're going to search your heart and tell me if that's what you're really feeling."

And judging from the arctic look on Jason's face, she wouldn't like his answer.

JASON WANTED NOTHING more than to dismiss Lilly's question, but he couldn't.

Hell.

One minute, they were all wrapped up in each other's arms, sharing hot kisses and on the verge of having equally hot sex. Now, he felt as if he were facing a firing squad.

And facing a moment of truth.

Lilly had simply asked what had been on his mind for days, and it was time to deal with it.

"If a relationship of convenience is what it takes for us both to be with Megan, will you consider it?" he asked, hoping she didn't slap him.

But if she had intentions of slapping him, Lilly didn't follow through on them. That's because they heard the sound at the end of the hall. Little footsteps. A moment later, the owner of those little footsteps appeared, and Megan toddled toward them.

Lilly did a double check to make sure they were both decent. They were. And she smiled at Megan. The little girl returned the smile. A sleepy one. She had woken up a little too early from her nap.

Megan stopped when she was just a few inches away

and gave each of them a considering look. Obviously she felt she had some sort of decision to make. It didn't take her long, though. She went to Jason, sank down next to him and rested her head against his arm.

It was one of those magic moments that he'd been lucky enough to share often with Megan. He treasured times like this. However, he knew these were no longer just Megan's and his moments. He picked up Megan, kissed her cheek and deposited her onto Lilly's lap.

Jason didn't know which of them was most surprised by that.

Megan look confused. Lilly, stunned. And he was sure he was both. Still, Megan didn't protest the new arrangement. She settled against Lilly and closed her eyes to finish her nap.

Lilly lifted her eyes to meet his. *Thank you,* she mouthed.

He braced himself for some feelings of jealousy, but those feelings thankfully didn't come. Progress, indeed.

"Well?" he prompted. "Would you consider a relationship of convenience?"

Lilly moistened her lips and looked down at Megan. "I'd consider almost anything for her sake. But we're already facing an obstacle or two in the convenience department. Sometimes the fire and heat burn out and leave a lot of bitterness. When that happens, it doesn't make anything convenient."

Jason didn't have to ask her to clarify. He knew. And unfortunately, he also knew she was probably right. But was there enough common ground between them to overcome anything? He didn't get a chance to pose that question to her because the phone in the living room rang. Since it could have something to do with security or the investigation, Jason quickly got up to answer it.

"Detective Lawrence, it's me, Corinne Davies," the caller said. "We met the other night at Lilly's office."

"I know who you are," he informed her. After the incident with the stolen car, both her name and voice were imprinted on his brain. What he couldn't figure out was what the heck she was doing calling him. "How can I help you?"

She didn't answer right away. "I hope I haven't made a mistake by contacting you, but I think I might have found some information you need."

That got his full attention. "I'm listening." And so that Lilly could do the same, he turned on the speaker function of the phone.

"I was going through some old files I had from when I worked for Lilly. I found some e-memos that Raymond Klein sent to Lilly's father." Her words were suddenly rushed, as if she was trying to hurry. "They seem to suggest that they were about to do something illegal. Something to do with paying off a city official so they could undercut other bids for a building project. One of those other bids appears to belong to your brother, Greg."

Jason met Lilly's gaze. She didn't appear surprised, but concerned. She pulled Megan protectively closer to her.

"I'll want to see these memos," Jason told Corinne.

"I thought you would. But there might be a problem. The files might have been tampered with." Corinne's voice dropped even lower. She was either very nervous and frightened about this call, or else she was putting on a good act. "I can't verify that this e-memo even came from Klein. I'm usually pretty good at unraveling the e-mail addresses and identities of the senders, but this one has been blocked. I can't be sure if this information in the memo is correct or if someone planted it to make it look as if something illegal was going on."

After hearing that, Jason had a dilemma of his own. Was Corinne up to something? He certainly didn't trust the woman, and that lack of trust cast some serious suspicion on what she was saying. However, he couldn't just dismiss potential evidence either, especially if that evidence could be used to convict Raymond Klein.

"Take what you have to police headquarters," Jason instructed Corinne. "I'll pick it up there."

"I can't do that."

"And why not?"

More hesitation. Jason could practically see the woman wringing her hands, or else pretending to wring them. "I think someone's watching me. Maybe it has something to do with what happened to Lilly. The shooting, I mean. I don't want to go walking into police headquarters because I believe someone will try to stop me from doing that."

Well, he could understand her concern. Jason could also understand his own concern. "You can fax or copy the files and e-mail them," he suggested.

"No, I can't. Some are handwritten, and the ink is very pale. I tried to copy a few, but they're barely even legible in places."

Oh, man. He didn't even want to know where this was leading.

"I want to meet with Lilly and you so I can give you the files in person," Corinne insisted.

Lilly made a frustrated sound and shook her head.

Jason agreed. "It wouldn't be safe for Lilly to be out in public."

"I can meet you someplace safe," Corinne insisted.

But Jason knew there were no real safe places. Especially not for a meeting with a suspect.

"You choose the location," Corinne continued. She no longer sounded just afraid. She sounded desperate. "You bring along extra cops. Guns, whatever. Do what you need to do to secure the place, and I'll give you what I found."

Jason quickly thought that through and came up with a solution. "All right. Let's meet in the parking lot of police headquarters, but Lilly won't be coming with me."

"She has to, or else I'll call the whole thing off. I don't really know you, Detective Lawrence, but I know Lilly, and I know she wouldn't do anything to hurt me. That's why I insist that she be there."

"Okay," he heard Lilly say.

Glaring at her hardly seemed enough to convey his displeasure for her okay. "Lilly won't be coming with me," Jason insisted.

"I'll be at the parking lot of the downtown police headquarters at 8:00 p.m.," Corinne said. "If Lilly's not there, I won't be, either."

And with that ultimatum, she hung up.

"We have to meet her. You know we don't have a choice about this," Lilly said immediately.

"Oh, but we do, and that choice is for you to stay

put. I'll go to the meeting and get those memos and files from Corinne while you stay here under police guard."

Lilly's frown probably meant she didn't agree with his plan. "What if she means what she said? What if she won't meet with you if I'm not there?"

Jason considered that, and dismissed it. "What if she's up to something?"

"What if she's not?" Lilly argued.

He huffed. "How long are you going to keep countering a question with a question?"

She made a show of pretending to think about it. "Forever?"

That didn't improve his mood. "Smart-ass."

"So I've been told. But here's the deal, Jason. Corinne wants to meet in the parking lot of police headquarters. If she had murder on her mind, she wouldn't have chosen a place where she'd likely get arrested. Pardon the question, but would she?"

Maybe. Or maybe this was one smart ploy to get them to cooperate.

And a ploy to get them killed.

"I don't like this," Jason told her.

"Neither do I. That's why I'll stay in the car. In fact, we both will, and we'll let Corinne come to us."

Jason stared at her. And glared. He hoped it conveyed his displeasure. But what it probably also conveyed was that Lilly had a point. Corinne might have something they needed.

"You won't meet face-to-face with Corinne even if she insists?" Jason asked.

"I might have a smart mouth, but I'm not stupid."

Lilly brushed a kiss on Megan's forehead. "Besides, I have a very important reason for staying alive, and I'm holding that reason right here in my arms."

Jason looked down at Megan. Before he ever switched on the speakerphone, he'd known that she'd fallen asleep. Megan seemed totally unaware of what was happening. Thank goodness. That was something at least. The stress and worry of their situation hadn't spilled over to her.

"Those memos that Corinne found could be the very thing we need to put an end to all of this," Lilly pointed out.

And she was right. Jason knew it. So did she.

That didn't make this easier, though.

"I'll get another officer to stay here with Megan," Jason finally said. "I'll also arrange for us to use an unmarked vehicle with bulletproof windows. You and I will drive to headquarters, but you won't be getting out of the car. Right?"

"Right," she promised.

That promise might keep her safe. *Might*. But Jason couldn't help but wonder if he was about to lead Lilly straight into a deadly trap.

CHAPTER ELEVEN

"I'M KICKING MYSELF," Jason mumbled. Though his voice carried almost no sound, Lilly heard him loud and clear. She also felt the knotted muscles in his arm as they sat side by side on the seat of the unmarked car. "You know that, right?"

Lilly knew.

She was kicking herself, as well.

This meeting with Corinne could be important, critical even, but she hated leaving Megan for any reason. It didn't matter that her daughter was in safe hands with not just one cop, but two. It also didn't matter that one of the cops, Sgt. Garrett O'Malley, was someone that she knew and trusted.

Nope.

This didn't have to do with trust. It had to do with leaving her little girl while she tried to figure out who wanted Jason and her dead. High stakes. But with an equally high possibility of failure.

She glanced around the parking lot again and checked her watch. "No sign of Corinne," she pointed out.

Lilly didn't have to add that the woman was nearly a half hour late. Jason was well aware of that. He was probably also well aware that Corinne wasn't going to show with the evidence and this had perhaps been some sort of wild-goose chase.

But why would Corinne have done that?

Lilly couldn't come up with a good answer, but there were possibilities that made her uncomfortable. In addition to the wild-goose theory, maybe someone had blackmailed Corinne into arranging this meeting. And that led Lilly right back to Wayne Sandling and Raymond Klein.

"She's not going to show," Jason declared.

Even though it was dark, there were enough security lights in the parking lot for her to note his frustrated, impatient expression. Sighing and feeling equally impatient and frustrated, she leaned her head against the glass of the heavily tinted window.

"Maybe the officers you sent out to check the area will find her," Lilly answered. "Maybe she's out there, waiting to make sure it's safe before she comes into the open."

"Maybe," he said, not sounding as if he believed that. She didn't believe it, either. "Don't sit so close to the window."

She glanced at the window. Frowned. "I thought they were bulletproof."

"More like bullet resistant. If the shooter is using armor-piercing bullets, the shot could still get through."

He didn't have to say that twice. Lilly immediately slid across the seat toward him, until her arm was squashed against his again. He felt warm. Comforting. Something she desperately needed.

"There are too many things that could go wrong," Jason said under his breath. "That's obviously why I didn't want you to come."

"But if something goes right, and we get these memos

from Corinne, you might have the evidence you need for an arrest. Then we won't be in danger anymore."

He stayed quiet a moment. "If this doesn't work, maybe you could try going about this from a different angle. During some investigations when the witness has been traumatized, sometimes we use a psychiatrist to hypnotize the person, to see if they recall anything."

Lilly considered that. "And it's been successful?" she asked.

"Sometimes."

"Well, sometimes is better than nothing. I'll do it. Just let me know when and where." In fact, she wished they'd already arranged it. Recalling the face of the person who'd tried to kill her might lead them to the person who was behind all these latest attempts on their lives.

"Let's get past this rendezvous first," Jason reminded her.

If there was a rendezvous. And if it would amount to anything. They could be back at square one, and that meant all of them were in danger.

Including Megan.

Only hours earlier Jason had asked her if she would consider a relationship of convenience. Ironic. Because with the danger staring them right in their faces, she should be considering just the opposite. To keep her child and Jason safe, she might have to consider doing the unthinkable.

She might have to leave.

In some ways that was unimaginable. And yet in other ways, it seemed irresponsible not to do it. If she left, maybe the person trying to kill her wouldn't go anywhere near Megan. It broke her heart just to consider it, but it would break her heart even more to lose her daughter.

The movement caught Lilly's eye, and she looked up to see two uniformed officers cut across the parking lot. They approached the car, and Jason lowered the window a fraction.

"We found something," one of the officers said to Jason.

"Is it Corinne Davies?" Jason asked.

The rookie shook his head and cast an uneasy glance at Lilly before bringing his gaze back to Jason. "Not exactly. But, trust me, you'll want to see this."

THE ROOKIE'S *You'll want to see this* might have been vague, but it was more than enough to get Jason moving. Obviously, his fellow cop had something to say, and he didn't want to say it in front of Lilly. If that was the case, there wasn't much chance of this being good news.

"I want you to wait here with Lilly," Jason ordered the rookie. He glanced at the other uniformed officer. "You'll come with me."

Jason checked his weapon and opened the door "Don't let her get out of the car, and don't let Corinne Davies or anyone other than me get anywhere near her, understand?"

The rookie nodded.

Lilly didn't agree quite so quickly. "Wait a minute," she said, grabbing Jason's arm to stop him from leaving. "What if I don't want you to go to check on this 'thing you'll want to see'?"

"It's my job to go," Jason countered.

She pointed first at the rookie and then at the other officer. "It's their job, too. Why can't they go?"

"Because I'm a detective and they're not. Besides, this is personal for me. If Corinne is out there, I want to see her face-to-face, to see if I can figure out what's really going on here."

She frowned. "I don't suppose it'd do any good to ask if I can go with you?"

He didn't even have to think about that. "No good whatsoever. You're staying put."

Jason turned to leave, but she latched on to his arm again. "Don't do anything...stupid, okay?" And with that, she leaned forward and hurriedly brushed a kiss on his cheek.

It definitely wasn't one of those lusty foreplay kisses they'd shared in the foyer of his house. But in some ways, it packed an even greater wallop. Because it was the kind of kiss that people gave each other when they were more than just two people with a child in common.

How much more? Jason asked himself.

But he pushed the question aside. He was about to venture into what could essentially be a kill zone, and he needed a clear head for that. He didn't want the distraction of his feelings for Lilly to cloud his judgment.

"Stay put," he ordered Lilly one last time, and he got out of the car before she could stop him again.

Or before he felt compelled to return that kiss.

"So, did you find Corinne Davies or not?" Jason asked the officer once the door was closed and Lilly could no longer hear what they were saying. If it was bad news, he wanted a chance to process it first before he told her.

"No, but we found a car parked just up the street." They headed in that direction, and Jason looked over his shoulder to cast one last don't-get-out warning glance at Lilly and a watch-her warning glance at the rookie who was now guarding the car.

"The car we found is a rental," the officer continued. "We called the company, and it's Ms. Davies' name on the rental agreement."

Maybe she'd used a rental because she was concerned about being recognized. Or maybe because her other car had been stolen and she hadn't had a chance to replace it. Still, the situation made Jason uneasy. Of course, everything was making him uneasy at this point.

With his hand on his gun, Jason and the officer proceeded out of the headquarters' parking lot and onto the sidewalk. He spotted the silver-gray car right away. It was parked in the center point between two streetlights. In others words, in the spot with the least visibility.

There was another uniformed officer waiting by the vehicle. "No sign of Ms. Davies yet," the officer volunteered. "She's not in the car, but we haven't made a thorough search of the area yet."

Jason looked around at the street jammed with buildings on each side. There were plenty of places to hide if Corinne had gone inside one of them. Maybe inside and on the roof with a high-powered rifle? He glanced up, half expecting to see her standing there, with a gun aimed right at him.

But Corinne wasn't anywhere in sight.

Temporarily satisfied that he wasn't about to be ambushed, Jason turned his attention back to the rental car.

He borrowed a flashlight from one of the uniformed officers and checked the interior.

Nothing.

No purse, no jacket, no cell. No sign of a struggle.

That didn't mean there hadn't been one.

He put his hand over the hood of the car. He didn't touch the surface in case it became necessary for them to dust for prints. But he could feel no heat coming from the engine. The car had no doubt been parked there for a while. Perhaps even for several hours.

Jason swept the milky light over the exterior of the car, and when he didn't see anything out of the ordinary, he began to examine the street and the sidewalk. It didn't take him long to spot what he'd hoped he wouldn't see.

"Secure the area," Jason ordered the officers. "And get the CSI guys out here now."

Cursing under his breath, Jason angled the flashlight, moving it along the black asphalt. Despite the dark color, he had no trouble seeing the wet spots. Though he already knew what they were, he stooped and touched his index finger to one of the drops.

It was blood.

CHAPTER TWELVE

"BAD NEWS?" Lilly asked. She was lying on the hospital bed, her forearm draped across her forehead.

Jason realized she'd been asking that a lot in the past twenty-four hours. Probably because they hadn't gotten good news about, well, much of anything.

It had been a long day.

And it was going to get a lot longer.

First, there was the hypnosis and then later Lilly was scheduled for one of those marathon physical therapy sessions at the hospital. But it wasn't the hypnosis and the physical therapy that concerned him most. His biggest concern was that it was next to impossible to keep her safe while they were away from the house.

"It must be bad news," she mumbled.

She was right, of course.

Jason pocketed his cell and debated how much he should tell her. After all, she was supposed to be relaxing, waiting for the drug to take effect so she could be hypnotized. She was drowsy, no doubt about that, but since he knew she was anxious for an update, Jason proceeded with the recount that he'd just gotten from a fellow detective.

"Still no sign of Corinne, and the crime scene techs estimate there's about a half a pint of blood on the trail leading away from the car." A trail that stopped one street over. Which meant Corinne had likely gotten into another vehicle. Now the question was, had that happened voluntarily or had she been forced to go? And if it'd been voluntary, why hadn't she gone to the ER? There was one just a few blocks from the scene, yet there was no record of anyone matching her description.

"They're sure it's Corinne's blood?" Lilly asked.

"It's consistent with her blood type. She's not in any of the data banks, so the CSI guys will first need to obtain a sample of her known DNA to compare to what they collected from the scene."

She nodded. Or rather tried to, but it was obvious the drug was taking effect. "She could have faked her injuries."

Jason was surprised she could come up with that theory while under sedation. But he'd already considered it. "You mean, maybe Corinne stockpiled some of her blood and used it to make us think there was foul play?"

Another shaky nod.

It was possible, but if Corinne had done that, it was because she was scared and wanted to make them believe she was no longer alive. Or else she wanted her fake death to allow her the lack of scrutiny from the police so she could finish what she had started. It sent a chill through him to consider what Corinne *might have started*.

"I learned something else," Jason continued. "It's not good news, either. The lab got the results from the clothes that Sandling and Klein were wearing the night of the shooting, and neither showed any signs of gunshot residue."

That proved nothing, of course. There'd been time before their interrogation so they could have changed clothes and given themselves a thorough scrub-down to remove any residue.

The door swung open and Jason automatically reached for his weapon. He stopped, however, when he realized it was the shrink. Dr. Malcolm McCartle. Tall, imposing. A dark tan with a shiny bald head that was less indicative of age than the fashion trend. Thankfully, the doctor had dealt with enough cops and police situations that he didn't even question Jason's actions.

"Lilly, how are you doing?" Dr. McCartle asked. He rolled over a chair, plopped down right next to her bed and took the notepad from the nightstand.

"Fine," she mumbled without even opening her eyes.

The doctor looked up at Jason. "Since she gave permission, you're welcome to stay, but I'd prefer if you didn't ask questions. And don't say anything, for that matter. I have your list of things here that you'd like to know, and I'll go from there."

Jason nodded, took a seat and listened as the doctor murmured words of reassurance to Lilly. It took McCartle several minutes to finish, and then he glanced down at the notepad, where Jason had written the questions. Jason only hoped they were the right questions and that Lilly could answer them.

"Lilly, I want you to think back to the night of your car crash," the doctor instructed, his voice soft and flat. "Nineteen months ago. You leave your office. It's night. The air is chilly because it's winter, and it's drizzling. Do you remember that?"

"Yes. I have on my coat. The black wool one with the silver buttons."

Well, that was a good start. Jason hoped it continued because there were some difficult questions on that list.

"You're walking through the parking lot and you get in your car," Dr. McCartle prompted. "And then you start driving on San Pedro. You head north on Highway 281 to Anderson Loop. Think about that drive, Lilly. Take yourself back to that night. Can you see if anyone is following you?"

Even though her eyes were closed, he could see the movement beneath her lids. "No. I don't think so."

"Look around the inside of your car. Do you have the computer disk with you?"

"Yes," she said quickly. "It's on the front passenger's seat, next to my purse. It's important. It has a lot of information about my father."

"What kind of information?" the doctor asked.

"Copies of forged and altered agreements and deals. There are some bids and paperwork that he stole so that competing companies wouldn't get city contracts that he wanted. He bribed people. He intimidated them. And I have proof of all of that."

Jason didn't doubt that such proof existed. It was just too bad that the cops hadn't realized just how much danger Lilly was in because she possessed such evidence. If they'd known, they likely could have given her protection and saved her from the accident and the coma.

"Lilly, are you nervous about the disk?" Dr. McCartle questioned.

"Yes." Another fast answer, and her face became tense. "I'm going to take it to the police."

"Does anyone know you're planning to do that?" the doctor asked.

No fast answer that time. Lilly gave it some thought. "I told my secretary, Corinne."

Oh, hell. Now that was a bit of info that Corinne hadn't volunteered. That lent some credence to the theory that Corinne might have faked her own death or injury. Of course, maybe the woman simply forgot to inform them of what she knew. But then, that seemed such an important thing to forget.

"Does anyone else know that you have the disk?" Dr. McCartle read from the list.

"Maybe." Another pause. Her forehead bunched up. "I kept the blinds in my office open all day, well into the evening. Corinne said something about having the feeling that we were being watched, and she was nervous."

Yet another new piece of the puzzle. It didn't exonerate Corinne, but it sure as heck explained how someone else might have known what Lilly was about to do.

"You're in your car now," the doctor continued. "You're driving on Anderson Loop. Traffic is light. You're going through an area where there aren't many businesses. Look around you again. Check the rearview and side mirrors. Is anyone following you?"

Before the doctor spoke the last word of his question, Lilly gasped. Jason bolted to his feet, but without looking at him, the doctor motioned for him to sit down.

"The car's coming right at me," Lilly said, her voice high-pitched and strained. So were the muscles in her face and neck. And she had a death grip on the side of the bed. "My God, it's going to hit me."

Jason couldn't sit. Not listening to that. Not hearing the terror in Lilly's voice.

"Describe the car," McCartle insisted.

She frantically shook her head, and for a moment Jason didn't think she could answer. That this had all been for nothing. But then, the head shaking stopped and her grip relaxed a little. "It's maroon. Dark windows. Four doors. It's coming at me. Fast. So fast. And I'm swerving to get away from it. There's a bridge. God, a bridge!" Lilly's hand flew up to cover her face, and Jason could only imagine how terrified she was. "I slammed into the guardrail."

"It's all right," the doctor assured her. "You won't feel any pain."

"No pain," Lilly repeated several times, as if trying to convince herself. "But I touch my fingers to my forehead, and I see the blood. I'm hurt. I'm dizzy."

Dr. McCartle gently rubbed her arm. "Look around you, Lilly. Do you still see that car that ran you off the road?"

"No. I can't see anything. Everything's spinning around."

The doctor leaned closer to her and lowered his voice to a whisper. "Listen, then. What do you hear?"

She waited a moment, and the movement was almost feverish beneath her eyelids. "Someone's there. Someone's opening the door on my side of the car. But I can't see a face."

"Look carefully," the doctor prompted. "Try to focus."

Jason held his breath. Waiting. And praying this would soon be over so that Lilly wouldn't have to go through any more.

"I can't see the face," Lilly whispered, her voice weak. "It's getting dark. And I can't feel. I don't think I can breathe." She hesitated. "And then everything stops... I stop."

The coma had taken her—and at such a crucial time. A few more minutes, a little better light, and Lilly might have been able to make an ID. Still, Jason wasn't ready to give up.

"Lilly, I want you to go back in time," the doctor instructed, looking at the notes. "Before the crash. What were you thinking about just before you saw the maroon car?"

It took her a moment to answer. "I was thinking about the disk. About all the problems my father had caused. And I was thinking about Greg."

That got Jason's attention. He motioned for the doctor to continue with that thread of questioning.

"Why Greg?"

"I found some information." Lilly paused, and judging from the way her mouth tightened, she was concentrating hard. "I think maybe Greg had some run-ins with one or more of my father's former business associates."

Well, that confirmed what Corinne had said. And what Jason had suspected.

"I was also thinking about the night Greg and I slept together," Lilly continued. "It was a mistake."

The doctor started to say something, but Lilly spoke before he could.

"I didn't love Greg," she volunteered. "And I told him

that. He was angry. Furious. Yelling. He said I didn't love him because I wanted his brother. It was true. I couldn't deny it. I've always been attracted to Jason." She made a dismissal sound deep in her throat. "But I'm not his type."

If he hadn't heard the words come from her mouth, Jason wouldn't have believed them. Whoa. That was a powerful confession. Definitely not the earth-shattering revelation of the identity of a would-be killer, but it was earth-shattering still the same.

So, now he knew. She hadn't been in love with Greg. Instead, she'd been attracted to him.

Him.

Now, the real question was, what was he going to do about it?

LILLY WASN'T HAVING much luck getting Megan to take a nap. Partly because she hated to lose even a couple of hours of time with her daughter—even if a nap was a necessity. On the other hand, judging from Jason's somber mood, he was waiting for Megan to fall asleep so that they could discuss some things. Things she'd no doubt disclosed while under hypnosis.

On the drive back from the hospital, Jason had said something about Greg being connected to one or more of her father's business associates. Before he could explain, he'd gotten a call. Then another. By the time he'd finished his conversations, they were at the house.

The interruptions hadn't stopped there.

They'd barely made it inside when she heard Megan rather loudly demand a bottle and some attention. Lilly had given Detective Sarah Albright, the "on-duty" nanny, a reprieve and had taken the crying child from her arms. She'd then given Megan a bottle, changed her, had even sung her a lullaby, but her daughter was still whining and obviously exhausted, reacting to all the recent changes in her life and the stress.

As was Jason.

He wasn't rubbing his eyes, but he had that surly, bruised expression. Mercy, she hoped she hadn't talked about sleeping with Greg. Jason shouldn't have been subjected to that.

Lilly pulled herself away from her mental brow-beating and kissed her daughter's cheek. Megan smiled. Not a bright-eyed grin as she often did. It was a lazy kind of smile that was a precursor to her eyelids drifting down. Lilly hummed softly to her, rocked her gently, and Megan finally surrendered to the dreaded nap.

Most would consider getting her daughter to sleep to be a small accomplishment, but for Lilly it was a huge milestone. There'd be many times like this. Milestones of all shapes and sizes, and she intended to be there for all of them.

Lilly struggled when she tried to get out of the chair in the nursery, and she silently cursed her still-weak legs. She was tired of being in recovery when she had so many important and dangerous things happening around her. Heaven forbid if she actually had to outrun a bad guy.

It wouldn't be a pretty sight.

When Jason noticed that she was struggling, he came to the rescue. He gently scooped up the sleeping Megan and eased her into her crib. Lilly gave Megan one last kiss, one last look before she covered her with a blanket, and Jason and she stepped out of the room.

"Okay," Lilly started, "what's wrong?"

He didn't answer her question. "Any leftover effects from the drug the shrink gave you?"

"I'm doing fine." Not exactly the truth. She was exhausted, but she had too many things to do to nap, including the physical therapy appointment that they'd have to leave for within the hour. There'd be time for naps once this rifle-wielding psycho was caught. "I don't think I can say the same for you, though. So, why the glum mood?" Rather than fishing for the answer, she went for the direct approach. "Did I say something about Greg that I shouldn't have?"

He blinked and shook his head. A denial that didn't quite convince her. "You said you thought maybe Greg had had some run-ins with your father's former business associates."

Not exactly news-at-five. Corinne had already said as much.

Jason looked around the hall and made a glance at the living room. "Let's go to my office," he insisted, already leading her in that direction. They passed through the living room where Detective Albright was taking a much-needed break on the sofa.

"I have the files we took from your office the other day," Jason continued. "And I think I might have found the connection."

Okay. So, maybe there was news, after all, and maybe this was the real reason for his puzzling mood.

Jason's home office was on the other side of the house, next to the kitchen. Lilly had glanced in there a time or two, but she hadn't gone in before now. It was a man's room. Wood floors, ceiling beams, a darkly colored Turkish rug and a desk that dominated the space. She looked around and spotted the baby monitor on the corner of the desk. A little green light indicated it was on, which meant they'd be able to hear Megan if she woke.

"Here," Jason said, pulling up a chair for her. She sat next to him, and he handed her a single sheet of paper. "It's the police's theory that the person who stole the disk from you after the car crash also went through your office and took the files you'd copied. I think the person missed this one. It's a handwritten memo from your father to Wayne Sandling."

She remembered the memo and remembered that she'd copied it onto the disk. It was one of literally hundreds she'd read when she'd been trying to determine the extent of her father's illegal activities. It was basically a vaguely worded "suggestion" for Wayne Sandling to make sure that their latest bid for a municipal contract was accepted. In other words, do whatever necessary to ensure no one else outbid them.

"Check the dates," Jason prompted. "And then look at the date of this correspondence from Greg."

Greg's correspondence was a week after her father's memo. Greg had written a letter to the city council, expressing his concern, and fury, over the selection process for a specific contract. A contract he'd lost, even though he'd insisted he'd put in a lower bid than the winning company—a business represented by her father.

Of course.

"There's more," Jason continued. "While you were

in recovery from the hypnosis drug, I made some calls. I had one of the detectives read back through Greg's accident report. An eyewitness reported that there was a maroon, four-door car with tinted windows in the vicinity."

Lilly shook her head, not making the connection.

"Under hypnosis, you said the car that hit you was maroon with heavily tinted windows."

She was so glad she was sitting down. No, it wasn't clear-cut evidence, but she couldn't dismiss it as a co-incidence, either. "You think Greg might have been murdered?" she asked, holding her breath.

"I think it's a strong possibility."

"Oh, God. Oh, God." She couldn't help it. She dropped her head onto his shoulder and the tears came. The grief was fresh again, as if his death had just happened. "And here all this time, I thought this was my fault. I've been blaming myself."

"And I've been blaming you."

She was aware that along with all the pain they were both no doubt feeling, there were several issues and revelations that had to be dealt with. Greg's death. Jason's and her past.

Maybe even their future.

"What are we going to do about this information?" she muttered, lifting her head from his shoulder.

"*You're* going to do nothing but stay safe. I've already turned all of this over to the lead detective. He's planning a database search to try to identify the car. Of course, it has been nineteen months…"

In other words, it might be too late. The car could be

anywhere by now. Still, she had to hold out hope that they'd get lucky.

Since Jason had broached the subject of his brother, Lilly decided to continue it. "While I was under hypnosis, did I say anything else about Greg?"

Jason eased away from her, and he dodged her gaze. "What do you mean?"

Uh-oh. That eluded gaze couldn't be a good sign. Yep, she'd no doubt mentioned sex. Great. Nothing like reminding him of the huge sore spot that was between them. "I just got the feeling that I'd said something to make you uncomfortable."

"No. Not uncomfortable," he insisted. But his hesitation said otherwise. "You just clarified a few things for me."

Another uh-oh. "Like what?"

He shrugged, moved away another inch. "Like how important it is for us to solve this case."

Lilly sighed. She couldn't fault him for his evasive answer. If their positions had been reversed, she wouldn't have wanted to discuss his previous sexual activity. She didn't even want to *think* about it.

"So, we're back to vague responses, chitchat, et cetera?" she mumbled.

"What do you mean?" Jason asked. And he asked it with a straight face, too. Had she misinterpreted his ambiguous response? Or maybe she hadn't said what she thought she'd said while under hypnosis.

"Why won't you tell me what I said that's made you so standoffish?" She heard herself and wanted to wince. Mercy, it was time to drop this. So what if she never learned his—

"I care about you," Jason said, interrupting her thoughts. Thank goodness. Because she truly hadn't wanted to finish that. "But we don't have a clean slate, Lilly. We never will. And I don't know how we deal with that. If—"

"Wait a minute." She slapped her palm on his chest. "Back up to that part about you caring about me."

He looked at her as if her nose were on backward. "Of course I care about you."

"Of course," she repeated. She held up her left index finger. "Give me a minute for that to sink in."

He shook his head, obviously surprised by her reaction. "I wouldn't have kissed you if I didn't care."

She grunted. "Kissing and caring aren't always related. Sometimes kissing is just about lust and nothing else."

"And sometimes, kissing is about kissing."

Lilly stared at him, trying to figure out what he meant and where this was going. After several long moments, she decided she didn't have a clue.

Did she?

She kept staring at him and unfortunately got a little distracted by his face. His mouth, in particular. And she nearly lost her train of thought. That mouth certainly had her hormonal number.

"So, when we were on the floor by the front door, were we just kissing, lusting…or were we doing something else?" Lilly asked.

He stared at her. Deadpan face. No expression other than maybe slight bewilderment. Then he laughed. Only then did she realize just how suggestive that last part must have sounded.

"I think it falls in the 'something else' category," he said.

Mercy. That sounded suggestive, too. Better yet, his eyes had filled with a warmth that softened the angles of his face. It softened her, too. The man was magic. He could improve her mood with just a look.

"That 'something else' category is a little broad," she stated. "And scary."

Jason nodded, looped his arm around her and pulled her closer. "I'm trying to take things slow. *Slower,*" he amended.

He no longer had that soft, amused look in his eyes. Subtle. But she noticed them, all right. She was aware of everything about him. The edginess that now tightened his mouth. His nostrils flared slightly. He brushed against her.

"Slow can be good, I suppose," she heard herself say. But she had no idea if that was true.

"I suppose," he repeated. More changes. She felt the muscles in his arms tense. The pulse on his throat raced. "Even though I've considered us just having sex to see if it'll burn this energy from us."

Her breath vanished. Just like that. It was gone. And just like that, she was his for the taking.

"That's an interesting theory." Lilly tried to keep her voice level. And failed. "You think that'll work?"

"No. But my body keeps suggesting it just to give my mind some kind of rationalization for wanting you."

She nearly laughed. "And you need a rationalization…why?" She didn't wait for him to answer. She spilled what had been gnawing away at her for hours.

"Because of something I said about Greg while I was under hypnosis?"

Jason loosened his grip a little so he could inch back and meet her gaze. "You don't remember?"

"No, and believe me, that's not a good feeling because I'm afraid I said something that hurt you."

"You said you didn't love Greg."

"I didn't love him," she added cautiously.

He paused. And paused. It went on so long that Lilly started to squirm, both literally and figuratively. "When you told Greg that, you said the two of you argued and that he accused you of not loving him because you were attracted to…well, me."

Oh. She'd really turned chatty during that hypnosis. Chatty about things she'd barely admitted to herself.

"Is it true?" Jason asked.

Well, at least she didn't have to think about the answer. "It's true."

And she braced herself for the fallout. What he must think of her. Sleep with one brother while being attracted to the other. Not exactly the start to a long-term relationship—if that's what either of them wanted, that is.

Was it?

Lilly didn't get an answer to her question. Nor did she get any fallout from her chatty revelation during hypnosis. There was a knock at the door; Detective Albright waited for Jason to tell her to come in before she opened it. Jason and Lilly had plenty of time to move away from each other. However, she figured they both looked guilty of something. She certainly felt guilty, anyway.

"Sorry to disturb you," Detective Albright said. "But I just got a call from the security guard at the gate. Your former nanny, Erica, just tried to use her access code to get inside the gate."

"The security company changed the codes," Jason advised.

Albright nodded. "Don't worry. Erica didn't get in, but she says it's urgent and that she's not leaving until she speaks to you."

But the detective wasn't looking in Jason's direction when she said that. She aimed the *you* right at Lilly.

CHAPTER THIRTEEN

"You don't have to do this," Jason reminded Lilly. He didn't know why he was wasting his breath—it was obvious he wasn't going to get her to change her mind—but he wasn't backing out of the garage to leave for her physical therapy appointment until he'd gotten his point across.

And his point was that meeting with Erica just wasn't a bright idea.

"We have to drive through the security gate anyway," Lilly explained. "Erica will be there, and she wants to speak to me. We might as well take a minute or two to see if she'll confess to trying to kill us. Then, you can arrest her."

Somehow she managed to keep a straight face when she said that, but Jason doubted he could do the same. "And you see what's wrong with that logic, right?"

"You mean, the possibility that this is a ploy so she'll have another opportunity to try to kill us?"

"Yes, that."

Lilly shook her head. "You think Erica's willing to do that in broad daylight in front of witnesses and with you carrying that big gun in your shoulder holster? Because she must have known you'd be with me."

He didn't want to point out that if Erica was en- raged, on a rampage for revenge, then she might not be thinking straight. Still, it didn't make sense for Erica to start shooting at them. Even though she was a suspect, Jason had her at the bottom of the list. The woman had loved and cared for Megan for more than eleven months. She'd been a good nanny. It was hard to dismiss that. He only hoped his dismissal wasn't a mistake that he'd come to regret.

Realizing he'd just talked himself into this meeting with Erica, he cursed under his breath, backed out of the garage and started the drive to the security gate.

"What if this isn't about a confession?" he asked, playing devil's advocate both with Lilly and himself.

"What else could she possibly have to say to me? Don't answer that," Lilly quickly insisted. Probably because she knew this might not be some earth-shattering revelation or confession but a rehashing of the uncomfortable goodbye they'd already had with Erica.

Jason hoped that was all there was to it.

When he approached the gate, Jason looked around for Erica's car but didn't see it. In fact, he saw no vehicles other than the white truck with the security company's logo. Instead, Erica was standing on the concrete platform in front of the small structure that housed the guard.

Jason stopped next to her, but he didn't get out. He lowered the window and then slipped his hand inside his jacket in case he'd been wrong about her and had to reach for his gun.

"Erica," he greeted. He made a visual check and didn't see any weapons. Thankfully, she wasn't dressed for concealment. Hard to conceal anything while wearing shorts and a cotton top that barely made it to her waist. Still, that didn't mean she hadn't stashed a weapon in her vehicle. "I don't see your car. How did you get here?"

That question seemed to unnerve her. She shifted her feet and folded her arms over her chest. "I parked up the street. I figured I'd use my access code to walk in because if you saw my car pulling up in front of your house, you probably wouldn't have even answered the door."

He would have, but he darn sure wouldn't have let her inside. "What's this visit all about?" Jason asked.

Erica barely spared him a glance, her attention focused on Lilly. "I don't know if you're still trying to take Megan away from Jason, but I've been doing some thinking. And I've decided that I can't give her up."

Jason hadn't forgotten about the custody issue, but he no longer believed that Lilly was out to gain total custody of Megan. Or maybe that was wishful thinking, too.

"Was that just an FYI comment?" Lilly asked. "Or did you have something specific in mind?"

"Oh, it's definitely specific. I found a lawyer who's willing to help me petition a judge for visitation rights. I raised her. I was more than a nanny." Now her gaze drifted in Jason's direction. But it not only drifted; it lingered a bit and turned into a heart-tugging stare. Jason didn't want Erica's pain and emotion to get to him, but he wasn't impervious to it, either.

"A lawyer?" Lilly repeated in a flat tone.

"I won't be shut out of Megan's life, understand? And I won't stand by while you continue to endanger her."

That was not the right thing to say. Jason tried to hold on to his temper. "Care to explain that?"

Erica pointed to Lilly. "Someone's trying to kill her, and that person isn't likely to stop until he or she succeeds. That means, every minute she spends in your house is a minute where Megan is in danger. Believe me, my lawyer plans to let the judge know that." Erica didn't wait for them to respond. Nor did she issue a goodbye. She spun around and hurried away.

"Well, that was pleasant," Lilly said sarcastically. "You were right. No confession."

While he wasn't happy about that, Jason was pleased that it hadn't turned into a shoot-fest. Still, Erica's threatened lawsuit and criticism of Lilly was yet something else on a plate that was already way too full.

"No judge will give her visitation rights," Jason assured Lilly. But he wasn't so sure. As a cop, he'd seen judges do the surprising and the unthinkable. And this certainly qualified as unthinkable.

"Erica's right, you know," Lilly concluded as Jason drove out the gate and onto the street.

He checked the rearview mirror but didn't see Erica anywhere. "About what?"

"About me endangering Megan."

Jason knew where this was going and tried to stop her, but Lilly was obviously determined to be heard.

"It's not only irresponsible of me to stay at your house," Lilly conceded, "it's selfish. And it's wrong."

Oh, how a few days could change things. A week ago he would have jumped at the chance to have Lilly far away from Megan. Now he wasn't jumping. Well, not that kind of jumping, anyway. "Please don't tell me you're even thinking about leaving."

"I shouldn't be just thinking about it. I should be doing it."

"No, you shouldn't."

"You think I want to do this?" she asked. "It'd break my heart to leave, but if this is the way to keep Megan safe, then I'll start packing as soon as we get back."

Jason glanced at her. "And you're letting Erica's opinion convince you to do this?"

She turned in the seat to face him. "Erica only stated the obvious."

Okay. He had some talking to do here. He only hoped he was persuasive enough. "Think this through, Lilly. If you leave, what's to keep this monster from trying to use Megan to get to you?" Jason didn't stop there. "And what if your ploy works? What if by leaving, the killer comes after you and succeeds? What then? Greg's already dead, so you've essentially made Megan an orphan."

"She has you," Lilly pointed out after she swallowed hard.

"She has you, too, and it'll stay that way. There's no safe place. Not for Megan. Not for us. The only thing we can do is work together to catch this guy. That's it."

Lilly shook her head, turned back around in her seat so they no longer had eye contact. "I want to agree with you, because I want to be with my daughter, but I think we have to consider my leaving as the right thing to do."

Jason didn't miss that *be with my daughter* part. He

couldn't blame Lilly for not including him. Heck, he couldn't even include himself.

Not for a real, permanent commitment anyway.

But maybe something else.

Less than a half hour earlier, Lilly had admitted that she was attracted to him. He was attracted to her. They even cared for each other. To what extent that caring was, he didn't know. However, he did know that they both loved Megan.

Maybe that was enough.

Maybe with Erica's legal threat, it had to be enough. This was definitely a united-we-stand kind of situation.

"We could get married. For Megan," he suggested. Jason didn't even look at Lilly. He kept his attention fastened to the road. However, he had no doubt he'd just shocked her to silence.

Unfortunately he didn't know how to continue after that. Since they'd kissed and come close to having sex, such a proposal might seem an insult. Of course, offering her a real relationship would be a lie. He cared for her. But they weren't in love with each other.

Still…

He glanced at her to see if she was dumbstruck at his pseudo-proposal, but instead she had her attention fastened to the side mirror. There wasn't alarm in her eyes, but just the fact that she was staring at it had Jason whipping his gaze at the rearview mirror.

There was a car behind them.

Not a maroon four-door. Thank God. It was dark green, and it had heavily tinted windows so he couldn't see the driver inside. It was the only other vehicle on the road. And it was following a little too closely for his comfort.

Hell.

Was this yet another threat? Was this the person who was after Lilly? And had he already let him or her get the advantage by getting so close?

Testing a theory he didn't want to prove correct, Jason sped up a little. So did the other car. And then he knew for a fact that this was not going to be fun.

"Is your seat belt on?" he asked Lilly.

"Yes." He didn't have to see her face to know what she was feeling. He heard the fear and the concern in her voice. He tossed her his phone. "Call for backup and get down on the seat."

The words had hardly left his mouth when the car behind them sped up. But it didn't just involve speed. It was a lurching motion, and the vehicle rammed into them, jolting their SUV forward so that Jason had to fight to maintain control.

His adrenaline level was already high, but that sent it soaring. He went into combat mode and hoped his training and blind luck would be enough to get them through this.

There was another ram. Harder than the first. Then another. Jason cursed. His SUV jerked to the right when he strayed onto the rim of the sidewalk. He corrected and then corrected again so that he wouldn't broadside a car parked on the otherwise empty residential street.

He forced himself to stay focused. Forced himself to rely on his training. Especially since it might be minutes or even longer before backup arrived. He scanned the area to make sure there were no more immediate threats or innocent bystanders who could be hurt. It was as clear as it possibly could be: no bystanders, which also meant no witnesses. Whoever was in that car behind them probably knew that.

"Should I try to drive so you can shoot at him?" Lilly asked.

He didn't have to think about that. "Too risky." Jason wasn't just referring to discharging his firearm in a residential area, either. He was referring to Lilly. Her body probably wasn't strong enough to make the switch to the driver's seat, much less keep control of the SUV.

And speaking of keeping control, Jason latched on to the steering wheel to brace himself for the next slam. It wasn't a moment too soon. The car behind them crashed into the back bumper, and Jason let the forward momentum career him into a side street. Fighting with the steering wheel, he spun his vehicle around, screeched to a stop and drew his weapon.

"Get down on the floor!" he shouted to Lilly.

Thankfully, she listened, though by getting onto the floor, it didn't mean she was safe. Not even close. Bullets could easily penetrate the metal and glass, and she could be hurt.

Or worse.

Jason was counting heavily on that worse not happening.

Using the meager cover of the steering wheel and the dash, he ducked down just slightly in the seat and slid his finger over the trigger. He was ready to fire.

Ready to kill, if necessary.

But he didn't get a chance to make that kind of life-

and-death decision. The other vehicle didn't wait. The driver slammed on the accelerator and sped away.

Jason threw off his seat belt and jumped from his SUV. He aimed his weapon and got off one shot. The bullet hit the back tire, but the driver kept on going.

He re-aimed and was ready to deliver a second shot when he saw a female jogger move onto the sidewalk right next to the escaping car.

Cursing, Jason lowered his weapon. He wasn't finished. He was going after the SOB responsible, and one way or another, this would end *now*.

CHAPTER FOURTEEN

LILLY HAD NO DOUBT about what she would see when she walked into Jason's office.

Yep. No surprises.

His jacket was slung over the back of his chair. His black T-shirt was now tucked. His hair mussed, no doubt from where he kept plowing his hand through it in frustration. And he was still on the phone, barking out orders to one of his fellow officers and sprinkling those orders with demands and profanity.

With the phone squashed between his shoulder and his ear, he was pacing. Like a riled tiger ready to strike. He was also checking the magazine of ammunition in his backup gun. His primary weapon, his Glock, had been sent to headquarters, because he'd discharged it in the line of duty. There'd be reports to do. Questions and more questions. An investigation. All necessary because of that one futile shot Jason had fired into the tire of their attacker's vehicle.

She stood there, using the door frame as support, and waited for him to finish his latest call. Every muscle in his body was iron-stiff, and she could practically see flames in his eyes. Lilly understood the pacing and even the ammunition check. However, while she was feeling the same emotions as Jason, he obviously had her beat in the intensity department.

Lilly could thank a hefty amount of fatigue and Megan for the semicalmness she was now experiencing. She'd just fed her daughter a bottle and settled Megan into the playroom/panic room. That brief time with her child had lowered Lilly's anxiety level enough for her to try to help Jason lower some of his.

A huge undertaking, no doubt.

He'd already done her a favor just by staying put. She knew how hard it'd been for him to do that. His every instinct had probably demanded that he go in pursuit of the car that'd rammed them.

But he hadn't.

After a fierce battle with himself, and with her not-so-gentle coaxing, Jason had taken them back to his house so he could make an initial report of the incident. And so he could sequester himself in his office to make phone calls. Unfortunately, both the initial report and the phone calls had only made the tension in him worse.

"Is something wrong?" Jason asked the moment he ended his call.

"Everything's fine. Megan's playing with Detective O'Reilly," Lilly told him. "She's discovered the joys of pulling off her socks and tossing them into the air." She hoped the news about Megan's cutesy milestone would cause him to relax a bit.

It didn't.

"And the other officer arrived to relieve Detective Albright?" Jason asked, reholstering his gun.

"Yes, about ten minutes ago." Despite the feeling that she was now living in a police compound, she welcomed the officer's presence. Having three cops in the house might allow her to breathe a little easier. Or at least it would take some of the pressure off Jason so that he might not feel totally responsible for Megan's and her safety. Of course, he'd no doubt feel that way if they had the entire police force in his living room.

"I don't want Megan out of the playroom," Jason continued. "And I also don't want either of you in any part of the house without an officer nearby, got that?"

"Agreed." He'd already told her that twice. With Jason's anxiety obviously near the boiling point, Lilly figured she'd hear it again soon.

"By the way, how are you holding up?" Jason asked. Not just a question, though. It was edgy and raw, like everything else about him.

Lilly sighed. Much more of this and he'd explode. It was time for action. Or rather, a good old-fashioned lecture. She shut the office door and leaned her back against it. "I want you to stop beating yourself up about all of this."

"I can't," he snapped. "This is my fault."

That answer didn't surprise her. "Noo-oo, it's not. It's the fault of that idiot in the other car."

Jason grumbled something she didn't want to interpret and started to pace again. "We can't keep going through this. We've been lucky, but we might not be so lucky next time. That's why I'm arranging for a safe house. An undisclosed location that only a handful of trusted cops will know about. It should be ready tonight. It'll have a solid security system. Plus, another officer and I will be with Megan and you at all times."

"That's good." Well, the security part was, but it meant they'd have no privacy. No real life. No real anything. They'd be on hold and all because of some unknown moron who wanted her dead. That moron wouldn't be shut away in some safe house, either. He or she would be out there, free, doing everything possible to find them.

So, just how safe would a safe house be?

"Nothing about this is *good*." Jason shoved his backup weapon into his ankle holster. "It's too little too late. Just how many sleepless nights will you have because I haven't been able to catch this guy?"

That did it. Lilly had had enough. She couldn't bear to see him like this. "How many sleepless nights will *you* have because of this nightmare that I brought to your doorstep?"

He dragged his hands through his hair again. "I'm not in the mood for sympathy and comfort."

"Tough. You're going to get it anyway." She snagged him by the arm when he started to pace by her.

Jason stared at the grip she had on him and then lifted his eyes to meet hers. "My advice? Back off, Lilly. I've got a lot of dangerous energy inside me right now, and you don't want any part of this."

"Oh, really? That sounds like a challenge," she said, because she thought they both needed a little levity.

The levity backfired.

Big time.

Adrenaline was high. Emotions, higher. Coupled with the attraction between them, touching him was indeed a dangerous prospect. She immediately thought of ways to defuse that tension. Well, one way in particular. Too bad it would have huge consequences.

Lilly tried to fight her way through her exposed emotions, the leftover fear and the fatigue. She tried to do the logical thing.

And failed.

When she realized her body wasn't going to cooperate with her attempts to think this through, she finally said to heck with it. She looked at Jason. At his face. At those intense gray eyes that were piercing into hers. And she knew exactly where this moment had to go.

Suddenly everything was crystal-clear. Razor-sharp. Powerful and honed. Like the energy spearing through her. She had the power to help him, to help them both. Human contact, human touch could undo a multitude of troubles. She wouldn't even think about the new troubles that it would create.

Before she could change her mind, or before he could stop her, she tightened her grip on his arm and pulled Jason closer.

Closer.

Closer.

Until his chest brushed against her breasts.

He stared at her, the intensity in his eyes going up another serious notch. "Think this through," Jason managed to say. Not easily, though.

"I already have."

Without further words, she put her mouth to his.

And Lilly kissed him.

OH, MAN. This was *so* not good.

At least that's what Jason's mind told him. But the rest of him heartily disagreed. It wasn't just *good*. It was better than good. Exactly what he wanted.

Just when he thought he couldn't take any more

without breaking, Lilly stopped the kiss. Maybe to catch her breath. Maybe to give him time to do something about this. And she stood there, staring at him, looking better than any woman had a right to look.

Her hair was loose, resting at her shoulders on the thin straps of her mist-green dress. And her eyes were making offers that he couldn't refuse. Everything about her, that face, those eyes, her mouth, called to him.

Cursing himself, cursing their situation, cursing fate and just plain cursing, Jason did the very thing that he knew he'd almost certainly regret. He gave in to the moment. Gave in to all the wants and all the primitive needs that were clawing their way free. He gave in to *her.*

He pulled Lilly to him. Knowing there was no turning back. Not caring. And knowing he would care and have regrets later. Still, that didn't stop him.

With the slight shift of movement, their bodies came together again. His pressed against hers. Her right leg wedged between his. They adjusted. Moved. So they could get as close as two people could possibly get. So they could do something about this ache. This need.

And the battle started.

Her mouth took his. Her lips moving against his. Not a soft gentle kiss of comfort. Not this. There was no comfort in the sensual moves of her mouth. This was all heat, fueled with lethal adrenaline and emotion.

Because he wanted more, and he wanted it now, he somehow managed to get her dress unzipped. It wasn't easy. His hands weren't too steady, and Lilly made things more difficult with the kisses that she was lavishing on his neck. A definite sensitive spot for him, and she'd figured that out right away. She kissed, using her tongue, pulling him tightly against her body. Drowning him in her scent.

Jason shoved her dress down to expose her bra. White lace. Definitely not modest, either. It kicked up his heart rate. Revved his body. Nearly made him beg. He took a moment to admire it and the woman beneath it before he caught the straps and lowered them, as well, to expose her breasts. She was small, firm.

Perfect.

Keeping his gaze connected with hers, he slowly lowered his mouth to one of her rosy nipples and nipped it with his teeth. A sharp gasp and Lilly grabbed him by the hair and pulled him to her, forcing him, until he took that nipple into his mouth. Leaving it shiny wet and pebbly hard, he gave the other one the same attention. She gasped. A sound of pleasure. And actually did some begging of her own.

It still wasn't enough.

Jason had to have more of her. All of her. Lilly obviously felt the same because she suspended her kisses, and struggling for position, went after his T-shirt. Like his, her movements were fast and frantic. It was a race. Against what, Jason didn't know, but it didn't matter. All he knew was that they had to have each other.

While she dragged his T-shirt off him, Lilly moved against him. Body against body. It was like striking a match. What little control he had left went straight out the window. He grabbed her by the hips and brought her roughly and precisely against him, aligning them.

"Jason," she whispered. She made a throaty sound of approval. "Yes."

He'd never been happier to hear a yes, and he was especially pleased that it had an urgency to it. He completely understood that urgency.

"I can't wait," she said. And she meant it.

Lilly kicked off her strappy sandals and went after his zipper. She succeeded. And she didn't stop there. Locking her arm around his neck, she freed him from his boxers and took him into her hand. Jason was fairly sure his eyes crossed, and the pounding pulse in his ears made it seem as if they were surrounded by primitive war drums.

"Now," she insisted.

Jason obliged. He hoisted her up and wrapped her long, lean legs around his waist. He pulled off her lace panties and in the same motion, repositioned her so that her back was against the door.

Though his vision was blurred, he forced himself to focus so he could watch her. So he could see her face. Her eyelids lifted when he pushed into that heat. Into her. Into her moist, welcoming body. And a kiss caught their collective sighs of pleasure and relief.

The kiss lingered a moment so she had time to adjust to him. But Lilly obviously felt she needed no such adjustment or time.

"Don't stop," she insisted. Lilly shoved herself against him. Sliding against his erection. Taking every inch of him.

Jason took everything she was giving, as well. The passion. The sensations of their bodies joined.

No longer wary of her response, he pinned her hands to the door and was pleased when she jerked and twisted against him. Her legs tightened around him. Forcing him closer. Forcing him to penetrate her even deeper.

They matched each other. Move for move. Trying to hang on to every second, every sensation. Until the friction and the pleasure were unbearable. Until all Jason could see, hear, feel, smell and taste was Lilly. She became the pinpoint of his focus, of his universe.

She became everything.

She whispered his name in rhythm to the frantic strokes, Jason waited a moment. Holding off as long as he could so he could hear every syllable, so he could watch his name shape her lips.

"Now, Jason," she said.

He agreed. It was time. His body couldn't hold back any longer. Not with this intensity. Not with the fierce need he had for her. So, with Lilly's whispered pleas brushing against his mouth, with her heartbeat pounding against his, with their bodies damp with sweat sliding against each other, Jason gave them both what they needed.

THE SENSATIONS slammed through her, leaving Lilly hazy and feeling as if everything were right with the world. She didn't leave that hazy place immediately. She stayed there a few moments, letting her body slowly come back to earth.

Even though earth wasn't where she wanted to be.

She wanted to linger in that haze. And to linger in Jason's arms, a safe place where there were no problems and no one was trying to kill them.

"That was amazing," she whispered.

Even though Jason was looking directly into her eyes,

he blinked as if trying to focus. And probably was. She wasn't anywhere near 20/20 yet, either. Sex with Jason apparently had the potency to blur vision—in a good way, of course.

His breath was coming out in hot gusts. "I can't believe we just did that."

"Please don't tell me you have regrets."

He shook his head and eased her legs from his waist. "No condom."

Those two words rang through her head and she nearly fell when she put her feet back on the floor. "Oh, sheez."

"But you're right, it was amazing. And this might be the lust talking, but it was worth the risk."

Lilly thought so, as well. She only hoped they both felt that way days or even weeks from now. She had too much on her mind to consider an unplanned pregnancy.

"I don't even know if it's the wrong time of the month," she concluded. "But with everything my body's been through, I doubt I'm ovulating."

Famous last words?

She hoped not. And while she was hoping, she added other issues to that proverbial list.

"I've considered just beating around the bush with this, but since time seems to be an issue here, I'll just come out and ask." Lilly fixed her dress, sliding it back into place, and she discreetly stepped back into her panties. She didn't continue until she was done and until Jason's gaze met hers. "Having sex with me wasn't your way of working out our custody issues, was it?"

Jason blinked again, but this time he actually focused. "I'm going to pretend you didn't ask that."

"All right, so if that wasn't about custody, was it anger sex?"

He zipped his jeans as if he'd declared war on them. "Are you trying to pick a fight?"

"No. But it probably seems that way to you. I'm actually trying to understand what just happened."

"You tell me, Lilly. If I'm not mistaken, you're the one who started it by kissing me." He held up his hand in a defensive, wait-a-minute gesture. "Oh, are you trying to tell me it was sex to stop me from leaving?"

She was on shaky turf. "It started that way, yes," Lilly admitted. "But then it sort of took on a life of its own, wouldn't you agree?"

Jason was no doubt spoiling for a fight. Not necessarily with her. But with the person who'd been trying to kill them. Still, he couldn't help those emotions erupting. And she was right in his path.

"I'm not sorry for what happened," she said. However, it didn't ring true. Not totally. She might not be sorry, but she'd no doubt regret it. Sex complicated things, but it wasn't that complication that bothered her the most.

It was her feelings for Jason.

Mercy. How was she supposed to deal with all the other things they were facing when all she wanted was to pull him back into her arms and kiss him again?

Lilly gave that question some thought, and she didn't like where that thought was leading. This sexual encounter hadn't solved anything. In fact, it'd done the opposite. It'd made her realize just how empty her life would be without him.

Yes, empty.

Jason made her happy, and as silly and cliché as it sounded, he completed her. She understood that now. Understood what was truly at stake here. Not just Megan. Not just Jason. Her future with both of them was at stake.

Before Lilly could even begin to think about spilling what was in her heart, there was a tap at the door. "Jason?" It was Detective O'Reilly. "Did Lilly tell you that the other officer is here to assist with security?"

"She told me." Jason lifted an eyebrow. Lilly lifted hers, as well. "What about the suspects? Have they been located?"

"Not yet."

That sent Jason to the door. He opened it with a fierce jerk. "*None* of them?"

Lilly had to hand it to Detective O'Reilly. He looked as if he wanted to take a huge step back, but he held his ground. "Wayne Sandling and Raymond Klein aren't at their residences. Erica Fontaine isn't at her hotel. And there's still no luck finding Ms. Davies, dead or alive."

Jason obviously didn't care for that information. "What's the latest from the lieutenant?"

"I just got off the phone with him," O'Reilly said. "He needs you to come down to headquarters and fill out your report about discharging your weapon."

Lilly groaned and shook her head. "Can't that wait?"

"I don't want it to wait." Jason reached for his jacket. "Now that the other officer is here, I'll do the report and then see if I can find our suspects."

Lilly went to Jason, blocking his path toward the door. "I thought I'd talked you out of doing this."

In fact, that was what she'd done for the first half hour after they'd arrived back at the house. However, Lilly wasn't under any misconception that she'd been able to convince him to stay put. His staying probably had less to do with her convincing than it did with the fact that his departure would have left Megan and her alone at the house with just one cop—O'Reilly. Now that the other officer was in place, that was no longer an issue.

"I'm going to find them," Jason insisted.

Her hands went to her hips. "Excuse me, but how do you plan to do that?"

"I'd like to know that, too," Detective O'Reilly added. But his comment only earned him one of Jason's prize-winning glares.

"I don't know how just yet, but I can't sit here and do nothing." Jason made a vague motion toward the outside. "I want to find them, and I want them to tell me everything they know about any of this."

A dozen arguments came to Lilly's mind. Good arguments, too. But she didn't get to voice any of them. Jason pressed a kiss to her mouth and moved her aside. O'Reilly didn't hold his ground this time. He stepped out of the doorway so Jason could leave.

"I have to do this," Jason said as his goodbye.

And because Lilly knew she couldn't stop him, she just stood there and watched him walk away.

"Oh, God," she whispered as a prayer.

The fear and dread were immediate. A sickening feeling that knotted her stomach. The taste was suddenly bitter in her mouth. Because Lilly had a feeling that something terrible was about to happen.

That was her first thought.

Quickly followed by another that was equally unnerving.

She hoped she got the chance to tell Jason something that she'd just realized.

She was in love with him.

CHAPTER FIFTEEN

"HAVE I MENTIONED that this is probably a huge waste of my time and yours?" Jason heard Sgt. Garrett O'Malley say.

The question didn't stop Jason. He simply gave his phone headset an adjustment so he could respond, and he kept on driving through the upscale neighborhood that Wayne Sandling called home. "Yeah. But a possible waste of time is better than nothing."

O'Malley made a sound to indicate he wasn't so sure of that.

Jason countered it with a grumbling sound of his own. "I guess that means there's no sign of Raymond Klein?" Jason asked.

"Nothing. And I do mean nothing. Not even a dog walker or a jogger." Garrett was several miles away, driving through Klein's neck of the woods, and though they'd both been at it for nearly an hour, things weren't looking good.

Their suspects had seemingly disappeared.

Of course, in Corinne Davies' case, she was possibly dead, but that left three others—Wayne Sandling, Raymond Klein and Erica Fontaine. Jason wanted to speak to all of them, and he didn't want to wait another minute to do it. Too bad waiting seemed to be on the agenda tonight.

"Why don't you go home to Lilly and Megan?" O'Malley suggested. "I'll keep looking around. If any or all of our suspects surface, I'll call you."

Considering that it was the sergeant's night off and that he was doing this surveillance as a favor, Jason didn't want to take him up on the offer. Still, he didn't want to leave Megan and Lilly alone any longer. Not that they were alone, exactly. There were two officers standing guard at the house. Jason knew the cops would do their job, but it wasn't personal for them.

It *was* personal for him.

He would do whatever it took to protect Megan and Lilly.

"Thanks," Jason told O'Malley. "I think I will go back to the house and check on things. I won't be long. Oh, and call me the minute you have any information."

"Will do. And while you're checking on things at home, why don't you get some rest?"

Before he ended the call, Jason assured him that he would. It was a lie. There'd be no rest tonight. Not with the suspects at large. Not with so many things unresolved.

Yes, this was indeed personal.

On the drive home, that one sentence kept going through his head, and though he knew he should be focusing solely on catching a would-be killer, he couldn't help but think of what had happened earlier.

He'd had sex with Lilly.

Unprotected sex at that.

If there was a name worse than idiot, that's what he should call himself. No, he didn't regret the sex part. Though he should have regrets. He didn't.

He couldn't.

Making love to her, even in that heated, frantic rush, was exactly what he'd dreamed about doing since Lilly had first set foot inside his house. And that need he had for her didn't have anything to do with Megan. What had happened between Lilly and him was about two people who couldn't keep their hands off each other.

Part of that disgusted him. The lack of control. Yet, another part of him wanted to lose control with her all over again.

Hopefully, this time with a condom.

It had been reckless to have unprotected sex. Here she was, just recovering from the coma. She would need lots more physical therapy before she was a hundred percent, and yet he'd risked getting her pregnant.

He frowned at the reaction that caused deep inside him.

A baby. A brother or sister for Megan. Why did that sound so damn appealing when it could cause nothing but problems for Lilly? She was just getting used to being Megan's mom. She didn't need any more pressure.

She didn't need him.

There.

That was it.

The niggling thought that kept at him. Day by day, Lilly was getting back to her old self, and once she was no longer in danger, she would be on the road to a full recovery. She'd resume her business, balance it with motherhood. Lilly was a pro at balancing. At efficiency. At being self-reliant.

She wouldn't need him.

But he would still need her.

Worse, that need was growing, and he was certain it wouldn't simply go away. With that thoroughly depressing revelation, he took the turn into his neighborhood and stopped at the security gate.

"Please tell me it's been a quiet night," Jason said to the guard as he punched in his security code.

The guard nodded. "Just a few people coming home from work and a pizza delivery."

That snagged his attention. "You checked them all out before you let them in?"

"I did. I had the residents show picture IDs, and I called the folks that ordered the pizza and had them confirm it."

Though Jason was appreciative of those security measures, he didn't relax. He drove home, wondering how in the name of heaven he was going to put an end to all of this. Because without an end, Lilly and he didn't stand a chance at having a beginning.

He approached the house with his cop's gaze on full alert. And maybe it was that full alert that had him concerned when he noticed that the lights were off. Then, he checked his watch.

10:00 p.m.

Well past Megan's bedtime, and as tiring as the day had been, it was no doubt past Lilly's, as well. He pulled into the garage and sat there for a moment, listening. He was still listening when the sound shot through his SUV.

The sound nearly caused him to jump out of his skin. Before he realized it was his phone ringing.

"Sheez. Settle down," he warned himself. He'd snap if he kept up this intensity.

"It's Garrett," Sgt. O'Malley said when Jason answered the call. "And before you ask, no, I didn't find any of the suspects. But we've had a Corinne Davies sighting."

Well, Jason hadn't counted on hearing that, ever. "I take it she's alive?" He used the remote to close the garage door and got out of his SUV.

"According to her neighbor, yeah. He says this afternoon he saw Corinne going into her house through the back door. We sent a unit out to see if she was there, but there was no sign of her."

Which made her all the more dangerous. Well, dangerous if she was guilty of anything. Maybe Corinne was simply a victim, like Lilly. A case of learning a little too much and now having to pay the consequences.

"Thanks for the update," Jason said, clicking the end button on his phone. He unlocked the door that led from the garage into the house and went inside.

And he came to a complete stop.

Two things immediately struck him as totally wrong. The security alarm didn't kick in, and the house was much too quiet. It was bedtime, he reminded himself. But that reminder did nothing to stop the slam of adrenaline. That instant jolt of fear.

His stomach dropped to his knees.

Jason pocketed his cell and drew his weapon. Because the sense of urgency was growing stronger with each passing second, he hurried. Running, he made his way through the utility room and into the kitchen. No one was there. Including the officers he'd left to guard the place. But there was a half-eaten sandwich and a nearly full glass of milk sitting on the counter.

He considered calling out to them, but his instincts told him it was already too late for that.

Trying not to make a sound, he made his way across the kitchen and to the hall that led to the back of the house. With each step, his heart pounded, his focus pinpointed and his body prepared itself for the fight. Maybe, just maybe, he wasn't too late.

But he was.

Jason confirmed that when he saw Lilly.

There she was. At the end of the hall. Just outside the door of the playroom.

The only illumination came from the night-light on the wall halfway between Jason and her. But it was more than enough for him to see the stark expression on her face.

The fear.

No. The terror.

That's when Jason realized she wasn't alone. There was someone behind her. With a gun that'd been rigged with a silencer.

And the gun was pointed right at Lilly's head.

LILLY THOUGHT she couldn't have possibly been more frightened, but she wrong. Her fear went up a significant notch when she saw Jason step into the hall.

Another minute or two, and this could possibly have been avoided.

Of course, another minute or two, and she might have been dead, but at least Jason wouldn't be in danger.

He was definitely in danger now.

Jason stood there. Not frozen. Not panicking. He inched toward them, his gun aimed and his wrist bracketed with his left hand. He was ready for anything.

Well, maybe not this.

There was no way he could be ready for this.

"Put down the gun," Jason said, his voice hardly more than a whisper. Probably so that he wouldn't wake up Megan. Lilly was praying the same thing. She wanted to keep her daughter sheltered from this.

"I can't," the woman behind Lilly answered.

Now, that stopped Jason. Lilly completely understood his reaction. She'd experienced a similar reaction about ten minutes earlier when she first realized that someone had gotten into the house.

And *who* that someone was.

"Erica?" Jason questioned.

Behind her, Lilly heard Erica's breath shudder. Not good. While Jason seemed relatively unruffled, she couldn't say the same for Erica. It wasn't just the woman's voice that was shaking. Erica was shaking, too. Lilly didn't care much for a jittery person with an equally jittery hand holding a gun to her head.

"She's trying to kidnap me," Lilly confirmed, not surprised that her own voice was trembling. Oh, she was scared. But she was even more frightened of staying put, where Erica could do heaven knew what to Jason or Megan.

There were worse things than dying.

Lilly knew that now. And losing Jason and Megan would be far worse than anything Erica could do to her.

"Is Megan okay?" Jason asked. No calmness that

time. He had to get his teeth unclenched so he could speak.

"She's asleep," Erica volunteered. "I wouldn't hurt her."

Not intentionally, anyway. But Lilly knew if bullets started flying, then good intentions weren't worth anything.

"Put down the gun, Erica," Jason warned, the grip tightening on his own gun.

"I can't. Not now. I have to stop this. I have to stop her."

"None of this is Lilly's fault. All she did was wake up from a coma."

"All she did was ruin my life," Erica snapped. "I love you, Jason—"

"Put down the weapon," Jason repeated. "And think this through. Megan is in that room right next to where you're standing with a loaded gun. If she wakes up, she'll be scared. Is that what you want?"

"No." Erica repeated it several times, her voice becoming edgier with each syllable. "All I want is to leave. With Lilly. I have to take her with me."

"You don't have to do anything but put down the weapon and step to the side." Jason inched closer.

"Stop," Erica said, pushing the gun even harder against Lilly's temple.

Jason stopped, and Lilly could almost see him thinking this through. She only hoped he had a better solution than anything she'd been able to come up with—which was exactly nothing. If she fought back, Erica might shoot and accidentally hit Megan. If she remained passive and cooperated, the same might happen.

"How did you get in here, anyway?" Jason asked Erica.

Lilly shook her head, indicating that she didn't know. She'd literally come out of the playroom to discover that she was looking down the barrel of a gun.

"I paid off the pizza delivery guy. He let me hide in the trunk of his car. Then I used my key to get in the house," Erica explained. "I turned off the security system."

Even in the darkness, she saw the flash of anger in Jason's eyes. "Where were the two police officers during all of this?" he snarled.

"I, uh, used a stun gun on both and tied them up."

There, she saw it. The skepticism on Jason's face. It would have been next to impossible to get close enough to two trained officers and surprise them with a stun gun. Lilly didn't know for sure, but she suspected both officers were probably dead. And that meant Erica had shot them with her gun fitted with a silencer.

Would she try to do the same to Jason?

It was too painful for Lilly to consider. Here, she'd just gotten back her life, and she might lose everything.

She frowned.

Listening to herself.

What the heck was she doing standing here, waiting for the worst to happen? So what if Erica had a gun on her? She had something that Erica didn't. She loved Jason and Megan. And it wasn't Erica's kind of psycho possessive love, either. It was the kind of love that could make her do anything to protect them.

Anything.

Lilly stared at Jason. Hoping that her now unyielding

expression conveyed that she was about to do something to get them out of this dangerous situation. He obviously got the point, and didn't approve, because he narrowed his eyes.

Jason's change in facial expression must have alerted Erica because Lilly felt the woman go stiff. "Don't do anything stupid," Erica warned.

Lilly didn't have anything stupid in mind.

She hoped.

Of course, anything could qualify as stupid if it wasn't successful.

Lilly gave Jason one last glance, and she gathered all her fear, all her energy, all her anger, and focused those emotions right into the elbow that she rammed hard into Erica's stomach.

Erica gasped and made a kind of garbling sound that indicated she was fighting for air. Good! Lilly did some fighting of her own. She turned, ignoring the wobble in her legs, and slammed her hand against the gun to try to dislodge it. Erica somehow kept control of it.

Jason charged toward them and, fearing that Erica would turn her gun on him, Lilly grabbed the woman's wrist and put it in the tightest lock she could manage.

Erica reacted. Mercy, did she ever. With the strength of ten men, she shoved her entire weight against Lilly, off-balancing her. Not that it was that hard to do. Wobbly legs didn't give her much of an advantage.

Lilly felt herself falling, and she couldn't do anything to stop it. She reached out for anything, but her hands only grabbed at the air. She landed hard on the floor just inside her bedroom.

Thankfully, Jason didn't fall right along with her. He

launched himself at Erica. They both crashed into the wall. But the crash didn't cause Jason to loose focus. When the scuffle was over, Lilly could see that he now controlled both weapons.

The breath of relief that Lilly was about to take stalled in her lungs. Before she could take that breath, she heard the sound behind her.

But it was too late for her to react.

Too late to stop what was happening.

The arm curved around her neck, and Lilly felt the barrel of a gun jam into the back of her head.

CHAPTER SIXTEEN

JASON HAD KNOWN this situation could quickly get out of hand. That was why he'd been so anxious to get the gun away from Erica. During all his concern about doing that, while also being worried about how to keep Lilly and Megan safe, he'd overlooked one important detail.

That Erica might not be working alone.

And she wasn't.

He became painfully aware of that when he came up off the floor with Erica in tow, and he saw Lilly. She didn't have a triumphant, we-got-her expression. But a frightened one.

Lilly was in the doorway of her bedroom, and even though the room itself was pitch-black, Jason could see the shadowy figure behind her. It took a moment to figure out why he couldn't distinguish any facial features.

The person was wearing a ski mask.

In addition to the ski mask, he or she had a gun aimed at Lilly. Like Erica's weapon, it, too, was rigged with a silencer. So, who was the brains behind this operation: Erica, or this person who had seemingly come out of nowhere?

The person didn't speak, but Jason saw the arm-grip

tighten around Lilly's neck, and he saw the slight gesture with the gun. The gesture was directed at Erica.

"Jason, give me those," Erica insisted, obviously responding to the gesture.

She reached for the guns that Jason had in his hands, but he sidestepped her. He could have easily brought her down with one hard punch. Or with one shot. And, man, he wanted to do that after what she'd just pulled. However, the person holding Lilly would retaliate.

"Think of Megan," Lilly whispered to him. A warning for him to do whatever it took to prevent gunfire. Drywall wasn't much protection against bullets, and he couldn't risk Megan getting hurt.

But he could say the same for Lilly.

He couldn't risk her life, either.

Now, the problem was how was he going to convince her to play it safe? That elbow ploy had worked on Erica, but Jason had a feeling that the success had been more luck than anything else. He didn't want to rely on luck to keep his family safe. And it didn't matter that Megan wasn't his biological daughter, or that Lilly wasn't his wife, they were his family in every way that counted.

"I want the guns," Erica prompted, motioning for Jason to hand them over.

Jason said a prayer and made his move. He reacted as fast as his hands could react. He tossed one of the guns aside and, in the same motion, he latched on to Erica. He shoved her in front of him and put the remaining gun to her head.

"Drop your weapon," Jason ordered the person in the ski mask.

The person made a slight huffing sound. "Not on your life. Or rather, should I say, not on Lilly's life."

Jason didn't have any trouble recognizing that voice, and obviously neither did Lilly. Her eyes widened a fraction, and her mouth tightened. "Raymond Klein," she mumbled.

Another huff and Klein loosed his grip around Lilly's neck so he could peel off the ski mask. Jason almost made a lunge for him then and there, while he was briefly distracted with the mask removal, but never once did Klein take the gun from Lilly's head. Jason figured he was fast, but he wasn't faster than a finger already poised on the trigger.

"I'd hoped to avoid all of this," Klein said in a discussing-the-weather tone. He aimed his attention at Erica. "We need to do this quickly. We don't want those two cops waking up."

"They're alive?" Jason asked.

"For now. I used a stun gun on them once Erica had them amply distracted. Then, I gave them each a dose of barbiturates that should keep them out for a while longer."

Jason processed that information. And it didn't process well. With that ski mask, the two cops probably hadn't seen their attacker's face. But they'd sure as heck seen Erica's. Jason figured that meant Klein planned to set Erica up so she would take the blame.

Erica obviously hadn't figured that part out yet.

"Drop your weapon, Detective Lawrence," Klein insisted. "Or I'll kill Lilly before you've even had a chance to say goodbye to her."

Jason wasn't immune to that threat. It cut through

him like a switchblade. But he pushed aside his fear and concern and focused on being a cop. Somehow he had to get Lilly and Megan safely out of this.

"Have you forgotten that I could do the same to Erica?" Jason fired back at Klein.

"Be my guest," Klein calmly said.

Because he still had hold of Erica, Jason felt her body tense. The quick, almost frantic intake of breath was an obvious clue that she'd just realized she was expendable.

"What are you saying?" Erica asked, frantically shaking her head. "The plan was to kidnap Lilly. That's it."

"The plan has changed," Klein informed her. "I can't leave witnesses behind, now, can I?"

"No!" Erica shouted. "We were going to kidnap Lilly, that's all. You said you could get her out of the country and put her somewhere so she wouldn't be able to come back. And she'd be out of the way so I could move back in here with Megan and Jason."

"I lied," Klein said, and he angled his eyes toward Jason. "Put the gun down now."

Jason knew he couldn't do that. "No way. You've already said you won't leave any witnesses."

"Go ahead, Jason," Lilly said. "Shoot him."

"If he does, you'll die," Klein reminded her.

"And then Jason will kill you," Lilly countered.

Jason must have conveyed his displeasure about that because Lilly nodded, as if trying to convince him that she was doing the right thing. "This way, one of us will survive," she told him. "Do it for Megan."

It was dirty pool. And it was a useless plea. Because if Lilly had her way, that plea would get her killed.

He had no plans to let her die.

Jason quickly went through the possible scenarios; he didn't like any of them. The risks were sky-high, but they were risks he couldn't do anything about. Doing nothing was just as risky. So he said another prayer and hoped like the devil that he could pull this off.

He shoved Erica forward, slamming her into Lilly. It had the domino effect that Jason hoped it would. Both Lilly and Erica flew back into Klein. All three went backward onto the floor.

Jason didn't waste even a second. With his gun aimed and ready to go, he launched himself at Klein so he could kick the gun from the man's hand.

He failed.

Jason heard the sound. Not a blast. But a muffled slash of noise. It didn't have to be loud, though, for it to be deadly. Because Jason knew that Klein had just fired the gun rigged with the silencer.

LILLY KNEW that sound.

A gunshot.

It instantly fed the terror that was already snowballing inside her. That bullet could have hit Jason. Or Megan. God. She couldn't lose them.

She came up off the floor. Or rather, she tried to, but a punch to her jaw sent her sprawling. Lilly felt the warm, wet sensation on the side of her face but ignored it so she could launch herself at Klein. She couldn't let him fire again. No matter what the cost, even if it meant dying, she wasn't going to let him shoot Jason or Megan.

In the darkness, she saw the tangle of their bodies. Hers, Jason's, Klein's and Erica's. Erica and she were on the floor, and Klein and Jason were standing, more or less, and were about to square off in what looked to be a gun battle.

Except Jason was no longer armed.

Somewhere in the scuffle, he'd lost his gun. Oh, God. That meant Klein would no doubt try to kill Jason.

Lilly ignored the stinging pain in her jaw and reached out. She managed to grab Klein's leg, and she tried to drag him to the floor with her. She wasn't successful, but for a split second, she'd distracted him.

Klein looked down.

Aimed his pistol right at her.

And he would have shot her point-blank if Jason hadn't rammed his body into the man. Somehow, Jason stayed on his feet, and it became a struggle for control of the gun.

Lilly decided to put the odds in their favor. She spotted Erica's weapon on the floor and scrambled toward it. Her legs suddenly felt like a deadweight, and she cursed her lack of mobility. It was no longer just an inconvenience. It was a handicap that could get them killed.

If she let it happen.

She wouldn't.

She fixed the image of Megan and Jason in her mind, and she used that image, her love for them, to force herself to move forward. One inch at a time.

Behind her, she could hear the sounds of a struggle. Fist against muscle. Did that mean that Jason had somehow managed to get the gun away from Klein? Or, heaven forbid, had Erica joined the fight?

With her heart pounding and her breath so thin that her lungs felt starved for air, Lilly stretched out her hand and scooped up the gun from the floor. She came up and was face-to-face with Erica.

"I can't give up Megan," Erica said as if it would change what Lilly was feeling.

It was on the tip of Lilly's tongue to tell her that she had already lost Megan, but the slash of movement from the corner of her eye had her looking up. At Klein.

Once again, he had the gun pointed at her.

"If you move, Detective Lawrence, I'll kill her."

Normally those words would have terrified her beyond belief, but this time they didn't have the effect that Klein had probably intended.

Why?

Because Lilly heard Megan. Her baby was not only awake, she had begun to cry, and those cries were quickly turning to sobs.

Lilly made eye contact with Jason. Mere seconds. To let him know this was about to end. He gave a crisp nod.

Her cue.

Or at least Lilly made it her cue. She ignored her limp muscles and pulled back her leg. She focused all her energy and rammed her foot into Klein's thigh.

Klein reacted all right. He howled in pain. But that didn't stop him from re-aiming his gun. Jason yelled for her to move, but she couldn't, and everything seemed to crawl in slow motion. She heard the sound, like someone blowing out a candle, and felt the sensation of pressure against the right side of her head. It didn't stay merely a sensation.

It quickly turned to pain.

And Lilly realized she'd been shot.

She dropped back onto the floor. Around her, there was a flurry of motion. Jason cursed and grabbed Klein, knocking the man's gun away. Jason seemed enraged, and he landed a hard fist in Klein's face.

Klein went down like a rock.

Jason didn't stop there. He snatched up his Glock and aimed it right at him.

"Move and I'll kill you." That was all Jason said. All he had to say. Because anyone who heard the threat knew that he meant it.

Lilly wanted to help Jason. She wanted to make sure that neither Erica nor Klein had managed to regain control of one of the weapons. She also wanted to thank Jason for saving her life.

But she couldn't do any of those things.

The dizziness came with a vengeance. The room began to spin out of control, and though she was aware that Jason was speaking, she couldn't understand what he was saying. Worse, she knew she was losing consciousness. Lilly fought it.

But she lost.

Because she had no choice, she shut her eyes and the darkness came again.

CHAPTER SEVENTEEN

JASON HAD ALREADY said at least a thousand prayers for Lilly, but he added another one before he opened the door to her hospital room. He braced himself for the worst, and he hoped for the best.

He got the best.

There she was, not in bed, but sitting on the edge of it, dangling her bare feet off the side. She had a small white bandage on her forehead. That was it. No bruises. No other indication that Klein's bullet had come much too close to killing her.

Things had not seemed so promising during the frantic ambulance ride from his house to the hospital. Then, Lilly hadn't been conscious, and she was losing blood from the head wound. In those moments, Jason would have bargained with anything or anybody just to have her safe.

"You're here." She smiled at him.

That smile warmed the bitter cold that had seeped into his body. "I'm here."

Because he didn't trust his legs to move, he stood there a moment and savored the view. "The doctor said the bullet didn't do any serious damage, just a graze, and that you were going to be okay."

Lilly gave him a contemplative look. "You didn't believe him?"

"I had to see for myself."

Her smile returned. "You can see for yourself if you come closer."

Jason did. No uncertain legs this time. Now that he knew Lilly was truly all right, he made it to her in just a few steps. He leaned down, put his arms around her and pulled her to him.

"I'm fine, really," she promised.

He eased back so he could kiss her. Jason meant for it to be quick and reassuring, but Lilly obviously had other plans. She slid her arms around his neck and kissed him back. She lingered a bit and left them both a little breathless. That was fine. Jason preferred her kisses to breathing any day.

Lilly ran her tongue over her bottom lip and made an *Mmm* sound to indicate she liked the taste of him there. "How's Megan?"

He had to get the goofy smile off his face before he could answer. "She's out in the hall with Detective O'Reilly. I wanted a few minutes alone with you, first."

"Uh-oh." There was suddenly strain in her voice, on her face. "Bad news?"

Some of it, yes. But other parts were very good. "Klein is behind bars," Jason said.

Lilly pumped her fist in the air. "Hallelujah. Did he happen to say why he wanted to kill me?"

Her question had come easily, but Jason didn't have such an easy time with the answer. Every memory of what Klein had said and done would haunt him. "He did. He's talking because he's trying to make a deal to cut down his prison time."

Lilly's relief faded. "He won't be getting out soon, will he?"

"Not for at least thirty years." Forty, if the D.A. had his way. "Thanks to a tough interrogation, Klein admitted to trying to kill you and running Greg off the road that night."

"I see." She cleared her throat and blew out a choppy breath. "So, he killed Greg?" she clarified, wanting to be sure.

Jason nodded.

The relief returned to her face, but it was intensified. She even blinked back tears. Jason understood her reaction. For nearly two years she'd blamed herself for Greg's death. For two years he'd blamed her, as well. That blame belonged solely on Raymond Klein's shoulders.

"They can get Klein for manslaughter for Greg's death," Jason explained. "But they'll charge him with attempted murder and kidnapping for what he did to you." He paused. Heck, he wasn't sure he could say this out loud, but he knew that Lilly would want to know. "Klein wanted you dead because he thought you would eventually remember that he was the one who ran you off the road that night."

She flexed her eyebrows. Paused. "Well, at least it's over." Lilly stared at him. "It is over, isn't it?"

He nodded. "Erica will be arrested as soon as she's out of the hospital."

"She was hurt?" Lilly immediately asked.

"Not badly. Klein shot her in the arm. Like you, she'll make a full recovery, only she'll be doing time while she's at it. For attempted kidnapping, among other things. The D.A. isn't pleased that Erica endangered the lives of a child and several police officers."

Jason wasn't pleased about that, either. In fact, it might take a couple of lifetimes for him to get over the sheer terror he'd felt when he'd realized that Megan could be hurt and that Lilly had been shot.

"More good news," Jason continued so he could lighten the quickly darkening mood. "Corinne surfaced. She got scared and went into hiding when someone tried to kill her."

"Let me guess—Klein was behind that, as well?"

"He was. He wanted to make sure she didn't go to the police with the info she found in some old files. Klein wasn't just altering bids, he was creating false contracts for repairs and maintenance to municipal and state buildings. He was getting paid a small fortune, too. And he's the one who stole her car so he could try that break-in at the security gate. His attempt to kill Corinne will tack on another few years to Klein's prison sentence."

Jason considered that the end of his official update, and he took her by the hand.

"Oh, no. Not more bad news." Lilly groaned.

"I hope not. I'm hoping you'll consider it good news." He rethought that. "Or I at least hope you'll consider it."

Because he was so close, he could see the pulse jump on her throat. "Okay, you have my attention."

"Don't say no until you've heard me out." Jason gathered his breath and his courage. This was really going to hurt if she said no. "When Klein had his gun on you—"

"This doesn't sound like the start of good news," Lilly interrupted.

"It is. Trust me. When I realized your life was in danger…" He had to take another moment. More breath gathering. Another prayer. "I also realized that I wanted you to marry me."

She blinked.

Not exactly the reaction he was hoping for.

"Did you hear me?" he asked. "I want us to get married."

Still no answer. She waited for what seemed to be an eternity before she finally spoke. "For convenience? Because of Megan?"

He made a deep sound of frustration. "No way. In fact, I can promise you that being married to me will be anything but convenient. I can also promise you that I'll do anything to make you happy."

Another blink. No smile. Just a blank stare. "Anything?"

"Anything. And I mean that. Groveling, foot massages, great sex—"

"How about love?"

Oh.

Jason tried to sort through what he'd already told her, but there was a big jumble in his head. He blamed it on the nerves and the total lack of sleep. "Didn't I mention that I'm in love with you?"

She shook her head. "No."

Oops. That was a biggie. "Well, I am."

No blink this time. But her breath trembled and her eyes watered.

"Oh, man." Jason pulled her into his arms. "You're crying."

"They're happy tears, I promise."

Happy tears, he mentally repeated, and it took several tries for it to sink in. The relief he felt was overwhelming, and he hoped he didn't disgrace himself by crying, too. Since he didn't want to risk that and since she still hadn't said yes, he kissed her. Really kissed her. He took all his feelings, all his love, and poured it all into an intimate show of affection.

"Yes," she whispered against his mouth.

"Yes?" And he hoped he hadn't misunderstood her.

"Yes, because I'm in love with you, too."

Okay. He mentally repeated that to himself, as well.

Jason's first reaction was to whoop for joy, grab her and swing her around in circles. Since she might not be ready for that, he laughed. Hugged her. And kissed her. This was what he wanted, and until a few short hours ago, he hadn't even known it.

"I do have some…news," Lilly said, inching just slightly away from him.

Because of all they'd been through, his first thought was that this wasn't going to be good. Lilly's puzzling expression only added to his reaction. "You're not changing your mind about marriage?"

"No. It's not that. It's this whole pregnancy thing."

"Excuse me?" he asked, certain he'd missed something. "You're pregnant?"

She shook her head. "No. I talked to the doctor about our unprotected sexual encounter, and he did a few tests. Turns out that I wasn't in the whole ovulation zone." She paused. Stared. Moistened her lips. "This is going to sound a little crazy, but I was actually a little disappointed."

So was he. A real shocker of a reaction. "We can try again when the time is right. Hey, I'm always up for a round of unprotected sex."

She smiled. "Against the door of your office."

"Anywhere. Anytime," he promised, smiling with her. His mouth came to hers again. A kiss. And that kiss might have lasted for hours if there hadn't been a knock at the door. "Are you ready for a visitor?" he heard Detective O'Reilly say.

Jason looked back at his fellow officer and spotted not just O'Reilly but Megan, who was already making her way toward them.

Since Megan was a little wobbly, Jason went ahead and picked her up and brought her to the bed. O'Reilly, probably sensing the need for privacy, stepped back into the hall and shut the door.

Lilly wiped away her happy tears and reached out for Megan. "You know what, your da-da and I are getting married. That's a great deal for all of us."

Jason didn't let go of Megan just yet. He whispered in her ear what they'd been practicing on the drive over. Megan looked up at him and beamed with one of those precious smiles.

"Ma-ma," she babbled.

Since the first attempt was aimed at him, he turned Megan in Lilly's direction. "Ma-ma," Megan repeated. Not just once. But she strung those syllables together, giggled at her accomplishment and made a dive for Lilly. She landed in her mother's arms.

More happy tears came, and Jason had to choke back a few of them himself.

"Da-da," Megan said, snuggling against him.

"Jason," Lilly whispered, snuggling, too.

And Jason knew that this was the life he'd always wanted. He reached for both of the ladies that he loved, gathered them into his arms and held on.

* * * * *

LEGALLY BINDING

Ann Voss Peterson

To Denise O'Sullivan, Lynda Curnyn and Allison Lyons.
Thanks for inviting me to Mustang Valley.
To Susan Kearney and Linda O. Johnston.
Thanks for exploring Mustang Valley with me.
And a special thanks to Jack, Sandy, Kevin
and Troy Jones
for introducing me to the state of Texas
all those years ago!

CHAPTER ONE

BART RAWLINS FORCED one eye open. Late-morning sun slanted through his bedroom window, blinding him. Pain, sharper than his old Buck knife, drilled into his skull. He gripped the edge of the mattress and willed the room to stop spinning.

He hadn't had that much to drink at Wade Lansing's Hit 'Em Again Saloon last night, had he? Not enough to warrant a hangover like this.

He remembered hitching a ride to the bar with Gary Tuttle, his foreman at the Four Aces Ranch. Remembered wolfing down some of Wade's famous chili and throwing back a few beers. Not enough to make his head feel like it was about to explode. Not enough to make his mouth taste like an animal had crawled in and died.

Damn, but he was too old for this. At thirty-five, he always thought he would be settled down with a woman he loved, raising sons and daughters to take over the Four Aces Ranch. Instead he was lying in bed with his boots on and a hangover powerful enough to split his skull.

He raised a hand to his forehead. His fingers felt sticky on his skin. Sticky and moist and smelled like—

His eyes flew open and he jerked up off the mattress. Head throbbing, he stared at his splayed fingers. Something brown coated his hands and had settled into the creases of work-worn skin. The same rusty-brown flecked his Wranglers.

Blood.

What the hell? Had he gotten drunk and picked a fight? Was a well-aimed punch responsible for his throbbing head?

Bart pushed himself off the bed and stumbled to the bathroom. Peering into the mirror, he checked his face. Although his nose was slightly crooked from a fall off a horse when he was ten, it looked fine. So did the rest of his face. And a quick check of other body parts turned up nothing, either. The blood must have come from the other guy.

The doorbell's chime echoed through the house.

Who the hell could that be? He tried to scan his memory for an appointment this morning, but his sluggish mind balked.

The doorbell rang again. Whoever it was, he wasn't going away.

Bart turned on the water and plunged his hands into the warm stream. He splashed his face, grabbed a towel and headed down the stairs. He'd better answer the door before the bell woke his dad. Good thing the old man was a heavy sleeper. Bart would get rid of whoever it was so he could nurse his hangover in peace. And try to remember what in the hell had happened last night.

He reached the door and yanked it open.

As wide as he was tall, Deputy Hurley Zeller looked up at Bart through narrowed little eyes. The sheriff's right-hand man had a way of staring that made a man feel he'd done something illegal even if he hadn't. And ever since Bart beat him out as starting quarterback in high school, he'd always saved his best accusing stare for Bart.

Bart shifted his boots on the wood floor. "What's up, Hurley?"

"I have bad news."

Bart rooted his boots to the spot. If he'd learned one thing about bad news in his thirty-five years, it was that it was best to take it like a shot of rotgut whiskey. Straight up and all at once. "What is it?"

"Your uncle Jebediah. He's dead."

Bart blew a stream of air through tight lips. Uncle Jeb's death meant there would be no reconciliation. No forgiveness to mend the feud in the Rawlins clan that had started the day Bart's granddad died and left his son Hiriam a larger chunk of the seventy-thousand-acre ranch. Now it was too late for a happy ending to that story. "Well, that is bad news, Hurley. Real bad. How did he die?"

Hurley focused on the leather pouch on Bart's belt, the pouch where he kept his Buck knife. "Maybe I should ask you that question."

Bart draped the towel over one shoulder and moved his hand to the pouch. It was empty. The folding hunting knife he'd hung on his belt since his father gave it to him for his fourteenth birthday was gone. Shock jolted Bart to the soles of his Tony Lamas. "You don't think I killed—" The question lodged in his throat. He followed Hurley's pointed stare to the towel on his shoulder.

The white terry cloth was pink with blood.

A smile spread over Hurley's thin lips. "I think you're coming with me, Bart. And you've got the right to remain silent."

LINDSEY WELLINGTON adjusted her navy-blue suit, tucked her Italian leather briefcase under one arm and marched toward the Mustang County jail and her first solo case. She hadn't been this nervous since she'd taken the Texas bar exam. At least her years at Harvard Law School had given her plenty of experience taking tests. This was a different story. This was real life.

This was murder.

She'd explained to Paul Lambert and Donald Church, senior partners of Lambert & Church, that she hadn't specialized in criminal law. She'd also reminded them she didn't have trial experience, that either of them would be far more qualified. But they'd insisted she take the case anyway. Even though both Paul and Don had backgrounds that included criminal law, Lambert & Church didn't have a true criminal attorney on staff. Not since Andrew McGovern had died in the annex fire last month. Not since Andrew was *murdered,* she corrected herself. A murder that wouldn't have been discovered, let alone solved, if not for her dear friend, Andrew's sister Kelly, and Kelly's new husband Wade Lansing.

Lindsey pushed into the air-conditioned lobby of the jail, checked in at the desk and followed a deputy back to a small visiting room to wait for her client.

Her client.

A shiver crept up her spine at the thought. She tried to quell it. She couldn't afford to be nervous. This case was the opportunity she'd been waiting for. Over fifteen hundred miles from her well-meaning family's influence and penchant for pulling strings to help her, she was finally getting a chance to prove herself on her own terms.

She set her briefcase on the table and took a calming breath. She couldn't let her client know how nervous she was. Or how little experience she had. If she wanted to prove herself a professional, she had to act like one.

The door swung wide and a deputy led a tall man wearing an orange jumpsuit into the room. Lindsey looked up into a tanned face and sparkling green eyes, and struggled to catch her breath. It was a good thing she was sitting because her knees felt weak.

When she'd imagined defending an alleged murderer named Bart Rawlins, she'd pictured Black Bart, the infamous outlaw. Big and mean, with coal black hair to match his black hat. But the man who folded his big frame into the chair opposite her couldn't be further from that image. With the body of Adonis and blond visage to match, he looked more like a hero straight from the silver screen.

"You must be Lindsey Wellington." He held out a hand. "I'm Bart Rawlins."

She shook his hand, a thrill skittering over her skin at the touch of work-roughened fingers. "Don't worry, Mr. Rawlins. I'll get you out of here immediately." Her voice sounded breathless in her ear. As breathless as she felt. She inwardly cringed.

"Call me Bart. Paul and Don said you were the best criminal lawyer in the firm."

The best? So they hadn't told him they'd handed his case to a lawyer who'd just passed the bar. "Paul and Don exaggerate. But I'll *do* my best, Bart. I promise you that."

"I'm sure you will." He tilted his head to study her, the fluorescent lights overhead gleaming off his sun-bleached hair. "They forgot to tell me you were the prettiest lawyer in the firm, too. Hell, I'd be willing to bet you're the prettiest lawyer in the whole damn county."

To Lindsey's horror, a warm flush inched up her neck and burned her cheeks. "I—we should—I mean, thank you," she finished lamely. What was wrong with her?

She was blushing and stammering like a teenager with a crush.

"So where do we start?" he asked.

She looked at Bart, her mind a blank.

"My defense. Where should we start?"

She snatched herself out of the idiot-trance that had grabbed her the moment he'd strode into the room. She had to pull herself together. She was a professional. "Tell me what happened last night."

He ran a big hand over his face and shook his head as if he'd already told the story more times than he cared to remember. "I went to Wade Lansing's place, a saloon down on Main Street called Hit 'Em Again. I shot some pool, downed a few beers and found myself at home with a hangover to wake the dead."

"What time did you leave the bar?"

"That's the problem. I don't remember."

"You don't remember the time?"

He grimaced. "I don't remember leaving."

She tried to keep her surprise from showing on her face. Bart Rawlins didn't strike her as a heavy drinker. In the high-pressure world of law in which her family lived, heavy drinkers abounded. But all the heavy drinkers she'd known in her twenty-six years had an air of despair about them that was lacking in Bart. "How many beers did you drink?"

"Three. Four, tops."

She looked him up and down, trying to ignore the tightening sensation low in her stomach at the sight of his long, lean legs and broad muscled shoulders. With his size, three or four beers shouldn't lead to a blackout. But then, people often underestimated their alcohol consumption. "Are you sure you didn't have more?"

"To tell the truth, the whole night is kind of fuzzy.

But I usually only drink three or four. Maybe I did have more."

"How did you get home?"

He shook his head, obviously at a loss for an answer.

"You didn't drive, did you?"

"I didn't have my truck. I hitched a ride to the tavern with my ranch foreman. Maybe I left with him. I don't remember."

"I'll talk to him. And a talk with the bartender might shed some light on exactly how much you drank." Lindsey jotted notes on her legal pad. "Of course there's always the possibility that you were drugged."

His eyebrows shot up. "Drugged?"

"Rohypnol or something similar. The date-rape drug."

"Date-rape drug?"

"It's an illegal tranquilizer that causes blackouts."

"I've heard of it in the news. But who would give me something like that?"

"Someone who wanted to make sure you took the fall for your uncle's murder."

He nodded, a frown claiming his brow. "Then what about the blood? Where did that come from?"

She clamped her bottom lip between her teeth. "What blood?"

"When I woke up, I had blood all over my hands and clothes. At first I thought I must have gotten in a brawl. But I don't have any scrapes or bruises."

"Did the deputies take samples of the blood?"

"Sure did. A load of pictures, too."

The start of a headache pulsed behind her eyes. If the prosecution tied the blood on Bart's hands and clothes to his uncle by DNA tests, Bart was as good as convicted.

Only O.J. had beaten evidence like that. And he hadn't been tried in Texas.

"There's another thing."

She almost flinched. "What?"

"My knife. A Buck Model One-Ten. It's missing. And from the look on Hurley Zeller's face when he arrested me, he knows where it is."

"At the murder scene."

"That's my guess." His voice was heavy, as if his charm and good humor had finally given way under the weight of the evidence against him. Or maybe he'd just read her face.

She forced a confident smile. "We'll find the answers. Don't worry."

He nodded, but judging from the pallor under his tan, he wasn't buying her strained optimism.

"The first thing we have to do is get you out of here. Do you have money or property to put up for bail? It'll be pretty high."

He waved a hand. "I can come up with the money."

She nodded, grateful for a development that was positive, even if it was merely a matter of available cash. "I'll push for a bail hearing. Then we need to get you to a doctor as soon as possible to test for drugs. If we can prove you were drugged, at least we'll have something to fight with."

"I didn't kill him, Ms. Wellington."

The naked honesty aching in his voice brought tears to her eyes. She blinked them back. "You don't have to tell me that, Bart."

"I want to. No matter what differences I or my father had with my uncle, I didn't kill him. I wouldn't kill anyone."

"Your father?"

Bart's eyes narrowed. "My daddy is sick. Even if he wasn't, he'd never kill his own brother any more than I would kill my uncle."

"Of course." Lindsey nodded. "We just have to prove it. And we will."

"Am I looking at the death penalty?"

"No. They'll charge you with first-degree murder. Only capital murder carries the death penalty in Texas, and for this case to be classified as capital murder, there would have to be other factors involved."

"Other factors?"

"Like the victim was a police officer. Or the murder was intentionally committed in the course of another felony. Or more than one person was killed as part of the same scheme or course of conduct. The most severe sentence you can get for a first-degree murder charge is life in prison."

"That sounds the same as death to me." Elbows on the table, he tented his fingers in front of his mouth and blew a stream of air through them. "Give it to me straight. My chances don't look good, do they?"

If she had more experience, maybe she would have been ready for the question. She'd have a prepared spiel that was both comforting and realistic. As it was, she didn't have a clue what to say.

"That bad, huh?"

"No. Not that bad. We'll get to the truth, Bart. I promise."

He dropped his arms to his sides and looked deeply into her eyes. "Thank you, Ms. Wellington."

"You can call me Lindsey."

"Thank you, Lindsey."

A shiver crept up her spine at the sound of his Texas drawl caressing her name. But this time the shiver wasn't only the result of physical attraction, it was one of fear. Because this time, losing didn't mean embarrassing herself in moot court or lowering her grade point average.

This time losing could cost a man his freedom.

CHAPTER TWO

BART GRIMACED AS the needle sank into the tender spot at the inside of his elbow. Once the needle was in place, Doc Swenson attached the vacuum tube, filling the vial with deep red blood. His blood. Blood that, if he was lucky, might still be spiked with Rohypnol or some other drug. "Damn."

Lindsey Wellington leaned her sweet body close. The scent of roses tickled his nose. Her shiny chestnut hair draped over one shoulder and brushed his arm despite the clips securing it back from her face. "Does it hurt?"

"What, the possibility of being a victim of the date-rape drug? Damn straight it hurts. It hurts my sense of manhood."

A smile teased the corners of her soft-looking lips. "I doubt your sense of manhood is that fragile."

"Maybe not when you're around. You're ladylike enough to make even a gelding feel like a stud."

That pretty pink color stained her cheeks again. God, she was a beautiful woman, delicate as a China doll with her clear blue eyes, porcelain skin and long, silky hair. But that wasn't all. In addition to looks, Lindsey Wellington had intelligence to burn and a refined Boston accent that reminded him of the Kennedy family.

And she was his lawyer. Amazing.

With the possible exception of Paul Lambert and Don

Church, he'd grown up with a healthy belief that lawyers were bloodsuckers at best, sharks at worst. But Lindsey Wellington had destroyed every preconceived notion in his head the moment he laid eyes on her.

It was a damn shame he hadn't met her last week, last month. Before he had a murder charge hanging over his head. Maybe he wouldn't have been at Hit 'Em Again last night. Maybe he would have been too busy trying to win her to be hanging out at the local watering hole. It was a twist of fate too cruel to be believed that he'd finally found a woman who set a spur in his side when he couldn't do a damn thing about it.

Doc Swenson pulled the filled vial from the needle in his arm, capped it and attached an empty one in its place. More blood flowed.

"Are you planning to drain me dry, Doc?"

The crusty old coot peered at him over little reading glasses. "Word has it you're the one draining people dry, Bart. The whole town is talking about what you did to your uncle Jeb."

He should have known. He'd been arrested just this morning, but waiting for a bail hearing had taken much of the day. He shouldn't be surprised that the news of his arrest for murdering Jeb had already swept through town. Gossip traveled fast in Mustang Valley. Especially gossip over something as juicy as family feuds and murder. Of course Doc would have learned about Jeb's murder even without the gossip. Jeb's body was probably waiting in the autopsy room this very minute for Mustang Valley's only doctor and coroner to poke and prod. "I didn't kill Jeb, Doc."

Doc waved a hand, as if he hadn't believed it from the beginning. But the sharpness in his old blue eyes suggested different. He nodded at Bart's arm. "What do you want this blood for, anyway?"

"We want to have it tested for any kind of drug that might have altered Bart's consciousness. We also need a urinalysis done for Rohypnol or any similar tranquilizer," Lindsey explained.

Doc capped the second vial, pulled out the needle and snapped off the rubber tourniquet wrapping Bart's biceps. Rummaging through stacks of supplies on the adjacent counter, he grabbed a plastic specimen cup. He held it out to Bart. "Fill this."

Bart looked down at the cup and shifted his boots on the floor. Discussing bodily functions had never bothered him before. He was a cowboy born and bred, used to dealing with anything cattle or horses could come up with. But somehow with Lindsey looking on, his bodily functions took on an entirely different meaning. And focus. He forced himself to take the cup from Doc's hand.

"So you think he got drugged up the night of Jeb's murder?" Doc smiled stiffly at Lindsey, the old buzzard's best shot at charm.

Lindsey ignored the doc's question. "When can you have the results?"

Doc's smile faded. "We don't have a lab here. Got to send the sample out."

Lindsey nodded and fished a card from her briefcase. She scrawled something on the back and handed it to the doc. "Here's the lab I'd like it sent to. And on the back, I've written my home address. Have them send the results there and to my office. I want to make sure I see them as soon as they come in."

Doc took the card. "Could take a few days, could take a few months, depending on how busy the lab is.

Then there's always the chance the drug won't show up at all."

"What do you mean? If it's in his system, it should show up, right?"

Doc scowled down at Bart. "Boy, what time did you take those drugs last night?"

"I didn't take drugs, Doc."

"Well, what the hell is this good-looking lady asking me about then?"

"Someone might have put something in my beer last night when I wasn't paying attention. A drug to make me black out."

"More likely you just got a little too friendly with a whiskey bottle."

Bart expelled a frustrated breath.

"What were you saying about the drugs not showing up in Bart's system?" Lindsey asked.

The old man turned his attention back to Lindsey. "If too much time has passed since Bart took those drugs, they won't show up on the screens."

Lindsey worried her bottom lip between straight white teeth. "I thought it took twenty-four hours for the drug to clear."

"That's right. But Bart's a big boy, so it might take a lot less."

A weight descended on Bart's chest. The clock on the wall of Doc's little examination room read six o'clock. Twenty-one hours had already passed since his last memory of the saloon. If Doc was right about his size making the time shorter, they were cutting it close. Damn close.

He glanced at Lindsey and closed his fingers tighter around the plastic cup. "I'll be right back."

She nodded. Judging from the worry creases digging

into that pretty forehead, she'd noticed the time as well. If the substance was no longer in his system, he couldn't prove he was drugged. And if he couldn't prove his amnesia was real, he wouldn't have much of a defense, no matter how pretty and smart his lawyer was.

BART HELD THE DOOR of the Hit 'Em Again Saloon for Lindsey and followed her inside. The place was nearly empty except for a couple of regulars at the pool table, the cowboys and working men who filled the place nightly still hard at work this early in the evening. On the jukebox, Dale Watson belted out a real country song, the music echoing off the empty postage-stamp dance floor.

They crossed to the oak bar and bellied up. The smell of stale cigarette smoke warred with the bleachlike smell of bar sanitizer, but it was the soft scent of roses that held Bart's attention. He leaned closer to Lindsey and took a deep breath.

"You don't usually drink beer this early, Bart. Need a little hair of the dog that bit you?" Wade Lansing pushed through the swinging door leading back to the kitchen and took his usual spot behind the bar. Despite his flip statement, Bart could see the worry lining his friend's face. Worry focused on him.

Bart glanced at Lindsey. "Lindsey, this is Wade Lansing, the owner of this fine establishment."

"You mean beer joint," Wade said.

"Beer joint with the best food west of the Mississippi," Bart threw in.

Wade grinned. "Nice to see you again, Lindsey." Wade cleared a couple of highball glasses from the bar, the gold band on his finger shining in the bar's dim light.

"I thought you and Kelly were supposed to be on your honeymoon by now," Bart said.

"I'm training a kid to take over this place while I'm gone. Don't want to come back to find the till empty and the building burned to the ground."

Lindsey nodded. "Kelly said the two of you are planning to go to Hawaii. Sounds wonderful."

"We could go anywhere as far as I'm concerned. As long as Kelly is with me, I'm happy. I'm glad to hear you're representing Bart here, Lindsey. It'll keep me from worrying." He zeroed in on Bart. The grin turning his lips faded. "The whole town is talking about you."

"I didn't kill Jeb, Wade."

"I know that. But Hurley Zeller doesn't share my opinion. He was in here as soon as I opened, asking questions."

"Damn." Bart grimaced. Hurley sure had a leg up on them. Bart still didn't have a clue what had happened. He hoped Wade could give them some answers.

Lindsey set her briefcase on the bar, opened it and pulled out a pad of paper and pen. "We'd appreciate anything you can tell us about last night, Wade."

"Like what you told Hurley," Bart said.

"I didn't tell that prick anything."

Bart couldn't keep the grin off his face. Wade might be happily married, but he still hadn't shed his distrust for authority.

"What do you remember seeing?" Lindsey asked.

"I set up a few bottles of beer and served Bart up some chili. Then I had to duck out to change some big bills." Wade grabbed a dirty glass and plunged it up and down on a dishwashing contraption made of spinning brushes located in a sink behind the bar. "When I got back, you were fall-down drunk, Bart. I figured you must have been doing some serious whiskey-drinking while I was gone. Though I've never known you to drink more than a few beers."

Bart and Lindsey exchanged looks. Wade's description jibed with their theory that Bart was drugged. Unfortunately, it could also be a description of a man who'd simply sucked down too much whiskey.

"Who served drinks while you were gone?" Lindsey asked.

"The kid I'm training to fill in for me," Wade jotted something on a cocktail napkin and handed it to Lindsey before resuming glass-washing. "That's his name and number. He has tonight off, but otherwise you can also find him here."

"Thanks." Lindsey stowed the napkin in her briefcase. "When did Bart leave and who did he leave with?"

Wade stopped the plunging motion and glanced up at Bart. "Blackout?"

Bart nodded.

Wade looked at Lindsey. "The place was hopping last night, but best I can remember, he left around midnight. I just assumed he rode back to the ranch with his fore man, Gary Tuttle, same way he came. I can ask around tonight, see if anyone saw different." Wade dipped the glass in the sink full of sanitizer and set it on a mat to drip-dry. "Are you going to tell me what was going on last night, Bart? You aren't one to drink till you black out."

"We think Bart was drugged," Lindsey supplied. "Maybe Rohypnol or something similar."

Wade didn't look surprised. "There's something strange going on in Mustang Valley. First Andrew and now this."

Bart couldn't agree more. The revelation that Andrew

McGovern had been murdered by Mustang Valley's mayor had been a shock. And now Jeb. Two murders in two months. Not to mention the mayor's fatal car accident. "The problem is, I don't know if I can prove I was drugged. Hurley might have kept me tied up in jail too long for the tests to show the drug in my system."

"What if you could find the bottles you were drinking out of?"

Lindsey leaned toward Wade. "You said the bar was busy last night. There must be hundreds of bottles. Can you really find the ones Bart drank out of?"

"My friend here has an annoying habit of peeling the label off every bottle of beer he drinks." He glanced at his watch. "This place will be full of cowboys soon, so I don't have time to look. But if you want to sort through the bottle bins out back, be my guest."

"It's worth a shot." Lindsey looked to Bart. "Do you want to help me search through empty beer bottles?"

"I'll sort through a thousand bottles if it will help prove I didn't kill Jeb."

"Then let's get started."

They slid off their bar stools and followed Wade through the prep kitchen and out Hit 'Em Again's back door. Wade pointed toward a Dumpster in the narrow alley. On one side of it was a row of large trash cans. Wade nodded toward them. "Have at it." Turning, he ducked back into the bar.

Bart glanced at Lindsey's sharply pressed suit, gossamer stockings and polished nails. "I'll do the searching."

Lindsey set her briefcase on the ground and pushed up her sleeves. "It'll go a lot faster if we both search."

He held up a hand. "I insist. A lady like you shouldn't be rummaging around in garbage."

Lindsey flashed him a pointed grin. "You forget. I'm no lady, I'm a lawyer."

Bart couldn't keep a laugh from bubbling out. "All right, then. But as far as I'm concerned, you're a lady. A real smart one."

She looked away from him before he could see if she was blushing again and set to work picking through the brown-glass bottles.

Suddenly footsteps and voices rose above the clank of glass hitting glass. Bart turned just in time to see his cousin Kenny round the building and stride into the alley, his black felt Stetson slung low over his eyes. "I heard you were here. I should have known you'd be hiding in a back alley," Kenny slurred, his voice rough with cigarettes and soggy with booze.

Bart hadn't spoken to Uncle Jeb's son in years. And he sure didn't want to start tonight. But it looked like he had no choice. "What do you want?"

"I want to know why the hell you aren't in jail."

"I don't want trouble, Kenny."

"You can take a knife to an old drunk's throat, but when it comes to fighting an able man, you don't want trouble?"

A good-looking blonde walked into the alley and stopped a few steps behind Kenny. Frowning, she folded her arms across her ample chest, like she was turned off by the prospect of her boyfriend picking a fight. A smattering of other spectators who'd apparently followed Kenny's bluster hung back in the shadows, content to watch from a distance.

Bart glanced at Lindsey. She watched Kenny the way a person eyed a car crash, repulsed but unable to look away. Bart shook his head. He didn't want to get into a family brawl in front of her. Hell, he didn't want her to know Kenny was family at all.

He pulled his gaze from Lindsey and focused on his cousin. Kenny had been an ornery cuss since the day he was born. But he'd also just lost his father—a father he despised, but his father, nonetheless. It was probably natural he'd want to blame Bart. Especially when the law was blaming Bart, too. "Listen, Kenny. I didn't kill Jeb."

"And you expect me to believe you?"

"I'm telling the God's honest truth."

"The same truth your daddy told when he talked Grandad into leaving him most of the Four Aces Ranch?"

Bart almost groaned. It was still about the ranch. "When Grandad died, Jeb didn't want any part of working the ranch. He never did. He just didn't want my daddy to have it. Look what he's done with the land Grandad gave him. Nothing."

"He didn't have it as easy as your daddy."

"And why was that? Because he liked to drink more than he liked to work?" Bart tried to bite back the words, but it was too late. He'd had it with Kenny's whining and excuses for his good-for-nothing daddy and himself.

Kenny balled his hands into fists and swaggered closer. "Maybe Jeb was a bastard and a drunk. Maybe he deserved what he got. But that doesn't mean I shouldn't get my fair share. Or are you planning to kill me, too, and take it all?"

Bart held up his hands, palms facing Kenny. "I didn't kill Jeb, Kenny. And that's all I'm going to say about it."

Kenny stepped closer. The stench of cheap whiskey wafted on his breath. He jabbed a fist at Bart. The punch missed. "Gonna pull out your knife, Bart? Oh, that's right. The police confiscated it after you used it to kill your own flesh and blood."

Lindsey stepped forward. "How do you know about Bart's knife?"

Kenny didn't bother to give her a glance, as if she wasn't important enough to answer.

Bart tried to keep a lid on his simmering temper. Getting into a fistfight with Kenny wouldn't do anyone any good. "Go home and sleep it off, Kenny."

"Won't change anything. When I wake up, my old man will still be dead, and you'll still be the one to blame." He threw another punch. His fist plowed into Bart's arm, connecting solidly this time.

Bart's arm throbbed with the blow. His own hands clenched into fists. Grieving or not, one more hit and Kenny was history. "I wouldn't do that again if I were you."

"Or what? You going to sic your whore on me?" He leered at Lindsey and drew back his arm.

Bart didn't wait for Kenny's next punch to fall. His own fist was already flying.

CHAPTER THREE

LINDSEY STARED IN horror as Bart's big fist plowed into Kenny's middle.

Kenny hunched over and stumbled to the side. He slammed into a bottle bin and fell. The receptacle tipped over. Glass shattered. Bottles scattered along the ground, brown glass everywhere.

The blonde who'd entered the alley with Kenny ran to his side. "Kenny? Are you all right?"

Kenny sputtered, as if trying to catch his breath. "You saw that. He attacked me. He tried to kill me."

Bart loomed over him. "If I'd tried to kill you, you'd be dead. Now get the hell out of here."

The blonde grabbed Kenny's arm, pulling him to his feet and toward the mouth of the alley. "You heard him, Kenny. Let's go."

Kenny shrugged off her hold. "I ain't going nowhere. He tried to kill me. You saw it. I want the sheriff. Somebody call the sheriff. I want to press charges."

Lindsey almost groaned. The last thing Bart needed was for the sheriff's department to get involved. The court could decide to revoke his bail over this. He'd be locked in jail awaiting trial. "You threw the first punch, Mr. Rawlins. I think you'll be hard-pressed to prove Bart tried to kill you."

Kenny's mouth flattened into a hard line. His eyes narrowed. "What do you know about it?"

"Plenty." She fished a card from the pocket of her suit jacket and thrust it at him, hoping her profession would give him pause. "I'm a lawyer."

He squinted at the card, then looked up at Bart. "So she's not your whore after all. She's worse. She's your goddamn lawyer."

Bart charged Kenny.

Spinning on his heel, Kenny scampered from the alley. Once he was a safe distance away, he looked over his shoulder. "I'll get you, Bart. You won't get away with what you've done."

The door of the tavern flew open and Wade Lansing stepped out. Assessing the situation through narrowed gray eyes, he walked over to Bart. "What the hell is going on out here?"

While Bart explained what had happened, Lindsey watched the small crowd that had followed Kenny to the alley disperse. A single woman stayed and stepped out from the shadows, the light from the setting sun turning her curls to fire. She scribbled notes on a pad of paper.

Cara.

Under normal circumstances, Lindsey would be happy to see one of the few good friends she'd made since moving to Mustang Valley. But these circumstances were anything but normal. Cara Hamilton was a reporter for the *Mustang Gazette*. And next to the sheriff or one of his deputies, a reporter was the last person Lindsey wanted to see right now. Even if it was Cara.

She darted around Wade and Bart. She couldn't do anything to change what had happened between Bart and Kenny, but maybe she could appeal to Cara not to splash the news all over Mustang Valley. "Hey, Cara."

Cara brushed a curl from her forehead and looked up from her notebook. "Hi, Lindsey. How are you mixed up in this? Are you representing Bart Rawlins?" Cara's eyes flashed with inquisitiveness, her pen poised over paper.

Great. Lindsey hadn't taken into account that *she* might be part of Cara's story. "Are you covering Jeb Rawlins's murder?"

"Of course not." Cara rolled her eyes. "Beau is keeping the good stories to himself as usual."

Lindsey nodded. Cara's editor, and owner of the *Mustang Gazette,* Beau Jennings, had covered every major story in Mustang Valley for the past forty-some years. "He knows once he gives you a major story, the Dallas papers will snatch you up in a heartbeat."

Cara tilted her head. "Of course, having a friend representing Bart Rawlins might just give me the break I need. So are you Bart's lawyer, Lindsey?" she asked again.

Lindsey should have known changing the subject wouldn't throw Cara off. Once her friend smelled a story, she didn't give up until she rooted out the truth. Lindsey sighed. "Yes."

"Why the heavy sigh? Is his case that bad?"

"No."

"He has a strong case then?"

She gave her friend a warning smile. "Quit fishing, Cara."

"Then talk to me."

"Off the record?"

"Okay."

"Don't print anything about this ridiculous fight."

"You're kidding, right? This is news, Lindsey. I can't just pretend I didn't see what happened."

She let out another sigh. "No, I suppose you can't. I'm just worried about poisoning the jury pool."

"I don't know what it's like in a big city like Boston, but gossip travels like dust in a strong wind around here. Even if I don't write about what happened, people will hear about it. And there's no telling what kind of twisted version they'll get."

"I suppose you're right."

"Damn straight." Cara's hazel eyes twinkled with humor.

Lindsey tried to return her smile, but her attempt fell flat.

"But you don't have to worry, I'll tell the whole story."

She gave Cara a questioning look.

"Meaning, I'll be writing that Kenny came looking for Bart and threw the first punch. I'll also include a bit of background, like Kenny's conviction for fraud."

"He's been convicted?"

"Kenny Rawlins is a master of the get-rich-quick scam. He's cheated a lot of people in Mustang Valley, a fact my readers won't easily forget."

Lindsey pressed her lips into a line. It wasn't a great situation, but she could live with it. "Thanks, Cara."

"For what? Telling the truth?" Cara smiled. "If you really want to thank me, give me a few quotes about Bart's case."

Lindsey took a deep breath of evening air. She supposed it was only fair she give her friend a quote. "He's an innocent man. You can print that. And I'll give you the scoop on who's guilty as soon as I find out."

BART WATCHED a single set of approaching headlights play across Lindsey's flawless skin. His attention trailed to her long, elegant fingers wrapped around the steering wheel of her little white sports car. On her right hand, a platinum ring with some kind of red stone glowed in the dashboard light. Her left ring finger was free of jewelry.

He tried to concentrate on the ribbon of highway stretching from Mustang Valley to the Four Aces Ranch. He shouldn't be noticing Lindsey's skin and fingers and whether she was wearing a wedding ring. She was his lawyer, not a pretty young thing he'd met at some honky-tonk.

Besides, he had more pressing things to deal with than a crush he couldn't do anything about. Like being accused of murdering his uncle. Like the real possibility he would be spending the rest of his life behind bars. Even if Lindsey wasn't his lawyer and far out of his league, he couldn't do a damn thing about his attraction to her. Not with the prospect of spending the rest of his life in Huntsville hanging over his head.

After Kenny had left the alley, he and Lindsey had resumed their search for beer bottles with missing labels. All they'd come up with were two bottles and a few shards of glass from the bin Kenny had tipped over. Tomorrow morning Lindsey planned to drive to Fort Worth to drop off the bottles and shards at the same lab where Doc had sent the other samples. A long shot, but better than nothing.

Of course, if it hadn't been for Lindsey's theory about the drug, he wouldn't have a shot at all.

His focus drifted back to her face. Her eyebrows knit together. She gnawed on her lower lip. All in all, she looked as worried as he felt. "What are you thinking about?" he asked.

She started at his voice, then glanced at him briefly

before bringing her attention back to the road ahead. "Your cousin, Kenny. Cara Hamilton said he's been convicted for fraud."

"I suppose Cara's going to write an article about what a hothead I was tonight."

"She promised to be fair and accurate. Under the circumstances, it's the best we can hope for."

"Fair and accurate is still going to make me look like a hothead. I doubt that will help my case with the good people of Mustang County."

"The article probably won't help, but something she brought up to me tonight might. What can you tell me about the scams your cousin pulled?"

Bart searched his memory. He'd tried not to pay too much attention to Kenny's dealings. Just thinking about them made his cheeks burn with shame that he and his cousin shared the same blood. "He was into everything from selling lame horses to spreading stories that local legend Shotgun Sally was born and raised on Jeb's ranch, the Bar JR."

"My friends Cara and Kelly like to talk about Shotgun Sally. Kelly is one of Sally's descendants." Her elegant eyebrows dipped low over those intense blue eyes. "How could Kenny profit from saying Sally was born on the Bar JR?"

"If there was a way, he found it. He sold worthless tin plates claiming they were from Sally's homestead. Tried to promote tours of Jeb's property. He even sold jars of dirt saying it came from Sally's grave."

"But that's all pretty harmless. Why was he charged?"

"After he gave up on cashing in on Shotgun Sally, he sold cemetery plots to old folks. A lot of cemetery plots. Only the plots weren't his to sell. He did three years in Huntsville. That was the end of his scams, far as I know. Though I'm sure he's still finding some way to make a quick buck."

"How far would he go to make money?"

He cocked his head at her question. "What are you thinking?"

"From the way he talked about his father, I assume they didn't get along."

"You assume right. Kenny had no use for Jeb. The only people Kenny blamed more than Jeb for his failures were me and my daddy."

"Because your father inherited more land?"

"Yes. And because my father was a success with the land he inherited. Jeb started with a nice cattle operation. It only took him about two years to drink it away." He could see where she was going. Her mind was heading down the same path his had since his run-in with his cousin. "You're thinking Kenny might have killed Jeb."

"I keep wondering how he knew your knife was the murder weapon."

"Unless he used it himself?"

"Is it possible? Would Kenny kill his own father if it meant a big inheritance?"

"I wish I could say no. But I wouldn't put it past him. If he inherits."

"He might not?"

"Like I said, there wasn't much love lost between them. Jeb might have written Kenny out of his will, for all I know."

"I'll find out. Our firm is handling the estate."

"And defending me. Isn't that a conflict of interest?"

"I'm not handling Jeb's estate. Don Church is."

Bart nodded. Donald Church was a specialist in wills and trusts and a full partner of Lambert & Church. Back before Bart's dad had gotten sick, he'd always sworn Don was the most honest lawyer in Texas. Bart gestured ahead to the next turn off the highway. "You'll want to take a right up here."

Lindsey swung the car onto the road. Juniper groves flanking both sides, the drive twisted up a gentle hill overlooking the most beautiful country this close to Dallas/Fort Worth. Too bad it was way past nightfall. He would have loved to show her the view.

Still looking worried, she squinted her eyes at the road ahead. "How about that blonde with Kenny tonight? Who is she?"

"You got me. Last I kept track, he was dating Debbie West. But that was years ago. Before she married that other loser."

"Debbie West?"

"A girl who grew up on a ranch bordering the Four Aces."

"That blonde last night sure didn't look like the girl next door."

Lindsey was right about that. "She's built like the women Kenny usually goes for—long legs, lots of curves—but something isn't quite right."

"Like what?"

"Her clothes. Her attitude. She has too much class to be hanging around Kenny. Of course, anyone who saw you and me together might say the same thing."

She pulled her eyes from the road and gave him more than a quick glance. "What do you mean?"

"Look at you. Sophisticated, smart, a real lady yet sharp as a barbed-wire fence. If you weren't my lawyer, you'd never be hanging around an old cowboy like me."

"Says who?" A smile softened her pretty lips. "If I wasn't your lawyer—" She pressed her lips together and looked out the window, like she was embarrassed by the unprofessional blunder she'd almost made.

If she wasn't his lawyer...

Did she mean she would be interested if... Bart shook his head and smothered the hope sparked by her comment. It didn't matter. He sure as hell wasn't going to be doing much dating. Not where he was headed. If they didn't find some evidence they could use for a defense, the last thing he would have to worry about was his love life.

He looked at the white pipe corrals and sprawling ranch house, apartment building, bunkhouse and barns ahead. A red dually pickup stood parked in its usual spot next to the main horse barn. He tilted his watch to read the face in the dashboard glow. It was plenty late, but this was important. "Gary's home."

"Your foreman?"

"You said you wanted to talk to him?"

"Very much. If he didn't drive you home last night, maybe he knows who did."

LINDSEY FOLLOWED Bart around a metal pole barn and toward the ranch foreman's place. White buildings and a maze of pipe fence glowed in the moonlight and stretched as far as she could see. Even in the dead of night, the ranch was impressive. "Beautiful place."

"Wait until you see the whole thing in the daylight." He motioned to the barn they were circling. "This is the horse part of the operation. It's my addition."

"Addition? Don't all ranches use horses?"

"People in these parts don't like to talk about it, but a lot of ranches rely on helicopters and four-wheelers to move their cattle. With the cost of labor and the difficulty in finding qualified cowboys, it's more economical than using horses. And these days, we in the beef industry need all the economy we can get. We even have a helicopter here at the Four Aces."

"Do you use horses at all?"

"We use them most of the time. The helicopter just helps out. But most of the horses in this barn spend more time in the show ring than on the range."

"I used to show horses when I was growing up. Pony Club."

"No kidding? I'd like to take you riding."

"Do you have a hunt seat saddle handy? Or do your horses just ride western?"

"Honey, quarter horses can do everything worth doing. And you can bet my quarter horses can do it better than anyone else's." He turned and gave her a teasing smile.

Her heart lurched sideways. He was something, this cowboy. Proud as any red-blooded Texan one minute, yet self-deprecating the next. And through it all, his green eyes shone with a sparkle that made her wish...

She stopped herself. What would she wish? That she could toss her career out the window and fall into his arms? The arms of a client, for crying out loud?

She'd kept her focus solely on proving herself in her career since she was eighteen. She wasn't going to let a little Texas charm turn her head now that she was on the cusp of proving herself. And saving him from a life behind bars.

Looking straight ahead, she focused on the long, low apartment building. On the other side of a large paddock, another good-sized building that appeared to be more living quarters perched on top of a gentle swell of land. And if she turned around, she knew she'd see the roofline of the main house. "This place is like a mini city. How many people live here?"

"Me, my daddy, my daddy's nurse, Beatrice, my foreman, Gary, and eight full-time hands, more during roundup. Daddy and Beatrice live in the house with me. The others live in the apartment building if they have families, and in the bunkhouse if they're single or just here for roundup."

She looked at the low stretch of apartments. All the windows of the long building were dark. Except for the bark of a dog, the place was quiet as a tomb. "Is everyone gone?"

"Don't let the quiet fool you. After working from can't see to can't see, there's not much a body wants to do most days but eat and fall into bed. Come sunrise, this place will be hopping." He strode to the first apartment and rapped on the door. "Gary? You awake? I need a word with you."

No answer.

Bart knocked again. Still nothing. Finally he turned away from the door and shrugged. "Old boy's probably worn-out after doing my work today along with his own. And probably being raked over the coals by Hurley Zeller to boot. Guess we'll have to wait for tomorrow. I'll walk you back to your car."

They'd just circled the barn when Lindsey spotted her car. It lurched at a strange angle. As if the tires on one side were flat. "My car."

Bart picked up his pace, long legs striding straight for the vehicle.

Lindsey half ran alongside to keep up. As they

approached, her breath caught in her throat. Red spray paint slashed across the windshield and white hood, and dripped down like blood. *Stay away from the murderer or die.*

CHAPTER FOUR

DEPUTY HURLEY ZELLER leaned on the hood of Gary Tuttle's dually and picked his teeth with a dirty fingernail. "I still can't believe you called me all the way out here to report a prank."

Bart had been trying to reach Deputy Mitchell Steele all night. Finally, he'd given up and asked the dispatcher to send whoever was available. He wasn't surprised when Hurley showed up. Hell, he wouldn't be surprised if the little bastard had conspired to keep Bart from reaching Mitch—the only fair-minded deputy in the county.

Bart narrowed his eyes. He hadn't liked Hurley Zeller since high school. But after taking the brunt of the deputy's sarcasm and bad attitude since his arrest, he was damn close to hating the man. "Seems more like a threat than a prank, Hurley. The car won't start, either. Whoever did this took the distributor cap."

Hurley shrugged. "Committing murder will win a few enemies. For you and your lawyer."

Exactly what Bart was afraid of. He glanced at Lindsey. Despite her brave front, he could tell by the rigidity of her spine she was upset. "I want protection for Lindsey."

Lindsey stiffened. "I don't need protection. You're the one in danger."

Hurley scoffed. "You're both kidding, right? We ain't got enough deputies in Mustang County to haul all the drunks off the highways on Saturday night. We don't have the manpower for baby-sitting."

Bart forced himself to take a calming breath. Hurley might be right. It might be nothing. Whoever vandalized Lindsey's car had the opportunity to hurt them, after all, and hadn't taken it. But whatever the vandal's intentions, Bart wasn't taking chances. "Lindsey is a lawyer with Lambert & Church. I doubt Paul Lambert and Don Church would be happy if something happened to her. And last I knew, they were big political supporters of Sheriff Ben."

The grin fell from Hurley's lips. If there was anything the deputy believed in, it was keeping his boss happy. "Fine. I'll arrange for a car to drive by her place every hour or so."

Lindsey shook her head, her eyes shooting bullets at Bart. "I don't need protection. I can take care of myself."

"That may be, darlin', but I want to make sure." Bart glanced back at Hurley and nodded. "I'll let Paul and Don know you're handling the situation. Also, you might want to stop at my cousin Kenny's house and ask him where he's been tonight. And while you're there, keep your eye out for red paint."

Hurley looked like he wanted to spit. He turned and walked to his car.

"And another thing," Bart added.

Hurley stopped in his tracks. "Don't push your luck, Rawlins. I'm warning you."

"You wouldn't know what happened to my shotgun and hunting rifles, would you?" While waiting for the deputy to arrive, he'd gone into the house for his shotgun. He wanted to be able to protect himself and Lindsey in case the vandal decided to turn to more serious crime. But all he'd found was an empty gun case, its door gaping.

"We confiscated them when we searched the property this morning."

Lindsey's glower moved off Bart and onto Hurley.

The deputy nodded in her direction. "The warrant included all weapons. I'll get you a copy."

"You do that."

"When can I get them back?" Bart asked.

"After you've served your time in Huntsville. I guess that would be twenty-five years to life." Grinning, Hurley climbed into his car, slammed the door and hung an arm out his open window. "If you'd like, Ms. Wellington, I'll drive you back to town, make sure you're safe." He glanced at Bart with that damn grin, as if he expected points for the offer.

BY THE TIME Bart fell out of bed the next morning, it was almost five o'clock. If he wanted to talk to Gary before the foreman left for the south pasture, he'd have to hurry.

He showered, shaved, downed a cup of coffee and made it to the barn just as Gary was saddling his little bay mare. "Hey, Gary. Can I have a word?"

Face deeply creased by sun, wind and hard living, Gary Tuttle looked and moved like a man twenty years older than his forty-five. He tossed his prized saddle, which he'd won on the rodeo circuit when he was young, on the mare's back and squinted at Bart with tired gray eyes. "You're the boss."

Bart frowned. Gary had been like a big brother when he was growing up on the ranch. He'd taught Bart how to rope a steer from horseback, how cattle break when they're on the move and how to fly the ranch's Enstrom

F-28F piston helicopter. He'd put so much work into the Four Aces, Bart's dad had given him a chunk of the place as a reward. But ever since Bart's dad had gotten sick, Gary was like a different man. Tired. Distant. And he'd talked more than once about retiring from the ranching business.

Bart had hoped a night together shooting bull at the Hit 'Em Again would bring back some of the brotherly camaraderie they'd lost. Unfortunately he didn't remember how his plan had turned out. "I suppose you heard about the goings-on yesterday."

Gary settled the saddle on the mare's back and flipped the near stirrup up. "Hurley Zeller told me you were arrested for killing Jeb. He asked me a bunch of questions."

"What did you tell him?"

"Nothin' much."

"I didn't do it. You know that, don't you?"

"If anyone deserved it, it was Jeb."

Bart shook his head. "As miserable as that son of a bitch was, no one deserves to die."

Gary flicked a shoulder in a half shrug. Avoiding Bart's eyes, he grabbed the cinch and fastened it around the mare's girth. She took in air, bloating her belly so he couldn't tighten it.

"I tried to wake you up last night."

"Oh?"

"I wanted to ask you about our night at the Hit 'Em Again."

"What about it?"

"How did I get home?"

"You blacked out, huh?"

"Something like that."

Gary kneed the little bay in the belly. Pinning her

ears, she let out the air with a grunt. He pulled the cinch tight, slipped the latigo into its keeper and let the stirrup fall against her side. "When I went to leave, you were already gone. I figured you must have left with that fine young thing you were talking to at the bar."

"Fine young thing?"

"You would have to black out to forget her. Blond. Legs longer than this mare is tall. Former Dallas Cowboys cheerleader, according to your drunken babble."

The same blonde who was with Kenny in the alley? There couldn't be two long-legged mystery blondes in Mustang Valley. Had she been the one to drug his drink? Provided the date-rape drug was responsible for his memory loss. "Did you see me drinking whiskey?"

Gary shook his head. "Just beer. But I wasn't watching over you like a goddamned nursemaid."

Too bad. A nursemaid was apparently what he'd needed that night. Maybe he should have asked Beatrice, his daddy's nurse, to go to the saloon with him instead of Gary. "What else did I say about the blonde?"

"You were too busy to have much conversation with me. But I got the impression she was hitting on you and not the other way around."

At least he wouldn't be known around town as some kind of womanizer. Just a drunk and a murderer. "Who was she?"

"Don't know. But you might want to check out yesterday's *Mustang Gazette*. They put out a special afternoon edition. There's a picture of her in it with Jeb."

"You have one?"

Gary nodded toward the tack room.

Bart stepped inside. The scent of horse sweat mingled with well-worn leather. He spotted the paper lying on a saddle rack. Bracing himself, he picked it up and looked under the headline proclaiming Mustang Valley's second murder in two months. His gaze landed on a picture of his uncle. Thin-lipped mouth set at a mean angle, Jeb stared at the camera as if challenging it to a fistfight. And on Jeb's arm was the blonde who'd accompanied Kenny to the alley last night.

The jingle of spurs jolted him out of his surprise. He glanced up from the paper as Gary leaned in the tackroom door, holding his saddled and bridled horse by a single rein. "She's something, ain't she? Can't figure out for the life of me what she'd be doing with old Jeb."

Neither could Bart. But he was damn well going to find out.

LINDSEY LOOKED UP from her paperwork as Bart laid a copy of the *Mustang Gazette* in front of her. Propping a hip on the edge of her desk, he watched as if waiting for her reaction.

She had a reaction, all right, but it wasn't to the newspaper.

Dressed in a denim shirt, jeans, tooled belt complete with big silver buckle and a well-shaped straw hat that blended with the sun-kissed blond of his hair, Bart looked like a lonely woman's cowboy dream. And his scent. Mmm. He wore the rugged scent of leather, honest work and fresh air. She breathed deeply and struggled to keep her composure.

What was it about being around this man that made her lose her equilibrium? She'd felt off balance since the moment she'd first touched his hand in the jail's visiting room. His attempt to protect her last night after her car had been vandalized hadn't helped matters. It had only made her feel helpless on top of fluttery. An unwelcome reminder of the way she'd always felt when her parents and brothers had hovered over her as she was growing up—the way they would still be hovering if she hadn't moved halfway across the country. As if she were incompetent, helpless, dependent.

As if she were still a little girl.

She shoved her insecurities to the back of her mind and tried to focus on the faces in the newspaper photo. Her past feelings didn't matter. Nor did her attraction to her client. She was on her own now, and the chance to prove herself was right in front of her. All she had to do was reach out and grab it by the throat. "I saw the picture about ten minutes ago. I would have called, but I figured you were already on your way here to keep our appointment."

"I've never seen that blonde around Mustang Valley before. Suddenly she's everywhere."

She nodded and studied the woman's attractive features. "At least, everywhere with Jeb and Kenny."

"And me."

"You?" Adrenaline jolted through her bloodstream, partly due to surprise, partly due to something she couldn't quite put her finger on. "When was she with you?"

"I caught up with Gary this morning. He said she was sitting with me at Hit 'Em Again the night Jeb was killed."

"The same woman? Is he sure?"

He nodded.

Another jolt.

Jealousy. That was it. Plain, simple and inappropriate. She shook her head, trying to clear her mind, trying to reclaim her professional demeanor. "Does Gary know who she is?"

"Nope."

"I gave Wade a call at the bar this morning. He didn't remember seeing her at all that night. And neither did the kid he's training. Of course, the kid was concentrating so hard on serving drinks, he didn't remember much of anything." Lindsey bit her bottom lip. "Maybe the blonde's working with Kenny."

He tilted his head and waited for her to go on.

"Say Kenny did kill his father in order to inherit the ranch and he wanted to make it look like you're responsible. How would he do that? I mean, he could never get close enough to slip Rohypnol in your beer. Not without you being suspicious. But he could hire the blonde to do it."

"If Rohypnol was in my beer."

"I borrowed Cara's car to take the pieces of bottle to the lab this morning." She didn't want to think about what she would do if the drug didn't show up in any of the tests. She knew Bart was telling the truth about blacking out that night. And she knew he was innocent. She could feel the honesty in every word from his lips. But faith and trust weren't exactly accepted as evidence in a court of law. And as much as she didn't want to admit it, she wasn't an unbiased judge where Bart Rawlins was concerned.

No, she needed evidence. And she needed it now.

"There's one thing that bothers me," Bart said, his gentle mouth turning down in a frown.

Lindsey pulled her gaze from his lips and met his eyes. "What?"

"A scam like the one you're talking about would take a lot of planning on Kenny's part. I'm not sure he has it in him."

She didn't know Kenny Rawlins, but from the limited exposure she'd had to him, she was inclined to agree.

"Okay. What if he didn't hire the blonde? What if she was the brains behind the brawn? It would explain how they know each other. It might even explain that picture of her and Jeb. She could have been setting him up for murder."

Bart tilted his head, as if weighing her arguments, then nodded. "I could see that."

"All we have to do is show a connection between Kenny and the blonde. And dig up evidence showing means and opportunity."

"A tall order."

It was. And at this point, it was pure speculation. But if they could find something concrete—

The sound of knuckles rapping on wood cut off her thoughts. "Come in," she called.

The door swung open and Paul Lambert popped his head inside. "Excuse me, Lindsey. I need a word with Bart."

"Sure, Paul, come in." She waved him inside.

Paul Lambert was a year or so shy of sixty. But with the touch of silver at his temples, his casual confidence and his friendly brown eyes, it was no wonder Dot down at the sandwich shop chatted about him incessantly, even though he was married. But more important to Lindsey than his looks or confident air was the aggressive way he'd recruited her right out of law school. As if he truly believed she was capable of becoming the lawyer she wanted to be.

Paul crossed the plush money-green carpet that covered all the floors at Lambert & Church and held out a hand to Bart.

Bart gave it a firm shake. "What's up, Paul? You aren't here to ask me if I want to sell the Four Aces again, are you?"

Paul grinned. "Naw. I gave up hope years ago."

Lindsey glanced at Bart. "You aren't thinking of selling, are you?"

Bart shook his head. "Not a chance. It's kind of a joke. When my daddy signed over the ranch to me, not a day passed that Paul or Don didn't ask me if I wanted to sell."

"We weren't that bad. But if you've reconsidered, I do have a client who might be interested." Paul's grin widened.

"You'd be the first to know. Unless Don beats you to it."

"Speaking of Don, have you talked to him yet?" Paul's grin subsided, his business demeanor taking over.

"Don? I can't say I've seen him. Why?"

"Your uncle stipulated that your father be present for the reading of his will."

Bart took a step backward, his surprise evident. "You sure about that?"

"Quite sure."

Bart shook his head. His lips flattened into an ironic half smile. "When I was a kid, I used to hope my daddy and Jeb would work through their differences one day and bring the family back together. I should have known one of them would have to be dead for it to happen."

"Do you think your father will be able to attend?"

"Daddy? Not a chance."

Sympathy furrowed Paul's brow. "I suppose his only brother's death is something of a shock."

"I'm sure it would be, if I'd told him."

"You haven't told your father?" Lindsey sat up in her chair, surprise riffling through her. "Why not?"

Bart looked at her, the sparkle in his green eyes muted by obvious pain. "He hasn't been well."

"I know he's sick, but wouldn't he want to—"

"He just lost Mama a year ago. He doesn't need to know."

Paul cleared his throat, bringing their attention back to him. "If you want to represent your father, I'm sure that would be in keeping with the spirit of the will."

Bart shook his head. "I won't be there, either."

Lindsey bit her lip. Murder was usually committed for one of two reasons—love or money. Finding out to whom Jeb had left his possessions could serve to illuminate both his love life and his finances. "It might be a good idea to attend."

"Jeb didn't leave my daddy anything. And Daddy probably wouldn't want me to accept it if he did." Bart's gaze bored into her, as if he was trying to make her understand. Or simply get her to back off.

She returned the eye contact. Despite his discomfort, she couldn't back off. Not when so much was at stake. "But it might be interesting to see to whom Jeb *did* leave his possessions."

Bart glanced at the floor and pushed a stream of air through tight lips as if he saw her point. "I'll think about it."

Paul gave Lindsey an approving nod before turning to Bart. "Don has scheduled the will reading for Tuesday, three in the afternoon."

"That soon?" Lindsey asked.

Paul shrugged. "I know. It's a little irregular. But it's what Jeb wanted." His attention riveted to the newspaper lying on Lindsey's desk. To the photo of Jeb and the blonde. He looked away, the planes of his face hardening.

"Do you know her?" Lindsey asked.

"Who?"

"The woman in the photo with Jeb Rawlins?" She pointed to the paper.

Paul bent over her desk and studied the woman's features. He lifted his shoulders in a stiff shrug. "Can't say I do." He looked up from the paper, careful not to meet Lindsey's eyes.

An uneasy feeling skittered over her skin. Paul knew the woman. Lindsey would stake her career on it. But why would he lie? "I think she's involved with Kenny in some way."

Paul casually crooked a brow. "Hmm."

"She was with him last night at Hit 'Em Again. We thought maybe she was involved with Kenny in some of his scams."

He nodded but still didn't meet Lindsey's eyes. "Before I forget, Nancy wanted me to tell you she has the files you wanted."

Lindsey nodded. The office administrator, Nancy Wilks, had promised to have an intern copy every file that had been subpoenaed by the prosecution to present to the grand jury. No doubt Lindsey had a late night ahead of her. "Thanks, Paul."

Paul nodded, glanced at his watch and focused on Bart. "I have to run. I have a meeting. I hope you re-consider coming to the will reading. You might find it illuminating."

As soon as Paul disappeared through the office door, Bart glanced at Lindsey. "That was strange."

Lindsey nodded. "Paul obviously knew who the blonde was. But why wouldn't he admit it?"

"Hell if I know. But I think you were right. I think I

should probably go hear what Jeb put in his will." He let out a stream of air. "But I'll do it on one condition."

"What's that?"

"I want to bring my lawyer with me. I don't like to make a move without legal advice I can count on." A grin spread over his lips and a twinkle appeared in his green eyes.

She returned the smile despite herself. "I think that can be arranged."

He really was an amazing man. He seemed to know just what to say, just how to smile to disarm her. Yet his warm grin and unassuming phrases didn't seem like merely an attempt to manipulate her. They seemed true and honest and a genuine part of who he was.

"Do you need help toting those files Paul mentioned?"

"That would be great."

Feeling stronger and more confident than she had in a long time, she walked out the door and down the hall to the main office, Bart by her side. She had a lot of work ahead of her. She just prayed she would find something useful soon. Because if she didn't, a very good man would pay the price.

CHAPTER FIVE

LINDSEY RUBBED HER eyes with her thumb and fore-finger and glanced at the clock hanging on her kitchen wall. Almost eleven o'clock at night. For two days she'd been sorting through the files she and Bart had picked up, and she still hadn't found anything.

She trained her eyes on the paper in front of her. Figures from the last year Jeb had cattle on his ranch swam on the page. Number of head sold, maverick rate, shrink-age rate—a regular crash course in cattle ranching and none of it seemed to lead anywhere. Luckily Bart had spent a couple of hours explaining the terminology to her over dinner. If it weren't for him, she would really be lost.

As if finally gaining permission to go where it wanted, her mind latched on to thoughts of Bart. His honesty, his sincerity and his disarming smile.

The phone rang, cutting through her thoughts. She punched the Talk button and held it to her ear. "Hello?"

"Hey, Baby."

Lindsey flinched. All her brothers called her Baby. When she was a kid, the name had made her feel spe-cial, like her four older brothers really noticed her. And cared. Now at the age of twenty-six, she'd re-evaluated. "What's up, David?"

"What's up? Why does something have to be up? Can't I just call my little sister occasionally?"

"If you, Michael, Rich and Cameron only called occasionally instead of every night, it might be nice. As it is, your calls are bordering on harassment."

"I'm just doing my part to save your career, Baby."

"My career doesn't need saving."

"Come on, Lindsey. You're a Wellington. You have a brilliant legal mind. Why waste it out in the sticks?"

His patronizing tone made her nerves stand on edge. "I'm not wasting anything. I'm making a career for myself. The same way the rest of the Wellingtons did."

"But you didn't have to travel halfway across the country to do that."

She blew a frustrated breath through pursed lips. She'd been through this argument countless times with each of her brothers. Even her mother and father chimed in on occasion. "I want to make it on my own. Why is that so hard for everyone to understand?"

"Maybe because we've given you an open invitation to join our firm here. In your home. And you won't be defending drunk drivers and reading real estate contracts on the side. Or you can clerk for Dad, specialize in constitutional law, work on what you care about. Hell, maybe someday you can make it to the bench. Follow in Dad's footsteps. That's what you want, isn't it?"

David knew darn well that was what she wanted. But that wasn't all she wanted. "I want to make it on my own," she repeated. "I want to earn my own way just like the three of you did when you started the firm from scratch. Like Cam did. Like Mom and Dad did in their careers."

"You don't have to do that, Lindsey. That's my point.

There are advantages to you being so much younger than the rest of us. Mom and Dad are established in their careers now. We're all established. Why not cash in on that? We all respect you. You don't have to earn anything."

"You respect me? That's a new one. That must be why you don't trust me to make it on my own." David, Michael and Rich had started their own firm. Cameron had risen to the ranks of federal prosecutor. Her dad was now a judge. Even her mother had finished her degree and landed a job teaching law after years of raising a family.

"Come on, Baby. Not that whole 'make it on my own' thing again."

"Why shouldn't I make it on my own?"

"Because you don't have to."

He would never understand. None of her family would. They all wanted to take care of her. To protect her. To coddle the baby sister. To give her all the advantages they never had. Advantages they didn't believe she could earn for herself. "I don't have time to talk about this, David. I have a big case I'm working on."

"Don't tell me, a drunk driver who dented someone's pickup truck *and* ran over a dog?"

She set her chin and scowled into the phone. Maybe in a way, she needed Bart as much as he needed her. Because by proving his innocence, she would also prove herself. To her family, to the world.

She just hoped she was as brilliant as her family liked to think.

TRUSSED UP in a white shirt with pearl snaps and a black tie to match his black Wranglers, Bart felt about as uncomfortable as a boy dressed for Sunday school. But he sure didn't feel like a boy around Lindsey Wellington. Far from it. Every glance from those intense blue eyes made him feel all man.

Her baby blues bored into him now. "Ready?"

He clapped his Resistol straw hat on his head and forced his thoughts to the will-reading ahead. He didn't know why he bothered dressing up. If the situation was reversed, he had no doubts Jeb would walk in with tattered jeans and manure on his boots. But somehow it didn't seem right to wear work clothes while attending the only last rites a man would ever have.

Not that any part of this felt right. "I still don't like this. I never wasted much time on good thoughts about Jeb when he was alive. I feel like a damn hypocrite suddenly showing up for the will."

She pushed back her chair and stood. "I know. But your uncle put your father's name in his will for a reason. We need to know what it is. Besides, the last several nights I went over the files Nancy copied for me, and I found absolutely nothing. We need a break."

Bart sighed. Good points. Not that Lindsey had to make them in order to convince him. Hell, he'd follow her anywhere. All she had to do was crook one of those ladylike fingers. "Let's get it over with, then."

With a decisive nod, Lindsey strode out the door of her office and led him down the hall.

Even though the annex fire, which had burned Andrew McGovern's body, had happened weeks ago, the scent of smoke still permeated the building. Especially in the area near the now-boarded-up entrance to the annex. Bart tried not to think about Andrew or the fire or the subject of murder as he swung through the open door of the conference room behind Lindsey and looked straight into the angry black eyes of his cousin.

"What the hell are you doing here?" Kenny bellowed. He balled his hands into fists, as if threatening to take Bart on in the middle of the conference room.

A challenge Bart would be happy to oblige if they were back in the alley behind the Hit 'Em Again. "I wouldn't be here if Paul hadn't asked me to come."

Kenny threw a scowl in Paul's direction.

The firm's partner leaned against the table, his eyes moving over a file in his hands, clearly unfazed by the likes of Kenny Rawlins.

At the end of the long table, Donald Church, the other half of Lambert & Church, stretched to his full five-foot-and-a-sliver height and cleared his throat. Dressed in his usual starched white shirt, French cuffs and two-thousand-dollar suit, Don reminded Bart of a round little peacock the way he preened and strutted in his fancy clothes. But the man also had the warmest smile Bart ever remembered seeing. He turned that smile on Kenny. "I'm sorry, Kenny. I know it's hard to have Bart here. But Jeb stipulated that Bart's father attend this reading. And since Hiriam can't be here, Bart has agreed to take his place."

Kenny growled deep in his throat like a dog on the end of a fat chain. "The old bastard must have done it to torture me. One more kick from beyond the grave."

Paul tossed the file he was perusing onto the table and clapped a hand on Kenny's shoulder. "Have a seat, Ken. This will all be over soon enough."

Kenny sank into a chair, his glower still focused on Bart.

Bart couldn't blame him. If the situation was reversed, he'd probably be across that table with his hands around Kenny's throat before either of the partners could say their first cajoling word.

Turning away from Kenny, Bart grasped one of the chairs and pulled it out for Lindsey. Flashing him a small smile, she lowered herself into the chair and set her briefcase on the floor beside her. Legal pad in hand, she crossed her long legs and looked to Don, waiting for him to begin.

Bart folded himself into a chair beside her. The faint scent of roses teased the air between them. He fought the urge to lean close and breathe her in.

Paul was the last to find a chair. Once he had, Don treated the whole table to one of his smiles and chewed over a long preamble about Jeb being of sound mind—which Bart had always doubted. Then he cut into the meat of the will. "To my only son, Kenneth B. Rawlins, I leave the case of whiskey in the basement of the house."

"Case of whiskey? He drank every drop of that a long damn time ago."

Don held up a hand. "I also leave him the contents of my safe-deposit box at First Texas Bank, Mustang Valley branch, and my 1995 Ford pickup."

Kenny leaned forward in his chair. "What about the ranch? What the hell does it say about the ranch?"

Paul laid a hand on his shoulder. "Let Don continue, Ken."

Eyes drilling into Bart, Kenny grasped in his shirt pocket, pulled out a pack of cigarettes and shook one from the pack.

Flipping the cigarette between his lips with one hand, he searched his pocket for a lighter with the other. Finding a red Bic, he lit the smoke and took a deep drag.

Don blinked his eyes a few times and looked back down at the document in front of him. "I leave the acreage and buildings that make up the Bar JR ranch to—"

Bart shifted in his chair. He drew a breath and held it.

"—my brother, Hiriam Rawlins."

A wooden feeling crept through Bart's limbs. He glanced at Lindsey. Shock was written all over her face, the same shock that had him numb from hat to boots. He forced his gaze to Don. "You've got to be kidding."

"It's all right here."

He shook his head, trying to cut through the sluggishness in his brain. "I don't believe it. It doesn't make sense."

"It all makes perfect sense to me."

Bart winced at the rasp of his cousin's voice.

Leaning back in his chair, Kenny's lips twitched into a smirk. He blew smoke from his nostrils, a thickening cloud circling his head.

CHAPTER SIX

BACK IN HER OFFICE, Lindsey set her briefcase on the desk and struggled to hide the anxiety threatening to overwhelm her. Judging from the look on Bart's face when Don had read Jeb's will, he was already unnerved. The last thing he needed was to see that his lawyer was struggling with worries of her own.

Bart sank into one of the chairs in front of her desk. Grasping his hat by the crown, he lifted it off his head and raked a hand through his hair. "Jeb's will doesn't make a lick of sense. Hell, if I didn't know the old coot better, I'd think he set me up and killed himself just so I would take the fall."

Her stomach clutched. "Is it possible?"

He blew out a frustrated breath. "Jeb was a miserable son of a bitch, but he wasn't suicidal. Not unless you count trying to drink himself to death."

Lindsey shook her head. "The facts of the case don't point to suicide anyway. Suicide victims don't slash their own throats. I guess I was just grasping at straws."

"The way things are stacking up, I'd give about anything for a few of those straws."

Lindsey gave a heavy sigh and leaned back against the desk. So much for hiding her apprehension. Not only was she grasping at straws, she'd just admitted it to her client. "Nothing has changed. We still have to find who had most to gain from Jeb's murder. And Kenny is still tops on the list."

"Maybe if he'd inherited Jeb's land. But he didn't."

"That doesn't matter. He probably didn't know what Jeb planned any more than you did."

Bart shook his head. "He knew. The thing I can't figure out is why he wasn't more angry about it. He was more upset about me being in the room than about the ranch going to me and my daddy."

Lindsey thought about the smirk on Kenny's face. Bart was right. Kenny knew. And he seemed more amused than upset.

Bart shook his head. "Why the hell would Jeb will the land to Daddy and me? He never cared much for me, and he outright hated my daddy."

"Would your father know why?"

Bart dropped his focus to the carpet. "No."

"Maybe it's something in their history. Maybe your grandfather made them promise to reunite the ranch when one of them died."

"If that's it, we'll never know."

"Why not?"

"My daddy…" He trailed off.

"Your daddy what?"

He shook his head. "Nothing. He won't remember, that's all."

She was pretty sure that wasn't all, but Bart obviously wasn't planning to come across with more. And without knowing more, she would have to take his word that asking his father was a dead end. "If only we knew how the blonde fit into all of this. Or if she fits at all."

"Maybe I could take her picture and ask around."

"That might tell us who she is."

Reconsidering his idea, Bart shook his head. "But it

might also let Hurley Zeller know exactly what we're up to. And we still won't know how she fits in with Kenny's schemes."

"True." She tented her fingers and tapped them against her lips. "So what if we come at this from another angle?"

"What angle would that be?"

"Both Jeb and Kenny were clients of Lambert & Church, right?"

"As far as I know."

"Then what if we have a chat with the lawyer who handled Kenny's criminal case?"

"Can we do that? Isn't there some kind of attorney-client privilege?"

"For the lawyer's dealings with Kenny, there would be. But unless the blonde is a client of Lambert & Church, confidentiality doesn't extend to her."

"Who worked on Kenny's case?"

By the time the question crossed Bart's lips, she was already starting for the door. "Let's find out."

THE WAY OFFICE administrator Nancy Wilks watched over the offices of Lambert & Church reminded Bart of a mother hen keeping tabs on her chicks. She clucked out orders to everyone from employee to partner. She fussed over each detail with motherly intensity. She even bobbed her head when she was upset. She was bobbing her head now as she sorted through a stack of file boxes, her severely cut dark hair swinging against her cheeks. "I swear interns these days have no idea how to file anything. I had a case last week where one filed a brief under the client's first name. Can you imagine?"

Lindsey gave her a nod and an understanding smile. "I have a question for you, Nancy."

"Can it wait until I straighten out this mess?"

"Actually, no."

Nancy dragged in a put-upon breath. "Let me find one thing, and I'll be all yours."

Despite the frustration crawling over his hide, Bart tried to hang on to his patience. No point in getting Nancy's back up. Besides, she seemed like a nice enough person, poultry tendencies aside.

He helped her shove around a few boxes, placing them where she directed. Finally she seemed to locate what she needed. Once she'd finished her business, she lit a cigarette and focused on Lindsey. "Okay, what can I do for you?"

"Do you remember Kenny Rawlins's conviction for fraud?"

"Sure. He was convicted for selling cemetery plots."

Lindsey nodded. "Who acted as his lawyer?"

"It had to have been Andrew. He handled all the criminal work back then."

Bart jolted. "Andrew McGovern?"

"He's the one."

"Damn." There would be no asking Andrew McGovern about the details of Kenny's scam. Not since the mayor had murdered him a month ago.

Lindsey let out a sigh that echoed with the same frustration that wound in Bart's gut. "Thanks, Nancy."

"That's it?"

"That's it. Good luck straightening out the filing system."

"Thanks. It looks like I'm going to need it." She took a drag off her cigarette like she was preparing herself for the ordeal ahead.

They walked back to Lindsey's office. As soon as

they stepped inside, she closed the door behind her and turned those intense blue eyes on him. He could see the wheels turning in that pretty head.

"When I came to Lambert & Church, I took over Andrew's old office and he moved to the annex."

Bart nodded and waited for her to continue.

"He was busy with cases and I was busy studying for the bar, so it took forever to complete the move."

"And?"

"When he died and the annex burned down, some of his personal papers were still in my office."

"Do you have them?"

"No."

He let out a breath.

Lindsey held up a finger, a smile spreading over her lips. "I gave them to his sister, Kelly."

He nodded, his pulse breaking into a jog. Kelly McGovern Lansing wasn't only Andrew's sister, she was Wade Lansing's new wife…and Lindsey's friend.

Lindsey grasped the cordless phone from her desk and punched in a number. She gave Bart a little smile as she listened to the phone ring. "Kelly? It's me, Lindsey. Do you still have those notes of Andrew's I gave you a couple weeks ago? I need to take a look at them, if you don't mind."

IT DIDN'T TAKE Lindsey long to tie up her business in the office. And when Bart offered to give her a ride to Kelly's, she didn't argue. The garage had left a message while she was attending the reading of Jeb's will. They'd replaced the distributor cap and tires, but the new paint job would take longer to complete. Unless she wanted to drive through town with red spray paint slashed across the hood, she wouldn't have a car until tomorrow. Tonight she was stranded. Or she would be if it weren't for Bart.

He pulled the truck to the curb of a little house nestled on a quiet Mustang Valley street and threw it into Park. He climbed from the cab and circled to the passenger side. He held out a hand as Lindsey pushed her door open.

A little feminine shiver rippled through her at the touch of his callused fingers. She gritted her teeth. Wouldn't her brothers love this? Her client helping her from a truck as if she wasn't capable of jumping down herself?

Even so, she had to admit she liked the way Bart held doors open for her, helped her from his truck and took off his hat when she entered a room. She liked the roughness of his fingers and the gentleness of his touch. She liked the scent of fresh air and leather that emanated from him, more seductive than any cologne. As a matter of fact, there seemed to be nothing she *didn't* like about the cowboy.

And that's what drove her craziest of all.

Once her foot hit pavement, she pulled her hand from his grasp and stood on her own two feet. "Thanks for the ride. Kelly said she'd give me a lift back to my apartment."

"I can wait until you're done."

She drew another breath. As much as she wanted him to stay, she knew she needed to be away from him now. She needed to be on her own. "Not necessary. Kelly said she's dropping by Hit 'Em Again later to pick up Wade. My apartment isn't far out of her way. Really."

"All right. But if you get in trouble, I expect you to use that little cell phone of yours to give me a call."

She couldn't keep the tension from creeping up her

spine at his words. But if there was anything she'd learned while dealing with her brothers' protective streaks all these years and with Bart's the past couple of days, it was that she could tell him she'd be fine on her own until she was hoarse and it wouldn't make a difference. He would still hover. He would still worry. He would still believe she couldn't take care of herself. "I'll call if I need you."

"Promise?"

"I promise."

"And if you learn anything from the files—"

"You'll be the first to know."

A grin spreading across his face, he circled to the driver's door, climbed into the truck and waited until she entered the little house.

As soon as Lindsey stepped inside, Kelly, wearing a Hawaiian shirt that set off the blue of her eyes, swept her upstairs. "It took some digging, but I found Andrew's papers."

"Thanks, Kell. I owe you one."

"Don't be silly. What are friends for?" She shook her blond head and waved Lindsey into the master bedroom. Sparsely furnished with only a bed and a single dresser, the room was stacked with open boxes. "I'm still moving in. With everything that's happened and the wedding and Wade training Jerry to run Hit 'Em Again while we're on our honeymoon, we haven't had much time to unpack."

To Lindsey's amazement, Cara, the newshound, sat among the boxes in the middle of the floor, a folder open in her hands. A stack of folders and legal pads perched on a box next to her, obviously already perused. She looked up at Lindsey through her red curls. "Hey, Lindsey. Have a seat. These are a lot more interesting than trying to decide what image Kelly should project on her honeymoon."

Lindsey's stomach clenched. She shot Kelly an alarmed glare.

Kelly held up her hands in front of her as if to ward off the look. "She was here when you called. She helped me dig out the box. She had to look at the notes. You know Cara."

Lindsey knew Cara, all right. That's what had her worried. "You can't write about anything you've found in that box."

"Why not?"

"Have you ever heard of attorney-client privilege?"

"Have you ever heard of freedom of the press?"

"Have you ever heard of getting me in a lot of trouble at the firm? Maybe even with the state bar?"

"They aren't official legal files, Lindsey. Just Andrew's private notes."

"Depending on what's in them, they could be classified as attorney work product."

Cara closed the file in her hands. "I never thought of it that way. I'm sorry, Lindsey. I'd never do anything purposely to get you in trouble."

Lindsey plunked onto the floor beside her friend. "I know."

Kelly sat cross-legged beside them. "Cara got the papers from me, and I'm not bound by any kind of attorney-client privilege. Doesn't that count for anything?"

"Not really, since I gave them to you in the first place." Lindsey looked at the stack with dismay. There was no sense in being upset with Cara or Kelly. The situation was her fault.

"Hey, it's understandable, Lindsey," Kelly said. "The past few weeks have been tough for all of us."

Especially Kelly. She'd found the man of her dreams, but she'd also lost her brother. Lindsey laid a supportive hand on her shoulder.

Cara tapped the folder in her lap. "I won't write about any of this unless I can verify it through another source. And at that point, who's to say where I uncovered the idea originally?"

Lindsey nodded. Cara wouldn't violate her ethics any more than Lindsey could violate her own.

"Are we all friends again?" Kelly asked.

Lindsey looked at the two women next to her. She'd had friends back in Boston. But those friendships had mostly been based on family ties and political influence. Her friendships with Kelly and Cara weren't like that. Even though the two of them had been buddies since childhood, as soon as they'd met Lindsey, they'd opened their arms to her without reservation. And since then, the threesome had formed a strong bond simply because they liked and respected each other. Friendship for friendship's sake. "Of course we're friends."

"How about a hug then?" Kelly reached out her arms.

They rose to their knees, put their arms around each other and hugged. When they finally sat back on the floor, all three had tears in their eyes.

Cara was the first to recover. "Well, now that we have that out of the way, let me show you what I found." She reached for a file marked *Rawlins,* flipped the manila cover open, pulled out several pages and handed them to Lindsey.

Lindsey skimmed the pages. "These look like stories."

Cara nodded, her eyes bright. "Local legends, actually. Most of them are about Shotgun Sally."

Lindsey remembered Bart mentioning that Kenny had tried to pass off the Bar JR as Shotgun Sally's original homestead.

"Here. You've got to read this one." Kelly plucked one of the legends from the pile and slipped it in front of Lindsey's nose.

She started to read. In the legend, Shotgun Sally was a lawyer back when women weren't yet allowed to join the Texas bar. When a cowboy named Zachary Gale was wrongly accused of murder, Sally stood up to defend him when no one else would. And she fell in love with him. Believing in him and laying her life on the line, Sally finally saved Zachary from hanging. And at the end of the story, married to the cowboy she loved, Sally became the first female lawyer to officially pass the Texas bar.

"Sounds a little like you and your good-looking cowboy, Bart Rawlins, don't you think?" Cara's eyes twinkled with humor.

Heat crept up Lindsey's neck and pooled in her cheeks. She remembered the look Cara had given her and Bart in the alley. If her attraction to Bart was that obvious, she was in trouble. "That's ridiculous. He's my client."

"Client, schmient. He's hot." A teasing smile curved Cara's lips. "Maybe even hot enough to tempt *you* into his bed?"

"Cara!" Lindsey protested. Her cheeks felt like they'd burst into flame. She never should have confessed to her friends she was still a virgin. That she'd been so busy focusing on her career she hadn't had the time or interest to get involved with a man.

"Don't mind Cara. She's a hopeless matchmaker," Kelly said.

"Hey, I was right about you and Wade, wasn't I?"

Kelly gave Cara a knowing half smile. "Yeah. Even though it took a shotgun to convince him." The two of them broke into laugher.

Lindsey shook her head. She still couldn't believe Kelly had held a shotgun on Wade to get him to agree to marriage—as if he'd really needed convincing. Lindsey was lucky she wasn't defending Kelly in court, too.

"It was Shotgun Sally's blood in me. And now I'm a saloon owner just like Sally." Kelly grinned and lowered one eyelid in a playful wink. "A saloon owner by marriage, anyway."

Lindsey frowned. "I thought Shotgun Sally was a lawyer."

"Actually—" Cara piped in "—she was an investigative reporter. All the other things she did were just covers so she could get her scoop."

"Now you've really confused me."

"Look." Cara spread the pages out on the floor. "There are a dozen or more Sally legends, all of them different. But in each one Sally gets her man, Zachary Gale, and metes out justice on her own terms."

Lindsey nodded. "On her own terms. I can identify with that ambition."

"See? You've been bitten by the Shotgun Sally bug already."

Lindsey looked down at the legends covering the bed. Legends Cara had pulled from a file marked *Rawlins*. "Did you find the legends in that folder originally?"

"Yeah."

"Why would Andrew keep them in a folder marked *Rawlins?*"

"I wondered that same thing," Cara said.

Kelly shrugged.

Lindsey flipped open the file's cover. The rest of the folder seemed to be filled with scribbled notes about the Bar JR. "It doesn't make sense. Unless..."

"Unless what?" Kelly asked.

"Bart said Kenny Rawlins tried a few get-rich-quick schemes to cash in on the Sally legends."

Cara nodded. "I remember. It was before his cemetery plot scam."

"Could the legends have something to do with that?"

Cara tilted her head and regarded the folder. "Maybe. But the rest of the notes don't have anything to do with Kenny's scams."

Kelly compiled the legends into a stack. "Maybe they were just misfiled. Andrew was a wonderful lawyer, but no one in her right mind would describe him as organized."

Lindsey nodded. Maybe Kelly was right. Maybe the legends had found their way into the file through nothing more intriguing than sloppy filing.

"I might know someone who can answer your questions," Cara said. "One of the professors at the community college specializes in local folklore. Della Santoro. If there's any kind of a connection between the Sally legends and the Bar JR or Kenny Rawlins, she would know. You can meet Kelly and me for lunch tomorrow and then I can take you down to the campus and introduce you."

"That would be great, Cara. Thanks." Lindsey took the papers from Kelly and stuffed them back in her briefcase. At least she had a direction.

"No problem. But you have to repay me by answering one question."

Lindsey groaned. "Cara the investigative reporter rears her ambitious head again."

Cara smiled, unfazed. "What were you hoping to find in these files? I know you want to find some dirt on Kenny Rawlins, something to show he killed old Jeb, but what *specifically* are you looking for?"

Lindsey sighed. It probably wouldn't do any harm to tell Cara. And maybe her friend could help. "Off the record?"

"Of course."

"The blonde with Kenny in the alley the other day was also in the bar with Bart the night Jeb was killed. And she was hanging around Jeb before his death. I hoped Andrew's notes could tell me how she's connected."

"You mean Brandy Carmichael?"

"I know Brandy," Kelly said.

Brandy Carmichael. So that was her name. "I thought there was a chance she'd been involved with Kenny in his past scams."

Cara frowned. "I doubt it. Unless the scam had something to do with real estate."

"Real estate?"

Kelly nodded. "Brandy is a real estate broker. She has her own company in Dallas. I met her when I was toying with the idea of going into real estate after college."

Lindsey nodded, her mind whirring with possible implications of this new information. "Thanks. I should have known I could count on you guys."

Kelly grinned. "Like I said before, what are friends for?"

BY THE TIME Kelly dropped Lindsey off at her apartment, it was well past ten o'clock. Except for the low rumble of CNN coming from the open window of one of the ground-floor apartments, the building and surrounding landscaped grounds were silent as death. Other than the news junkie, Lindsey's fellow tenants in the mid-priced eight-unit had either not realized it was one of the rare June nights that was cool enough to do without air-conditioning, or they had turned in early to catch some sleep before work the next day.

Letting herself into the glassed-in foyer, she turned and waved to Kelly, who was waiting at the curb for Lindsey to get safely inside before she drove away. After collecting her mail from the locked box in the foyer, Lindsey climbed the stairs, unlocked the door and slipped into her apartment.

The air was dead and stuffy. Setting her briefcase on the floor and her mail and cell phone on the telephone table in the little alcove just inside the door, she eyed the blinking light on her answering machine. She hit the Play button. Sure enough, there was a call from her brother Cam. Add the call David made to her at work, and that qualified as a call from each of her four big brothers in the past two days. A full-scale barrage. No doubt it would be Mom and Dad's turn to call her tomorrow.

After erasing the calls, she walked to the sliding glass door overlooking the quiet street below, opened it a crack and breathed in the fresh air. There was nothing like fresh air to remind her of all Mustang Valley offered that she couldn't find in Boston. It wasn't that her brothers and parents didn't want what was best for her. The problem was they assumed only *they* could provide it. That she couldn't find it on her own. That she couldn't make it without help.

She strode into her bedroom to change into the New England Patriots T-shirt she always slept in. Slipping the red-white-and-blue-logoed shirt over her head, she laughed. Maybe she'd even trade it in for Dallas Cowboys sleepwear. That would be sure to get her brothers' goat.

And she could imagine the smile on Bart's face.

Cara's comment about Bart tempting her into bed teased at the back of her mind. She shook her head. She couldn't let herself think about Bart as anything but a client. If she wanted to prove herself, she had to confine her thoughts to the framework of his case.

After washing her face and brushing her teeth, she padded back into the living room to lock the patio door before she went to sleep. She had another long day ahead. Hopefully her meeting with Della Santoro and an investigation into Brandy Carmichael's real-estate business would yield results. If not, she didn't know where to turn.

She closed and locked the sliding glass door. She had just flipped off the lights when a thud caught her attention.

Her heart lodged in her throat.

Someone was in her apartment. Someone—images of paint, red as blood, flashed through her mind. She had to get out of here. She had to call for help.

As quietly as she could, she padded for the door. If she could wake one of her neighbors, use their phone—

A dark shadow lurched toward her from the alcove.

Panic shot through her. She threw up her arms, trying to protect herself, trying to fend off the assault.

Something hard and flat hit her.

She stumbled backward, grabbing the wall to keep herself from falling.

Another blow landed against her head.

She hit the phone table and crumpled to the floor, mail scattering on the tile around her.

CHAPTER SEVEN

LINDSEY CURLED INTO a ball on the cold tile, her arms shielding her face. Her pulse thundered in her ears. She was afraid to move, afraid to breathe.

The shadow loomed over her. A man. He clutched her briefcase in his fist.

She braced herself for another blow.

But instead of hitting her, he spun and bolted for the door. Throwing it open, he dashed into the hall. Heavy footfalls echoed the length of the hall and down the stairs. The thump blended with the frantic beat of her heart.

He could have killed her.

She struggled to her feet. Her legs wobbled. Her stomach rolled. Grasping the wall, she struggled to rein in her panic.

The table in the little alcove lay on its side. The mail she'd gotten from her box was scattered upon the floor. The telephone lay next to her cell phone. And judging from its broken casing, her answering machine was history.

Her briefcase. It was gone. The intruder had hit her with it and taken it with him. Was that what he was after? Was that why he'd broken into her apartment? She didn't buy for a moment that this was a simple burglary. He hadn't gone near the television or expensive stereo equipment her brothers had given her for a passing-the-bar gift. He'd sneaked into her apartment for something specific. And as far as she could tell, the only thing he'd taken was her briefcase.

Hands shaking, she picked up the cell phone. She needed to call the sheriff's office, tell them someone had broken into her apartment, attacked her, stolen her briefcase. But somehow she couldn't force her fingers to punch 9-1-1. She couldn't deal with Hurley Zeller's cruel laugh and mind games. Not when she was feeling so vulnerable. Not when she was feeling so weak.

Bart.

He'd told her to call if she needed him. And she needed him now. Needed to hear his voice, needed to see the strength in his eyes, needed his warm arms to fold around her and stop her from shaking.

She found his number in the Mustang Valley directory and punched in his number with trembling fingers. The line rang, pulsing in her ear.

Finally his sleepy voice answered. "Hello?"

"Bart—" A frightened sob stuck in her throat and cut off her breath.

"Lindsey? What's wrong?"

Her mind whirled with relief, with fear, with confusion. She struggled to find the words to tell him what had happened—struggled and lost. "I—I need you."

"I'll be right there."

BART HADN'T HIT ninety on the highway leading to Mustang Valley since he was seventeen and driving his dad's old Ford pickup. But he buried the needle now.

The fear in Lindsey's voice when she called had hit him like a kick to the gut. Her voice had sounded so small, so vulnerable, so afraid. His first response had been to get to her as fast as he could, to pull her into his arms and make her safe. His second was to kill whomever had made her sound that way.

He roared onto Main Street and checked his speed. Thank the good Lord, the town's sidewalks rolled up by nine o'clock during the workweek. Once he passed Hit 'Em Again, the street was clear until he made the turn that led to Lindsey's apartment complex.

The street outside her building was quiet. No deputy in sight. Damn that Hurley Zeller. If he'd been protecting Lindsey like he'd promised—

Bart shook his head, cutting off the thought. It didn't matter what Hurley was up to. Bart was here now. And he'd damn well make sure Lindsey was okay. And that she stayed that way.

He pulled to the curb, switched off the engine and threw open the door. Boot heels echoing on pavement, he dashed to the front door and hit the doorbell button next to her last name.

"Bart?" Lindsey's shaky voice filtered through the speaker.

Relief tumbled through him. "It's me, darlin'."

"Second floor, apartment B." She buzzed him in.

He raced to the top of the stairs and found her door. She opened it before he had the chance to knock.

Her face was pale and she clutched the doorjamb for support. But she wasn't bleeding. She wasn't hurt.

Bart stepped into the apartment and gathered her into his arms.

Her body trembled against him. Her arms tightened around him. She felt as substantial as a flower, as delicate as a petal. Her lips pressed against his neck, right above his shirt collar. "I know I should have called the sheriff, but I just couldn't."

"I'm here. I've got you." He rubbed his hand over the

length of her back and kissed her hair. "Tell me what happened."

"Someone broke into my apartment. When I spotted him, he hit me with my briefcase and ran."

Rage twisted in Bart's gut. What kind of a coward would hit a woman? If he got his hands on the son of a bitch— He forced himself to take a deep breath. "All I know is, I'm awful glad you're okay. You could have been killed." His voice cracked. His chest tightened. Even hearing those words come from his own lips was too much.

Lindsey pulled back and looked up at him. Her eyes locked with his.

He smoothed her satin cheek with his fingers, wanting to reassure himself she was all right. Wanting to feel her, to smell her, to draw her in. Tilting her head back, he lowered his head and fitted his mouth to hers.

She tasted like warm honey and smelled like roses. He pulled her closer, joining his tongue with hers, soaking in the feel of her, the heat of her, until he was drunk with the contact.

He'd wanted this so much. Ever since she'd walked into the county jail with that classy lift to her chin and raw determination in her eyes. She was his lawyer. He was accused of murder. Nothing could ever come of this, but he wanted it all the same. Wanted the heat of her, the taste of her. Wanted to hold her in his arms and be her hero.

He wanted Lindsey.

And she needed him. She circled his neck with her arms, pulling him closer, deeper into the kiss. Her thighs brushed against his.

Heat shot straight to his groin. What he wouldn't give to carry her to bed, strip her clothes off and run his hands over every inch of that smooth skin. He stepped farther into the apartment, pulling her with him. Something crunched under his boot.

He drew back from the kiss and looked down. A smattering of letters and a mail-order catalog were strewn across the floor. A battered answering machine lay on the tile, its plastic casing in shards under his feet.

A groan of pleasure died in his throat. What was he thinking? Lindsey was attacked here tonight. She could have been hurt. She could have been killed. She needed him, all right. But not to kiss her, not to make love to her. She needed him to keep her safe.

He looked up, peering into the intense blue of her eyes. "Pack your things."

A little crease formed between her elegant eyebrows. "My things?"

"You're moving out to the ranch."

THROUGH THE ARDUOUS process of filling out a police report about the break-in and the long drive to the Four Aces Ranch, Lindsey tried to silence the nagging voice of doubt whispering in her ear.

The effort was a waste of time.

She'd moved to Mustang Valley to be self-sufficient, to build a career and a life on her own, and she'd already blown it. Big-time. She might be able to take care of herself when her life was well ordered and predictable, but as soon as something out of the ordinary happened, she needed a big strong cowboy to save her.

And Bart Rawlins was definitely the man who fit that bill.

She stared at the lines of fence and juniper groves whizzing past the truck window, drew in a deep breath of fresh country air and tried to purge memories of his strong, safe arms and passionate kiss from her mind.

It was no use.

But even though his arms had sent a thrill through her body as strong and jolting as an electric shock, and his kiss had caused her whole system to overheat, she couldn't let the sensations short-circuit her mind. She was a lawyer. A professional. And Bart was her client. She had fallen into the role of damsel in distress tonight, but that didn't mean it would happen again. And even though she'd agreed out of fear to stay at the Four Aces Ranch, nothing had changed. She wanted to kiss him. Heck, she wanted more than a kiss. But she hadn't gotten where she was by giving in to sexual attraction every time it heated her blood. She would handle her attraction to Bart the way she'd always handled the appeal of sexy men. By ignoring it.

The truck passed under the archway proclaiming the Four Aces Ranch and rattled through the open gate designed to keep cattle inside. Lindsey glanced at Bart, his face illuminated in the dashboard's glow, his head bobbing slightly in time with Merle Haggard on the CD player. She looked ahead at the sprawling white house and ranch buildings crowning the top of the hill. The ranch was as quiet as the last time she'd visited. All the lights in the apartments, barns and the bunkhouse were dark. The only sign of life was a single light blazing from the main house.

As if following her gaze, Bart's eyes flicked over the house before landing on her. "Someone must be up."

"Your father?"

"Or Beatrice."

"The nurse?"

Nodding, he swung the truck into the driveway

leading to the house and pulled in front of the garage. Switching off the ignition, he turned to her. "It's been a rough day. Let's get you settled so you can get some sleep."

He climbed out of the truck and circled behind. When he joined her at the passenger side, he was carrying her suitcases. She held out her hand for them.

He looked down at her open palm. "Don't be ridiculous. What kind of a man would I be if I let a lady carry her own bags?"

"I can do it."

"I know you can. But that doesn't mean I'm going to let you." He strode away, leaving her to catch up.

The main house was a rambling affair, the kind she'd seen on television westerns. The long roofline was broken by half-a-dozen dormer windows. On the main floor, double-hung windows peered out on a wood porch that ran the length of the structure.

Bart led her to a side door instead of continuing down the porch to the main entrance. "I'd bring you through the front door, but around these parts, the only people who use them are the politicians."

"The only thing worse than lawyers."

"Damn straight."

She followed him inside, smiling. She liked that he took her through the door he regularly used himself.

The door opened into a utility area connected to the kitchen. As soon as they stepped inside, a rough voice echoed through the dark hall. "Where's my money?"

Lindsey followed Bart into the kitchen. Although a light glowed from somewhere deep in the house, this room was dark. He flicked on the light. At the table sat a man almost as tall and probably once as strapping as Bart. But time had obviously taken its toll on his body, leaving him bony instead of lean, worn instead of vital. He frowned at Bart, confusion pinching his bushy gray brows. "Who the hell are you? Did you steal my money?"

Bart walked over to him and laid a gentle hand on his shoulder. "Your money is in the bank, Daddy. It'll always be there, whenever you need it."

"Then give it to me. I can't even buy a newspaper around here."

Bart glanced at Lindsey. She remembered him mentioning he hadn't told his father about Jeb's death. He probably didn't want him to see a newspaper, either. The last thing the older man needed was to read in a headline that his brother was dead and his son was accused of his murder. Especially if he was confused in the first place.

"I'll get you a newspaper, Daddy."

Bart's father looked at him with blank eyes, as if his demand for a newspaper had already slipped away. "Where's Abby?"

Bart's lips tightened with obvious pain. "Mama is gone."

"When she gets back, tell her I need more socks."

"I will." He smiled and patted his father's shoulder. "Daddy? This is Lindsey. She's a friend of mine."

The older man squinted at her.

"Nice to meet you, Mr. Rawlins." She held out a hand to shake.

He stared at it, as if he didn't know what the gesture meant. "This morning Abby made me scrambled eggs. I love scrambled eggs."

"That was Beatrice," Bart corrected, his voice patient.

"Who?"

"Beatrice. Your nurse. She's the one who made you the scrambled eggs."

"Abby makes the best scrambled eggs."

Bart sighed. "Mama always knew just how to take care of you, didn't she?"

"I'm tired."

"Why don't you go back to bed then? What were you doing sitting in the dark anyway?" Bart looked down a long hallway on the other side of the spacious family room. "Is Beatrice here?"

His father stared at him. "Who the hell is Beatrice?"

"Somebody has to get you to bed." Bart let out a heavy sigh and glanced at Lindsey, as if asking her to excuse him.

She nodded her go-ahead.

He helped his father up from the table.

"I'll take him, Bart." A soft Southern accent drifted through the room. Standing at the mouth of the hallway was an equally soft-looking woman. Pleasantly plump, with gray hair framing a wide face, the woman shuffled into the room in a blue housecoat. Her sharp blue eyes focused on Lindsey.

"Lindsey, this is Beatrice."

Lindsey returned the woman's smile. As soon as they exchanged introductions and pleasantries Beatrice looped her arm around Bart's father and ushered him down the hall.

Bart turned to Lindsey. "Now let's get you upstairs."

"It must be tough for you."

He looked at her like he had no idea what she was talking about.

"Him not remembering you. It must be tough."

"Sometimes. Truth is, he hasn't remembered me for a long time. I'm kind of used to it."

"He has Alzheimer's disease, doesn't he?"

A muscle in Bart's cheek flinched. He lowered his eyelids and nodded.

"I'm sorry."

He swallowed hard and shook his head. Stepping to the table, he picked up the suitcases. "Let me show you where you'll be staying."

She could understand his reluctance to talk about his dad. Just seeing Hiriam Rawlins tonight, she could get a sense of the man he used to be. The man who was fading away bit by bit. But she couldn't truly understand the pain of watching that horrible disease ravage someone she loved. She hoped she would never truly understand that.

She rose from her chair and followed Bart up the stairs to the second floor. The hallway ran the length of the house, at least a half-dozen doors opening onto it. "This house is huge. How many bedrooms are up here?"

"Five bedrooms, two baths. And there are two bedroom suites downstairs."

"Do you have a lot of brothers and sisters?"

"Nope. Just me. My parents wanted a whole houseful, but after I was born, my mama couldn't have any more. I always hoped I would fill these rooms with kids someday." A bittersweet smile flickered over his lips before he turned and walked halfway down the hall.

Lindsey followed, Bart's yearning and regret ringing in her ears.

He halted at a closed door. Using his elbow, he pushed the door open, then stepped to the side so she could enter. The room was spacious and airy. The yard light streamed in through two oversize dormer windows dressed with a pretty chintz fabric. Between the windows, a wide bed stood, piled with pillows and covered with a handmade quilt of the same chintz. Sweet and comfortable and just a little feminine. Even though the room was worlds apart from the sleek, contemporary house she grew up in, it felt like home. "It's beautiful."

"My mama. She could have decorated for one of those fancy home magazines, I swear."

"I bet she could have."

Bart shifted his feet, boot soles scuffing on the hardwood floor. There was pain in his mother's memory, too. So much sorrow.

"How did she die?"

"Doctors say it was heart failure."

"And you don't believe the doctors?"

He didn't answer.

"What do you think it was?"

"It might sound sappy, but I'd say her heart broke."

Her own heart pinched. "Your father's illness?"

He set her suitcases down and plucked his hat from his head. He ran his fingers over the brim as if intent on checking its shape. "She always believed he'd get better. Like if she waited long enough and loved him hard enough, the disease would give up its hold. I think when it became clear he was never going to improve, she lost the will to go on."

The sadness in his voice seeped into her soul. She ached to wrap her arms around him, to hold him, to kiss him, to make his pain go away. The way he'd held her earlier tonight until she'd stopped shaking. The way he'd kissed her until his strength had made her whole. She barely stopped herself from reaching out to touch him.

"I'm sorry about your parents," she whispered lamely. "I'm so sorry."

He pressed his lips together in a sad smile. "Me, too."

"I wish I could do something."

"You can't. No one can." Leaning forward, he fitted his hat on his head and peered at her from under the brim. "I'm glad you're here, Lindsey. And I'm glad you're safe. If you need me, I'll be in the next room."

The next room. Images bombarded her. His broad chest naked. His long, bare legs tangled in the sheets. His strong arms open and waiting for her to crawl into them. She took a deep breath and ruthlessly pushed the visions from her mind.

But she couldn't push away his quiet anguish over his father's illness and his regret for the empty bedrooms he'd hoped to fill with children. Nor could she banish the ache she'd seen in his eyes as he told her of his mother's death. And his mother's love.

She might be able to fight her physical desire for him. She might even be able to ignore it. But she couldn't ignore his vulnerability. His decency. The real man with secret dreams and secret pains. She closed her eyes and willed herself to stay rooted to the spot.

"Good night." His low drawl washed over her like a warm Texas breeze.

She summoned a deep breath. "Good night."

She didn't open her eyes, not when she heard his footfalls move into the hall, not when he closed the door softly behind him. It was only when he was safely on the other side of that oak barrier that she allowed herself to stare at the door.

Staying at the Four Aces was going to be harder than she'd ever imagined.

CHAPTER EIGHT

THE MORNING SUN stretched through the kitchen window and fell on the side of Lindsey's face, making her skin and hair glow with the soft light of an angel. "More coffee?" She held up the pot.

Bart tore his eyes away. Picking up his cup, he thrust it toward her. God knows, he needed the caffeine. Though he couldn't say if his lapse into staring had more to do with his sleepless night or the awe that something as exquisite as Lindsey Wellington was under his roof.

"I talked to the sheriff's office this morning about the break-in at my apartment."

"Let me guess, the deputy in charge of the case is Hurley Zeller."

"How did you guess?"

He blew out a disgusted breath. "And did he find anything?"

"Not yet."

"Don't hold your breath."

She gave him a somber smile. "How early did you get up?"

"I look that tired, huh?" He concentrated on watching her graceful hand pour steaming coffee into his cup.

"You should have woke me. I would have helped with chores. I have plenty of experience feeding horses and mucking stalls."

"Pony Club, right?"

She smiled. "How early?" she repeated, as if the answer was important.

"Sunrise. Not any earlier than usual." Hell, who was he trying to kid? He had gone out to the barns around sunrise, but he hadn't fallen asleep all night. He'd spent the hours listening for Lindsey's quiet breathing in the next room and wishing he was in that big bed alongside her, instead of hunkered down in his own room. Alone.

"Is your father up yet?"

"He usually sleeps late and through anything. Especially when he's been knocking around the house in the middle of night." He glanced down the hallway that led to his dad's rooms. When he turned back to Lindsey, she was watching him intently. As if she could see straight through him and into his heart. He forced a chuckle. "So how are we going to keep my hide out of prison today?" He meant the comment as a joke, but the words fell like a roped-and-tied calf.

"Cara's taking me to visit an expert on local folklore later on."

"Local folklore? Am I missing something?"

She filled him in on the Shotgun Sally legends she, Cara and Kelly had discovered in Andrew's files. But though she didn't seem to be holding back any of the details, the way blood tinged her cheeks when she mentioned the legend about Sally as a lawyer suggested otherwise. "After we talk to her former professor, Cara will take me to the garage to pick up my car. It's supposed to be ready today. But do you have time to drive me into town this morning?" She flinched as she asked, like the question caused her pain.

"I'd be glad to give you a ride. Are just you and Cara going to the college?" Damn. He'd meant to make the question sound innocent, but his concerned tone left little mystery to what he was really thinking. And how worried he really was.

She raised her chin. "I'll be safe. Cara is one tough cookie. And I'm no pushover myself. If anyone messes with us, we'll make him wish he was never born."

"I don't doubt you will." He forced another chuckle, though he was far from convinced. He did know one thing, though. Lindsey Wellington didn't like him worrying about her. Not one damn bit. Too bad backing off wasn't in his nature. "What else are you planning for today?"

Lindsey eyed him warily. "I found out who the blonde is."

He crooked his brows and waited for the punch line.

"Her name is Brandy Carmichael. Cara and Kelly said she's a Realtor. She has a company in Dallas."

"A Realtor? Interesting."

"Interesting that Paul insists he doesn't know her."

He nodded. "It also makes me wonder if Jeb was planning to sell before he died."

"I thought I'd ask Brandy that very question."

"Are you planning to do that with Kelly and Cara?"

"Kelly is getting ready to leave on her honeymoon tomorrow morning. And Cara has work to do. I can't take up all of her day."

The tension was back in his gut. "You planning to go by yourself?"

That pretty chin raised back up a notch.

Tough. "I'll meet you at your office after lunch. We'll go see Miss Brandy together."

Lindsey opened her mouth to protest, then closed

it without uttering a word. As if she could tell arguing
would do no good. Especially when Bart had only to
point to the break-in at her apartment last night to make
his case. Finally she nodded. "Okay. After lunch."

"After lunch." Only a few short hours, but it seemed
like an eternity. An eternity where anything could
go wrong. At least he never promised he wouldn't be
early.

"ARE YOU OKAY?" Blue eyes wide with concern, Kelly
looked at Lindsey like she might keel over at any
moment.

"I'm fine," Lindsey said in what she hoped was a
casual tone. Resisting the urge to touch the scuff on
her chin, she filled her friends in on the events of the
night before, keeping her voice low so none of the other
patrons at the diner could overhear. "The whole ordeal
scared me more than anything."

"No wonder." The news of the intruder in her apartment last night even seemed to shake Cara. "You should
have called us. You could have spent the night at my
place. Where did you sleep? You didn't stay in your
apartment after that attack, did you?"

Lindsey had contemplated not telling her friends for
fear of worrying them. But she'd discarded that idea
before Dot had brought their drinks. Friends didn't hold
things back from one another. Not important things in
their lives, such as this. And truthfully speaking, Lindsey needed to talk to someone about last night. She
could discuss the intruder with Bart, but she could only
talk to her friends about the rest of the night. "I called
Bart Rawlins on my cell phone. He came over."

"And?" Cara prompted.

"He took me back to the Four Aces. I spent the rest of the night there."

A grin broke over Cara's lips. "Hot dog!"

Kelly smiled, shaking her head. "He rescued you? How romantic."

Despite the conflicting feelings waging war inside her, Lindsey couldn't keep the smile from her lips at her friends' enthusiasm. She had to admit last night had seemed like an unreal dream. The intruder. Bart's arms around her, keeping her safe. Going back to the ranch with him. It didn't seem like it really happened until this moment—when she told her friends.

Cara smiled over her drink. "I told you, Lindsey. I know about these things. You should listen to me."

"I hate to disappoint you two, but I slept in an extra bedroom. Nothing happened."

"Too bad," Cara said. "You've got to be more aggressive, Lindsey. Though I doubt Bart will need much of a push. Maybe if you just wander over to his room in the middle of the night. Tell him you were looking for the bathroom."

"Yeah, and do it naked."

"Kelly!" Now Lindsey's cheeks were burning.

"Oh, don't act so offended, Lindsey." Cara was grinning ear to ear. "You want him, that's obvious. So why don't you go for it?"

Cara was half right. Lindsey wanted Bart more than she'd ever believed she could want a man. But she couldn't go for it. For many reasons. "He's my client, for one thing."

"Maybe you have a bit of Shotgun Sally in you, too," Kelly said in a singsong voice.

Cara nodded, her eyes brightening the way they always did when she talked about one of her favorite subjects.

"That's right. In the story where Sally is a lawyer, she saves her love, Zachary Gale, from hanging."

"Maybe it's fate," Kelly added. "The Shotgun Sally legend repeating. Maybe you're meant to be together. He keeps you safe, and you save his life. All the while, falling deeply in love."

Lindsey shook her head at her friends' romanticism. Part of her might want to believe every word they were saying, but the other part was rational. And focused. "I came to Mustang Valley to prove I could make a career—a life—on my own. I've only been here a few weeks and I'm already depending on a man to take care of me. No matter what kind of romantic twist you two give the situation, it's not what I want. I might as well have stayed in Boston under my brothers' protective wings."

Kelly shook her head. "Your brothers and Bart Rawlins are not the same."

Cara nodded. "You can say that again. Nothing against your brothers, since I've never met them, but I don't think Bart is protecting you out of some sense of brotherly responsibility. Or because he doesn't think you can take care of yourself. I think he wants to jump your bones."

Lindsey almost groaned at the teasing, but that would give Cara too much satisfaction. Besides, she could accept the sexual attraction explanation far more readily than talk of fate and true love. So instead of protesting, she nodded her head. "And I want to jump his bones, too. But I can't. Not unless I want to undermine everything I've come to Mustang Valley to build—my independence, my career. So what do I do now?"

Both Kelly and Cara looked at her, as if this time neither had a quick quip or a piece of advice to give.

Finally, Kelly spoke up. "I guess you just wait and see what happens."

Cara nodded. "And get Bart acquitted. No matter what happens, you can't fall in love with him or jump his bones if he's behind bars."

CARA AND LINDSEY made it to the community college right after Professor Della Santoro's lecture ended. They caught the professor outside one of the square, institutional-looking buildings that made up the Mustang Valley Community College campus.

"Cara. It's so nice to see you." Professor Santoro cradled a stack of books in one arm. She reached up with her free hand to brush back a strand of dark hair that had escaped from the neat bun at her nape.

Cara gave the professor a fond smile. "It's nice to see you, too, Della. I've been meaning to ask you to lunch again. Maybe next week?"

"I'll check my calendar. What brings you here today?"

Cara nodded to Lindsey. "My friend Lindsey Wellington. She has a few questions about local legends, and I told her you were the one to ask."

Della Santoro scrutinized Lindsey through silver-framed glasses perched on the end of her nose. "I'd certainly love to help, if I'm able. What local legends are you interested in?"

"Shotgun Sally."

The professor shared smiles with Cara. "Our favorite," the professor said. "And perhaps the most controversial legendary figure in the area."

This was the first time Lindsey had heard of any controversy surrounding Sally. "Controversial? How so?"

"Because there are so many different versions of the Shotgun Sally legend, many people believe she never really lived. That she was actually a composite of many different women."

"But you don't believe that."

"There is ample evidence that she lived. Whether she did all of the things in the legends is another question. The most important thing about Shotgun Sally is that she represented a role model for women in an age where women weren't encouraged to do things like take part in cattle drives or own businesses."

"Or be lawyers," added Lindsey.

"Or muckraking reporters," said Cara with a smile.

Professor Santoro nodded. "Exactly."

Sally was a noble figure, indeed, real or composite. But that didn't address the questions Lindsey had come to ask. "What I'm really interested in is how she's tied to the area. Specifically whether she has anything to do with Jebediah Rawlins, his son Kenny, or the Four Aces Ranch."

The crease deepened between the professor's thin brows. "I'm not sure what you're looking for."

Lindsey gave her a quick description of Andrew's notes about the Bar JR and the legends found among them. "Is there anything that would explain why the legends would be inside that file?"

"As far as I know, Shotgun Sally has no direct link to the Rawlins family."

"Or the land?"

Tapping manicured pink nails on the books in her arms as she walked, Professor Santoro shook her head. "I'm sorry. I don't know what else to tell you."

Cara let out a sigh. "I guess Kelly was right. It must

have been a misplaced file. Or it had something to do with Kenny's penny-ante Shotgun Sally scams."

Frustration settled like a cold lump in Lindsey's stomach. Everything related to this case seemed to be a dead end. And although she really didn't have cause to hope a few legends stuck into Andrew's files had any real significance, she had let herself hope. It just showed how desperate she was.

They reached a low office building at the far end of campus. Della Santoro paused at the base of the steps and motioned to the glass doors with her free hand. "I have office hours now. You're welcome to come in and continue our chat. If you have any other questions, I'd be glad to try to answer them."

Lindsey gave the professor a grateful smile. She'd already wasted enough time hoping a few legends were the key to Bart's case. There was no point in wasting more. "I appreciate the offer, but I'm sure you're plenty busy. Thank you so much for your time."

After Cara also thanked her friend, the professor continued up the stairs and through the door of the building. Lindsey and Cara walked back to Cara's car.

Tilting her curly red head, Cara studied her. "Sorry."

Lindsey forced a shrug. "If there's no connection, there's no connection. I knew it was a long shot."

"What are you going to do next? Off the record."

"Bart and I have an appointment to talk to Brandy Carmichael. I want to see if her connection to Jeb is merely a false lead, too." If it was, Lindsey didn't know what she'd do next.

BART GUIDED HIS truck into the circle cobblestone driveway and eyed the huge white stucco house perched on the tiniest scrap of land he'd ever seen. He glanced at Lindsey sitting in the passenger seat. "I don't understand it."

She furrowed that beautiful brow and looked at him questioningly. "Don't understand what?"

"People who shell out money for a house like this. It might be big and ritzy, but if they flex their elbows, they're in danger of poking their neighbor in the ribs."

She laughed, the musical sound filling the truck's cab. She grabbed the handle of the truck's door. "On that note, let's go in."

Bart frowned at the empty horseshoe driveway. "Are you sure she's here? I don't see a car."

"Her office said she's here. She's supposed to be getting ready for a broker's open house." Lindsey nodded to the red sign in front of the house with the name Brandy Carmichael and Associates printed on it in fancy letters.

"All right." He dismounted from the truck and circled to Lindsey's side. When he reached her, she was already jumping down from the runner. He had to content himself with steadying her when her heels hit the pavement.

They walked to the door together, Bart slowing his stride so he could stay close beside her. Even in the outdoor air, he could smell the scent of roses. It wasn't strong. Not like some women's perfume. Lindsey's scent was subtle, classy. Like the woman herself.

They reached double front doors so grand he felt as small as an awkward boy standing in front of them. He looked around for a side door, but there wasn't one to be had. Not surprising. Anyone who would live in a house with no land to call his own and no connection to the earth that spawned him had probably never used a side door in his life.

Lindsey extended a graceful finger and pressed the bell. A gong sounded from inside. The sound was followed by the clack of heels on marble floor and the door opened.

Brandy Carmichael peered out at them. She looked older than she had in the alley that night, but still every inch the cheerleader. Her bouncy blond hair glistened in the afternoon sun. Red lips stretched into a smile, parting slightly to show the whitest teeth Bart had ever seen. "If it isn't Bart Rawlins and his lawyer..." She paused, waiting for Lindsey to fill in her name.

"Lindsey Wellington."

"Lindsey, of course." Brandy stepped back and swung the door wide. "Don't tell me, you're looking for a house."

Lindsey looked the woman straight in the eye. "We'd like to ask you a few questions."

Brandy's smile didn't fade as she motioned them into a white marble foyer as big as Texas Stadium. "Come inside. Please."

They obliged. She led them through the stadium and into a room with a view of the neighbor's pool. She motioned to a couple of white chairs and perched on a white stool next to a bar that had probably never served something as working-class as a plain old beer. Brandy turned on her smile. "So, Lindsey, how are things at Lambert & Church?"

Lindsey lowered herself into one of the chairs and crossed smooth legs. "Are you familiar with my firm?"

"Let's just say there's a history."

Just what they were looking for, a history. Hopefully

fraudulent and including Kenny. Remaining on his feet, Bart focused on Brandy. "What kind of history?"

"I know Don Church and his wife. And, of course, Paul Lambert." Her voice ran huskily over Paul's name. She shot a sly woman-to-woman look in Lindsey's direction. "Though I can't say I know his wife."

"That's interesting. Because Paul said he doesn't know you."

Brandy's smile seemed to grow wider and more slinky. "Not surprising, considering the circumstances of our many meetings."

"The circumstances?" Lindsey prodded.

"It's a long story. A long, *personal* story. And one I'm sure he doesn't want his wife to know about."

So Paul had had an affair with the ever-fetching Brandy. No wonder he didn't want to own up to knowing her. Bart glanced around the house's interior. "Might as well tell your story. It doesn't look like the good people of Dallas are lining up to buy this monster."

"Some of the top real-estate agents in the area are joining me for cocktails. And don't worry. Once they get a look at this monster, as you put it, they'll be falling all over themselves to tell their clients about it." She lowered one made-up eyelid in a sexy wink and didn't volunteer more.

Just as well. Paul's sordid love life wasn't what they were after anyway. But Brandy's, on the other hand, might yield some answers. "How about Kenny Rawlins? Is there a long, personal story behind your relationship with him?"

"Not as long and not personal at all, thank God."

Lindsey raised a skeptical brow. "The two of you seemed pretty friendly in the alley behind Hit 'Em Again the other night."

"Appearances aren't everything. Listen, I play up to potential clients. That doesn't mean I sleep with all of them." Brandy tilted her head, her smile still in place. "Not Kenny Rawlins, at any rate."

"So he's a potential client?" Lindsey said, not missing a beat.

"I have a buyer who's interested in obtaining a large piece of land in the Dallas/Fort Worth area. The Bar JR fit the bill."

Lindsey nodded. "And Kenny wanted to sell?"

"He and Jeb wanted to sell. I wanted to accommodate them."

A piece fell into place in Bart's mind. The explanation for the photo in the *Mustang Gazette*. Brandy schmoozing a sale. "So what did this accommodation include?"

She frowned like she'd bitten into a sour apple. "Not what you're thinking."

He was thinking murder. But he doubted that was what she was talking about.

"I wanted to list the ranch before my buyer got it in his head to approach Jeb directly. That's it."

"So you want us to believe you were hanging around Jeb, and later Kenny, just to get a listing?" Lindsey asked.

"That's right. If I were a man, you wouldn't even question it."

Lindsey's elegant eyebrows lowered as if she was considering Brandy's statement. "So why were you playing up to Bart at Hit 'Em Again the night Jeb was murdered?"

Brandy turned her white smile on Bart. "That was for pure pleasure."

Lindsey stiffened.

Bart watched Lindsey out of the corner of his eye. After their kiss last night, he'd like to think her reaction to Brandy's quip meant she was jealous. But try as he might, he couldn't see a reason why she should be. Lindsey was so far beyond Brandy's league, it was like comparing Emmitt Smith in his prime to some skinny high school kid who couldn't make junior varsity.

"Of course, Kenny assumed the same thing you're assuming—that I'd sleep with him to get the listing." She shuddered slightly. "It wasn't until after he realized I wasn't going to that he came clean."

"Came clean?" Lindsey prodded.

"He admitted the Bar JR wasn't his problem."

Bart must not have heard her right. "His *problem?*"

"That's right." A smile of realization spread over those red lips. "You don't know, do you?"

"Know what?" Lindsey asked.

"That the Bar JR is mortgaged to the hilt. That the cash you'd get from selling it wouldn't even come close to paying off the debt old Jeb ran up on the place."

The news hit Bart with the force of a mule kick to the head. No wonder Jeb had left the ranch to his dad and him. It made perfect sense. Jeb didn't want to reunite the original ranch. He wanted to saddle them with the tab for the past twenty years of his miserable life. And he knew Bart and his dad would pay that tab rather than give up the land. Bart shook his head, a grin tweaking his lips despite himself. "That crafty old buzzard."

Lindsey focused like a laser on Brandy. "Kenny told you this?"

Brandy nodded. "He laughed about it. Thought it was a big joke that Jeb planned to shift his debt to his brother when he died."

"Why would he tell you this?"

She shrugged. "Once he realized a roll in the hay didn't come with the listing, I guess he wanted to show me how stupid I was for hanging around him when he was dead broke."

"And when did this happen?"

"I don't know. A day or two ago. After Jeb was murdered." Brandy glanced at Bart.

Lindsey leaned forward, bringing the woman's attention back to her. "Was it before yesterday?"

"Before yesterday? You mean, did he know he wasn't going to inherit the ranch before the will was read?"

"Did he?" Bart asked.

"He told me about it the day after the murder. Right after we ran into the two of you in that alley behind the bar. He said you were as stupid as me." She gave a dry laugh. "Nice guy, your cousin."

The mule kicked again. Kenny was a nice guy all right. And now they couldn't prove that nice guy had any reason to kill Jeb.

Beside him, Lindsey seemed to droop. She held out a hand to Brandy. "Thank you for your time."

"No problem. Say hello to Paul for me, would you?" She winked again. "Oh, and Don, too."

After Bart shook Brandy's hand, as well, they left the mansion and started walking back to the truck. Bart's gut churned with acid. "So much for our notions about Kenny. If he knew the ranch was worthless and he knew he wasn't going to inherit it anyway, he had no reason to kill Jeb. Other than the fact that Jeb was a miserable old bastard and the world would be better without him, of course. But everyone in town had that motive."

"Not so fast." Lindsey stopped in her tracks and turned wide eyes on Bart.

Bart's muscles tensed the way they always did when he sensed the cattle were about to make a break for it. "What?"

"If you are convicted, what would you do with the Four Aces?"

"I suppose I'd have to sell. Gary is aching to retire from the ranching business. So without me, there would be no one to run the Four Aces. Besides, I'd need the money to take care of Daddy."

"So you'd sell the ranch and put the proceeds in a trust for your father?"

"That's how Don set up my will if I died, so I guess that's how I'd have him handle it if I was convicted, too."

She pressed her lips together, deep in thought. "And if something were to happen to your father before you went to trial?"

His tension ratcheted up a notch. "I suppose I'd still have to sell the Four Aces."

"And the Bar JR?"

"Daddy's will leaves everything to me." Maybe her point was as clear as the broad side of a barn, but he couldn't see it. "Even if I was convicted and something happened to my daddy, both ranches would just go back to me."

"The Four Aces would."

"But not the Bar JR?"

"That's what I'm telling you. If you're convicted of Jeb's death, Texas law says you can't inherit Jeb's land."

That barn was broad, all right, and it was staring him in the face. "Then the Bar JR would go to Kenny. And by the time I came to trial and was convicted, Jeb's debt would already be settled."

She nodded.

Dread plowed into Bart's gut. "But he would only get his hands on the Bar JR if I was convicted…and Daddy was dead."

CHAPTER NINE

"DADDY!" BART RACED into the kitchen with Lindsey on his heels. Lindsey had used her cell phone to call the house and barn numbers repeatedly on the hour drive from Dallas. No one had answered. Still, he'd hoped by the time they'd gotten to the ranch, Beatrice would be back from a simple grocery shopping trip, his father in tow.

No such luck.

The house was dead quiet. No sign of his father. No sign of Beatrice. He raced down the hall to his dad's bedroom, his boots thundering on the wood floor. Maybe he'd find him taking an uncharacteristic afternoon nap. Maybe all his worry was for nothing.

He threw open the door. In the dim light, he could see the plain, dark spread smoothed over the bed. Untouched since morning. He spun around and started for the bathroom. "Daddy?" He pounded on the door, the wood trembling under his fist. "Daddy? Are you in there?"

No answer.

He turned the knob and pushed the door open. Holding his breath, he looked to the floor first.

White tile gleamed back at him. A quick glance around the empty room yielded nothing. No body, no blood, no Daddy.

He crossed the hall and knocked on Beatrice's door. No answer there, either.

"Maybe Beatrice took him somewhere," Lindsey said from behind him. "The doctor's office? The barber? Did she say anything to you or write his schedule on a calendar?"

Bart forced his mind to slow down. He had to concentrate. "I don't know. I don't remember." Damn him for not keeping better track of what his father was doing.

"You've had a few things on your mind. Like being accused of murder."

"That's no excuse. If anything happens to Daddy…"

"Can you reach Beatrice? Does she have a cell phone? Someone who would know where she might be?"

What was wrong with him? Why hadn't he thought of that before? "She doesn't carry a cell phone. But she does have a sister."

He found a phone and a phone book and punched in the number.

On the other end of the line, the phone picked up on the second ring. "Hello?" Beatrice's sister's cigarette-roughened voice carried over the line.

"Mary. It's Bart. Is Beatrice there?"

"Bart? Why would Beatrice be here?"

"Because she's not here. And neither is my dad."

"You're at the Four Aces?"

"Yes."

"Odd. Beatrice said she was going to be home all day. In case I wanted to call and chat."

Bart's heart froze. "Are you sure about that?"

"Yes, I'm sure. What's going on, Bart? You're scaring me."

He was scaring himself, too. His dad was confused,

weak, helpless. He couldn't fight for himself. Hell, he didn't even know who he was half the time. And Beatrice. She was missing, too. Pressure bore down on his head until he thought his skull would split. He managed to mumble a few reassurances to Mary and dropped the phone into its cradle.

Lindsey touched his arm. "We'll find them."

"If anything has happened to my daddy and Beatrice, I'll kill Kenny with my bare hands."

"Do you want me to call the sheriff?"

"Would you?" As if it would do a damn bit of good. Hurley Zeller was more concerned about convicting Bart than finding the truth or protecting the public. And Sheriff Ben was too busy starting his campaign to replace the mayor to do his current job. He handed her the phone and headed for the door. He couldn't rely on the sheriff. He had to do everything he could to find his dad and Beatrice. And he had to do it now.

Bart reached the barn just as Gary and a new hand rode up. He flagged the foreman down. "Daddy's gone. Did you see anything the last hour or two? Anyone creeping around the house that shouldn't be?"

A stricken look spread over Gary's face. "Kenny."

Bart's pulse raced. "You saw Kenny?"

"I ran him off. About the time you left for town. I can't believe he'd do something to your daddy."

"Your daddy? Older man, a little shorter than me?" Tall, thin and strong as a steel fence post, the new hand riding with Gary wasn't old enough to grow a mustache. Though from the look of it, he was giving it a damn noble attempt.

"Did you see my daddy?"

The kid used his tongue to tuck his chaw into a cheek and spat into the dirt. "I seen an old man east of here when I was out looking for strays. Down by Shotgun Creek."

Bart lunged forward. "Wearing jeans and a—" He paused and tried to picture what his dad had been wearing this morning. "Blue button-down shirt?"

The kid nodded. "And a Dallas Cowboys cap."

That was him. It had to be. "Was anyone with him?"

The kid shook his head.

"He was alone?"

"Far as I could tell. He acted kind of strange. Said he didn't need or want my help. Called me Jeb."

"That's him." Wandering by himself. Maybe someone hadn't kidnapped him. Maybe whoever was behind this just let him out of the house and let his dad's confused mind do the rest. But if that was the case, what had happened to Beatrice? "What time did you see him?"

"'Round noon, I guess."

Just after Gary saw Kenny at the ranch. Damn. His daddy could have wandered miles by now. Bart focused on Gary. "How many hands are here right now?"

"Three, counting me and Billy. The rest are vaccinating calves in the south pasture."

Only three. Not enough to do a sweep of thirty thousand acres, that was for damn sure. "Take the horses down to the creek and look around the spot where Billy here saw him last." Bart glanced at the helicopter sitting out on the ranch's makeshift helipad.

"You taking the Enstrom?" Gary asked.

"Damn straight. Is it topped off?" Bart had used the helicopter in the south pasture this morning to round up cows and their new calves for vaccinations.

Gary nodded. "It's ready to go. But there's supposed to be a storm west of here, moving in slow."

Bart checked the horizon. Sure enough, the dark shadow of rain clouds topped the gently rolling hills. "Then we'd better get a move on. I sure as hell don't want Daddy wandering out there in a thunderstorm."

Gary nodded again. "I'll get the other hand." Gary set a spur into his mare's side and sent her loping for the corral. Billy followed on his big gelding. They'd be out on the range before Bart got the helicopter's engine idling.

He strode for the helipad. He always kept the copter in working order, fueled up and ready to go, whether they were using it to gather cattle to pasture or not. Even after spring roundup, he had to search for breaks in fence and monitor the streams and rivers running through the pastures during summer droughts. And you never knew when an emergency might crop up.

Like now.

Lindsey raced out of the house and joined him at the helipad. "A deputy's on his way."

"One of the hands saw Daddy wandering toward Shotgun Creek a few hours ago. No one was with him."

"So he wasn't kidnapped?"

"Doesn't appear so. Someone just let him out of the house and watched him disappear." Anger and dread mixed with the nausea swirling in his gut. "He'll never remember how to get back to the house."

"What about Beatrice?"

"No sign of her."

"I told the sheriff she was missing, too."

"Good." Bart tried to push away his worry. He sure as hell hoped the sheriff could find her, because he didn't have the first idea where to look. He directed his thoughts to his daddy out on the range. Helpless. Probably afraid. Bart had to find him.

He climbed into the helicopter and started the engine. It roared to life, the sound bouncing off nearby barns. Overhead, the rotor was still, the engine only idling at the moment.

Eyeing the craft, Lindsey set her chin, circled to the opposite side and opened the door.

What she intended suddenly came clear to Bart. "Where do you think you're going?" he yelled above the roar.

"With you."

He shook his head. "Stay here. The hands went with Gary to look for my daddy. You need to wait for the sheriff."

She held up her little phone. "I'll call and fill him in about the cowboy seeing your father by the creek." She punched in the number and did just that as Bart performed a hurried series of safety checks. After turning off the phone, she climbed into the chopper.

Bart glanced at the storm on the horizon before turning a frown in her direction. "You can't go with me, Lindsey. It's not safe. Flying a helicopter is dangerous in the kind of weather that's blowing in."

"You need help."

"No."

Her eyes sharpened. "You don't want me staying here by myself, do you? Kenny or whoever let your father out on the range might still be around."

He pressed his lips into a line. Damn. He knew she was playing him, but the hell of it was, she was right. He couldn't leave her at the ranch alone. "You don't give up, do you?"

"Not when I know I'm right."

He looked out at the dark horizon. Sucking in a breath, he forced himself to nod. "Strap yourself in."

She fastened her safety harness. Glancing at her, he slipped on his headphones and motioned for her to do the same. Then he started the rotors.

He increased power, set the antitorque pedals and centered the cyclic. As he increased power further, the helicopter began to lift off the skids. He made more adjustments and brought the craft up about eighty feet into a hover. Scanning the horizon, he moved the cyclic forward and headed in a different direction from where Gary and the hands rode out. It was just a guess, but if Daddy had called the kid Jeb, there was a chance his mind had gone back to his childhood. That might mean he was doing something he and Jeb loved to do as kids. And exploring the banks of the Brazos River topped the list. It was worth a shot anyway. Bart was damn short on other ideas.

And on time.

He tapped Lindsey on the shoulder and pointed to a set of binoculars he kept in the craft to spot stray cattle or broken fence. She grabbed them and raised them to her eyes. Bart trained his own eyes on the land ahead of them. Swells of grassland stretched to the horizon. In the middle of the land, the Brazos River slithered between hills like a silver snake.

His dad was down there. Lost. Confused. They had to find him. Before the storm rolled in. Before he hurt himself.

Before it was too late.

A flash along the dark horizon caught his eye. He studied an ominous storm cloud. Another bolt of lightning followed the first. Judging from the way the cloud blotted out the afternoon sun, it wasn't a gentle storm. Not a storm he should be flying a helicopter into, that was for damn sure.

And not a storm a confused old man should be wandering around in alone.

They flew low, skimming over the ground at about a hundred feet. Over prairie and creek, woodland and river. Bart pointed out groves of mesquite, so Lindsey could study them more closely. In some spots, the scrub trees grew so thick it would be easy for a cowboy to lose half-a-dozen steers behind a thicket of gnarled branches, let alone one man.

"There he is." Lindsey's voice reverberated in his headset. She pointed to a rough area near the river.

He followed her outstretched finger. Sure enough, a small blue speck was picking his way through rock and mesquite. Bart scanned the area for a place to set down the helicopter. The top of the swell, before the land sloped to the river, was his best bet. From there, they would have to backtrack, fighting through scrub to reach his dad. It would take time, but he had no choice. They couldn't land on mesquite. He moved the cyclic in the direction of the swell.

A light flickered inside the craft.

Heart jolting into his throat, he looked down. The fuel-pressure light glowed orange.

Adrenaline flooded his bloodstream. He cut back on the cyclic and reduced pitch. Too late. Another sound sent his pulse pounding like a stampede of cattle—the sound of the engine sputtering and stalling.

CHAPTER TEN

BART'S PULSE BEAT in his ears, louder than the slowing rotor of the helicopter. He kept the craft in perfect working order at all times. He knew he had fuel. He hadn't just taken Gary's word for it, he'd checked. It didn't make sense that the fuel pressure was low. It didn't make sense that the engine had stalled out.

Damn him for hurrying his safety checks before taking the craft up. He must have missed something. He must have been so intent on not letting Lindsey go up with him, so scared for his dad, that he'd cut corners. Corners that might mean their lives.

Bart shook his head. He couldn't think of that now. There would be plenty of time to blame himself later. As long as he got them safely to the ground, he could wallow in self-blame the rest of his life, if he chose. Now he needed to focus. He needed to remember everything he'd learned in helicopter flight training or blame wouldn't matter. They would be dead.

Although he'd read about autorotation landings and practiced them on a simulator, he'd never had to perform one for real. And with the stakes so high, he didn't have room for error.

He could feel Lindsey's eyes on him, as wide as the horizon. He wouldn't let her down. He couldn't. He had to think. He had to focus. He had to make sure they survived.

The first order of business was to use the airflow to keep the blades turning. If the blade slowed much more, they'd plummet to the earth like a stone. He reduced the pitch further. The craft inclined forward, the changing airflow powering the blades, speeding the rotation.

So far, so good. Now to bring the craft down.

He established a glide at fifty-five knots. He could hear the rotor spinning slightly faster than it had in powered flight, and as steady as his best ranch horse. The craft began its descent, approaching the ground at an angle of twenty degrees.

The ground loomed closer. The river wound to the side of them, its banks thick with mesquite. A little farther and he could have set down on the grassy plateau. A nice, clear landing. No such luck. It was mesquite tangles or nothing.

He had to reduce airspeed and rate of descent just before touchdown if he wanted to cushion the landing. He moved the cyclic to the rear. The helicopter tipped back slightly, increasing the wind hitting the bottom side of the blades. He applied collective pitch with the pedals. The ground came up fast. He felt Lindsey tense beside him just before the skids hit mesquite.

The copter jolted and bucked. Bart plunged forward. The harness kept him pinned to the seat with the force of a punch to the sternum. He battled for breath.

The helicopter settled back on its haunches.

And tipped to the side.

The ground came up to meet Bart. The binoculars and something else flew through the air and smacked him in the jaw. Mesquite punched through the side window, stabbing inches from his face. Finally the craft swayed and settled.

Hanging in his belt, Bart struggled to clear his mind.

He looked up at Lindsey, suspended above him. Eyes wide, she gripped the harness fastening her to the seat with frantic fingers, knuckles white. She gasped, chest heaving.

"You okay?"

"I think so," she coughed out.

Bart nearly groaned with relief. At least she hadn't been hurt. Shaken up, yes, but she'd recover. Now he just had to figure out a way to get them out of this mess. He grasped the radio. At least they could call for help. Help for them and help for his dad. He flipped on the switch.

The radio was dead.

"Damn."

"Did it break in the landing?"

"I doubt it." Their landing had been rough, but not that rough.

"Then what's wrong with it?"

He groped under the radio, feeling the wires. One hung loose. He pulled it out and looked at the abrupt end.

Lindsey's eyes flared. "It was cut."

"It sure as hell was. And I'll be willing to bet the engine was sabotaged, too."

"Sabotaged," Lindsey whispered under her breath, as if she couldn't quite believe it.

Bart shook his head. He couldn't believe it, either. Despite the vandalism to Lindsey's car and the break-in at her apartment, no one had tried anything this serious. No one had tried to kill them.

Until now.

"Whoever stranded my daddy out on the range probably knew I'd take the helicopter to look for him." Anger constricted his throat like a noose.

"And he sabotaged the engine to make sure you wouldn't return," Lindsey finished. "We have to reach the sheriff's department."

"The ELT should do that for us."

"The ELT?"

"Emergency Location Transmitter. It notifies the authorities when a craft goes down." He groped the spot where the little box was located. His hand grasped air. Another surge of adrenaline dumped into his bloodstream. "The only problem is that it's not here."

"He took it out?"

He nodded. "So when we went down, no one would know where we were." His head pounded. He squinted up at the sky. The clouds were growing thicker by the second. The air was charged with electricity. "We have to find Daddy."

"I have my cell phone. We'll use it to call for help." She groped around her seat. "If I can find it, that is."

"I think it flew past my face when we tipped." Bart peered into the tangle of mesquite pushing its way up through shards of glass. Sure enough, something small and silver glinted through the gnarled branches. "I see it."

"Can you reach it?"

He tried to fit his hand through broken glass and sharp branches. The phone rested a good four feet below. He couldn't move his hand more than four inches through the shattered window. It was no use. "This damn mesquite is too thick. We're on our own."

Lindsey pushed out a breath of air. But instead of giving in to the fear furrowing her brow and turning her skin to chalk, she raised her chin and met his eyes. "Okay. Let's get out of here and find your father."

"Can you open the door?"

"I think so." She yanked up on the release and pushed. The door opened an inch before gravity slammed it shut again. Gritting her teeth, Lindsey didn't waste a breath before trying again. She pushed harder, this time catching the door with a foot before it closed. She slipped her fingers through the open crack and grabbed the door-frame. "Release my belt."

"Are you sure you can—"

"Release my belt," she repeated.

He did as she asked, using one hand to free her and the other to help support her weight.

She shoved upward. The door flung wide and rested fully open on its hinges.

Bart grasped her waist with both hands, his fingers nearly circling her slender body. "I'll give you a boost. On three."

"Ready."

"One…two…three." He boosted her upward, through the door.

She grasped the skid and pulled herself onto the helicopter's side.

The craft tipped slightly on the scrub and then stilled. Bart released his own harness and scrambled so he was sitting upright in the tight space. He looked up where Lindsey was peering down at him, reaching her hand down to help. "Jump free of the chopper."

"Can you get out by yourself?"

"Yes. Just get free. This thing might tip when I climb out. The last thing we need is for you to get pinned underneath."

She nodded. Lowering herself over the skid, she disappeared from his sight.

The copter swayed on the unstable bed of mesquite.

Bart held his breath, afraid to move a muscle. One shift in weight and the thing would roll.

"All clear." Lindsey's voice drifted over the humid wind.

Scooping in a breath, Bart stood and grabbed the edges of Lindsey's door. Pushing off with his legs, he pulled himself out. The craft tipped under his feet. He leaped into the bramble just as the helicopter rolled onto its blades.

A hand closed around his arm before he could pull himself free of gnarled branches. "Bart. Are you all right?"

He looked into eyes bluer than Texas bluebells and scrambled to his feet. "Fine." He tried not to look at the helicopter lying nearly belly up beside him.

"Thank God we're safe."

"Thank God." He looked up. The sky overhead was darker, the air oppressive with humidity and alive with electric charge. After checking the ground around the helicopter in vain to see if the change in position would make it possible to reclaim Lindsey's cell phone, he focused on the storm. "We've got to find Daddy."

Lindsey squinted up at the clouds. "Maybe we can get him to some kind of shelter before the storm hits. Do you remember which direction he was heading?"

Before he could answer, a bolt of lightning split the air. Thunder crashed over their heads.

He'd gotten them to the ground, but they were far from safe. And somewhere out in the storm, his dad wandered alone.

RAIN PELTED Lindsey's face. Lightning split the sky, followed by bone-rattling crashes of thunder. She held up a hand, trying to block the raindrops' sting, trying to see through the deluge. It was little use. She could hardly make out Bart, and he was holding her other hand.

"Daddy could be within spitting range and we wouldn't see him," Bart said, echoing her thoughts. Rain collected in the brim of his hat and cascaded down his back in a waterfall. "And this damn lightning is dangerous. We need to find shelter. Wait this out."

"And leave your father out in this?" she yelled above the wind.

"Covering this ground isn't going to do a speck of good if we can't see him."

She knew what he said made sense. It was impossible to see. And the lightning was dangerous. But still, she couldn't block the memory of Bart's eyes when he realized his father was a target. His pain at the thought of losing him. His determination to make sure that didn't happen. She wouldn't let Bart quit now. Not when she suspected he wanted to find shelter for her sake. "If it was just you out here, you'd keep searching, wouldn't you?"

Bart's brow hardened into a frown.

Answer enough. "We keep looking." Gripping his hand like a lifeline, she stumbled on.

At first the dark shape on the riverbank looked more like a heap of clothing than a human being. She picked up her pace. As they drew closer, she caught a glimpse of a face and wet gray hair. "Bart!" Lindsey yelled, pointing.

Bart's head snapped around. He followed her gaze, his eyes growing wide. Releasing Lindsey's hand, he sprang into a run.

Hiriam Rawlins lay curled on his side. His arms were wrapped around his head as if he was protecting himself from blows. His knees were drawn up to his chest. And his whole body was shaking.

Reaching the bank, Bart fell to his knees and gathered his father into his arms.

The older man fought against Bart's embrace for a moment. Then his body seemed to relax. His eyes grew less panicked, his face less distraught. Finally he wrapped his arms around his son and lowered his head onto Bart's shoulder. A veined, work-worn hand gently patted Bart's back as if comforting a crying child.

Lindsey stopped in her tracks and watched until tears blurred her vision and mixed with the rain.

LINDSEY FITTED her back into a partially protected hollow in the side of a hill that sloped down to the river. Rain wicked down her hair and dripped from the end of her nose.

Bart lowered himself next to her. Hiriam curled on the other side, his body protected under a shallow shelf of rock. The blanket from the helicopter's first-aid kit wrapped tightly around him, the older man had finally stopped shaking. At least visibly. And at the moment, he appeared to be asleep.

Lindsey couldn't begin to guess all he'd been through today. How he'd gotten so far from the ranch, how frightened and confused he'd been, how cold and miserable and totally alone. How someone could victimize a confused, helpless old man was beyond her. She didn't even want to understand that kind of evil. She shivered and wrapped her arms tight around her middle.

"Here." Bart spread his arms, inviting her inside.

She snuggled against the hard plane of his chest. His arms encircled her. His heat soaked into her. His scent surrounded her and made her feel safe for the first time since the helicopter had gone down.

A miracle.

She thought back to the terror that had claimed her when the helicopter's engine had quit. The cold hand of fear choking her as they had careened to the ground. And the panic that had attacked when Bart pulled out the severed radio wire. "Who would sabotage the helicopter?"

"I have one guess."

"Your cousin." She had only to close her eyes to see Kenny Rawlins glaring at Bart through angry slits as Don read the terms of Jeb's will.

"If both my daddy and I died, Kenny would get his hands not only on the Bar JR, but the Four Aces to boot."

Lindsey nodded. "Would he know how to sabotage a helicopter?"

"He worked as a truck mechanic for a while."

"But that's not the same thing as a helicopter engine, is it?"

"It isn't similar enough for him to know how to *fix* a helicopter engine, but I'll bet it's similar enough to know how to *break* one. And he could take the ELT and cut the radio wires easily enough. It would also be easy for him to get Daddy out of the house unseen. He knows his way around the ranch. He used to live here when he was a kid, before Grandaddy died." Bart's shoulders jerked behind her in a shrug, the movement as tight as a wound spring. "There's only one thing that bothers me."

"What's that?"

"The whole thing seems a bit ambitious for Kenny."

"Working on a helicopter engine?"

"Figuring out who inherits, setting me up for Jeb's murder, the whole thing. He's always stuck to scams that don't require much planning or imagination. The thought of him pulling off something this complicated..." He shook his head. "I just don't know if he's capable. He has to be working with someone."

She had to agree. In the few times she'd met Kenny, she hadn't walked away impressed by his cunning. She searched her mind for possibilities and came up empty. "But it doesn't seem to be Brandy Carmichael. So who?"

"A damn good question."

The thought of one person out there who wanted them out of the way was scary enough. The prospect of two gave her chills. Not that she needed help with those. The rain and wind were doing a fine job. She snuggled against Bart's warmth.

He pulled her closer. "You were something today."

"Me?" She twisted in his arms to look up at him.

He gave her a half smile. "Yes, you. You didn't have to come with me in the helicopter. Hell, I shouldn't have let you."

"That's not your fault. I forced the issue."

"That's what I mean. And after the crash. Most people wouldn't have trudged through the rain looking for my daddy. Not with all that lightning. You never gave up. You never quit. No matter how scared you were, no matter how bad things looked, you wouldn't quit until we found him."

"Why would I quit?"

His smile grew wider. "Exactly. It doesn't even occur to you to quit. Not everyone is like that. In my experience there are damn few people like that."

She shook her head. "You were the one who was amazing. I had no idea a helicopter could still fly after the engine quit running. I thought we were goners."

"You could have fooled me. I'd say you willed me to land that chopper. Have you always stuck to your guns like that?"

Had she? She had to admit she didn't have any memories of throwing in the towel. Not over anything. A fact that no doubt had caused her parents more than a few headaches. "I suppose I have been pretty tenacious."

"I bet it served you well in law school."

She had to nod. "And with my family."

"Your family?"

"They're a little overprotective." She paused. "Well, a lot overprotective. That's why I moved to Mustang Valley. If I'd stayed in Massachusetts, they'd have built my career for me. I wanted to do it on my own."

"They sound like good people."

She drew in a deep breath. "The greatest," she admitted. "But sometimes they want to do too much. They don't believe I can take care of myself."

Bart nodded as if he'd just figured something out. "That's why you jump down my throat every time I try to help you. Or protect you."

Did she? Yes, she supposed she did. "I can take care of myself. No one seems to believe that."

"I suppose you have brothers."

"Four. All older."

"Ah, I see," he said, as if that explained it all. "So along with planning your career for you, did they follow you around when you went on dates?"

"I didn't go on dates."

"A woman as pretty as you? I can't believe that." He craned his neck to look into her eyes.

Her cheeks heated. She felt as awkward talking about this with Bart as she did with Cara and Kelly. No, *more* awkward. Much more. Bart made her wish she had gone on more dates. He made her wish she had more experience with men. Maybe then she'd know how to handle the feelings kindling inside her.

She took a deep breath. "I come from a family of lawyers. My father is a judge on the Massachusetts Supreme Court, three of my brothers have founded a successful legal firm and the fourth is a federal prosecutor."

"Don't tell me, they chased potential boyfriends away by threatening them with lawsuits."

A chuckle bubbled from her throat. "I wouldn't put it past them. But no, they usually behaved."

"In that case, I can't see any reason those Yankee boys wouldn't be knocking your door down. But then, I've never truly understood Yankees."

She almost shook her head. Bart was something, all right. She'd never been affected by flattery before. But with Bart, the flattery didn't seem like empty words. He made her feel as if every word from his lips had come straight from his heart. "It wasn't the Yankee boys, it was me. I wanted to focus on law school and establishing a legal practice. So I've never had a serious relationship. I've never—" She shook her head. This wasn't coming out right. "Dating was never as important to me as the law." Until now, looking into Bart's eyes. Until now, when she had no business thinking about dating.

"Then it's true." Bart grinned, a teasing glitter to his green eyes. "They really do force you to cut your heart out of your chest as soon as you pass the bar."

Another laugh broke free. It was amazing that Bart still had a sense of humor after all that had happened the past few days and the pressure they were under now.

But then, there were so many amazing things about Bart Rawlins, she'd lost count. "I don't want to have to trade my career for a family, that's all."

"Don't you want a family? Don't you want children?" He sounded shocked, as if he couldn't envision that kind of life.

Of course he probably couldn't. Family was what drove Bart. She had only to think of the row of bedrooms he'd planned to fill, of his tenderness when he gathered his father into his arms on the riverbank or of the ache in his eyes when he talked of his mother's death to know that. "Family is important to you, isn't it?"

"It's the most important."

She angled her body so she could look straight into his eyes. "So why aren't you married? Why don't you have children of your own?"

"I haven't found the right woman. With my daddy's illness and my mama…" Regret flickered briefly in his eyes. Then it was gone. He shrugged. "I haven't had a lot of chances to date. Not the last few years anyway."

"You've sacrificed a lot for your parents, haven't you?"

"Sacrifice?" He shook his head. "I wouldn't put it that way. Giving up things isn't sacrifice when you do it for someone you love."

"That sounds like something my mother would say."

"A smart woman. You must take after her."

A chill worked over her skin. She hoped not. She'd been working hard all her adult life not to take after her mother. "My mother is a wonderful woman. A brilliant woman."

"But?"

"But she and I don't see things the same way."

Bart crooked an eyebrow, but he didn't ask. He merely waited for her to go on.

Lindsey drew in a deep breath. "She was a star student at Harvard Law School when she met my dad. They had a real whirlwind love affair and ended up getting married at the end of her second year. By the time the fall semester rolled around, my dad was clerking for a Supreme Court justice and my mom was pregnant with my oldest brother. It wasn't until recently that she finished school and fulfilled her dream of teaching."

"And you figured if you didn't date, that would never happen to you."

"It's not that I don't want a family. I do. But I want to establish my career first. I don't want to grow to resent my husband and family, to blame them for my failure to do what I needed to do with my life."

"Is that how your mother feels about the delay in her career? Does she resent you?"

"No. But I would feel that way. I know I would. The law is too important to me. Proving myself is too important. When I find the right man, when I decide to start a family, I want to be able to give myself without reservation."

Bart nodded and looked into the darkness. Silence stretched between them, whipped by wind and rain. Finally he returned his gaze to hers, green drilling into blue. "And you're not afraid of never finding that special person? Of never having a family? Of being alone?" Deep and ragged, his voice ached with his own misgivings and penetrated a tender spot at the center of her heart.

She swallowed hard. "I'm scared to death." She'd never admitted that before. Not to her family. Not to Kelly and Cara. Not even to herself. She'd spent so much time and energy focused on her career, on proving herself, she'd never realized how much she wanted a man to love her, too. And how afraid she was that she'd have to choose between a man and her career. She suddenly felt as exposed as a raw nerve. She dipped her head and studied the muddy earth.

He reached out and touched a rough finger to her chin. He tilted her head back so she had to meet his eyes. "A woman like you, there's no reason you shouldn't have it all. The career you want, a husband who dotes on you and children as beautiful as you are."

Warmth bloomed in her cheeks and spread down through her body, radiating from his touch.

"You're one brave woman, Lindsey Wellington. Not many people even know what they want. Even fewer would risk moving halfway across the country on their own to get it."

She didn't feel brave. Not right now. She felt unsure and scared and, oh, so alive. She wanted him to kiss her again. To touch her. To make her feel like he had in her apartment that night—safe and wanted and as if she was facing incredible danger all at the same time. She parted her lips.

His eyes focused on her mouth. "I wish I could kiss you again." He traced a finger along her jaw and over her lower lip. "I wish I could make love to you."

She pursed her lips and kissed his finger.

His eyes seemed to darken. For a moment she thought he'd lower his head and claim her. Instead, he looked away. "The man who makes love to you for the first time should be able to promise you a future. I'm not going to make promises I can't keep."

A chill claimed her, colder than the rain pelting her face. She could reassure him that he'd be acquitted. She could try to convince him that she needed him far more than she needed any promise. But any argument she made would just be words. And right now they were beyond words.

She laid her head on his shoulder and breathed in his scent. She'd find a way to keep Bart from going to prison for a murder he didn't commit. She had to. The alternative was too tragic to contemplate.

WHEN THE STORM finally let up, armed only with the Maglite they retrieved from the helicopter, they climbed out of the protective hollow and trudged across the rolling land. It was slow going. On a good day, his daddy's arthritis didn't allow him to move very quickly. But now, exhausted from his ordeal, he was moving slower than a show horse's jog. Dawn was bathing the countryside in its gold glow by the time they reached the dirt road stretching from the Four Aces to the highway heading for Mustang Valley.

Bart paused to get a better hold on his dad before turning in the direction of the highway.

Lindsey propped up Daddy's far side. She nodded back in the other direction. "Isn't that the way to the ranch? Or am I all turned around?"

Bart shook his head. He was the one turned around. But not about the direction. The need to pull Lindsey into his arms, to kiss her, to make love to her had pounded through his bloodstream all night long. Even now walking alongside her, watching her face screwed up with concentration from supporting his dad's weight, her little pink tongue darting between her lips every two strides, all he could think about was fitting his mouth over hers and tasting her again.

He surveyed the road ahead. "The highway leading to

Mustang Valley is closer. I'm hoping we can flag down a truck to take us to Granbury."

"To the medical center?"

"That's right. Daddy needs a hospital."

As if to illustrate just how badly he needed medical attention, his dad sagged against him. Bart slipped his arms under his back and legs and scooped him into his arms, cradling him like a baby. His dad used to be strapping strong as any cowboy in the area. But though he wasn't two inches shorter than Bart, after nearly ten years of illness he had all the substance of a flake of hay.

Bart picked up his pace. He had to get help. His dad's health was fragile as it was, and a day of wandering the riverbed and a night of huddling out in a thunderstorm and trudging halfway across the ranch hadn't done a speck of good.

By the time they reached the paved highway, Bart's arms had begun to complain about his dad's weight, as unsubstantial as it was. They walked on the gravel shoulder for a good mile before an old blue pickup complete with a loaded gun rack finally rattled toward them. Lindsey stepped out into the road and waved her arms

The pickup slowed and pulled to the side of the road.

A grizzled man who looked like he was on the north side of sixty and had had a hard life peered out the dusty window. He smiled around a giant plug of chew tucked in one lined cheek.

Lindsey pulled the truck door open. "Thank God you stopped."

"What can I do you for? Need a ride?"

"We need to get to Granbury," Bart said. "To a hospital."

He eyed Bart and his daddy, as if he'd just noticed them. "I see that. Well, what are you waiting for? Pile in."

Lindsey opened the back door of the King Cab. Bart ducked inside, propped his dad gently on the seat and climbed in beside him. Lindsey closed the door and let herself into the front seat.

Obviously damn pleased with the seating arrangement, the man's smile grew wider, highlighting spectacularly stained teeth. He ground the truck into gear and pulled out. "Shep. Shep Davis is the name. So where are you folks from?"

"The Four Aces," Lindsey answered. "Our helicopter broke down out on the range."

"Had to pull an emergency landing, huh?"

Lindsey smiled and glanced back at him. "Bart landed it like the pro he is."

Bart tensed. Watching the man's face in the rearview mirror, he waited for him to link the Four Aces with the name Bart. After that it would only be a short skip to realizing he had a suspected murderer riding in his truck. If they were lucky, he might just toss them out on the side of the road. If not, Bart could very well find the barrel of one of those shotguns pointed in his face.

The guy behind the wheel just smiled at Lindsey as if the two of them were the only ones in the truck. "If you ask me, helicopters are ruining ranching. So loud and damn expensive. They scare the cattle and bankrupt the rancher."

Bart bit his tongue. He hadn't liked the idea of the helicopter, either. But the fact was, qualified cowboys were hard to find these days. It took years of experience to make a hand. Kids nowadays were more interested in learning to toss a football so they could be the next Troy Aikman than learning to rope cattle. Adding the helicopter to help out the horses and cowboys had saved the Four Aces from the labor problems that had devastated many other ranches in the area.

"Are you a rancher?" Lindsey tilted her head toward Shep, as if truly interested.

An unmistakable pang shot through Bart and settled in his chest. How could he be jealous of a sixty-year-old coot who had half a can of tobacco bulging from one cheek? It was ridiculous. Especially when he should be glad Lindsey was distracting the man and keeping him from adding one and one and tossing them out on the side of the road before they reached Granbury.

He concentrated on his dad's shallow breathing and tried to ignore the small talk in the front seat.

"I ain't a rancher. Not anymore. Used to work on one out here, though. The Bar JR."

Bart's ears pricked up. So much for his attempt at ignoring their conversation.

Lindsey nodded and glanced into the backseat. "The Bar JR? That's Jeb Rawlins's ranch."

"That's the one."

"How long ago did you work there?"

"A good twenty years ago. Old bastard quit paying me and stole my woman. By the time I moved down to Waco, I'd lost four months' wages and gained a broken heart."

"That's terrible." Lindsey's voice rang with sympathy. "Do you still live in Waco?"

"Nope, just moved back."

"I see."

Bart could see she was planning to fish for information

on Jeb. Anything that would point to someone else as the murderer. And old Shep's financial ruin and jealousy made good motives. Bart just hoped her prying didn't refresh Shep's memory and help him connect the dots. His dad would likely recover now with a little patching up and rest, but if they had to walk from here to Granbury, things wouldn't be so rosy.

Up in the front seat, Lindsey's strategy was working. Shep nodded, his head jiggling up and down like one of those bobblehead dolls. He spat out the open window before turning bright eyes back to Lindsey, obviously eager to share his life's story with his beautiful audience. "I guess now that Jeb's dead, I won't see a dime. Shame. With the economy the way it is, I could use the bucks. I suppose I'll sue the estate, but I don't expect that'll do me a hell of a lot of good. You can't get blood from a stone."

Bart nearly groaned. It looked like the Bar JR was turning into exactly what Jeb intended it to be: a black hole that would suck money from the Four Aces. Jeb's revenge.

Shep narrowed his eyes on Lindsey. "Know any honest lawyers?"

"Actually, yes. I'm with Lambert & Church in Mustang Valley."

"You're a lawyer? No kidding?"

"No kidding." Lindsey smiled and then stared at him with rapt fascination. "What about the woman you loved? Tell me about her."

"Beatrice? It didn't last with her and Jeb. At least that's what I heard."

A bad feeling crept up Bart's spine. "Beatrice? Not Beatrice Jensen."

The grizzled face peered at him from the rearview mirror. "You know her?"

Bart paused, not wanting to answer.

"What am I thinking? Of course you know her. She works at the Four Aces now, doesn't she?" The lines in his brow grew deeper. "What did you say your name was?"

Oh, hell. Hearing Beatrice's name in connection to Jeb's had surprised him so much, he'd plumb forgot to keep his damn mouth shut.

Shep adjusted the mirror so he could get a good look at Bart's face. "You're Bart Rawlins, ain't ya?"

Bart gave Shep a reluctant nod.

Shep turned in Lindsey's direction. "And I'll bet that makes you the lawyer who's fixing to get him off on those murder charges."

"Bart didn't kill his uncle, Mr. Davis. He's innocent."

"I thought I told you to call me Shep. Even my daddy was never Mr. Davis." He turned back to Bart, his eyes hardening. "And I don't care what you did to Jeb. He deserved what he got. But by pulling that knife on him, you took away any chance I had to get my money."

Bart held up a hand. "You make sure we get to the medical center in Granbury, and I'll see you get your money."

"You're serious?"

Bart nodded. "And on the way, you tell us everything you know about Beatrice Jensen."

CHAPTER ELEVEN

LINDSEY ACCEPTED THE steaming cup of bitter-smelling coffee Bart handed her and watched him sink into the hospital waiting-room chair next to her. Fortunately his promise of money had convinced Shep Davis to bring them to the Lake Granbury Medical Center and now Bart's father was getting the medical attention he needed. Unfortunately, Shep hadn't been able to tell them much about Beatrice that Bart didn't already know—at least not about the present-day Beatrice. After Jeb stole her affections, Shep had had little to do with the woman.

Lindsey peered at Bart over her cup. Her mind had been whirring since Shep had told them his story. "What if we've been thinking about Jeb's murder the wrong way? What if the motives involved are entirely different from what we've assumed?"

"You mean, what if he wasn't killed for his land?"

"That's exactly what I mean. What if there's some other motive behind his murder? A motive like jealousy?"

"You're thinking of Beatrice."

"Could she still be in love with Jeb?"

"Maybe. I don't know. Before today, I didn't have a clue they even knew each other. And now she's missing. Very suspicious." He frowned, his eyebrows pulling low over green eyes. "But isn't a murder due to jealousy usually done in a fit of passion? Beatrice finds out Jeb's been running around and confronts him with a knife? That kind of thing? Whoever killed Jeb had to do some fancy planning in advance or they couldn't have framed me."

Lindsey pursed her lips in thought. He had a point. "Maybe she didn't kill Jeb. But she could have left your father out on the range to lash back at you for Jeb's murder."

"It would explain how Daddy got out of the house without anyone at the ranch seeing him. But it doesn't explain the helicopter."

"Kenny?"

"Gary said he was at the ranch. But I can't think of one reason Beatrice would work with Kenny."

"Mr. Rawlins?" a deep voice said.

Lindsey looked in the direction of the voice. A rough-hewn man with black hair and skin the color of a copper penny peered down at Bart. "I'm Dr. Mendoza. I've just examined your father."

Bart sprang to his feet.

Lindsey rose beside him and placed a supportive hand on his arm.

He glanced at her, giving her a grateful smile.

Warmth curled through her. It must have been so hard for him, facing his father's illness alone, facing his mother's death alone. She was glad she could offer some comfort. Some support. Pulling in a deep breath, Bart looked back to the doctor. "How is he?"

"He's doing amazingly well under the circumstances."

"When can he come home?"

The doctor held up a hand. "Not so fast. I said he

was doing well *under the circumstances,* not that he was ready to go back to life as usual."

Bart tensed. "Spit it out, Doc."

"He needs to stay here for a while. Maybe a few days. After that, I suggest he goes to a rehabilitation center. He's going to need around-the-clock skilled care for a while."

Hospital. Rehabilitation center. Skilled care. Lindsey's head spun at the possible implications. Bart's father was in worse shape than she'd realized.

Beside her, Bart clenched his teeth. "Whatever my daddy needs to get better, he'll get." His voice was clipped, harsh, as if he was having trouble controlling his anger. Anger no doubt directed at the person who was responsible for his father's condition.

"We should know more in the next couple days," the doctor said.

"Can Bart see him?" Lindsey asked. "Before we leave?"

"Certainly."

"And Doc?" Bart said. "No one is allowed in my daddy's room besides the two of us and any medical staff that needs to see him. No one. Not friends and certainly not family. I've called an outside security firm to watch over him. They should be here within the hour."

The doctor hesitated for a moment and then nodded. "Whatever you wish, Mr. Rawlins." After exchanging thank-yous and goodbyes, the doctor left.

Once they were alone, Lindsey looked up at Bart, searching his eyes. She could feel anger pulsing off him in waves. Anger born from worry for his father and frustration at not having been able to protect him. But even though she understood where his anger was coming from, it concerned her just the same. "We'll find out who did this, Bart. And we'll make sure your father isn't hurt again."

Bart gave a sharp nod. "Damn straight we will. But before anything else happens, I need to talk to the sheriff first, and then Don Church."

"Don Church? About Jeb's will?"

"About changing my own."

"LINDSEY, BART, where have you been? I've been trying to reach both of you since yesterday."

Bart and Lindsey strode past Nancy Wilks and straight down the hall to Don's office. There was no time to stop and chat. He had to see Don. Kenny or Beatrice or whoever the hell was behind what had happened to his dad weren't going to get away with what they'd done. Not if he had anything to say about it. And although things weren't as clear-cut as they'd seemed when Kenny appeared to be the only one who would profit by Jeb's death, Bart's money was still on his cousin. Money he was going to make damn sure Kenny never got his hands on.

Beside him, Lindsey glanced at Nancy as she walked. "Nancy, we need to see Don," she explained "It's urgent."

"You need to listen to your voice mail. The grand jury came back with a true bill. Bart's arraignment is scheduled for tomorrow."

Bart nearly stumbled. He knew the chances were nearly one hundred percent that the grand jury would vote to indict. Lindsey had explained to him that a grand jury rarely acted as more than a rubber stamp for the prosecution. And in Bart's case, the district attorney had far too much evidence for any grand jury to ignore, even if they wanted to.

Lindsey gave him a worried glance but kept on walking. They rounded the corner and reached Don's office. The door stood open. No one was inside.

Lindsey whirled to face Nancy. "Where's Don?"

"Paul's office."

Lindsey met Bart's eyes, and the two of them started back in the direction of Paul's office.

"Wait!" Nancy scampered to keep up with them, her breath labored. "Paul and Don are in a meeting."

They reached Paul's closed door. Lindsey planted her feet in the hallway. "So we'll wait. We need to talk to Don right away."

"Suit yourself." Nancy eyed Lindsey and bobbed her head. "What happened to you?"

Lindsey looked down at her wrinkled suit and nearly shredded stockings as if she hadn't realized how she looked until this minute.

Bart cringed. In his urgency to find out who was responsible for his father's condition, he'd forgotten they'd spent the past twenty-four hours searching through mesquite in a thunderstorm and hiking halfway across Texas. "I'm sorry, Lindsey. I didn't even think of giving you a chance to clean up. Do you want to stop back at the ranch before we talk to Don?"

She smoothed a hand over her hair and raised her chin, a dignified expression gracing her face. "This is more important than appearances."

Just as he opened his mouth to tell her she didn't have to worry about appearances, that she always looked great, the mahogany door swung wide and Paul Lambert stood in the doorway.

Surprise registered in his face. His gaze traveled from Lindsey's drip-dried hair to the mud clinging to Bart's boots. "Lindsey, Bart, what happened?"

"We need to talk to Don," Lindsey said.

A young man, his hair the color of coffee with too much cream, stepped up beside Paul and leveled beaming brown eyes on Lindsey.

The surprised look still on Paul's face, he glanced at his client. "Roger Rosales, I'd like you to meet Bart Rawlins and Lindsey Wellington."

Rosales gave them a practiced smile. "Nice to meet you."

"Lindsey is a lawyer here at the firm and Bart is one of our best clients," Paul continued.

Ignoring Bart, Rosales horned in on Lindsey. "Wellington. Not one of the Boston Wellingtons?"

Lindsey nodded stiffly. "How do you know my family, Mr. Rosales?"

"It's Roger. My company has holdings in the Boston area."

"Your company?"

"Ranger Corporation. I'm in charge of regional development, so I'm based in this area. But I have occasion to travel to Boston."

Bart had heard of Ranger Corporation. Who hadn't? The company was huge, with its fingers in pies all over the world.

Lindsey looked down at her wrinkled suit. A flush of embarrassment stained her cheeks. "Please excuse my appearance. It's been a tough day."

"I hope it improves."

"So do I." She glanced past Rosales and Paul to where Don stood in the back of the office. "It was nice meeting you."

"Thank you. Meeting you has been an unexpected perk." He gave her a beaming grin.

Bart stiffened. He didn't like Roger Rosales, and it

wasn't hard to figure out why. The man was too good-looking, too charming, and the interest in his eyes when he looked at Lindsey made Bart want to clock him.

"Paul, Don…" Roger said. "I trust you'll get in touch with me."

Paul stuck out his hand and shook Roger's. "We sure will." Don gave a wave and a nod from across the room. As soon as the Ranger Corporation executive disappeared down the hall, Paul zeroed in on Lindsey. "Okay, what happened?" His voice was sharp with obvious concern.

Bart stepped closer to Lindsey. "Someone tried to kill us and my daddy. We're here to make sure it doesn't happen again."

"Tried to kill you?" Paul looked to Nancy, still hovering behind Bart and Lindsey. "Call Ben."

Bart turned to Nancy and held up a hand. "We already talked to him at the hospital."

"Hospital?" Paul repeated.

"My daddy is in rough shape."

"I'm sorry. I hope he'll be okay."

Joining them at the door, Don added his concern to Paul's. "So how can we help?"

"I need to change my will."

"What would changing your will…" Don trailed off, understanding dawning on his face. "You think Kenny did this. That he tried to kill you and your father so he can inherit both the Bar JR and the Four Aces."

"Damn straight. And the best way to keep that from happening is changing my will and my daddy's will so the son of a bitch won't get a single square foot of land."

Don nodded. "We can do that. Since you hold power of attorney, it won't be a problem. We'll set up a trust for your father, and stipulate that upon his death the holdings go to charity or wherever you'd like. Are you still planning to sell the Four Aces if…"

Bart let out a breath. Don didn't have to say the word *convicted* for Bart to know what he was getting at. "I suppose I am. I don't have much of a choice."

Don turned to Paul. "Do you want to make sure the paperwork is ready, just in case?"

Lindsey shook her head adamantly. "We won't have to go that far. Bart isn't going to be convicted." She stood with her chin raised, her spine straight as a fence post and the fire of an avenging angel burning in her eyes. Like she was ready to fight by his side to the end.

An uneasy feeling niggled at the back of his mind.

"You're right, Lindsey. He won't have to worry about selling the ranch. He's going to be acquitted," Paul said. He frowned at Don. "In the meantime, didn't you have another problem you wanted to discuss with Bart?"

Another problem. Bart almost cringed. He focused on Don. "What is it?"

"Someone is contesting Jeb's will."

Now it was Bart's turn to stare in surprise. "Not Kenny?"

"No, not Kenny."

Of course not. No one who knew the Bar JR's financial state would want the ranch. No one without a family legacy to protect at any rate. "Then who?"

Don shifted his feet on the thick carpet, as if he didn't want to answer.

"Who, Don?"

The portly lawyer sighed and looked at the floor. "Beatrice. Beatrice Jensen. She claims she married Jeb twenty years ago."

BOOTS THUMPING down the hallway of the ranch house, Bart headed straight for Beatrice's living quarters, Lindsey right behind him. His dad's nurse had a heap of explaining to do. He didn't care that she was contesting Jeb's will. Even though he'd love to reunite the original Rawlins ranch, he'd never expected to inherit the Bar JR in the first place. But the news that she'd been Jeb's estranged wife for the past twenty years and never told him had flattened him like a well-aimed fist.

He pounded a fist on Beatrice's door. "Beatrice? We need to talk."

Nothing answered him but the soft sounds of his and Lindsey's breathing.

He knocked again.

Still nothing.

"Damn." He grasped the knob. It turned easily under his hand. Pushing open the door, he flipped on the light.

The room was as barren as the day before Beatrice moved in. No clutter in the bathroom, no sheets on the bed, no sign a human lived here at all.

Lindsey looked up at him. "I guess we didn't have to worry that something bad happened to her. She just filed her claim against Jeb's estate and moved out."

He ran a hand over his face. "I'm glad I hired security for Daddy. If she was the one who left him out on the range…"

"Would any of the hands know where she might have gone?"

"I doubt it, but it's worth asking around."

They found Gary and some of the hands in one of the corrals. Covered with dust, Gary's bay mare was dark with sweat. Foam lathered where the reins touched her neck. "How's your daddy doing, Bart?" Gary said, looking from Bart to Lindsey.

"He's going to be in the hospital for a while. I'll let you know when he can have visitors."

Gary nodded. "Got word that the FAA is sending someone out to investigate the helicopter crash. You call them?"

"I imagine Sheriff Ben did." Bart was glad the FAA would investigate. At least he wouldn't have to rely on Hurley Zeller to get to the bottom of the helicopter sabotage.

"How about Beatrice? The sheriff find her?" Gary asked.

The sheriff. What a joke. Bart didn't even know if the sheriff had searched. "Looks like Beatrice moved out on her own. Any of you know anything about it?"

"Can't say I do." Gary glanced at the cowboys riding behind him. "You boys?"

A chorus of nopes and shaking heads answered.

"Anyone see her yesterday?" Bart glanced at the group of faces to the same result.

Gary's brow furrowed. "You can't be thinking Beatrice sabotaged the helicopter. She wouldn't know a blade from a cyclic."

"I'm thinking she may have done something to Daddy."

Gary shook his head. "I can't see it. Beatrice loves that old man."

That's what Bart had thought, too. Until his daddy's life had been put in danger. Until he'd learned Beatrice was married to Jeb.

Gary grunted. "Unless..."

Bart's pulse picked up its pace. "Unless what?"

"Something Kenny said when I ran him off the

ranch yesterday. Made it seem like he was here to see Beatrice."

A shot of adrenaline slammed into Bart's bloodstream. "Why didn't you mention this yesterday?"

"I didn't believe him when he said it. I thought he was just making up excuses to be here so he could cause trouble."

Anger throbbed in Bart's ears. But the anger wasn't directed at Gary. It was aimed squarely at Kenny. His cousin wasn't much of a planner, but somehow he'd stumbled on the perfect plan to ruin Bart's life and the lives of everyone he cared about.

And Bart damn well wasn't going to let him get away with it.

LINDSEY COULD SEE the anger work its way from Bart's hat to his boots, tensing every muscle and balling his hands into fists on the way. So when he spun on a heel, she was ready.

She stepped in front of him, blocking his path. "Where are you going?"

"I have to take care of something." He stepped around her without missing a beat. His long legs and rolling stride closed the distance to the truck with remarkable speed.

She ran to catch up. "Tell me you're not going to confront Kenny."

"I should have done it a long damn time ago." He yanked open the door.

Lindsey raced around the truck. She couldn't let Bart rush off like this. If she could keep him talking, maybe he'd calm down and see this confrontation as the mistake it was. Maybe he'd listen to reason. She opened the door and scrambled into the passenger seat.

Bart glanced at her out of the corner of his eye. His lips flattened into a hard line, as if he was unhappy she'd tagged along but not surprised. He slipped the key into the ignition and cranked the engine to life. Shifting the truck into gear, he accelerated down the driveway and out the gate.

Lindsey strapped herself in and held on. "You can't talk to Kenny. Not until you calm down."

He looked straight ahead, eyes hard. A muscle twitched along his jaw.

"This will just lead to a fistfight."

He pulled onto the highway and accelerated.

"Your arraignment is scheduled for tomorrow, Bart. You don't want the kind of headlines another fight between you and Kenny will cause. Not unless you want all of Mustang County to believe you're guilty. You have to report this to the sheriff, let the law deal with Kenny."

"The law has done nothing but railroad me for a murder I didn't commit."

She couldn't argue with him there. She could understand his growing cynicism. "Give the system another chance, Bart. You can't take matters into your own hands."

"Can't I? Daddy could have died out on the range. Hell, we may never have found him. And you were in that helicopter. You could have—" He stopped abruptly, as if he couldn't push the words past his lips.

"Your father is doing well, and I'm right here. You have to listen to me."

Bart stared straight ahead as if he hadn't heard a word. Reaching the city limits in record time, he slowed. A couple blocks later, he swung into the parking lot of Hit 'Em Again. The lot was filled with pickup trucks, nearly every one equipped with a gun rack. The windows and doors of the tavern stood open. A steel guitar wailed into the warm evening.

Bart swung the truck into one of the few free spaces, threw open the door and dismounted, slamming the door behind him. Hands hardened into fists, he strode for the tavern.

Lindsey scrambled to catch up. She grasped his hard biceps just as he reached for the door. "Don't do this, Bart. Please."

He looked down at her, his gaze sweeping over her face and zeroing in on her eyes. "Sometimes a man has to stand up, Lindsey, and protect the people he cares about. I can't sit by while Kenny tries to hurt you or Daddy. I wouldn't be much of a man if I did." He turned away from her, yanked open the door and strode into the tavern.

A shiver worked over her skin and settled in her chest. *Protect the people he cares about.* He'd included her in that select group. Her and his father.

She caught the door before it swung closed and followed him into the swirl of smoke and country music.

The place was packed. Couples whirled on the dance floor, their cowboy boots moving in the rhythm of a Texas two-step. A band crowded onto a bandstand in the corner. A short, wiry man stood center stage and belted out a heartbreak song in the deepest voice she'd ever heard. Through the smoke, music and laughter, she spotted Kenny. His back to the bar, he tipped a beer and stared through narrowed eyes at the people blowing off steam around him.

Setting his jaw, Bart headed in his cousin's direction.

When Kenny spotted him, he pushed off the bar and

stood on boots wobbly from booze. "You have some nerve, Bart." His voice boomed, rising above the music and noise.

Heads snapped around. Curious eyes followed the exchange.

Lindsey cringed. If this confrontation erupted into a fistfight, there would be plenty of witnesses. Just what Bart didn't need.

"I heard you stopped at the Four Aces yesterday, Kenny."

"The Four Aces? What are you talking about?"

"Don't play dumb with me."

"Dumb? You're the one who's dumb. Coming around me. I ought to grab that shotgun over the bar and put some buckshot in you right now for killing my old man. No one would blame me."

"Stay away from the Four Aces. Stay away from my daddy and Lindsey. I'm warning you."

"Well, thanks for the warning, cousin. I guess that's more than you gave my old man."

"Go to hell, Kenny."

"You planning to send me there like you did my daddy?"

"I didn't kill Jeb. But so help me God, if you do anything to hurt my daddy or Lindsey or the Four Aces again, I will kill you. And I won't need a knife. I'll do it with my bare hands."

Kenny turned to the people around him. "He threatened me. You heard that, didn't you? He said he was going to kill me."

Lindsey closed her eyes and prayed the scene wouldn't come back to haunt them.

CHAPTER TWELVE

SHIFTING IN HIS seat behind the defendant's table in Mustang Valley Superior Court, Bart watched people file into the courtroom and take seats in the gallery behind him. People who by now probably had heard all about his appearance at Hit 'Em Again last night.

He'd been damn stupid. Stupid to confront Kenny and stupider still to threaten to kill him in front of all those people. He should have listened to Lindsey. He should have held his temper.

As if that had been possible.

When he'd heard Kenny was at the ranch visiting Beatrice the day his dad disappeared and the helicopter was sabotaged, he'd lost all sense of reason. Kenny had tried to take from him everything he cared about, *everyone* he cared about.

And hell, he *would* kill his cousin and gladly do the time if it meant keeping his dad and Lindsey safe.

Lindsey.

She leaned forward in the chair next to him studying a legal document. Her hair draped over her shoulder like a silken veil.

He wasn't sure when she had worked her way under his skin. But he couldn't deny that she had. She had the refinement of a true lady, yet the tenacity of a coon dog. And the way she put herself on the line for him, for what she believed in, for all that was right in the world, truly humbled him.

He'd never killed more than a couple of coyotes in all his years, but he wouldn't hesitate to choke the life out of Kenny with his bare hands if that's what it took to protect her and his daddy.

"The Mustang Valley Superior Court is now in session," a bailiff barked out. "The Honorable Judge Enrique Valenzuela presiding. All rise."

Bart glanced back at the gallery. The seats were filled with concerned citizens, retirees with some hours to fill and reporters, not just from Mustang Valley but Dallas/Fort Worth, as well. The owner of the *Mustang Gazette,* crusty old Beau Jennings, peered over his glasses from the back of the room. And beside her boss stood Lindsey's friend, Cara Hamilton. Bart gave Cara a brief nod before turning his attention back to the front of the courtroom.

The distinguished-looking judge swept into the room in black robes and perched on the mahogany bench in front of the American flag and the Lone Star flag of Texas.

Bart stifled a smile. He'd gone to grade school with Enrique Valenzuela, or Rico as he was called in those days. He'd been a smart-mouthed little whelp back then. Who knew he'd grow up to be the youngest and most respected judge in the county. And one of the toughest.

Rico scanned the room through tiny rimless glasses. "We have two arraignments this morning, as I understand it."

The bailiff glanced at the docket. "Yes, Judge."

"Then let's have the first case."

The bailiff announced the name of a cowboy Bart had seen many times at Hit 'Em Again and the charge levied against him. Drunk driving. The cowboy pleaded not guilty. That bit of business dispensed, Rico looked at Bart point-blank and nodded to the bailiff.

Lindsey's hand found his under the table. Her soft fingers wrapped around his and squeezed.

The bailiff seemed to straighten, suddenly formal. "The court calls Bartholomew J. Rawlins."

Releasing his hand, Lindsey rose. Bart pushed to his feet beside her.

The bailiff continued. "In the name and by authority of the State of Texas, the grand jury of Mustang County, State of Texas, do present that Bartholomew J. Rawlins in said county and state did commit a criminal homicide of the first degree against the peace and dignity of the State."

Bart had thought he understood the charge he was facing. But hearing it read aloud in such a formal manner shook him to the soles of his Tony Lamas.

The judge focused on Bart. "How do you plead, Bart? Are you guilty or not guilty?"

Bart swallowed into a dry throat. "Not guilty, Your Honor."

Rico nodded. "And you're out on bail, as I understand it."

"Your Honor?" a voice said from the other side of the courtroom.

Bart snapped around to look in the direction of the voice. He hadn't noticed the man sitting at the other table until now. But he knew him. Fifty if he was a day, yet bursting with the energy of a squirrelly colt, Marshall Kramer had peppered the county with advertisements while running for the post of District Attorney. Hell, Bart had even voted for the guy.

"Yes, Marshall?" Judge Rico said.

Marshall adjusted his three-piece suit. Where one of Marshall's three assistants had handled the drunk driving case, the charge of murder clearly counted for enough to justify Marshall taking the case himself. "I have some concerns about the defendant's bail."

Next to Bart, Lindsey stiffened. She kept her eyes focused on the judge.

"And what would those concerns be?" Rico asked.

Marshall raised the *Mustang Gazette* with a flourish. The headline blared for all to see—Murder Defendant Makes Threat. "The defendant was overheard threatening one of the witnesses against him last night."

Judge Rico nodded as if he'd already heard the story. With the speed of gossip around Mustang Valley, he probably had. Many times.

Bart inwardly cringed.

"And?" the judge prompted.

"And we would like his bail revoked."

His words cut into Bart like a cold blade.

"Your Honor," Lindsey said in a controlled voice that belied the tension Bart could feel emanating from her. "May I address the court?"

"Go ahead, Ms. Wellington."

"My client was severely provoked to say what he did. If I could show you the mitigating circumstances, I'm sure you'd agree. So I'd like to request we delay this decision pending a hearing."

"I don't think that's necessary, Judge." Marshall looked around the room, like he wanted to pace but couldn't find the acreage. "The defendant said he was going to kill a man. The son of the man he's accused of murdering, no less. I have a dozen witnesses. He's a danger to public safety, and we need to get him off the streets as soon as possible."

Behind him in the gallery, Bart could hear reporters' pens scratching down every word. The blade of impending disaster sunk a little deeper.

"Your Honor," Lindsey said. "Bart is a lifelong resident of Mustang Valley. He's never been charged with anything until now. To assume he's a danger to public safety without a hearing—"

"Point taken, Ms. Wellington. We'll set a hearing date for early next week. That should give both sides a few days to interview the witnesses." He looked down at Bart, his black eyes deadly serious. "And, Bart? Use that time to get your affairs in order. If I find that you have indeed been threatening witnesses, you'll find yourself awaiting trial behind bars."

The blade filleted him from breast to belly. He had no doubt what the judge would find. And it was going to be awfully tough to protect Lindsey and his daddy while he was sitting in a jail cell.

LINDSEY SET DOWN her fork for the fifteenth time and watched the shadows in Bart's eyes. By the time they got back to the ranch, evening was closing in on the rolling hills. After she'd helped Bart feed the horses, they'd sequestered themselves in the kitchen to eat and discuss the upcoming hearing. So far they'd done little of either.

She looked down at the macaroni and cheese she'd made, congealing on her plate. She didn't know what she'd been thinking. The simple meal had smoothed over problems when she was a child, but it would take more than comfort food to fix things now. She pushed her plate away nearly untouched and returned her attention to Bart.

He was looking straight at her.

Her stomach gave a little jolt.

"What are you thinking about?"

She glanced at the table, noticing his plate was untouched, as well. "That I should have made something different to eat."

"It's fine. You could have whipped up a gourmet meal and I wouldn't have been able to choke it down. Not after today."

The jolt she'd felt in her stomach turned into a cold lump. Not after today. Today, when a hearing was the best she could come up with to deflect the prosecution's request to revoke bail. A hearing where a parade of witnesses from Hit 'Em Again would get up on the stand and testify that Bart had threatened to kill his cousin.

"Now what are you thinking?" Bart asked again.

She looked into his eyes and forced a confident smile. "I was just thinking of witnesses I could put on the stand at the hearing."

"And coming up empty?"

She opened her mouth to protest, but the words died on her lips. He wouldn't buy any slick answers she gave anyway. "I'm sorry."

"You're the last person who should apologize. If I'd listened to you instead of my hot head, I wouldn't be in this fix." His green eyes were dark, haunted. His rough features were twisted with regret.

She drew in a deep breath. "It's past, done. Now we have to move on, figure out what we can do from here."

"I'll hire a bodyguard for you and beef up security for Daddy. The two of you will be safe. I'll make sure of it, whether I'm here or in jail awaiting trial."

"I don't need a bodyguard because you're not going to jail."

He raised his brows. "How do you figure that? I did just what Marshall said I did. I threatened to kill Kenny."

"We'll show that you did it out of fear for your life, your father's life and my life. That you only did it to make Kenny back off."

"And how do we show that?"

"I'll call Gary. I'll call Brandy Carmichael. Both can tell the court a few things about Kenny's recent conduct."

"And mine. Gary saw how angry I was when I set out to Hit 'Em Again. Brandy saw me throw a punch at Kenny."

He was right. Each of them could testify to a piece of what Kenny had done to Bart, but they could also give damaging testimony. And she had no doubt Marshall would bring out the other side at the hearing. "What about me? I've been part of everything. I've seen what Kenny has done. I know you were just trying to protect us."

"You can be a witness and my attorney at the same time?"

"Well, no. I'd have to step down as your attorney."

"Then we can't do that, either."

"We can find another attorney, Bart. Someone with a lot more experience."

"No. Besides, if you stepped down as my attorney you could also testify to how angry I was that night. And that I threatened to kill Kenny. And coming from you, that's got to carry extra weight with the judge."

He was right about that, too. She blew out a frustrated breath and dropped her chin to her chest. Her hair swung over her shoulders and draped around her face. "I'll think of something. There has to be something."

He leaned forward. Reaching across the corner of the table, he smoothed her hair back from her cheek and tilted her chin up. His touch was so tender, shivers stole down her spine. "There isn't any way around the truth, Lindsey. They're going to revoke my bail. I'm going back to jail." He paused, looking into her eyes with such longing she thought her own heart would break. "I just can't help wishing…" He trailed off, his voice hoarse.

"What? What do you wish?"

He withdrew his hand and rested it on the corner of the table, as if gripping the solid surface for support. "It doesn't matter."

She laid her hand on his. His fingers were rough, the skin thick with calluses. But she could feel a slight tremor run through him at her touch. "It matters. It matters to me."

He raised his eyes to hers. He watched her for a long time, and when he finally spoke, it was in a whisper. "I wish I could look at you across a crowded dance hall and know that you were saving every dance for me."

The tremor traveled up her arm and settled in her chest. "What else do you wish?"

"I wish we could ride bareback together under a moonlit sky."

Her chest tightened. She struggled to breathe. "And?"

"I wish I could show you just how deeply and thoroughly a man can love a woman."

She leaned toward him, wanting the corner of the table between them to disappear, wanting his arms around her, wanting to feel the solidness of his chest pressed against her breasts. She stood and stepped around the table.

He rose beside her. His hands hung at his sides, his

fingers flexing and straightening, as if he wanted to touch her but couldn't. "And most of all, I wish we had a future stretching in front of us. A future a thousand miles long and a hundred years deep."

"We have tonight."

He sucked in a breath. "That's not enough."

"It's enough for me. Right now it's all I could ever ask for." She reached out and laid her hands on his chest. She could feel the steady beat of his heart under the crisp white cotton. A heart so strong. A heart so tender. She slid her hands upward until she could clasp them around his neck. Until her own heart pressed against his. Looking deep into his tortured green eyes, she pulled him down to her.

He let her guide him, as if he couldn't mount a fight. But when he claimed her lips, she could tell he wanted this as much as she did.

His lips caressed hers, warm and tender. But there was an urgency underlying the kiss. A desperation. An overwhelming need. A need for her.

And the need within her answered.

He slipped his tongue into her mouth and deepened the kiss.

Warmth rushed through her body, making her light-headed, making her knees weak. She sagged against him.

He pulled her into his strong arms. Breaking the kiss, he narrowed his eyes with unspoken questions.

"Make love with me, Bart. Please," she whispered.

He scooped her into his arms and held her tight against his chest. Boots thunking on wood, he climbed the stairs and carried her to his bedroom.

He didn't switch on the light, but moved into the darkness and set her gently on her feet near the bed.

He slid open a drawer in the nightstand and rummaged inside. Producing a book of matches, he struck one and set the flame to the wick of a candle next to the bed.

Light flickered over his face and shone in his blond hair.

She swallowed hard and forced her voice to function. "That's nice."

"I wish I had more. A wall of candles. Music. Flowers. Your first time should be special. Romantic."

"All I need is you. You make it special. Romantic."

He looked away, as if he didn't quite believe her.

She reached up. Grasping the brim of his hat, she lifted it off his head and set in on her own. It settled low on her forehead, nearly covering her eyes.

A small smile curved his lips.

She tilted her head back to peer up at him under the huge hat. "Sexy, huh?"

"You make anything look sexy." He grasped the hat's crown and lifted it off her head. With a flick of his wrist, he tossed it on a chair. Heat in his eyes, he gathered her against him and lowered his mouth to hers once again.

His lips and tongue nipped and played over hers. Once her mouth had been thoroughly kissed, he moved his lips over her neck to her collarbone.

Heat spiraled through her and centered deep within her body. She wanted to touch him, for him to touch her. She wanted to be closer.

As if reading her mind, he slipped his hands under her suit jacket, under her blouse, until his work-roughened skin scraped along her sides.

She wanted more. She wanted him to touch all of her, see all of her, kiss all of her. She arched her back, pressing against him, savoring the feel of his hands.

He moved his fingers over her ribs. When he reached her bra, he slipped his fingers underneath, pushing it up and out of the way. His hands covered her breasts, cupping, holding.

She sucked in a breath.

His fingers teased her nipples. His tongue and lips took her, devoured her. Finally he pulled his hands from her breasts and found the buttons of her jacket. The jacket hit the floor, followed by her blouse and bra until she stood before him naked from the waist up.

He stood an arm's length from her and drew in a shuddering breath. "Lord, you're beautiful."

Shivers pebbled her skin and raised her nipples to tight nubs. With him looking at her this way, she felt beautiful. She felt loved. She felt powerful. And she wanted more.

She held out her arms, but he didn't step into them. Instead, he peeled off his own shirt.

Candlelight flickered over his broad, smooth chest. Shadows hugged the ridges of hard muscle. She felt she'd swoon at the sight.

Before she had a chance, he was with her, his warm skin touching hers, his arms enveloping her. His lips descended on hers, teasing, claiming. Her nipples rubbed against his chest. His fingers stroked over her stomach and back, finally finding the zipper of her skirt. He pulled it down and pushed the skirt and slip over her hips. They puddled on the floor at her feet. But instead of removing her panty hose, too, he moved his hands over her, caressing her backside, the rough skin of his hands scraping nylon. He worked his hand lower, his fingers brushing between her legs.

A shudder rippled through her. His fingers moved deeper. His touch grew more intimate, tracing her tender folds, circling the tight bundle of nerves, teasing until she couldn't take any more.

She slipped her fingers under the waistband of her panty hose and began pushing them down.

He grabbed her wrists. "Not so fast."

"I want you to touch me. I want—"

"I'll give you everything you want and more. Believe me, darlin'. I want this to last all night." He touched his lips to hers, soft, hot and full of promises.

She released the panty hose and moved her hands around his neck.

His hand once again slipped down her back and between her legs. He caressed her through the nylon, stoking her desire until she thought she'd burn up from the heat. He scattered kisses over her neck and collarbone. Then his mouth moved lower, over one breast, claiming a nipple. His tongue teased. His fingers stroked.

Her body convulsed and shuddered. She dug her fingers into his shoulders, clinging to him as her knees threatened to buckle. Heat washed through her in waves.

When the sensations finally passed, she was breathless. He kissed her cheeks, her eyelids, her lips. Then he lowered her to the bed, stripping off her panty hose on the way.

She lay back on the softness. Her muscles felt limp, her energy spent. But her heart felt strong and full to bursting.

Maybe Kelly and Cara were right. Maybe she had a bit of Shotgun Sally in her, as well. Maybe Bart was her Zachary Gale, and she was meant to save him from this murder charge. Maybe fate had brought them together and led them to this moment. She reached out her arms to him, wanting him to join her on the bed. Wanting to curl into his warmth.

"Not yet. I want to look at you." He stood at her feet, his gaze moving over her the same way his hands had done. Over her breasts, down her belly and settling between her legs. Caressing, stoking the fire once again. Finally he moved his hands to his waist and unhooked his silver buckle.

Lindsey watched, anticipation building like a coil tightening inside her.

He unzipped his fly and pushed jeans down powerful legs. Stepping out of his boots and jeans, he straightened and hooked his thumbs in the waistband of his briefs. Eyes locked with hers, he pushed them down, as well.

She lowered her gaze and swallowed into a dry throat.

She'd known from the bulge in his jeans that he was large. But she hadn't expected this. Warmth rushed between her legs. At the same time, her muscles clenched in apprehension.

The shadow of a smile played on Bart's lips. "Don't worry. We'll take it slow. I want this to be good for you." He leaned forward. Starting with her feet, he massaged his way up her legs, littering kisses along the way. By the time he reached the tops of her thighs, her apprehension was gone, and tingling warmth flowed through her body.

He gently parted her legs and lowered his head. His lips caressed her. His tongue opened her.

Tension once again built in her muscles. Except this time it wasn't caused by trepidation. This time it was urgency, need. She raised her hips to him.

Cupping her buttocks in his hands, he devoured her.

Another shudder ripped through her. And another. Finally, when she was certain she couldn't take any more pleasure, he kissed his way up her body, over her breasts. He reached past her and pulled a packet from the nightstand. Ripping the condom package open, he sheathed himself before settling his hips between her spread legs.

She could feel him nestle against her, long and hard and ready. Her body ached for him to fill her. She tilted her hips, opening to him.

Claiming her lips in a kiss, he eased into her. First just a little. Then a little more.

She stretched to receive him. Pain burned through her. She sucked in a breath.

Bart froze. "I'm sorry."

She grasped his shoulders. "No. Don't stop. Please, don't stop."

He eased in a bit more.

Her body warmed, accepting him a little at a time until he was fully inside.

He searched her eyes. "Are you okay?"

Raising her chin, she pecked his lips. "I'm wonderful."

He smiled. "Yes, you are." He lowered his mouth onto hers and began moving slowly.

The pain between her legs faded, replaced by heat and wetness and overpowering need. She moved with him, awkwardly at first, then with the rhythm of a perfect dance. Heat built between them, melding their bodies, their souls. And when the shudder claimed her this time, he was with her, calling out her name.

ARM CURLED AROUND a sleeping Lindsey, Bart stared at his bedroom wall. He breathed in the light fragrance of roses, his chest aching like he'd been stuck with a dull knife.

Making love with her had been even more than he'd imagined it could be. She had touched his heart, touched his soul. She had widened his world and opened up a future he'd only dreamed of. A future filled with love and children and happily ever after.

A future he doubted he would ever know.

She'd said she wanted him, needed him, even if it only meant one night. But he couldn't fool himself. He hadn't gone against his better judgment for Lindsey's sake. He'd done it for himself. Because he needed to feel her skin against his. Because he needed to look into her eyes as he entered her. Because he needed to lock the memory of making love to her inside his heart where nothing could take it away—not the law, not prison, not the bleak future he faced. And now he'd have to live with what he'd done.

And hope to God Lindsey didn't pay the price for his selfishness.

He drew in another deep breath of her. A faint scent registered in the back of his mind. Not just the sweet fragrance of roses, but a trace of smoke. An uneasy feeling spread over his skin.

Gently untangling himself from her, he slipped from the bed and padded to the open window on bare feet. The ranch sprawled in front of him, moonlight reflecting off white buildings and pipe corrals. He inhaled again. Definitely smoke. Smoke coming from the direction of the barns.

A panicked equine scream pierced the air.

Adrenaline slammed through his bloodstream. He spun from the window. Groping in the dim light, he pulled on his clothes.

Lindsey stirred and sat up in bed. "What's going on?"

Another whinny split the night.

Bart reached for a boot. "Smells like fire. I think it's coming from the barns. I'm going down to check it out."

She threw back the covers and jumped out of bed, the moonlight glowing on her skin. "I'm coming with you."

The thought of Lindsey anywhere near a barn fire rammed into his gut like a hard fist. "No, stay here. Call 9-1-1."

She nodded. Struggling into her white silk blouse, she grabbed the phone at the side of the bed.

Bart finished thrusting his feet into his second boot and charged into the hall. He raced down the steps and out the door. The smoke was stronger out in the open air. He launched into a dead run. By the time he reached the door of the main horse barn, a ruckus of whinnies had started up. It was a fire, all right, in the horse barn. He had to get the horses out.

He flattened a palm against the door. The steel was cool to the touch. A good sign. At least the fire wasn't right behind the door; he had a chance to get inside. He grabbed the door's handle.

"The fire department is on its way," Lindsey shouted breathlessly from behind him. "What should I do? How can I help?"

He spun around.

She was dressed in the white blouse and dark blue skirt she'd worn to court. Under the skirt, her bare legs tapered down to a pair of flimsy high-heeled shoes. Not exactly the gear for fighting fires. Not that he'd let her take one step inside that burning building even if she was dressed in full firefighter's gear. "Go wake Gary and the hands. If they aren't awake already."

She nodded and raced in the direction of the bunkhouse and apartments. The hands' living quarters were farther from the horse barns than the main house was, but Bart hoped they had heard some of the ruckus or smelled smoke and were on their way.

As soon as Lindsey had cleared out, he turned back to the barn and slid the big door open. Smoke billowed out. A wave of sound hit him. Horse snorts and screams. The thunk of hooves against wood. The low roar of flame.

He plunged into the smoke. Groping through the darkness, he located the switch box and flipped on all the lights. Even with the lights blaring overhead, the barn was dim. Smoke hung in the air and made his eyes sting and water. Smoke and something else.

The smell of gasoline.

Someone had set the fire deliberately. His gut clenched, tight as a fist. He pushed the anger from his mind. He had only minutes, maybe seconds to save the horses. He had to focus.

He raced down the barn aisle. Smoke billowed from the tack room and spread out along one wall. There were only thirty horses in this barn. Mostly his show horses, a few pregnant broodmares and a few mares with brand-new babies. The working horses and other broodmares were in the corrals outside, safe from the fire. Reaching the first box stall, he unlatched the door and yanked it open.

The mare inside nearly ran him over in her haste to get out. He stepped back and spread his arms, barring her from running deeper into the barn, directing her toward the open door and freedom.

She weaved, undecided at first. Then finally catching

a whiff of fresh air, she raced like a bat out of hell for the door, steel-shod hooves clattering and slipping on the cement aisle floor.

He moved to the next stall and the next, freeing each horse, directing them to the open door. As he got deeper into the barn, the smoke grew thicker, the heat more intense. Flames flickered and glowed, leaping over ceiling beams and huddling along the floor.

A male voice shouted through the thick smoke. *Gary.*

"I'm about halfway down!" Bart yelled back. His chest seized with the effort, sending him into a fit of coughing.

Suddenly many people were with him, pulling open stalls, herding the horses to safety. The smoke was so thick he couldn't see faces. All he could see were shapes.

One grabbed a hose in the wash stall and sprayed, flame cowering under the assault. Another sprayed a fire extinguisher. A smaller figure clad in white and dark blue slipped past, heading for the broodmare stalls at the far end of the barn.

Lindsey.

Fear clogged his throat and turned his stomach. He set out after her, racing deeper into the barn. White swirled around him, thick and lethal. He fought to see, fought to breathe. Lindsey was nowhere. It was like she'd disappeared into the white fog. Or like she'd never existed.

Had she really slipped past him into the smoke? Had he just imagined her? Imagined her because he was so scared she'd get caught up in the fire? That she'd be in danger? That he'd lose her?

Sweat poured down his face, salt and smoke filling his eyes. He fought on. If Lindsey was in here, he'd find her. Find her or die trying.

CHAPTER THIRTEEN

BART GROPED THROUGH the smoke, struggling to see. The stall doors gaped open like screaming mouths on either side of the aisle. Stall after stall was empty, each horse safely outside.

No sign of Lindsey.

Even through the thickening smoke, he could see the large sliding door at this end of the barn. If he opened the door, he could have more oxygen. He could breathe. Problem was, the fire could breathe, too. He had to check the last stalls before he opened the door. Because once he opened it, he'd better damn well be prepared to get the hell out.

He forced his feet to move to the end of the barn. In spite of the hands' success in beating back the flames with the wash-rack hose, the fire was still going strong. Heat assaulted him. His lungs ached with lack of oxygen and burned from smoke. He had to get out of here. And he had to get out now.

He made his way to the end of the aisle. The end stalls were broodmare stalls, extra large and reserved for mares either with foals or expecting. He liked to call them family double wides. They held two mares who could drop their foals any moment. He reached one stall and peered inside. Smoke burned his eyes. Tears streamed down his cheeks. But through the tears, he could see the stall was empty.

He started across the aisle to the other side of the barn. Before he reached the last stall, he could sense movement inside. He raced through the open door.

Lindsey stood near the head of the sorrel mare.

Bart's heart caught in his throat.

Her eyes were wide, her hair singed. She grasped the mare's mane with one hand, obviously trying to coax the frightened horse out of the false safety of the stall. When she saw Bart, a look of relief washed over her face. "She's scared. She made it halfway down the aisle and then turned around and headed back to her stall. I think she might be in labor. I can't leave her here."

Of course she couldn't. Not Lindsey. Hell, neither could he.

The mare's wet sides heaved. Her eyes rolled white in their sockets.

He slipped into the stall and joined Lindsey at the mare's head. "We need something to cover her eyes. If she can't see the fire, she won't know what she's going through." He stripped off his shirt and tied it over the mare's eyes.

The mare tossed her head, trying to rid herself of the blindfold. He grasped a handful of mane. Using it as a lead rope, he guided the mare to the mouth of the stall while Lindsey encouraged her from behind.

The mare balked at the door. Lindsey raised a flat hand and brought it down on her haunches in a loud slap. The mare surged out the door and into the aisle.

Bart gripped her mane tighter and circled an arm under her neck to bring her back under control. He guided the blinded horse to the barn door. He glanced at Lindsey. "Open it. And as soon as you do, get out. I'll be right behind. This side of the barn is going to be a fireball."

She nodded. She grabbed the handle of the door. At Bart's nod, she yanked it wide and jumped out. The mare shot through the opening, pulling Bart with her. Flame roared behind them, heat licking at their heels.

BART SURVEYED the ranch, anger hardening in his chest. Red and blue light throbbed in the night, bouncing off the whitewashed buildings and fence like the sign announcing some damn sale at the local discount store. The county's fire truck, all five county sheriff's cars and an ambulance crowded around the charred skeleton that was once the horse barn.

The hands who weren't being treated by the EMS for burns and smoke inhalation had gathered the horses into one of the far corrals. Their frightened whinnies cut through the low rumble of human voices.

He turned from the wreckage and focused on Lindsey. Perched inside the open back door of the ambulance, she stared at the activity with shell-shocked eyes. Despite the warm night, a blanket was wrapped around her shoulders. She held it tight at her throat with trembling hands.

It'd been damn foolish, the way she'd plunged into the smoke to save that mare without thought of the risk to herself. And damn brave. But he'd come to expect nothing less from her. He just hoped to hell her bravery didn't get her hurt. Or dead.

A sheriff's car pulled up to the ambulance on its way out. Bart recognized the black hair and sharp cheekbones of Deputy Mitchell Steele behind the wheel. He motioned for Mitch to stop.

Mitch hung an arm out his open window. "Bart."

"Mitch, I need a word."

The deputy looked up at him, narrowing his unusual golden eyes. "What is it?"

"I smelled gasoline. In the barn. When I opened the door it hit me like a damned blanket."

"So you think it's arson?"

He nodded. "Listen, could you do me a favor? Could you check on Kenny's whereabouts tonight? A lot of things have been happening around here since Jeb's death, things I suspect Kenny is behind, and Hurley won't look into any of it."

Mitch nodded as if he wasn't surprised. "I'll check up on Kenny and see what else I can do. But I can't promise much. Sheriff Ben and Hurley have been keeping me out of the loop lately. Probably has something to do with the upcoming election. Ben has his eye on the mayor's job, and Hurley doesn't want me as competition for the sheriff post."

"He's worried you're going to follow in your daddy's footsteps?"

A shadow of pain passed over Mitch's hard face. Pain, no doubt, from the rumors surrounding Mitch's father's death. Rumors of scandal and suicide.

"I'd appreciate it if you'd do whatever you can, Mitch. You're the only lawman in this county that I trust."

"And we all know how much the trust of a murderer is worth, don't we?" Hurley Zeller strode toward them on short legs. He turned his mean little eyes on Mitch. "This is my case, Steele. Don't you have a call to get to?"

The planes of Mitch's face hardened. He glanced at the beat-up sedan pulling up the road to the ranch. Cara Hamilton's red hair shone in the passenger seat, her boss Beau Jennings hulked behind the wheel. "Don't worry, Hurley. I'm not planning to steal your headlines.

We'll talk later, Bart." Mitch raised the car's window and drove away.

Hurley cursed at the departing car and then swung his attention back to Bart. "So what were you talking to Steele about? Confessing you set the fire yourself to direct attention away from your uncle's murder? You know, make yourself look more sympathetic and heroic to the public?"

"I hope you either have facts to back up those charges or you keep them to yourself, Deputy," Lindsey said as she stepped beside Bart. Her voice challenged despite the pallor of her face and trembling of her hands. "That is unless you want to be looking at a lawsuit once Bart is acquitted."

"I'm just calling it as I see it. I'm sure you two have some scheme cooked up, but I sure as hell ain't playing along." Hurley's lip curled in a sneer.

A sneer Bart would love to wipe off with his fists.

Lindsey shook her head like she couldn't believe what she was hearing. "What is it with you? What do you have against Bart?"

"Other than the fact that he murdered a man?"

"He didn't kill Jeb Rawlins."

"Right. What you and this whole damn town don't seem to understand is that just because Bart was a football star in high school, and he's been Mustang Valley's goddamn golden boy all the years since, doesn't mean he's better than the rest of us. Doesn't mean he gets away with murder, either. And I'm going to make damn sure of it."

Bart's blood heated to boiling. "So that's what it comes down to, Hurley? You've been waiting all these years to pay me back for beating you out for quarterback in high school?"

"I didn't put the knife in your hand and aim you at Jeb's throat. I'll enjoy bringing you down, but you're the one who made it happen. And if the fire inspector finds you had anything to do with this, I'll be right there to arrest you for insurance fraud and arson." The deputy walked away, each stride exaggerated like a puffed-up rooster.

Bart raked a hand through his hair. "Hell, I wouldn't put it past Hurley to frame me for the fire."

She raised her chin. Determination glinted in her eyes. "I'm going to have a talk with Cara. Maybe Hurley isn't concerned about the life and property of a defendant in a murder trial, but I'll bet Sheriff Ben will care about what the press has to say. Especially with an election coming up in the fall."

Bart watched her stride off. The blanket flared out behind her like some damn superhero cape. If anyone could twist Ben's and Hurley's arms, it would be Lindsey and Cara. They were just lucky Kelly Lansing had left on her honeymoon, and they only had two of the dynamic trio to contend with.

Bart looked down the driveway in the direction of Mitch Steele's fading taillights. He hoped Mitch could dig something up to nail Kenny. Of course, even if he did, Sheriff Ben was still in charge. And press or no press, the sheriff would favor Hurley's word over Mitch's any day. Hadn't his failed attempts to reach Mitch before this already proved that? Hadn't Mitch himself said the sheriff and Hurley had purposely kept him away from Bart's case?

A chill worked over his chest and back. The truth was, no matter what Cara wrote in the paper, no matter which deputy was on the case, Bart couldn't expect protection from Sheriff Ben. Not for his dad or Lindsey or the cowboys, horses and cattle who lived on the Four Aces.

He thought of Lindsey. Of the way she'd given herself to him last night. Of the way she'd risked her neck to save the broodmare. Of the way she'd stood toe-to-toe with Hurley to defend him with all the fire of an avenging angel. If anything happened to her…if anything happened to Daddy or Gary or the other hands and their families…he would never forgive himself. If there was anything he'd learned through this ordeal it was that people were precious. More precious than unfulfilled dreams or family legacies. More precious than wide-open spaces and white pipe fence. A lot of people on this ranch relied on him, and it was up to Bart to make sure they were safe.

Or at least to take away the reason they were in danger.

"ARE YOU ALL RIGHT, Bart?" Paul Lambert's brow pinched in a concerned frown. He swung the door to his office wide and ushered Bart inside like he was royalty.

Or some kind of invalid.

"I'm fine."

"I heard about the fire at the Four Aces. It was a miracle you didn't lose any horses. Or people."

Bart nodded. It was barely ten o'clock in the morning, but by now he had no doubt every soul in Mustang Valley had heard about last night's fire. "Guess I've been providing the town's entertainment lately."

The pity on Paul's face stung.

Bart shifted his boots on the thick carpet. Hell, he didn't need pity. He, Lindsey, Gary and all the hands had gotten by unhurt. They'd managed to save all the horses. What they hadn't saved was the barn itself. Or Bart's confidence that he could protect his dad or Lindsey or anyone else, for that matter. Especially if he was operating from a jail cell.

A shiver worked its way over his skin. If he hadn't seen Lindsey through the smoke…

He shut the image from his mind. He couldn't think about how close he'd come to losing her. He could only focus on what had brought him to Lambert & Church. "I didn't come about the fire, Paul. I need to talk to you."

"What about?"

Bart took his hat from his singed hair and tried to beat back his misgivings. He hated not telling Lindsey what he was doing, but he couldn't take the chance that she would talk him out of it. "The other day you said you had someone interested in buying the Four Aces."

"You want to sell?"

Bart bobbed his head. Pain threaded through his chest with every beat of his heart.

"Why don't you sit down?"

Hat in hand, Bart forced himself to walk to the desk. The soles of his boots bogged down in the plush carpet. The office's air-freshener scent clogged his throat, still sore from smoke. When he reached the chairs in front of Paul's desk, he balked. Somehow the thought of sinking into one of those chairs seemed like he was giving up.

Paul circled his desk, his shrewd eyes sizing up the situation. "You seem hesitant."

Hesitant about selling his dreams? His legacy for future generations of Rawlins children? Rawlins children that would never be born? He shook his head. "I don't have much of a choice."

Paul arched his brows. "This isn't about your case, is

it? Lindsey might be a little green, but she's a competent attorney. The law is in her blood. You'll see when you get to trial."

"I don't doubt Lindsey. Not for one second."

"Then what's the problem?"

He didn't want to tell Paul more. Not today. Not when he felt that every word of explanation tore away a little bit of his soul. "Do you want to talk business? Or should I call Brandy Carmichael and list the ranch with her?"

At mention of Brandy's name, Paul froze. Guilt showed clear as day on his face along with a touch of anger. Apparently the cheerleader-turned-Realtor was telling the truth about their personal history. "I can call my client right now, if you like, set up a meeting."

The air seemed to rush from the room. Bart struggled to take a breath. He had to do this. If he wanted to keep Lindsey safe, keep his dad safe, keep the hands and their families safe, he needed to say goodbye to the only home he'd ever known.

A small price to pay. "Do it."

LINDSEY SORTED through the papers and unopened mail cluttering her desk. She couldn't stand working in this kind of mess. She liked the desktop clear, organized, professional. Especially since her life had been anything but clear, organized and professional since she'd walked into the Mustang Valley jail and shaken hands with Bart.

Her throat ached at the thought of him. His strength and cool head when he'd helped her rescue the broodmare from the fire. The pain she'd seen in his eyes as he watched the smoldering skeleton of his prized horse barn. The way he so obviously cared about every cowboy and horse and cow who lived on the ranch as if they were part of his family.

The way he cared about *her*.

A tingle traveled over her body. Last night he'd said he wanted to show her how deeply and thoroughly a man could love a woman. He had done just that and more. And now the future seemed more muddled than ever.

She picked up the stack of mail that had just arrived this morning and forced her mind off Bart and onto work. She flipped through the letters. A request for a court date here, a note from her mother there. A plain white envelope caught her attention. A Fort Worth postmark canceled the stamp. Her pulse picked up its pace.

Fitting a nail under the flap, she ripped it open. Tissue-thin paper spilled out. The drug report. Holding her breath, she unfolded it and skimmed the page. One word leaped out at her. The word listed in the results column of each test.

Negative.

She closed her eyes and covered her face with her hands.

"My God, Lindsey. Are you okay?"

Lindsey wiped silent tears from the corners of her eyes and focused on Nancy standing in the doorway. "I'm fine."

"I heard about the fire at the Four Aces. How terrible. Shouldn't you be home recovering?"

Although Nancy seemed like a nice woman, she had never acted personally concerned about Lindsey since she had taken the job at Lambert & Church. Wouldn't you know her maternal instincts would pick now to kick in? Now, when Lindsey desperately needed to be alone. "I'm fine, Nancy. Really."

The older woman tapped herself on the forehead as if remembering something. "The meeting, of course. I suppose you had to come in for the meeting this morning."

"Meeting?"

"With Roger Rosales from the Ranger Corporation."

She gave Nancy a blank look.

"Don't you know?"

Lindsey shook her head.

"I realize you're acting as Bart Rawlins's criminal attorney. But I just assumed you were involved with this, too. Or you'd know about it, at the very least." She shook her head, flustered, and pressed her lips tightly closed as if determined not to let another word escape.

"What was the meeting about, Nancy?"

The office administrator's eyes shifted to the door. She looked like she wanted to bolt.

"What was the meeting about?" she repeated. "I'm Bart's attorney. You can tell me."

"I don't know."

"Suit yourself. But if you don't dish, I'm going to have to walk down the hall and ask Paul. He'll want to know where I got wind of the meeting and..."

"All right, all right. It's about Bart's ranch, the Four Aces. He's selling."

"And Ranger Corporation is buying," Lindsey said flatly. She wrapped her arms around herself and willed her body not to start shaking.

CHAPTER FOURTEEN

"YOU CAN'T SELL the ranch."

Bart stopped in his tracks in front of the corral and turned to face Lindsey. He knew she'd find out. She was too smart, too resourceful for him to be able to keep her in the dark long. "I have to sell, Lindsey. It's the only way."

"The only way to do what?"

"Protect you, Daddy, Gary, the hands and their families, everyone. You read that message spray-painted on your car. My God, you were attacked in your apartment. Anyone who's around me is in danger. If I sell, it'll break the connection."

"It won't break the connection between you and your father. Or you and me."

"No." He looked past her and focused on the spot where Gary's bay mare stood tied to the corral fence, saddled and ready. "I'm still figuring a way to deal with that."

"You don't have to sell the ranch. Hire security."

"For the next twenty-five years to life?"

"You're not going to be convicted."

He shook his head and brought his gaze back to her. Determination burned in her eyes, hot as blue flame. Her hands balled into fists by her side like she was ready to challenge the entire Mustang Valley legal system to a brawl in order to save his hide. "You've seen for yourself how the law works in this county. Hurley might or might not be crooked, but he definitely has a grudge against me. And he has definitely stacked the deck."

Concern flashed in her eyes. She glanced away, a split second too late.

"What? What's happened?"

"I got the drug analysis from the lab. Blood and urine."

He didn't have to hear her answer to know what the report said. He steeled himself for the blow. "There was no Rohypnol, was there? Or anything else."

"No."

He met the news without flinching. "Selling the place is the right thing to do. The only thing I can do."

She shook her head and raised her chin. "No. I'll find another way to prove you're innocent. I can win an acquittal. You have to believe in me."

"I do believe in *you*. But I can't ignore the evidence stacked against me."

She shook her head. "My family always says they believe in me, too. But they don't act like it. You don't, either."

"It isn't a matter of believing in you, Lindsey. I just can't take the chance someone will be hurt. That you'll be hurt. People are more important than a ranch. Even this ranch."

She looked away from him, glancing past the horse tied to the fence and toward the apartments beyond. Two little kids galloped around like colts in front of the long, low building. When she looked back to him, the fire in her eyes was barely a smolder. "You're right. This has nothing to do with me. And you have no other choice."

A knife of pain stabbed into his chest at the defeat in her voice, in her eyes. He reached out and pulled her into his arms. "The way your family tries to protect you and help you has nothing to do with not believing in you, either, Lindsey. They worry about you because they love you."

She looked up at him and searched his eyes. "And you? Why do you worry about me, Bart?"

His throat closed. He touched her hair, her face, and then let his hand fall to his side. Swallowing hard, he pulled back and turned away. He couldn't look into her eyes one more second. Couldn't stand to see the love shining there. The kind of love he'd seen in his mama's eyes every time she looked at his daddy. The kind of forever love he'd have given his soul for before he'd been charged with Jeb's murder.

He focused on Gary's mare. A halter and lead rope secured her to the fence. A brand-new bridle draped over the saddle horn. The bit and reins rested against the pro rodeo logo tooled into the saddle's fender.

A dose of adrenaline slammed into his bloodstream. "That saddle."

Lindsey glanced at the saddle and then back to him, her eyebrows dipping low in question.

"The saddle on Gary's mare. It's the one he won back when he was riding the rodeo circuit."

"I'm not following."

"It's his favorite saddle. He kept it in the tack room of the horse barn."

Understanding dawned. Her eyes widened. "The saddle should have burned along with everything else in the tack room."

He nodded. "Unless Gary took it out…" He didn't want to believe where his mind was taking him.

"…before he started the fire…" Lindsey finished for him.

LINDSEY STOOD BEHIND Bart as he slipped his key into Gary's apartment door. Despite the fact that his horse was tied to the corral fence, the foreman was nowhere to be found. And he didn't answer the knock on his door.

She thought of the pain on Bart's face when he recognized what the saddle meant. Duplicity. Betrayal. If only they could call the sheriff, let the law deal with Gary. It would be easier on Bart than confronting his foreman personally. But Hurley hadn't taken the fire seriously in the first place. Calling him would yield nothing but the joy of dealing with his bad attitude. No, they had to get evidence of Gary's involvement. Once they did that, Hurley and the sheriff would have no choice but to pursue the case.

The knob turned under Bart's hand and he swung the door wide. The room was dim, blinds drawn against the morning sun. "Gary? You home?"

The apartment was silent as death.

Bart flicked on a light and stepped into the living room.

Lindsey followed, glancing around the room, looking for some clue to the man who lived there. But except for a worn couch and small television, the room was nearly empty. No sign of Gary. Not much sign of life in general. At least not much of a life. "How well do you know Gary?"

"He started working here when I was just a kid. He taught me practically everything I know about ranching. He's been like a brother."

Like a brother. His words tore at Lindsey's heart. The strain on Bart was worse than she'd imagined. Much worse. "Maybe he didn't do anything. Maybe there's another explanation for the saddle."

"If there is, I sure as hell can't come up with it. And I've been trying. God, have I been trying."

Her heart ached for him. "But why would he burn the horse barn?"

Bart flinched with obvious pain. "I wish I *couldn't* think of a reason."

She watched him with questioning eyes and willed him to go on.

"When my daddy passed the ranch to me, he gave a portion to Gary for his retirement. Sweat equity."

"So he'll profit when you sell."

Bart nodded. "He's been wanting to retire for a long time now. Bad back. He may have thought a fire would hurry up the sale. If he did, he was right."

"But if he wanted the money to retire, why wouldn't he just ask you to buy him out?"

"He did. Only problem was cash flow. I couldn't scare up the money to give him what his share is worth. And with beef prices the way they've been for the past ten years, the bank refused to loan me that much. The Four Aces is a successful operation, but that's only because we've cut the fat to the bone. It'll take me years to get the kind of money Gary deserved. He knew that."

"Why wouldn't he just sell to someone else?"

"My daddy stipulated that he could only sell back to a Rawlins. He wanted to keep the ranch in the family. Maybe he shouldn't have done that. Maybe he should have given Gary more of a way out." He drew in a pained breath. "I guess the only way we're going to get answers is to start looking."

She nodded. They needed answers, all right. She just hoped the answers they found wouldn't bring Bart more anguish.

They moved quickly through the apartment. The

place was painstakingly neat, making a search easy—a search that turned up a couple of sticks of furniture, a few dishes and some work clothes. In other words, nothing.

"There's one other place he stores things. Follow me."

They retraced their steps. Once outside, Bart headed for a garage to the rear of the apartment building. He pulled up the door. Sunlight flooded the space, illuminating everything from an old sofa and chair to stacks of boxes to spare tires.

Bart picked his way through the garage to a row of cabinets lining the back wall. "This one's Gary's." He opened one of the doors. Color drained from his face. "Damn."

"What is it?" Lindsey moved up behind him. A can of spray paint peeked out over some old truck parts on the top shelf. The cap was bright red. She sucked in a breath. Here, the entire time they'd been looking for Gary that night, he'd been vandalizing her car.

But Bart wasn't looking at the spray paint. His attention was riveted on a lower shelf.

She craned her neck to see around him. Tucked behind some odds and ends was a small black box. "What is it?"

"The ELT for the helicopter." He clipped off the words. A muscle twitched along his jaw.

"Gary sabotaged the helicopter?"

Bart closed his eyes as if struggling to hold on to his self-control. "How could he have done it? How could he have tried to kill us?"

"And your father? Do you think he let your father out on the range?"

Judging from the anger radiating from him, he did.

He grimaced and pressed a thumb and forefinger to his closed eyelids, as if by doing so, he could erase what he'd seen—he could erase Gary's betrayal. "After all Daddy did for him. How could he have done it? And for what? Money? When I get my hands on that bastard—" He opened his eyes and froze, staring at a spot among the clutter on the floor.

A trickle of fear ran down Lindsey's spine. "What is it?"

Bart closed his eyes again. "It's Gary."

She stepped around Bart. "Where is—" Her question caught in her throat.

Gary lay on his side among a jumble of boxes, an arm stretched out toward them. A pool of red puddled under his body.

Lindsey's stomach heaved. "Oh, God."

Before she could turn away, a car swung around the burned wreckage of the horse barn, gravel popping under its tires. Blue and red lights flashed from its roof. Another sheriff's car followed.

"Oh, hell," Bart muttered.

Hurley scrambled out of the first car. A deputy Lindsey didn't recognize climbed from the second and fell in behind him. Struggling to regain her composure, Lindsey took a step toward them. "We were just about to call you, Deputy."

Hurley looked past her. "What the hell do we have here?" Eyes narrowing, he rested his hand on the butt of his gun. Behind him, the other deputy did the same.

CHAPTER FIFTEEN

BART LEANED BACK in the hard chair and tried to smother the worry building inside him like a raging brushfire. The tiny office in the Mustang Valley police station closed in on him. The dark lens of the camera in the corner of the room stared down on him. It hadn't taken much to figure that Hurley would try to pin Gary's death on him. He'd seen that coming the moment the weaselly deputy had roared up the ranch road, lights flashing. What he couldn't figure out was how Hurley knew about Gary. And where he'd taken Lindsey.

Finally, after letting Bart stew for at least an hour, Hurley pushed open the door and stepped inside. Cradling a thick folder in the crook of his arm, he crossed the tiny room in two steps. He dropped the folder on the desk with a thump and stood over Bart, hands on hips. "Who'd a thunk it'd end like this, eh, Bart?"

Bart tried his best to stifle a growl. "Where's Lindsey? I want to see my lawyer."

"We'll get to that. First you got to tell me why you killed Gary. Did he find out about your plan to kill Jeb and take his ranch? Or was Gary in on it with you?"

"Gary was the one who vandalized Lindsey's car. He sabotaged the helicopter. He burned down the horse barn. He may have killed Jeb, too, for all I know. Look in his garage space. The evidence is all there."

"And that's why you killed him? You thought he did all these things?"

"I didn't kill Gary."

"Don't play me for a fool, Rawlins. I know damned well you killed Gary. I drove up while you were busy stashing the body, remember? Or did you kill him earlier, and you were just planting the evidence you mentioned when I drove up?"

Bart's head throbbed. "When you drove up, I'd just discovered the body."

"Right."

"Ask Lindsey."

Hurley rolled his beady eyes. "I'll just rush off and do that."

"Where is she?"

"That shouldn't be your concern right now, Bart. You should be focused on explaining your ass out of this mess."

Bart narrowed his eyes. "How did you happen to be out at the ranch at just that moment anyway, Hurley?"

"I came to question you."

"If you didn't know Gary was already dead and you weren't setting me up to take the blame, what were you planning to question me about?"

"You really are a good actor, Bart. You should have gone out for theater in high school instead of football."

"I'm telling the truth, damn it."

"Right." The deputy stroked his chin. "But then, I suppose you don't know we found her."

"Found who?"

Hurley stared at him, a smug grin on his face.

Bart wanted to wipe that grin off more than he wanted air. "Tell me, damn it."

"Like you don't already know. Unless there are more bodies out there we ain't found yet."

A body. Someone else was dead. *"Tell me."*

"Pretty smart to send us on a wild-goose chase looking for Beatrice Jensen when she's been in the Squaw Creek Reservoir all along."

Beatrice. He tried to catch his breath. Jeb, Beatrice, Gary...all dead. And Hurley wanted to believe *he* had murdered them. His mind spun. He gripped the chair arms.

"You'd be better off confessing, Bart," Hurley said, his voice suddenly soft with kindness. "The whole thing will go easier on you if you tell us what happened. Make us understand."

"I didn't kill Beatrice, Hurley. You've got to believe me."

Hurley let out a frustrated breath. "You have no idea what you're up against."

Bart's gut clenched. "What? What am I up against? Who's doing this? Who's paying you to railroad me?"

The little deputy looked down at him and shook his head, the disgust at Bart's suggestion plain on his face. "The justice system, Bart. You're up against the Texas justice system. Murderers don't go free around here like they do in bleeding-heart states like California. Here they get the needle. And that's what you're going to get if you don't do something to help yourself."

Bart knew all about the Texas death penalty. He'd even been in favor of it once. Before he knew how easily a man could be railroaded for a crime he didn't commit. Before he knew how easily *he* could be railroaded. "Where's Lindsey? I want to talk to my lawyer."

"No lawyer is going to get you off. You've killed more than one person now. And the way I see it, those murders are all linked to your scheme to get your hands on Jeb's land. I just talked to the D.A. before coming in here. And he promised me he was going for the death penalty."

Bart gritted his teeth. He remembered Lindsey's explanation of the capital murder laws the day he'd met her in the Mustang County jail. And far as he could tell, Hurley was telling the truth. "I want to talk to my lawyer, and I want to talk to her *now*."

"You can talk to your lawyer all you want, but it ain't going to be Lindsey Wellington no more."

Fear stabbed into Bart's gut. "Why not? What happened to her?"

Hurley leaned back against the wall, the smile on his face bigger than the state of Texas. "Lindsey Wellington is in the next office chatting with the sheriff. Too bad you got her involved in this. Seems she's facing charges now, too."

"I GOT HERE as fast as I could." Paul Lambert stepped into the sheriff's station office and took the chair next to Bart. He gave Bart a tight smile, clearly meant to be reassuring.

Bart didn't bother smiling back. "Is Lindsey okay?"

"Don's talking to her in the next room. He'll be taking her case. I'll take over yours, if that's okay with you."

"Doesn't Don just do wills? Does he know how criminal law works?" He'd never had cause to distrust Don Church and his abilities, but with the stakes so high, he had to be sure.

"Lindsey will be fine, Bart. From what I've gleaned, the sheriff's evidence of her role in the actual murder isn't too convincing."

Maybe not, but Bart wasn't willing to take that chance. "If the evidence isn't convincing, why is she being arrested?"

"She hasn't been arrested. And neither have you. Not yet, anyway. You're both merely here for questioning."

"Why is she being questioned?"

"Because the sheriff has some physical evidence that suggests she helped you dispose of Beatrice Jensen's body."

Bart sat forward in his chair and gripped the chair arms. "That's ridiculous. What kind of evidence?"

"That I don't know."

"Well, you'd better damn well find out, Paul."

Paul stuck his hands out, palms to Bart, fingers splayed. "Don is handling Lindsey's case. He'll take care of her. You need to calm down."

Bart couldn't calm down. Not with Lindsey in trouble. It was one thing for the law in this county to railroad him, but he wasn't going to sit by and pretend to be civilized while they railroaded Lindsey. "What is she facing?"

"Possible accessory-to-murder charges."

Bart jolted from the chair. This couldn't be happening. He stepped forward to pace, but there wasn't enough space in the cramped room to take more than a couple steps.

"Don't panic, Bart. I can't see this going too far. The idea of Lindsey being involved is ludicrous. They're just rattling their sabers."

He spun back to face Paul. "You don't think they'll indict her?"

The lawyer grimaced. "They might. But that doesn't mean they have a case. The grand jury is the prosecution's own private dog-and-pony show. Marshall could

probably convince the grand jurors to indict a ham sandwich, as the courthouse saying goes."

"She could face a trial? Prison?"

Paul held up a hand. "I doubt the charges will stick.
Not from what I've heard of their evidence."

"What about her career?"

"It depends on a lot of factors. If she's indicted, she
could face disbarment."

Paul's words hit him like a mule kick to the head.
He tried to breathe. Lindsey's career was her life. Being
disbarred would kill her. He couldn't let that happen.
"What if I confess? What if I say I did it all without
Lindsey knowing about any of it?"

Paul shook his head. "You're facing the death penalty
now, Bart—multiple murders committed pursuant to the
same scheme or course of conduct. You confess, and
you're putting yourself on death row."

"Isn't there a good chance of that happening no matter
what I do?"

Paul grimaced again and looked to the floor, obviously not wanting to answer.

"Isn't there, Paul?"

He let out a deep sigh. "I suppose there is."

"Then I have nothing to lose." Bart drew himself up.
God forgive him for the lie, but he had to do what he
had to do. "Call in the D.A., Paul. I want to confess."

FINALLY ALONE, Lindsey hunched in the police station's hard wooden chair and let Don Church's visit wash
through her memory. The partner had been nervous, his
voice pitched a bit higher than it usually was. Especially
when he got to the part about Beatrice Jensen's murder
and evidence that Lindsey had helped Bart cover it up.

The way Don had looked at her, she could tell he

had his doubts about her innocence. No wonder he was never a poker player. Or a litigator. Don didn't have the nerves for high-stakes games.

She pushed her hair back from her face. What Don thought didn't matter. The truth didn't seem to matter. All that mattered was seeing Bart.

What she was facing was nothing compared to what he must be going through. A triple-murder charge would qualify Bart for the death penalty. And the State of Texas took that designation seriously.

She lowered her face into her hands and stared at the floor between her fingers. A sob worked its way up her throat, emotion choking her, threatening to drag her under.

Footfalls outside the door cut through her despair. The door to the little office swung wide. But instead of Hurley Zeller's smug sneer or Don's dapper smile, a dark and handsome deputy she recognized from the aftermath of the barn fire peered down at her with the most unusual gold eyes she'd ever seen. "Lindsey Wellington?"

"Yes?"

"You're free to go."

His simple phrase sent a shock wave through her. "I'm what?"

"You're free to go."

"I'm not going to be arrested?"

"No."

Relief sagged through her. But the relief was short-lived. It didn't make sense they would let her leave just like that. Not after what Don had told her. He said they'd found her date book in the reservoir near Beatrice's body. He said they'd found mud consistent with the reservoir on a pair of shoes in her apartment. The police didn't let that sort of thing go. It just didn't happen. "Why am I not being arrested?"

Surprise registered on the deputy's strong face. "You want to be arrested?"

"Of course not. I just want to know why I'm not, Deputy…"

"Steele. Mitchell Steele."

"Deputy Steele."

"I can't tell you why, ma'am. I don't know. The district attorney just told me you aren't."

Lindsey's mind raced. Maybe they believed Don when he told them the date book was in her stolen briefcase. Maybe the mud hadn't ended up matching that at the reservoir. But somehow she got the feeling it wasn't that simple. "What about Bart Rawlins? Is he being charged?"

The deputy pressed full lips together.

She lunged to her feet. "If I'm not being charged as his conspirator, then I'm still his lawyer. I need to know."

A muscle worked, flexing from jaw to sharp cheekbone. Finally he gave a single nod. "Bart met with the district attorney about fifteen minutes ago."

Bart met with Marshall Kramer? All Don had said was that Bart was talking to Paul. He hadn't mentioned anything about a meeting with the D.A. "And?"

"Bart cut a deal."

Her head spun. Her stomach swirled. It didn't make sense. Bart hadn't killed anyone. Why on earth would he plead guilty? "A deal? What kind of deal?"

"I don't know," Deputy Steele said. "You'll have to ask Bart. I'll take you to him."

Foreboding gripped her throat like a strong hand. She nodded.

Turning on a heel, Deputy Steele led her out of the room. He stopped at the next door in the hall, rapped on it twice and pushed it open. He stepped to the side so Lindsey could enter.

From the hard chairs to the small desk to the camera peering down from the corner, the room was identical to the one she'd just left. Bart sat beside Paul. He looked tired, drawn, his skin pale under his tan. And instead of the straightforward way he'd always met her gaze, he dodged and looked away.

A tremor shuddered through her. "Bart, I need to talk to you."

Paul pushed himself up from his chair and stepped toward her. "This isn't a good idea."

"How can it not be a good idea to talk to my client?"

"It's all right, Paul. It's only right that I tell her myself."

Paul glanced back at Bart briefly before returning his scrutiny to Lindsey. Finally giving a nod, he stepped past her and out of the room. The door thunked closed.

Lindsey dragged in a breath. "What is going on, Bart? What kind of deal did you cut with the D.A.?" Her voice came out in a choked whisper.

His lips flattened. He focused on a spot in the corner of the room, as if he couldn't bare to look at her. "I'm going to have to let you go, Lindsey. Paul is representing me now."

Her heart stuttered. She didn't know what she'd expected him to say, but this certainly wasn't it. "You're firing me?"

"Yes."

The room whirled around her. "Why?"

"Things have changed. I need a lawyer with more experience."

She staggered back. She'd always known this was a possibility. Hadn't she suggested it to Bart herself? The fact was, criminal law wasn't her specialty. She'd never taken a case solo, let alone a murder case. She was in over her head from the beginning. The smart thing, the prudent thing for him to do would be to find a lawyer with more experience. And although Paul's current specialty was real estate law, he'd worked criminal cases before. Bart needed a lawyer like Paul.

Then why did his decision feel like the thrust of a blade into her heart?

She studied Bart. His shuttered expression. The way he looked everywhere but at her. There was more to this than he was telling. Much more. "I can understand your decision. But if that's truly how you feel, why can't you look me in the eye?"

As if to prove her wrong, he focused on her. His eyes ached with sadness, hopelessness. And underneath she sensed something more. Something tender. Protective.

She knew Bart. And she knew what he was doing. "You're protecting me."

He shook his head and looked away.

"The sheriff has evidence that I was involved in disposing of Beatrice Jensen's body, and yet they didn't arrest me. They let me go." Her mind swam. Dread inched up her spine. "Bart, what did you do? What kind of deal did you agree to?"

"I'm already going to prison for killing Jeb."

"What did you do?"

"I confessed."

Lindsey tried to breathe, but she couldn't draw air through her pinched throat. "You can't confess."

"I'm not going to let them go after you just to save myself from a couple more murder charges."

"A couple more murder charges?" Panic swamped her. "Being convicted for killing three people in Texas is worlds different from being convicted for killing one. Life-and-death different."

His face was fixed as stone.

Realization closed over her head like cold, black water. "Oh, my God. That's what you want, isn't it? You want to be executed."

He dipped his head. "I'm confessing to the murders. That's all."

"That's not all, and you know it. Marshall is going to argue that those murders were committed pursuant to the same scheme or course of conduct. He's going for the death penalty. And you're giving him a confession. That's the same as committing suicide."

"It's not suicide, damn it."

"Just because it's state-sponsored and disguised as justice doesn't mean it's not suicide." She studied Bart's face. "But you wouldn't see it that way, would you? You'd see it as sacrifice."

Bart looked up. His eyes narrowed to green slits. His expression warned her to back off.

"No. Not sacrifice. It isn't sacrifice when you do it for someone you love, is it?" She threw his words back at him with all the force she could muster. Rage stormed through her. Her heart ached. Bart loved her. She knew that now. Knew it with more certainty than she'd known anything in her life. And because he loved her, she was going to lose him.

"Life in prison is the same as death."

It all fell into place. It all made some kind of twisted sense. His need to protect her. His seeing life in prison as a death sentence. A sentence he didn't want to visit on her. "You don't want me waiting."

The planes of his face hardened.

"That's it, isn't it? You don't want me waiting like your mother waited for your father."

"Leave it alone." Every muscle in his body tensed for fight. He wasn't giving in.

God help her, the stubborn, self-sacrificing fool wasn't giving in. "For God's sake, Bart, all they have against me is a date book that was stolen with my briefcase and a little mud on a pair of my shoes—mud that hasn't even been tied to the reservoir. The best they can hope for in a case like that is a hung jury."

"But that might be enough."

"Enough for what?"

"Enough to disbar you. Enough to ruin your career."

Her career. Numbness stole through her. Numbness and despair. Once she'd thought her career was the most important thing in the world. Only now could she see how wrong she'd been. Her career was nothing without her family's love. It was nothing without Kelly and Cara's unconditional support. But most of all, it was nothing without Bart. "If saving my career means losing you, it's not worth it."

"You're a good lawyer, Lindsey. A great lawyer. You've worked so hard, wanted it so—"

"No. My mother is the one who had it right. My mother knew a career could wait, that some things are more important, some things have to come first. That all the success in the world doesn't mean a thing if you don't have someone to share it with. I want the success, Bart. But it doesn't mean anything if I can't share it with you."

"They're going to convict me anyway. I'm just trying to keep them from ruining you in the process."

Tears clogged her throat. "I'm not going to let you do this."

"You have nothing to say about it, Lindsey. You're not my lawyer anymore."

"Maybe not. But I'm not going to sit by while you let them put a needle in your arm. I'm going to the D.A. I'm going to tell him the whole thing is a lie."

"And what would that do? He won't believe you. He thinks you were helping me cover up, for God's sake."

He was right. Marshall wouldn't believe her. Not unless she had evidence to back her up. Strong evidence. Evidence that didn't seem to exist.

Panic threatened to choke her. "I'll challenge the allocution. Judge Valenzuela won't proceed with sentencing if your former lawyer challenges the validity of your confession."

His hands opened and closed by his sides. "You can't do that."

"Actually, I can."

"And what good will it do? You'll be charged for helping me, and the D.A. will use my confession against me during the trial. The jury will convict me without a second thought." He was right. Oh, God. Her knees wobbled. And folded. She reached out, supporting herself on the back of a chair.

Suddenly Bart was beside her. His gentle hands, his fresh scent, his tenderness. He propped her up and guided her into the chair. "I'm not going to let you sacrifice your career for no reason. Please, Lindsey. Let it go."

She looked into his eyes, soaked in his touch. He was so tender, so caring, so giving. Her heart squeezed. "It really isn't a sacrifice when you do it for someone you love, is it?"

He flinched. Tears sparkled in his eyes. "Please, Lindsey."

She shook her head. "I'll explain your confession to the jury. We'll find more evidence. Evidence that exonerates you. I'll show the jury that you didn't kill your uncle, that you could never do such a thing. I'll hand them reasonable doubt on a silver platter." She waited, breathless. Wanting him to agree with her. Wanting desperately for things to be different.

"There is no evidence, Lindsey. No silver platter." Running his fingers through her hair, he pushed the stray tresses over her shoulder and smoothed his hand down her back. He leaned down and pressed his lips to the top of her head. "It's over, Lindsey. I want you to forget it and move on. For me."

She wrapped her arms around his waist and pressed her cheek against the hard muscle of his stomach. He felt so strong, so solid. She inhaled the essence that was his alone.

She couldn't forget. She couldn't move on. She didn't care about her career. She didn't care about her future. All she cared about was Bart, hearing him say her name…breathing in his clean, honest scent…loving him.

With all her heart, loving him.

Tears broke free, coursing down her cheeks. "You're wrong, Bart. It's not over. Not by a long shot. You said once that I never give up. Well, you were right. I don't give up. And I'm not going to give up on you."

He sucked in a sharp breath. "That's what I've always been afraid of."

CHAPTER SIXTEEN

LINDSEY SLUMPED IN her office chair and tried not to look at the clock on her desk. The effort was wasted. She knew what time it was. She could feel every second tick by, drawing closer and closer to the scheduled time of Bart's allocution—the hearing where he would confess to three murders he didn't commit and receive his sentence. By agreeing to a plea bargain with the D.A., he had given up his right to a trial.

She'd worked so hard since she'd last seen him, spending countless hours overturning every stone she could in an effort to find evidence to clear him. But except for the report on the bottles and glass shards from Hit 'Em Again, she'd come up with nothing. And even the report had turned out to be negative for any kind of drug except alcohol.

The only thing she was left with was her faith. In Bart. In his goodness, his honesty. And in the court system. And stacked against Bart's confession, that didn't add up to much.

Or did it?

The last time she'd talked to Bart, she'd threatened to go to the judge, to challenge Bart's confession, to tell him everything she knew, whether she could prove it or not. Bart had been right that a move like that wouldn't solve the problem. That the best they could hope for was for the judge to throw the question to a jury—a jury that would probably look no further than Bart's confession. It certainly wasn't the solution she was hoping for, but at least it would postpone his sentencing. At least it would buy some time.

Pushing back from her desk, she stood and strode out of her office and down the hall. Maybe she could catch Paul before he left for the courthouse, tell him her plan.

The door to Paul's office was open. A good sign. She rounded the bend and stepped inside.

Nancy Wilks stood at Paul's vacant desk. Her dark bob, usually harnessed rigidly in place by loads of hair spray, looked mussed. Her eyes darted to Lindsey, as if she'd been caught going through Paul's private papers. She held up a cigarette in shaking fingers and bobbed her head. "Lindsey?"

"I need to talk to Paul."

"He already left for court."

Lindsey's heart dropped.

Nancy gathered up a stack of files on Paul's desk. Taking a drag off her cigarette, she started for the door. "I'm heading to the courthouse in just a few minutes. If you want, I can pass on a message."

Lindsey hesitated. An uneasy feeling crept up her spine. There was something about Nancy's tone. Something wrong. As if she suspected Lindsey was hiding something? As if she was hiding something herself? "Thanks anyway, Nancy. I'll just give Paul a call on his cell phone. He has it with him, doesn't he?"

Nancy raised a controlled eyebrow. "Of course."

Lindsey stepped to the side of the desk and picked up the phone. Her hand trembled as she held the cordless receiver. She quickly tapped in Paul's number. The ring on the line sounded in her ear, blending with the buzz of nerves. "Thanks, Nancy."

Giving her one last look, Nancy turned and walked from the room, leaving a trail of cigarette smoke behind her.

After several rings with no answer, Lindsey replaced the phone in its cradle. Leaving a voice mail would do no good if he didn't get his messages until after the hearing. She needed to get down to the courthouse, and she needed to get there now. She stepped away from the desk, her foot plowing into the metal trash can.

It fell to its side. Blackened ash spilled over the money-green carpet.

Ash? Paul didn't smoke. Why would there be ash in his wastebasket? She leaned closer. She could make out two slips of paper. Reports of some kind. Lab reports. The name of the lab to which Doc Swenson had sent Bart's samples was legible at the top of each page.

She lowered herself to her knees and blew a stream of air at the reports to clear away some of the ash. The half-charred name at the top of both was Bart Rawlins. One address was the office and the other was her apartment. Two copies of the same report. One must have been stolen from her apartment in the break-in. Farther down, a number indicated the level of Rohypnol in Bart's system. And even though she was no scientist, she recognized the number as being high.

Very high.

Her pulse beat a frantic rhythm. She grabbed an envelope from the desk. Poking and prodding, she pushed the slips of paper into it, careful not to destroy any fingerprints there might be. Ash floated into the air around her. The rest of the reports were destroyed, but she'd seen all she needed to see. The report she'd received earlier was a fake.

And if she hadn't interrupted Nancy, she never would have found the originals.

LINDSEY RACED up the steps of the Mustang Valley Courthouse. She had to reach Bart. She had to show him and Paul what she'd found. She had to tell them what Nancy had done before it was too late.

When she'd driven out of the Lambert & Church parking lot, Nancy's car had still been parked in its usual space. Lindsey had beat her to the courthouse, but there wasn't a moment to spare. Bart's hearing was drawing near.

Heels clacking on marble, she negotiated the maze of hallways leading to Judge Valenzuela's courtroom. People bustled and gathered outside the courtroom. The doors were open and flanked by bailiffs, and inside Lindsey could see a crowd of reporters and citizens.

She turned a corner and headed for the lawyer-client meeting rooms to the side of the courtroom. Only one was occupied. She rapped on the door with a shaking hand.

Paul pulled it open and peered out. "Lindsey?"

"I have to talk to you and Bart."

"Now's not the time. We're due in court soon."

"It's urgent."

He frowned but stepped back to let her slip inside.

Bart pushed to his feet on the other side of a small table, watching her through sad and wary eyes. He looked thin and pale in his jail jumpsuit, more like his father than the robust cowboy she'd met at the beginning of this ordeal. The cowboy she'd fallen in love with.

Her heart pinched.

Paul closed the door. "This had better be worth it, Lindsey."

It was worth it, all right. She kept her attention on Bart. She couldn't have done otherwise if her life depended on it. "I found the reports, Bart. The *real* lab reports. The ones that show high levels of Rohypnol in your system. The other one was a fake."

Lines dug into his brow. "What are you talking about, Lindsey?"

"Evidence. I'm talking about evidence that proves you couldn't have killed Jeb Rawlins."

His jaw tensed. His face hardened. As if he didn't believe what she was saying. Or he was afraid to let himself hope.

"It won't make the judge drop the charges immediately. But it will give us some ammunition to take to a trial. Strong ammunition. The kind that produces reasonable doubt." She drew a deep breath, forcing all her conviction into her voice. "You can't plead guilty. You have to help me fight this."

"Let me see those reports," Paul held out his hand.

Lindsey clutched the envelope. She didn't want to let it go, even to show Paul. She wanted to hand it directly to the judge. She couldn't take the chance that whatever evidence it carried would be contaminated. "We don't have time. I have to show this to Judge Valenzuela. Nancy will be here any minute."

"Nancy?" Bart echoed. "What does this have to do with Nancy?"

"I'll tell you later. Just promise me one thing. Promise me you won't plead guilty."

"Lindsey—"

"Trust me on this, Bart. If I'm wrong, you can plead

later. Just promise me you won't plead guilty. Have faith in me."

A full minute seemed to tick by. His eyes drilled into her. A muscle along his jaw flexed and released. Finally he dragged in a ragged breath. "I promise."

Relief spiraled through her. Forcing herself to turn away, she strode for the door on shaking legs, gripping the envelope like a lifeline.

"Lindsey?" Bart said.

She turned back. A shiver rippled up her spine. "What?"

"I've always had faith in you."

Tears welled in her eyes. She blinked them away. She didn't have time for tears now. She had to reach the judge. She had to give him the slip of paper that could save Bart's life. She reached for the doorknob.

A hand slammed against the door, holding it shut. "You're not going anywhere, Lindsey." Paul's voice was rough, strange.

She turned around and stared into the snub-nosed barrel of a gun.

CHAPTER SEVENTEEN

BART'S HEART JUMPED to his throat. He stared at the little revolver, its barrel leveled on Lindsey. "What the hell are you doing, Paul?"

Paul looked at the gun in his hand, as if just recognizing it was there. Then, his expression hardening, he took his free hand off the door and shoved it toward Lindsey, palm up. "Give it to me."

Lindsey's eyes flared wide and then narrowed on Paul, like she'd gotten a bead on him and not the other way around. "One of these reports is addressed to me at my apartment. You broke into my apartment that night, Paul? You stole my briefcase? But it wasn't my briefcase you were after, was it? It was my mail."

Paul's expression didn't change. "Give me the report."

"You knew all along Bart didn't kill Jeb. He couldn't have. He had too much Rohypnol in his system. Rohypnol Gary Tuttle slipped into his beer at the bar." Lindsey lifted her chin and met her boss's eye. "Who killed Jeb, Paul? You?"

Paul didn't answer. But he didn't have to. Bart could see the guilt etched in the lines of his face, hard as the callousness in his eyes.

"So it wasn't Kenny," Bart muttered. He couldn't quite believe his cousin was innocent, but the evidence was right in front of him, shoving a gun in Lindsey's face.

The gun. He had to get that gun away from Paul. But to do that, he needed to get around this damn table without Paul seeing him move. He focused on Lindsey, willing her to look at him, to know what he was thinking.

Her blue gaze flicked toward him. And then held. She set her chin and drew in a deep breath. Breaking eye contact, she focused on her boss. "Why did you do it, Paul?"

Paul glanced at him and then back to Lindsey.

"I can't imagine what would make you do something like that," she continued. "What's in it for you?"

Paul shook his head in disgust. "Isn't it obvious?"

Bart took a silent step.

Lindsey frowned, a tiny line appearing between graceful eyebrows. "Obvious? How?"

Paul shifted his focus to Bart. "It's all your damn fault."

"How is it Bart's fault?" Lindsey raised her voice, trying to draw Paul's attention.

It worked. Paul turned to her with a glower. "If Bart would have sold the Four Aces when I originally approached him with the Ranger deal, and if his damn ornery cuss of an uncle hadn't jacked up the price of his land beyond reason, none of this would have had to happen."

"The land? You killed three people over land?" Lindsey prodded.

"I didn't kill Beatrice. Gary did. She got in his way when he was taking the old man out on the range."

Poor Beatrice. She'd only been doing her job, trying to take care of his daddy, keep him safe. And Gary.

After all his daddy had done for Gary... Bart pushed away the sting of betrayal. None of it mattered. The only thing he could think about now was stopping Paul. And saving Lindsey. He took another step toward the corner of the table.

"So you and Gary did all this for what?" Lindsey continued. "Money?"

"The Bar JR and the Four Aces are worth a lot. More than you know." Paul scowled at her. "Maybe money doesn't seem like much for a Wellington or the owner of the Four Aces or for Don Church and his family millions. But some of us weren't handed money and influence at birth. Some of us had to scrape and scratch for every penny."

Bart shook his head. Despite the current success of the Four Aces, there had been plenty of lean times. He could understand the frustration Paul felt at not being raised with money, at having to see Don dressed to the nines in his designer suits every day while Paul had to claw to build his end of the partnership. And he could understand Gary's desperation to retire from ranching after suffering years of back pain. Maybe even his desire for a few luxuries. Still, none of it made a damn bit of sense. No amount of frustration or pain or envy could justify murder.

Lindsey glanced at him before zeroing in on Paul. "You *murdered* Jeb and Gary. And you would have let Bart take the lethal injection for it."

Paul's lips flattened, but there was no remorse in his eyes.

Lindsey shook her head. "I can't believe you almost got away with it."

"I did get away with it. Bart signed the papers. The

ranches belong to Ranger now, and the cut of future profits Roger promised is mine."

"Not yet. Bart isn't convicted. He isn't going to plead. I saw Nancy in time."

"What the hell does Nancy have to do with this?" Paul asked.

"She didn't burn the lab report or help you cover up evidence?"

"You think she's in on this? Please. Nancy is a glorified bookkeeper. She doesn't have the imagination or the ambition."

"Then what was she doing in your office this morning?"

Paul's brow furrowed. "I don't have a clue. Probably snooping. I'll deal with her later."

"How about Brandy Carmichael?" Lindsey pressed on.

Paul flinched at the name. "She's just a mistake from my past."

"She told us about your affair. She also told us she wanted to list Jeb's land. Was she after that deal with Ranger Corporation, too?"

Paul's brows shot toward his hairline. "You think you have this all figured out, don't you? Did you also figure out why I gave you Bart's case when you had no experience in criminal law, let alone murder?"

Lindsey sucked in a breath.

"That's right. I thought you'd blow it. And you did."

Bart clenched his teeth until his jaw hurt. Lindsey hadn't blown it. She'd saved him. Despite the way he'd played right into Paul's hands in a misguided attempt to protect her, she'd saved him. And he was damn well going to get the chance to thank her. He took another stealthy step.

Paul's eyes shifted, like he'd caught movement out of the corner of his eye.

Bart froze.

Lindsey reached for the door.

Paul grabbed her arm and jammed the muzzle of the gun into her ribs. "What the hell do you think you're doing?"

Every nerve in Bart's body screamed for him to jump Paul, to get that damn gun. But the table still blocked him. And though he'd seen such heroics in movies, in real life the move would probably only get them killed. He forced himself to take only a small step, a step Paul wouldn't notice. He had to get into position before he made a move. It was Lindsey's only chance.

Lindsey glared into Paul's eyes, like the gun in her ribs didn't even faze her. "We're in the courthouse, Paul. There are bailiffs just outside the door. You're not going to get away with this."

"That's where you're wrong. You and I are going to walk out this door and right under those bailiffs' noses. And you aren't going to try anything."

Bart's heart slammed against his ribs. Paul obviously didn't know Lindsey like he did. She would try something. He would bet his life on it. And Paul would shoot her. Fear clutched his throat. He couldn't let Paul take her out that door. He had to put an end to this now. He inched around the corner of the table.

"But how's that going to work?" Lindsey continued. "Bart will be here by himself. You really don't think he's just going to sit here politely while you're gone."

"That's exactly what he's going to do if he doesn't want me to put a bullet in you. And when I get back, he's going to go into that courtroom and plead guilty for killing Jeb, Gary and Beatrice. And he's going to make it convincing."

"How does he know you aren't going to put a bullet in me as soon as we step outside the courthouse?"

Paul smiled. "I guess he'll just have to have faith in me."

Not in this lifetime. Bart met Lindsey's eyes. He took the last step around the table.

Lindsey dropped to the floor.

Bart charged. Before Paul had time to swing the gun around, he drove into Paul's side like a linebacker.

Breath exploded from the attorney's lungs.

Bart plowed a fist into his jaw.

Paul raised his gun hand.

Bart chopped down on his arm. The gun clattered to the floor. He found the lawyer's face with another punch and another, until Paul lay still.

Grabbing the gun, Lindsey scrambled to her feet and rushed for the door. The noise of the crowds in the hall had probably prevented the bailiffs outside from hearing the fight, but Lindsey obviously intended to call them in now.

Bart caught her as her fingers touched the knob. "Wait."

She turned to him. Eyes bright and skin flushed that delicate pink, she looked as beautiful and strong as he'd ever seen her. She searched his eyes.

"Once you get the bailiffs in here, we won't be able to talk. And I have some things you need to hear."

She shook her head. "You have faith in me. You were willing to put your life on the line. You saved my life. That's all I need to know."

"Then there's something I need to say." He gathered

her against him. She was so soft and yet strong. Ladylike yet as tenacious as his best cutting horse. "I love you, Lindsey."

Tears sparkled in her blue eyes. "I love you, too, Bart. And I'll get you cleared. I promise."

He shook his head. "I only need one promise from you."

"Anything."

"Promise me that when this mess is over, you'll let me prove how much you mean to me."

"I promise, Bart. With all my heart, I promise."

Holding each other close, they moved toward the door as one.

EPILOGUE

"WHAT ARE YOU going to do now, Lindsey?" Cara's concerned voice rippled over Lindsey's cell phone.

The million-dollar question. Lindsey threw her car into Park but didn't open the door. Instead she sat in the air-conditioning and watched lights glowing from the house, apartment building and interim horse barn at the Four Aces.

Her head was still spinning. It was impossible to wrap her mind around all that had gone on in the past few days since Paul had drawn a gun on her and Bart at the courthouse. So much had come to light. So much had changed. And now the news Cara had just given her. None of it seemed real.

"Lindsey? Are you there?"

Lindsey brought her mind back to her conversation. Cara had asked what she was going to do now. What *was* she going to do now? Don had offered to keep her on while he sorted out the wreckage of Lambert & Church, but she hadn't given him her answer. "Is this Cara the reporter asking?"

"No. Cara the friend."

She blew a breath of air through tight lips. "I'm sorry. I'm still trying to recover from the bombshell you just dropped on me."

"Don't worry about it. Being called a reporter in any context is no insult to me. You know that."

Yes, she did. Cara was a top-notch reporter through and through. And she and Kelly were top-notch friends.

"Are you still staying at the Four Aces?" Cara asked.

Lindsey looked out the windshield of her parked car. "Bart has been insisting I stay here until he's sure I'm no longer in danger. That protective thing he's got going."

"Yeah, and I'm sure that's all it is," Cara teased. "As long as he's protecting you in bed at night, that's all that matters."

"Cara!"

"Don't tell me you're still living a chaste life. I'll have to come out there and slap you."

No, there was nothing chaste about the life she'd been living at the Four Aces since the sheriff had found so much evidence of Paul's wrongdoing hidden at his house that the D.A. had been forced to drop the charges against Bart. Just thinking about the nights since Bart had been released from jail brought heat to her cheeks and a silly grin to her face. "There will be no slapping, Cara."

"Good girl. Now back to my original question. What are you going to do now?"

"Ranger Corporation is threatening to sue Bart for backing out of the sale. I suppose I'll be busy working on that."

"What about long-term, Lindsey?"

"Long-term? I guess I have some thinking to do."

"Fair enough. I just don't want you deciding to move back to Boston."

Move back to Boston? She hadn't thought of that option. Maybe because it wasn't one. "Mustang Valley is my home. You're not getting rid of me that easily."

"Glad to hear it," Cara said with certainty, as if all her questions were answered. A remarkable feat.

Too bad Lindsey's questions weren't answered. And sitting in her car chatting with Cara wasn't about to answer them, either. "I have to go."

After exchanging goodbyes, Lindsey punched the End button on her cell phone and climbed into the warm Texas night. She needed to find Bart. She needed to tell him what had happened. Maybe then she could put her life in order in her own mind. Maybe then she could answer some of the questions plaguing her.

She spotted him walking from the barn, a big palomino horse trailing behind him. Although the horse wore a bridle, his back was bare. As soon as Bart spotted her, a smile spread over his lips. "Just the woman I'm looking for." He narrowed his eyes and studied her face. "What happened?"

Cara's news. Shock must still be written all over her face. "Cara called."

"And?"

"The grand jury indicted Paul for both Jeb's and Gary's murders and for drugging and framing you."

"After all the evidence they found at his house and office, it's no wonder."

She nodded.

"So if Cara called just to tell you that, why the long face?"

"That's not all she told me." She took a deep breath. "They found Paul in his jail cell after the news of the indictment came down. He hanged himself."

Bart's lips tightened. "I can't say I'm too sorry about that."

"Me, either, I guess. It's just that the whole thing is so sad. I took the position at Lambert & Church because

Paul seemed to believe in me. He made me think I could be a success."

"You are a success, Lindsey. You don't need Paul. You don't need Lambert & Church. You don't need anybody."

"That's not true. I need you. But not to believe I'm a success. I just need you to be happy."

"Damn straight. And I need you, too." He stepped forward and gathered her into his arms.

Warmth seeped into her bones and wrapped around her heart. She drew in a deep breath of leather and fresh air. He was something, her cowboy. Honest and tender and strong all wrapped into one sexy package.

He pulled back slightly and looked down at her. Mischief twinkled in his green eyes. "All this brings me to the reason for this horse." He raised the rein he held in one hand and the palomino stepped forward.

She gave Bart a questioning look.

"The other night I wished I could take you for a moonlight ride. Tonight I aim to make that wish come true."

Anticipation shivered through her. The thought of snuggling close to Bart while a horse's back rocked gently beneath them was more tempting than chocolate. "I'll go change into jeans."

"Don't bother. I don't envision us needing a lot of clothing for this ride."

Another shiver sent heat to her core.

"But before we go riding, I have a question to ask."

"A question?"

"Yes. And I want an honest answer, so help you God."

As if she could meet Bart's sincerity with anything less. She raised her right hand. "So help me God."

Dropping the rein, effectively ground-tying the horse, Bart fitted a large palm over his hat and lifted it off his head. "After that ordeal with Paul in the courthouse, I said I only wanted one promise."

She remembered. How could she forget? "You said you wanted me to let you prove how much you loved me."

"Yes. But I've decided that isn't enough."

She willed him to go on, to tell her what more he wanted, what more she would gladly give.

Holding his hat to his heart with one hand and taking Lindsey's hand in the other, he sank to one knee. "When I met you, I'd all but given up on finding a woman I wanted to spend forever with. But I found that with you. I don't know what the future is going to bring, but I do know I want to spend it with you. I want you to be my bride."

Joy spun through her, making her giddy.

"I know you want to build your career, and I'm fine with that. I've been a bachelor so long I can take care of myself and Daddy and you. We can do this, Lindsey. You won't have to sacrifice a thing."

"Oh, Bart. You don't have to convince me. I would be honored to be your bride. I would be honored to spend the rest of my days loving you." She reached down and smoothed her fingertips over his stubbled chin. Decisions fell into place in her mind, decisions she hadn't known she'd made until this moment. "I want to set up a practice to help people who can't help themselves. Children. And people like your father."

He nodded, pride spreading over his face in a wide grin.

"And after I establish my new law practice, I want

children of our own. I want to fill all the bedrooms in that big house of yours."

He pushed to his feet. Fitting his hat back on his head, he wrapped his arms around her. "You've just made me the happiest man in Texas, maybe the whole damn country. We can get the marriage license and rings tomorrow and be married by next week."

She pulled back from his embrace. "We have to wait for your father to get out of the rehabilitation center. He has to be at the wedding."

Bart's brow furrowed briefly as if considering this new wrinkle. He nodded. "He's doing better every day, so that shouldn't be too long."

"And we have to wait until my family can come to the wedding."

He looked at her out of the corner of his eye. "Of course."

"And Cara and Kelly. We have to wait for Kelly to get back from her honeymoon."

"Okay. Is that all?"

"It would be nice if you and Kenny could reconcile."

His grimace broke into a smile. "Well, I guess I can try. It's not sacrifice if you do it for someone you love."

Joy spread over her lips and burst in her soul like Fourth of July fireworks. Kenny aside, the thought of a wedding to the man of her dreams witnessed by all the people she loved filled her nearly to bursting.

He chuckled and folded her back into his arms.

She reveled in the feel of him, so strong, so solid, so warm. It didn't matter what the future brought. As long as she had Bart, she could weather anything. As long as she had Bart, every day for the rest of her life would be a stunning success.

* * * * *

Harlequin® Blaze™ brings you
New York Times *and* USA TODAY *bestselling author*
Vicki Lewis Thompson with three new steamy titles
from the bestselling miniseries SONS OF CHANCE

Chance isn't just the last name of these rugged
Wyoming cowboys—it's their motto, too!

Read on for a sneak peek at the first title,
SHOULD'VE BEEN A COWBOY

Available June 2011 only from Harlequin® Blaze™.

"Thanks for not turning on the lights," Tyler said. "I'm a mess."

"Not in my book." Even in low light, Alex had a good view of her yellow shirt plastered to her body. It was all he could do not to reach for her, mud and all. But the next move needed to be hers, not his.

She slicked her wet hair back and squeezed some water out of the ends as she glanced upward. "I like the sound of the rain on a tin roof."

"Me, too."

She met his gaze briefly and looked away. "Where's the sink?"

"At the far end, beyond the last stall."

Tyler's running shoes squished as she walked down the aisle between the rows of stalls. She glanced sideways at Alex. "So how much of a cowboy are you these days? Do you ride the range and stuff?"

"I ride." He liked being able to say that. "Why?"

"Just wondered. Last summer, you were still a city boy. You even told me you weren't the cowboy type, but you're…different now."

He wasn't sure if that was a good thing or a bad thing. Maybe she preferred city boys to cowboys. "How am I different?"

"Well, you dress differently, and your hair's a little longer. Your face seems a little more chiseled, but maybe that's because of your hair. Also, there's something else, something harder to define, an attitude…"

"Are you saying I have an attitude?"

"Not in a bad way. It's more like a quiet confidence."

He was flattered, but still he had to laugh. "I just admitted a while ago that I have all kinds of doubts about this event tomorrow. That doesn't seem like quiet confidence to me."

"This isn't about your job, it's about…your…" She took a deep breath. "It's about your sex appeal, okay? I have no business talking about it, because it will only make me want to do things I shouldn't do." She started toward the end of the barn. "Now, where's that sink? We need to get cleaned up and go back to the house. Dinner is probably ready, and I—"

He spun her around and pulled her into his arms, mud and all. "Let's do those things." Then he kissed her, knowing that she would kiss him back, knowing that this time he would take that kiss where he wanted it to go. And she would let him.

Follow Tyler and Alex's wild adventures in
SHOULD'VE BEEN A COWBOY
Available June 2011 only from Harlequin® Blaze™
wherever books are sold.

HBEXP0611

SPECIAL EDITION

Life, Love and Family

LOVE CAN BE FOUND IN THE MOST UNLIKELY PLACES, ESPECIALLY WHEN YOU'RE NOT LOOKING FOR IT...

Failed marriages, broken families and disappointment. Cecilia and Brandon have both been unlucky in love and life and are ripe for an intervention. Good thing Brandon's mother happens to stumble upon this matchmaking project. But will Brandon be able to open his eyes and get away from his busy career to see that all he needs is right there in front of him?

FIND OUT IN

WHAT THE SINGLE DAD WANTS...

BY *USA TODAY* BESTSELLING AUTHOR

MARIE FERRARELLA

AVAILABLE IN JUNE 2011
WHEREVER BOOKS ARE SOLD.